HIGHLAND DEW

HIGHLAND DEW

BARRETT MAGILL

SAPPHIRE BOOKS

SALINAS, CALIFORNIA

Highland Dew
Copyright © 2018 by Barrett Magill.All rights reserved.

ISBN - 978-1-948232-11-1

This is a work of fiction - names, characters, places, and incidents are the product of the author's imagination or are used fictitiously. Any resemblance to actual persons living or dead, business, events or locales is entirely coincidental.

Editor - Heather Flournoy
Book Design - LJ Reynolds
Cover Design - Treehouse Studio

Sapphire Books Publishing, LLC
P.O. Box 8142
Salinas, CA 93912
www.sapphirebooks.com

Printed in the United States of America
First Edition – April 2018

This and other Sapphire Books titles can be found at
www.sapphirebooks.com

Acknowledgments

First and foremost, thanks must be paid to my fellow travelers: my brother John, good friend Mandy as well as Bonnie, Mark, and Molly.

It's taken over two years to put all the pieces together. The research was extensive, intriguing, and quite delicious. The passion, history, and creativity of the distillers in Scotland have for generations, provided the world with the magic of Scotch Whisky.

The work slowed to a crawl until my publisher, Chris Svendsen, put some gentle pressure on me, "I want that book." Evidently, I work better under pressure, and here it is…finally.

Still, that's only the first half of the process. The critical work has been done by my crack beta readers. Mary Ann Bosworth has a wonderful eye for incongruence, typos, and just plain stupid mistakes. I appreciate the quick turnaround as well as her encouraging words.

Jane Morrison-my Scottish regional interpreter-went through the manuscript twice and provided me with some very astute observations that made my vision bona fide. She patiently explained the details that added a ring of truth and authenticity to the story. She recently sent me an article about a bartender in the Speyside region who sounded very much like someone who could've been in the book. She said the article gave measure to how much research I had done.

Bev Prescott took time to read through the manuscript

and give me some wonderful notes. She pointed out weaknesses and strengths. I am grateful for her insight and her wisdom.

I would be remiss if I did not give a huge shout out to the endlessly talented and professional Ann McMan and TreeHouse Studio. Once again, she was able to distill (no pun intended) the essence of the story into a magnificent cover. She even created the logo that was stamped on the barrel. That logo has been essential to promoting the book. Of course, she would prefer that I actually distill some Highland Dew.

Most importantly I want to thank my publisher, Chris Svendsen, along with Schileen Potter, and Lori Reynolds for their generous support. I'm amazed and relieved by the subtleties missed by so many pairs of eyes. Kudos to the proofreaders. I extend special gratitude for my amazing editor Heather Flournoy—for searching every corner and detail to make this the best story it could be. And she was able to do it with a minimum of bloodshed. Thank you!

The entire team/family at Sapphire Books Publishing provides wonderful support.

Special thanks to Melinda Mullet, author of the Whisky Business Mystery series—thoroughly entertaining.

The F.O.W.H Lodge #251 provided stalwart support in the endless task of testing whisky samples. After all, someone had to do it.

As always, these books are for you—the reader. No

matter how many hours an author spends writing, wringing her hands, and rewriting; the entire process is for naught without the appreciative engagement of the reader. Thank you!

Slàinte

Author's Note

I first landed in Scotland in 2000 with three close friends. We spent a week on a special bus tour from Glasgow throughout the Highlands, Inverness, and back through Edinburgh to Glasgow. We then leased a car and spent four days based in Oban doing day trips. It was wonderful.

Back home, I realized I was besotted with all things Scottish because of this trip to the "homeland." Along with the MacGills, I have some Ogilvies and Ramseys in my DNA.

Five years later, we made the trip again. This time I brought my brother and my friend brought her mom. We rented cottages and a car, and traveled the countryside at our leisure. It was glorious. To this day, I have flashes of that countryside, the people, and the beauty.

It's been twelve years now, and it's time for me to pay homage to the small country with such a bounty of talent, genius, and passion.

Come along and breathe the fresh, clean Highland air, the musty drafts, and intriguing scents in any of a dozen distilleries. Malted barley, spring water, and aged bourbon barrels continue to produce "Usighe Beatha"—the water of life.

This story is my tribute to all the Scots who labor to produce this magical Scottish whisky.

Chapter One

"Aromatic, a little floral, slightly smoky." Bryce Andrews held the Glencairn tasting glass up to the light and then inhaled the delicious aroma again. "Ripe fruit."

Leo Edelman smiled. "Very good, what else?" Leo, her boss, was CEO of Global Distillers and Distribution and her mentor for the past fifteen years.

The warm malt whisky rolled across her tongue and slid down her throat like silk on silver. She smiled. "This is good. Maybe some baked apple, with sherry?"

"I got much the same." He swirled the amber liquid around and took another whiff. "I'd like it better with some more age. It's a good start, though."

The exhibit hall of the convention center reverberated with conversation, laughter, and recorded video tracks from the dozens of booths. They both put down their glasses as Reggie Ballard rushed up.

"Guess what? A little start-up from Colorado is here and they have an interesting new single malt."

Reggie had been with GDD almost as long as Bryce. Their shorthand for the company was "god." Bryce was given a promotion to Regional Sales Manager when they expanded to the west coast nine years ago. With it came a generous raise and more responsibility. Reggie came on board because she was quick, smart, and hungry. Bryce smiled. She was also quite disarming with her slow southern drawl and blue eyes. A stereotypical cheerleader type and surprisingly calculating. The girl had an agenda for her future.

Leo looked at his watch. "Let's save that one for tomorrow. I think we ought to head to the dining room for lunch. I've got some people for you to meet."

Reggie looked at Bryce then nodded. "Good idea."

"Let's meet in the lobby in ten minutes." Leo adjusted his expensive wristwatch. He stood about the same height as Bryce at five foot six. His partial baldness, thick glasses, and pencil-thin moustache made him look like a cartoon detective. However, it belied a shrewd, sharp business man who seldom missed a good opportunity.

Bryce picked up her convention registration bag containing swag, program, and a dozen handouts and business cards.

They left the grand exhibit hall and passed under the huge banner for the American Craft Spirits Association 2010 Annual Congress. This was the first time Leo had invited her and Reggie to attend a trade show. This group represented a new direction for them and Bryce loved a new challenge.

⁂

When they returned from lunch, the Grand Exhibit hall vibrated with the buzz of a chorus of excited conversations. The afternoon session "Bringing Artisanal Distillers to the Main Stage" brought almost everyone to the sectioned-off theater area. Leo engaged the VP of a competitor in discussion, so Bryce moved off to a table and looked around at the faux opulence. It seemed every hotel exhibit hall hired the same decorators. Oddly patterned carpet and gold-and-white-striped wallpaper with alternating fleur-de-lis appliques were illuminated by multifaceted chandeliers.

"What do you think Leo has in mind with this craft distilling?" Reggie sipped her water and doodled on the side of her notepad.

"I'd guess it's a new market he wants to tap into. I'm thinking this idea would take off in the Far East region. Sam Davis loves this stuff." Bryce leaned back and stretched her legs. New changes were great motivators, especially when her job got so rote that it felt heavy. Some days felt like she'd been walking through waist-deep water for twelve hours.

The room quieted as the next speaker turned on his PowerPoint presentation which projected on a huge screen.

"After what we've tasted today, I think there may be some hidden gems," Bryce whispered.

"Yeah, I think you're right." Reggie turned the page and began taking notes. "You know, you get used to thinking Scotch is all pretty similar. But, just because it's been done one way for a couple hundred years doesn't mean there might not be something worth trying."

"It might be good to work on something new. Time to change things up." Bryce enjoyed her work, but lately she noticed restlessness.

Reggie smiled. "You mean another change." She bumped Bryce's shoulder. "Does this mean you're done with the relationship-mourning stage?"

A flash of heat covered her face and Bryce clenched her jaw. "We are not going there."

"Sorry, I was just teasing. Geez, Bry, it's been

almost a year. I can't believe you're still so sensitive. She's not worth it, really. Good riddance to the lying, cheating skank."

"Ladies and gentlemen, we're delighted to have Roger Cutler, editor of the Whisky Craftsman. Roger?"

Bryce flipped over the page on her legal pad and took a deep breath. It pissed her off that the thought of Gretchen's callous action could still punch her buttons. Maybe because they were back in Chicago where it all began. The mental grumbling stopped when the speaker made a comment about artisanal distillers needing to learn better marketing tools to get their brands discovered. She glanced at Leo, who smiled and nodded. They had always had some weird mental connection when it came to business. Like minds, she guessed. His skills with personnel were not quite as impressive. Fortunately, their HR director Glenda Houseman brought considerable skill to that area. At nearly sixty, she reigned as den mother and fire captain. Bryce wished her own mother had some of that warmth. She scribbled a few salient comments and underlined them.

Once the session ended, the exhibit hall came alive with activity. Elaborate and simple booths circled the outer walls, while smaller displays and equipment formed tight aisles. Lights, colors, laughter, and a cacophony of audio and video soundtracks filled the large exhibit hall. Along with the noise and hundreds of bodies, she felt claustrophobic.

Another nasty residual from her breakup with Gretchen. Breakup, hell. She was unapologetically dumped.

Reggie handed her coffee. "You okay?"

"Yeah, it's just so crowded in here." Bryce sipped

her coffee and let her shoulders relax.

"I have an idea. Leo's off gabbing again, why don't we head over to the Colorado booth. It's in a corner near the exit. It's cooler." She touched Bryce's shoulder.

Bryce appreciated the suggestion. Sometimes Reggie surprised her by being so sensitive. "Thanks, good idea. Tell me why they're unique?" She followed as Reggie pushed through the crowd.

"It's a small boutique company started by a husband and wife team. The financial crash in 2008 hit them hard. They took their savings and decided to follow a dream of home distilling." Reggie pointed to her right. "Over there. The one with the mountain panorama."

The display in front of them looked almost quaint. A large, paneled panorama of the Rockies screamed fresh air and pure water. Clever. A laptop ran a PowerPoint slide show of their process and equipment. Not original, but attractive in a simple way.

When two customers moved on, Reggie stepped forward. "Stan and Mary Clanahan, I'd like you to meet our Regional Sales Manager, Bryce Andrews. Bryce, this is Stan and his wife, Mary."

Stan stuck out his hand. "Pleased to meet you, Ms. Andrews. Reggie has told us good things about your company."

"Bryce, please." She took his hand. "Reggie has raved about your single malt. I thought I'd better get over here and see what she was talking about."

He relayed what Reggie had told her about the company and included the growth and expansion in the past two years. Bryce nodded and ran some numbers in her head about his sales. He certainly would benefit from better distribution, but they still needed to taste the quality and gauge the consistency.

"I imagine you'd be interested in a little tasting before any more talk," Stan said. "Mary will fix you up with our two specials."

Bryce took the glass and held it up to the light. Rich color. She swirled the amber liquid and took a long sniff. Sweet, caramel notes, leather?

Reggie had already tasted and was smiling. "What do you think?"

Bryce ignored her and let the warm liquid fill her mouth. After she had swallowed, she smiled. "This is very interesting." Another sip. "It's almost like a Madeira flavor."

Stan and Mary smiled at each other. To Reggie, Stan said, "She's good."

"What? Is that right?"

"For this batch, we did the final aging in Madeira casks. At first, it was a wild idea from our head distiller, but we all liked the result."

"I can see why. It's interesting and oddly warming." She finished her sample and nodded. "We'll need to get Leo over here, but I think you have a great product."

"Thanks, that's much appreciated." Stan beamed.

Sunday afternoon was the last chance to talk to prospective customers and all three fanned out to offer proposals to the contacts of interest. As planned, they had regrouped in the lobby bar.

"Nice work, team. I'd call this a successful trip." Leo held up his glass. "Reggie, I'll give you credit for the Clanahan deal. We'll see how they manage their first big order and go from there."

"Thanks, boss." Reggie toasted him.

"I have to say…" Bryce set down her glass. "This was my first experience at an artisanal distillers group and it exceeded my expectations. This is an exciting new movement in the industry."

Leo nodded. "I'm glad you said that. I was thinking along the same lines. We've got several really good leads from this group, and I'll be talking to the board about sponsoring something for next year."

Bryce and Reggie both smiled.

"Here's what I'd like you both to do." He pulled a leather notebook and fountain pen from his pocket. "Before too much time passes and we lose the window of opportunity, I'd like you to make a trip to Scotland. If we have over twenty artisanal distillers here, think how many might be under the 'registered but still unknown' category, in the home of single malts."

Silence as they all pondered the idea.

"When do you want to do this, and how?" Bryce shuddered when she thought of the number of possible locations.

"When you get back to the San Francisco office, gather your team and find out what possibilities are available, and draw up a plan. I want you both on a plane soon. I want regular reports, and I want you to find at least one completely unique single malt—a Cinderella product that can be distributed by our company."

❧ ❧ ❧ ❧

The week flew by as meetings and phone calls to the office in Scotland distilled into a game plan.

By the following Friday, they had tickets and reservations set up and had completed the first leg from San Francisco to Chicago. The two-hour layover allowed some time to navigate the enormous O'Hare International Airport—a living microcosm of the entire world's population.

The layover gave Bryce the time to make a call. She excused herself from Reggie and chose an empty gate area. It seemed to be the one thing she hated more than the dentist: calling home. When things blew up with Gretchen, her relationship came under fire with both her mother and sister. Her perfect military brother escaped to Afghanistan and was probably safer. But going overseas without calling would be suicidal.

"Hi, Mom. I'm just checking in." Bryce clutched the cell phone tight to her head to hear through the background noise of the busy terminal.

"Ellen, is that you? I can hardly hear you."

"Yes, it's me, and I don't go by El… never mind. Sorry for the noise. I'm at the airport."

"Honey, we haven't heard anything from you for six months. Why are you calling from the airport?" Her mother's voice sounded tense, as usual.

"I know. It's been a long time, but things have just been crazy at work." Bryce pinched the bridge of her nose and took a breath. "I wasn't sure when I would get the chance to call again."

Overhead speakers blared with competing announcements, and she saw Reggie walking toward her with two water bottles. "Oh, Mom, they just called my flight." She felt mildly guilty for lying, but she didn't want to get into it with her mother in front of her coworker.

"Your flight? Where are you going?"

"To Scotland." Now Bryce regretted making the phone call. "It's only for a few weeks. We need to do some research on small whisky distilleries. Leo got a great idea after a conference to find some new products."

Her mother's silence was the worst. "What conference? Where? Sometimes I just don't understand. You have a family that loves you, and you just keep getting farther and farther away."

"I know. I'm sorry. Maybe when I get back, I can take some vacation time. Please don't worry. I'm really okay." Her throat burned with sadness. "I love you, Mom. Got to go." She ended the call and slid the phone in her pocket.

"Your mom upset?" Reggie handed her a cold bottle. "When was the last time you talked to her?"

Bryce took a drink and tried to remember if she had told her mother about her last promotion. "I'm not sure. Let's change the subject, okay? Do you have any ideas about how to get small distillers to sign with a global distributor?"

Reggie shrugged. "Not offhand, but I remember some of the whiskies we tasted at the conference were outstanding. I'm looking forward to something new and different." Reggie recapped her bottle and stretched. Her perfect figure always looked relaxed. "Did you look at any maps? I haven't been to Scotland in so long, I don't remember where anything is."

Bryce smiled. "The only thing I remember is that the roads are about ten feet wide, there's barely room for one car let alone two, and everybody drives on the wrong side."

Reggie coughed and wiped her chin with a napkin. "You had to remind me of that!"

"Well, it was my fondness for curbs that wreaked havoc on the tires. Expensive lesson."

Bryce remembered their first business trip to learn the whisky business from the ground up. It made her smile—such a good time. "But the trip was a great experience. Do you remember that first distillery when we saw those big, round copper stills up close?"

Reggie laughed. "I couldn't believe they actually got fabulous whisky that way. I learned so much on that trip, and now, every time I talk to a client, I remember how the malting rooms smelled and how good that first sip of whisky was."

"I can't believe that was six years ago." Bryce took a swallow of water.

Overhead, another announcement blared through the speakers. "Flight 2103 to Glasgow will begin boarding in twenty minutes."

Chapter Two

*T*hunk!

"Ladies and gentlemen, we'll be making our final descent in a few minutes..."

Bryce blinked open her eyes and squinted out the partially open window next to her. Must've been the landing gear.

Flying business class had helped override the sensation of being fresh-packed tuna, but only slightly. Bryce initially enjoyed the travel, but the joy of it began to fade after a few years. She shifted her pillow and tried deep breathing to improve her circulation. Out the window, the sky ahead of them was orange and purple, but off to the west a crescent moon hovered over the horizon. Beautiful. A sleepy smile creased the corners of her mouth.

The first couple of hours had been good for reading reports, eating the chicken scaloppini, and talking with Reggie. They had met after Bryce transferred to San Francisco years ago. Reggie looked like a taller, short-haired version of Kristin Chenoweth. Perky, fun, and driven. Together they'd put together a stellar team for the west coast office of Global Distillers and Distribution.

Their CEO, Leo, seldom worried, but lately his tanned face had begun to show a more furrowed brow and some dark circles under his eyes. Leo would never discuss company problems, but the corporate counsel confided their concern to her about some hungry new start-ups. This new venture could be critical in bringing up their numbers. Bryce had an important task.

About halfway through the flight, she'd wrestled her team of fretting demons into submission for a few hours while the drone of the large turbine engines lulled her to sleep.

Now, window shades peeped open around her and Bryce slid her shade all the way up. The first glint of sunrise cracked the horizon with a neon nectarine glow in the purple-black sky. The plane banked right and began to descend. It wasn't long before she caught the first hint of green, likely the north of Ireland. It really was emerald green through the gossamer wisps of cloud. Beyond lay Scotland. Flying into Europe often awakened old history studies and maps from her memory. Newgrange, King Arthur, royal houses, and clans.

Bryce pulled a towelette packet from her messenger bag and wiped her face and hands. The lemon scent convinced her she was fresher, even if she didn't feel so.

The plane touched down with a jolt, and braked hard enough to steer. Bryce was grateful for the few hours sleep. The local time in Glasgow was nine twenty-five. Sun now streamed through the window. She rolled her shoulders and flexed her stiff ankles.

Reggie squinted open one eye. "Are we there?"

"Yup. Right on time. I'm guessing you slept?" Bryce turned on her cell phone.

"Like a baby. You know, I think brandy helps. And wine." She sat up. "Do you have any water left?"

Bryce raised one eyebrow and laughed. "Hmmm." She handed over a half full bottle. How she managed to sleep that long and not have one hair out of place was infuriating. Her short, blond hair looked sculpted. Bryce ran her fingers through her own hair several times, imagining it just might look combed.

Once they'd cleared customs, they found a young man with an iPad that read Global Distribution.

"I think that might be our Man Friday." Reggie nodded at the red-haired lad.

"Welcome to Glasgow," he said with a charming guttural brogue. "This way, if you please. We've a special waiting area for international visitors in the car park." He took charge of the luggage carrier and led them to the waiting car.

"Thank you, Leo," Reggie said. "I love being met."

"Your reservations are confirmed at the Hilton Strathclyde, just up the road a bit."

"Sounds perfect," Bryce said. "How's the weather been?"

He glanced in his mirror. "It's been warming up nice. Had a ton of rain two weeks ago. Where are you coming from?"

"California through Chicago, and across the pond."

"Sounds like a verra long way."

Reggie laughed. "Oh, believe me, it is."

The driver expertly navigated the arrival traffic out of the airport and around downtown Glasgow. Their office in Airdrie was a few miles east of downtown. "The regional manager will give you more information when he meets with you a bit later."

A short time later he pulled under a portico and hopped out. He set the bags on the brass carrier when a bellman wheeled it in to the lobby. The large sign read "Doubletree by Hilton."

"That was quick. I forget how close everything is over here," Reggie said. "Oh look, is it the same as the stateside Doubletrees? I could use a fresh, hot cookie."

Registration was quick, and the bags were efficiently taken to their double room. "I want to eat something before I go up, how about you?" Bryce said.

"Come to think about it, yes. Airline food didn't cut it, and without the cookie…" Reggie hooked her bag over her shoulder and pointed to the dining room. "I can taste that Scottish breakfast already."

Like the lobby, everything in the dining room was ultra-modern: furniture and décor in black and white with bright accents of lime green and eggplant. Stark, but attractive.

Within ten minutes, two plates loaded with the traditional items appeared. Eggs, sausage links, bacon, baked beans, tattie scones, black pudding, and cooked tomatoes. It smelled wonderful. Along with some good Scottish tea, it was the perfect welcome.

"I've died and gone to heaven." Reggie purred. "This tastes so good. I'd forgotten. Now if they'd add some grits…"

They both laughed.

"I know. I can't even remember our last real meal. I'll sleep for sure now." Bryce pushed back her chair and set her napkin by the empty plate.

The waitress brought another pot of tea and Reggie poured. "Have you thought of any way to locate and track down small distillers?"

"I think we should wait to see what Ian Smith has laid out. He's pretty detail oriented. Plus, it might be a handful and it might be dozens. It will also make a difference where they are."

"Hey." Reggie leaned forward and whispered,

"Listen, we're in Scotland now. I'm guessing there might still be some of that clan rivalry up in them bens and lochs. We'll have to do some hunting."

Bryce laughed at the reference, but thought there might be some truth in it. Scots were a proud people and had strong family ties, not unlike the small stills that bloomed in the Appalachians. "You may be right. Maybe we could contact Robert the Bruce?" She finished her tea. "If you've had your fill of bangers, I'd like to catch a nap before we meet Ian."

"You go ahead. I think I'll take a walk to settle my stomach." She grinned. "I'll be quiet when I come up."

"Please." Bryce shook her head and walked to the elevator. She smiled as she remembered why they usually had separate rooms on long trips. It had something to do with plastic bags. They shared a room at the Broadford on Skye several years ago. The first morning Reggie got up early and snuck around trying to get dressed quietly...until she started rummaging through a plastic bag or twelve. The rustling went on for hours and sounded like she had fallen into a bag of bubble wrap. *Dear God, please don't let that happen again.*

Sleep held a lofty position in Bryce's hierarchy of needs, and once she'd changed and crawled into bed, sleep stole her away.

❧❧❧❧

Dressed impeccably, Ian Smith sat posture-perfect at a corner table in the bar. Bryce could see why Leo had lured Ian from a large distiller in Edinburgh. He looked like he'd stepped out of a Marks & Spencer catalog. He stood when they approached from the entrance.

"Welcome back to Glasgow."

"Thank you. It's good to see you again. How've you been?" Bryce shook his hand and sat across from him. "Do you remember Reggie Ballard?"

"Of course. Ms. Ballard, a pleasure." He shook Reggie's hand. "I've taken the liberty of ordering some snacks or appetizers. In my experience, overseas flights are often disruptive to meal schedules."

They both nodded.

"You're right. We both had a good meal a few hours ago, and I'm still not sure what schedule I'm on," Bryce said.

He handed each a folder with maps, lists, and typed notes. "Well let me give you some information and you can continue to reset. I'm afraid this is as much as I could come up with on short notice. The Scottish Craft Distillers Association has recently got started. Their list is woefully small."

A waiter appeared with a tray of mixed appetizers including stuffed mushrooms, oatcakes, different cheeses, potato wafers, and smoked salmon.

"Will there be anything else?"

"Not at the moment. Thank you. Ladies, please help yourselves."

Bryce could feel her stomach growl with the delicious smells coming from the beautiful, dainty servings.

When they each had filled a plate, Ian continued with his briefing. "It appears that Mr. Edelman has set you a fair task to accomplish. I'm certain there are hidden gems out there, especially in the Highlands, however, getting those Highlanders to reveal their secrets may require some skill." He opened his folder and showed them his lists. "Aside from a few experimenters, all distilling enterprises must be registered. I've tried to break it down in areas—Highland and Speyside then the Lowland and Islands. The distance between stops, and the number of sites, are approximately the same."

"Wow. This is impressive." Reggie shook her head. "There are more than I thought."

"These are registered as of the end of the year. Many of these may no longer be open. I'd advise you check with locals first to get an idea of whether to bother." He pulled out a map. "There are two routes. I hope you don't mind, but I took the liberty to create separate tasks to save time. You may choose whichever you prefer. The first is the Lowland and Island distillers—marked on this map in red. The other is the Highland and Speyside distillers—in blue. The small boutique distillers will likely be in the same areas and known by the locals. I highlighted the ones that are part of the GDD group. Oh, and I took the liberty of leasing two cars, which can be picked up nearby."

Bryce and Reggie thumbed through the assembled information.

"You have done an amazing job, Ian. We had no idea how to begin. This is such a great help, I think we should celebrate with a wee dram—your choice, Ian."

He closed his folder and smiled with a look of great relief. "Wonderful. I'm so glad. I did notice an eighteen-year-old Dalwhinnie at the bar, would that do?"

"Perfect."

The next hour flew by as they sipped whisky and told stories of other travels. Bryce felt her eyelids drooping when Ian finally stood.

"I will take my leave now. I hope your journeys are successful, and please remember, I am only a phone call away."

"Thank you for everything. I'm sure it all will go smoothly from here on out." Bryce waved as Ian tipped his head and walked out through the lobby.

They headed toward the elevator.

"We might get this job done in a couple of weeks," Reggie said.

Might was the operative word. Bryce wasn't quite that optimistic. Scottish locals had their own time and didn't have the urgency Americans were used to. Patience.

⊰ ⊱⊰ ⊱

Bright and early they were up, bathed, and fed. Bryce felt energized and eager to start this challenge. The hotel shuttle drove them to the car rental office close to the main motorway. Morning sunlight helped warm the air, and Bryce zipped her fleece to conserve heat anyway.

"I just remembered all the damn roundabouts. Did Ian say anything about providing bail?" Reggie whispered.

"I know. Just remember, we don't need to rush. Relax and take your time. At least, you'll avoid the Glasgow traffic since you're going directly south."

The driver pulled up to the front of the office. They each climbed out of the van while he placed their bags on the curb. Bryce tipped him. "Thank you."

"We have two reservations, one for Ballard and one for Andrews," Reggie told the rental desk clerk. "So far so good. And we'll check in every evening?"

It took only minutes, since they'd confirmed the reservation and Ian had guaranteed it.

"Right. Of course, call if there are any problems." Bryce put her license and credit card back in her travel wallet. She glanced at the typed itinerary from Ian. "Looks like my first stop is Stirling. What's yours?"

"Looks like Kilmarnock. Huh, have you ever driven a Vauxhall Insignia?"

"No. I guess this will be another first." Bryce gave Reggie a quick hug. "Let's find some treasure."

"Stay safe, and happy hunting." Reggie turned toward the dark red car.

It took Bryce several minutes to reorient herself to having the controls opposite, but the decal on the dash "Stay Left" with a big red arrow helped. On her last visit to Scotland, she discovered slow speed seemed the safest as she navigated multiple roundabouts. She'd cleverly entered information on her cell phone and the directions were helpful as she merged onto Highway A725 north.

Bryce set the cruise control and began to enjoy the beautiful May morning as the highway rolled through neat little suburbs. Scotland had a wonderful sense of tradition and function. While it grew with technology, it maintained a strong link to its important history. She unzipped the fleece and began to relax. Spring in the Highlands would be lovely.

Chapter Three

Ms. Fiona, it's Murray. Sorry to bother you on Sunday, but I thought you'd need to know your da' is gettin' to be quite ornery. I'm forever hiding keys to keep him from running off."

Fiona MacDougall gripped the phone and clenched her jaw. It just kept getting worse. Ever since her mum died a few years ago, things had spiraled out of control. Damn. She pulled her sweater closer. "I understand, but what about Robert or Sam, can't they help?"

"No ma'am, there's no' enough to cover bills so they've gone."

Her dream job teaching in Edinburgh, a flat of her own, and some money in the bank. Why couldn't it be her time? A small headache crept into her temples.

"All right. I'll close up here and make some calls. I should be back in Cardow tonight."

"I'll mind him and do the best I can."

"Thank you, Murray."

Fiona hung up. She pressed her knuckles against her head. After a few minutes, she started a list: pack for a week, call Shirley to substitute teach this week, hold mail, leave a key with Jen and Mary.

This was the fifth trip home in the past eighteen months. At first, she attributed her dad's strange behavior to grief. After all, her mother's death was sudden and unexpected due to an aneurysm. Now she had to admit the signs of his changing were showing long before. Her dad seemed to lose his interest in the business and it was slowing down. They even had to lay off staff. No wonder Murray worried.

The whole situation made her mad, but there was no other option. She had to make some tough decisions.

Ian's first lead was a family-owned distillery west of Stirling. Bryce turned west on the A811 and followed the scenic route through farm fields and woodlands to the small village of Buchlyvie, where she slowed to look for signs.

"Excuse me, do you know where the Braehead distillery is?" Bryce said to a man loading a lorry with crates.

"Aye, turn just a bit past the post office, follow it past the oak grove. You'll see it."

"Thank you. Have a good day."

He doffed his cap and waved.

Bryce smiled. It was nice to get off the highway and wander. The rolling green hills dotted with small farms and the sun dancing between some fluffy clouds made everything look magical. Yes, Scotland felt like home. She felt a warm sense of belonging and almost missed the sign hidden between two huge oak trees on her right. She slowed and looked at the large barn and adjacent whitewashed single-story building. She parked in front of the building housing "Braehead Whisky."

A young man waved and came over to her. "Hullo, can I help you?" His brogue was soft but clear.

"Good afternoon, my name is Bryce Andrews. I

believe Ian Smith may have called you regarding my visit today?"

"Aye, he did. My dad is waiting in the tasting room." He led her toward the open door.

She glanced around at the chickens and ducks walking in the nearby yard. The older farmhouse had been there for at least a century. White sheets snapped in the breeze by the back door. The main office seemed dark by comparison, but the smell of dank, whisky-perfumed air filled her with curiosity. Could this be a gem?

"This is the American lady, name's Andrews." The young man gestured and a tall, muscular man stood. Dark brown corduroy breeches were held up by two bright red suspenders over a dark green plaid shirt. He held a pipe between his teeth with a big smile.

"Pleased to meet you. I believe we've got a few Andrews back in the family somewhere. Dusty Hamilton. This is my boy, Danny."

She shook his hand and gave him her business card. "Thanks for taking the time to see me. I'm sure Mr. Smith briefed you on why I'm here. My company is looking for small-batch whisky for international distribution."

"He did. Have a seat." He waved to a stool made with part of a barrel. The bar itself was only about four feet long. "Danny, would you set us up with a couple of glasses and the two bottles I set out?"

"So, how long has Braehead been operating?" Bryce opened a small notepad.

He poured a share into a whisky tasting glass. "Over fifty years. My dad started distilling small batches after he retired. The folks around here liked it well enough he had to keep increasing the batches he made. Within five years he had to expand. He built this addition, hired some local lads, and took out a loan for more equipment. By the time I graduated high school, I had a full-time job." Dusty beamed with pride.

Bryce sniffed the whisky and held it up to look at it. She added a splash of water from a small pitcher, smelled twice more, and tasted it. She scribbled a couple of notes.

"This is an eight-year-old single malt." Dusty took a swallow from his own glass and nodded. "We switched to a new cooperage five years ago. I think it'll make a difference in the flavor. The other barrel had a musty odor."

"I agree. This has a good nose but tastes a little green. Nice color."

Dusty reached across the bar for the next bottle. "This is our twelve-year. Used sherry casks for the second stage."

She dumped her glass, rinsed it, and watched as Dusty added the older Braehead. The color glowed dark amber in the light. She took her time to give it a chance to breathe. "Oh yes, this is lovely. Very nice." She took another sip and wrote more notes.

They chatted a bit before Bryce stood. "This has been a pleasure. As I said, when all the samples are in, we'll notify everyone the results."

"I'm glad you stopped by our little operation. It's nice to have American visitors."

Bryce opened her car door. "By the way, can you recommend a B and B around here?"

"The Garrique is up the road just outside of Kippen. Might have to check to see if it's available. Otherwise, the inn on the corner is good."

Bryce waved as she turned onto the road. She

headed east and her phone rang. She hit the Bluetooth.

"Hello."

"Hi, Bryce, it's Reg. I just wanted to check in. Where are you?"

"I just finished up at Braehead and I'm heading back to Kippen to find a room. How was your day?"

"Great. I visited the little place in Dungavel and the owner referred me to a…let me see…John Brown at a pub in Drumclog. He had some great stories and a couple of interesting leads. The guy knows his whisky."

"I'm glad. Where're you stopping?"

"I'm heading to the coast to spend the night in Ardrossan so I can get the early ferry to Campbeltown. I think from there I might as well continue up through the islands."

"Check in later if you want to."

"Will do. Hey, Bryce, how're you feeling?"

"Good. In fact, being back in Scotland has brightened my mood considerably. I'm sorry I've been so irritable lately. Let's blame the hormones." A weight had been lifted just by the change in scenery.

"Okay, if you say so. Take care, bye."

Bryce slowed down as she entered Kippen. She parked in front of a small pub and looked up Garrique on her phone. A woman answered on the second ring.

"Hello, I'm inquiring about a room for tonight?"

"I'm so sorry, we're booked for the weekend. Would next week do?"

"I'm afraid not, I'm on the road. Thanks anyway."

Bryce took the map inside to get a sandwich. It was nearly four and she hadn't had much since breakfast except a protein bar and some whisky. Inside was homey and warm. Some tea and a cheese sandwich sounded good.

"Could you tell me how long it would take to get to Perth?" She asked the barman.

"Won't be much traffic if you get on the M9 and avoid Stirling. Follow that, as it'll be the A9. Take you straight to Perth. Maybe an hour."

Spring nights meant it stayed light till very late. Refreshed, she drove north looking forward to stopping in Pitlochry and then visiting The Dalwhinnie the next day. How was it she had forgotten how good she felt driving through the countryside, stopping when she wanted, and not answering a constant barrage of questions?

Once she'd settled in someplace, she might even take a long walk. On a whim, she looked up the Atholl Palace, an elegant old manor house built in 1871. When they answered she inquired about a room for the night. "I'll see you before six."

She remembered stopping there once for lunch after visiting the Edradour Distillery—the smallest in Scotland at the time. Pitlochry oozed charm and authenticity—like time had stopped briefly. The streets still held fast to their history and each homeowner, like the one before, had kept their homes in pristine and well-loved condition. Freshly painted, window boxes filled with blooms. Then there was the illustrious Atholl Palace, which possessed old-world charm with a heavy dose of class. She smiled at the memory the the grand old building that resembled an ancient castle, including large turrets. The view from her room was breathtaking, and the rolling hills were scattered with fluffy white sheep.

This was the kind of treat she relished on a solitary road trip. In fact, she'd even be willing to dress for dinner.

Chapter Four

When she'd opened her eyes that morning, an unusual sensation had rippled through her body. She guessed it was excitement. Anticipation. And yes, eagerness. Those feelings had been dormant for a long time. Maybe this was what midlife felt like. Poor sleeping, lack of interest, weight gain. Ennui, pure and simple.

Rain. *Of course, it's Scotland.* Bryce leaned on the window frame as rivulets streamed down the pane, and sipped the steaming tea with added milk and sugar. This change in her normal daily business routine and a new diet of comfort foods, along with new scenery invigorated her. The time change from west coast caused a brain blip that changed her plans. She forgot it was Sunday. No appointments today. Might as well try to visit The Dalwhinnie Distillery on her way northeast.

She propped herself up on pillows with her tea, then picked up her phone to call Reggie.

"Hello?"

"Hi, are you up?"

Reggie grumbled something and dropped the phone. "What time is it and where am I?"

"It's just after eight, and I hope you're still somewhere in Scotland." Bryce smiled. Reggie was not a morning person.

"I just looked out the window and there's water.

It might be the ocean. Oh yeah, salty sea and peaty whisky, must be Scotland."

"Must be good whisky if you're not sure where you are." Bryce wasn't concerned; Reggie rarely did herself too much mischief.

"I made good time yesterday, so I continued to Islay and made a few more visits. Didn't get to bed until really late and then couldn't sleep. Overtired. Remind me why I said I liked peat?"

Bryce sipped the tea and gazed at the watercolor world of Pitlochry. "I'm not sure, I think it was the strong flavors."

"Hang on." Rustling and pouring. "A little carbonated sugar might help. Ran into a guy from Suntory. They're all over these Islay malts. Guess they're building their portfolio. What's on your schedule?"

Bryce yawned. "Turns out it's Sunday. No appointments. I switched my schedule around and I'm going up to the coast. I'll work my way back to eventually meet you."

"Okay. I can follow this route to Fort William then head east. I might as well get my notes in the computer for Leo. Have you done yours?"

"Some. I'll finish today. It's a grey and rainy day here, no sightseeing, might as well drive. It's only about three hours."

Reggie coughed. "Sorry. Wrong pipe. Will you stop to see Malcolm?"

"I forgot. Is he still at Tamdhu?" Malcolm Harris started at their company distillery in Airlie twelve years ago as a malt man and worked his way through the ranks learning every job. He left when the Tamdhu distillery needed a Master Distiller. She scribbled a note in her planner.

"I'm pretty sure. Listen, I need to get some food in me. I'll give you a call later—in case you're bored."

"Right. I'll try to be strong. Take care."

Bryce folded the map and put her files away. Hot porridge sounded perfect. Or was it parritch?

❧ ❧ ❧ ❧

The Highlands in the spring could be unpredictable. Even though it was May, the snow still covered many of the higher elevations. By midafternoon, the sun began to break through and warm things up.

Because of her late start, Bryce chose Aviemore to stop for a break. She steered off the A9 and followed the side road to the Old Bridge Inn. It looked much the same as it had four years earlier: a single-story stone building whitewashed clean, garnished with flower trellises and flower baskets. Inside was the rustic inn with sturdy wooden tables, an open fireplace, and a comfortable bar.

"What'll it be, lass?" The barman looked familiar, but she wasn't sure.

"What's on tap?"

"Belhaven."

"That's good. What's the special today?"

He set the full pint on a coaster, wiped the bar, and smiled. "If I'm not mistaken, we may still have some fresh spring lamb left."

"That sounds perfect." Bryce smiled at the charming old Scot as he headed into the kitchen. Already it felt like a neighborhood tavern, like Cheers, where everyone knows your name. The theme song began in her head.

The room contained a few tables and a dartboard in the back. Near the fire, a young man played a fiddle. She couldn't make out the tune, but it certainly added to the ambience. She hung her jacket on the back of the barstool and pushed up her sleeves.

The ale tasted good and hearty. It wouldn't be her choice in the states, but in Scotland it seemed perfect. Her neck and shoulders dropped with relaxation.

"What brings a pretty American up to Aviemore?"

She smiled. "Business and pleasure. My name is Bryce Andrews."

"Jamie Meigle at your service. What business might that be?"

This is perfect, Bryce thought. "Whisky, as a matter of fact."

"You don't say." He raised his bushy auburn eyebrows and smiled.

"I'm scouting for small-batch whisky. It's become popular in the States."

"We've been makin' small batches of whisky for a couple hundred years. I couldn't even count how many I've tasted." His laugh was deep and musical.

"That's why we're here. Nobody knows whisky like the Scots." She hoisted her glass. "Is there anyone you'd recommend?"

"Hmm, any special requirements?"

Bryce hadn't thought about that, but now wondered what could be waiting up in the hills. "I guess it would need to be someone serious about growing the business. They'd need something unique, legal, that they could replicate."

"I'll ask around. Will you be back this way?"

"Let me leave my card. I'm going on to Speyburn before I come back this way." She circled her cell number. "This has my email and phone number."

"Enjoy your visit."

❧ ❧ ❧ ❧

Bryce started the car and then jotted a note to remember Jamie Meigle in Aviemore. This felt like forward movement on a goal. The progress energized her. Well, that along with a delicious meal and good conversation.

The sun broke through the parting clouds and sparkled off the river. The bright blue sky highlighted the resplendent, rounded-shoulder mountains. The Highland scenery took her breath away.

The highway surged northeast, and after a few minutes, Bryce decided to get off and take the secondary road along the River Spey. Her GPS showed a short distance to the Speybridge roundabout and an entrance to the Cairngorms National Park, which covered over seventeen hundred square miles of breathtaking mountain scenery.

Her Bluetooth phone dinged and the helpful voice declared, *"Call from Leo."*

"Hi, Leo. What're you doing up so early?"

Leo laughed. "It's not that early. It's eight o'clock and somebody has to work to keep the business afloat."

Oh boy. "I'm sure you're managing just fine."

"I had to fly out to the west coast to help wrangle those juvenile delinquents you left in charge."

"You went in person? I certainly appreciate your sacrifice, but I think you'll be pleased with our scouting."

"Do tell? Anything mind blowing?" He sounded excited.

"Not yet, but the best info has come from the small village pubs. Their owners hear all the stories and get to sample any new efforts the locals produce. I met a couple of good contacts."

"Makes sense. Where are you now?"

"Since today is Sunday and I can't see any of the regulars, I'm on my way up to Speyburn in Rothes. I'll see the team tomorrow. Any messages?"

"Find out how the blend is coming along. I need to get the design team on it soon."

"I sure will." Bryce hoped he wouldn't ask about Malcolm. It was still a sore subject at the Chicago office.

"Okay. Bryce, you're doing a fine job and you sound much better…Maybe it's the change of scenery or…well, whatever it is I'm glad. You do your best work when you're breaking new ground. Make me proud."

"I will. Thanks, I do feel better."

"How's Reggie doing?"

"She's already moving through the islands. We'll meet up in a couple of days to compare notes."

"Be careful and be frugal!"

"Yes, sir." Bryce laughed. He always said that and never questioned her expense sheet. "Thanks for calling."

His concern was touching, and she knew how much he cared. They'd made a good team, and he was a terrific and generous mentor.

After graduation, Bryce thought she had the world by the tail with her fancy business degree. Once she entered the real world, it was clear how little she knew and how women were denigrated in the hospitality and beverage business. If it hadn't been for Leo making her his protégé, she might be working retail somewhere.

Instead, she had a big job with a comparable salary and was respected for her work.

Too bad Gretchen didn't appreciate the good life and chose an airline stewardess instead.

Next roundabout: six miles.

Bitch.

⁂

The secondary route required more attention as the road width became uncomfortably narrow. Once the traffic thinned, the countryside blossomed with gorgeous, spring-green growth everywhere. The road cut through the river valley, surrounded by wooded hillsides dotted with farms tucked neatly beside them. The air smelled of new grass.

The topography eventually flattened, and more farms appeared. When Bryce spotted a large lorry piled high with huge timbers coming around a curve ahead, she chose the next left-sided passing place to stop and wait.

Once it rattled past her, she slowly pulled out. She looked right, then saw a hidden driveway on her right with double white posts and a dangling, broken sign. Odd. When she passed it, she noticed faded black lettering: "MacDougall & Son Distillers."

Not especially welcoming. She smiled. Probably another of the small deserted stills of forgotten times.

Upper Knockando: 3 miles.

Might need to make a pit stop. She fidgeted in her seat. The seat belt pinched. Something about that hanging sign bothered her. Bryce wasn't much for superstition or psychics, but she'd always had a strong intuition about certain things, and she eventually learned to listen to it.

A wide driveway lay on her right just ahead. No cars in sight, she pulled in and turned around. *This is just crazy, but hey, I've got plenty of time.*

Weeds claimed most of the driveway, but she could see a small orchard on one side and a roof above the tree line up on the other. No livestock and no sounds. She slowed near the stone house and parked. When she got out of the car, a woman appeared on the front step. Bryce instantly regretted her impulse to trespass.

"Can I help you?" The woman asked. Her arm shielded her eyes from the lowering sun. Her clothes were casual: jeans and a large wool sweater that looked like one of those Lands' End Heather Brown numbers. It matched her hair.

"I'm really sorry. I was exploring and I thought this might be abandoned." Bryce swallowed and hoped she wouldn't be shot. Leo would be furious.

The woman laughed. Genuinely laughed.

"I can see why you'd make that assumption."

All Scottish brogues were appealing to Bryce, but this woman's voice was lyrical and soft—as was her appearance.

"I didn't mean to intrude. I'm scouting for small distilleries." Bryce gestured to the road. "The hanging sign read MacDougall & Son Distillers and I thought..."

The woman stepped down and walked closer. Up close she looked much younger. "I can't blame you, and there's no harm done." She stopped in front of Bryce and folded her arms casually. "If you'd stopped by a year or so ago, it would have been true. Not now."

"That's a shame." That was a stupid thing to say. "I mean this is a perfect location for a distillery... What a legacy. When did it close?"

"I'm not sure. It's been dying for some time because my father can no longer manage it. The staff left one by one until they were no longer producing whisky. The inventory dropped and with it, the income." The woman wiped her cheek. "I'm sorry to be going on. My name is Fiona MacDougall—the daughter—not the son."

"Please don't apologize. I appreciate you sharing it. Oh, I'm Bryce Andrews." She felt her face heat up with embarrassment.

"Do you mind if I ask why you're scouting distilleries?"

"Oh, no, of course not. I work for an international distributor and we were hoping to find some unique small distillers to market."

"Sounds fascinating. Sorry we couldn't help you, but good luck with your scouting." She smiled and held out her hand.

"Thanks, it was nice to meet you…Take care." Bryce took her hand then backed up. Fiona let go first and Bryce hit the car. "Whoops."

They both laughed and waved as Bryce turned the car around and made her exit toward the road.

Chapter Five

A few miles east of Knockando, as the sun dipped farther down, Bryce slowed the car and pulled off to find a room for the night. Craigellachie was near and she remembered it. After a quick call to confirm availability, she steered her car into the Highlander Inn lot.

The first time Leo had brought her to the Speyside Distillery, he explained that he had stopped there so she could experience a small pub with an extensive selection of single malts and a knowledgeable barkeep.

They had stayed for almost a week, and he took her around to the major distillers in the area. She smiled when she remembered their first evening when Leo offered the barman £40 for them to taste a wee dram of twenty single malts. It was a slow night, and the man agreed. Billy something. It took a couple of hours, and she had written the notes for every single one of them. It was a lesson and experience she never forgot.

Neither did the bar patrons. They watched in rapt attention as Billy explained each one. The other patrons also bought samples for themselves. Not a bad thing all the way round.

When they were ready to leave, the manager asked if Leo would like to come and do it on a regular basis. He declined, but filed the idea away for the future. *Remember to call Leo.*

"Thank you, that would be great." Bryce returned her credit card to her wallet and took the room key. More and more this trip felt like she was coming home. The old inn looked exactly the same—the wood-trimmed walls, slightly faded plaid carpet, and antlered ceiling fixtures. The faint smell of wood smoke and freshly baked pastries.

Her room was in the back facing the River Spey. There was a small deck and a slider to open for a fresh breeze. The handmade quilts, curtains, and doilies lent an unexpected warmth. Bryce had spent way too many nights and days in large, impersonal, modern corporate suites. "Sit and have a wee cuppa."

Bryce set down her things and smiled. It kind of felt like her new home.

❧❧❧❧

Monday morning dawned like storybook Scotland—"dreich," as the locals called it. A text from Malcolm said he'd meet her at The Highlander after work, so she called ahead to see Tom at Speyside.

"Just tea and a biscuit, I think." Her stomach still felt queasy. Probably all the driving. She checked her email from habit. Nothing. When had that ever happened? The dining room had a handful of patrons. Most looked like older tourists and a couple of singles.

Once outside, her fleece jacket helped keep out the chill and she readjusted the defroster in her still unfamiliar Vauxhall. Visibility was sketchy at best, but the GPS steered her onto the A941, the main road going north. The roadway lined by trees was probably lovely when the fog lifted.

Rothes presented like many small villages with neat, stone buildings lining the main streets, slate roofs with double chimneys. She waved at a woman with a pram, who waved back.

Gradually, Bryce was feeling better about the trip to Scotland. The stress and exhaustion from big-city living just leached away into the air of the ancient landscape. She laughed and rolled down her window. Even Reggie had sounded less cynical when they talked last night. Her route had taken her through Islay and now Jura. She'd be in Oban by tomorrow. Her territory looked smaller, but already she had made more stops and more contacts. *That's good. Means she's motivated.*

The road sign indicated a roundabout ahead, and the Speyburn Distillery was the third exit. *Remember to get on the inside lane.* She had time. Fortunately, no large vehicles made for a smooth turn. *Move out, left B9015, got it.*

Shit!

Damn curb.

She pulled over when she could to check the tire. She stood red-faced as cars passed. The tire looked okay, but she could detect a small scrape on the hubcap.

Could've been worse, she thought as she turned on the side road for the distillery.

❧ ❧ ❧ ❧

Tom Hobart took over Speyburn as general manager in 2001. He had started his career in Edinburgh at the fabled Whisky Shop on Princes Street. Another great find for Leo. He lured him away to Glasgow and the main office in Airdrie, and finally to Speyside.

"Bryce, my gosh! How long has it been?" Tom stood about six foot with long arms and legs, probably a runner. He strode across the waiting area with his hand outstretched and a smile on his face.

"Hi, Tom. Good to see you." She accepted his enthusiastic greeting. It felt good to be welcomed by a peer—it wasn't always that way. "It's at least four years. You look great. Are you enjoying the northern climes?"

"You know, I really am. This is so much different than the energy in Glasgow or Edinburgh." He steered her to a small lounge. "Would you like some tea or coffee?"

"Tea would be great. I don't want to take too much of your time, I just wanted to check in and see how things were going."

He leaned back and unbuttoned his tweed jacket. "Pretty well, I think. The economy up here took a dive a few years ago." He smiled. "I guess it did everywhere. But with fewer tourists on the trail, we had to rotate some staff to keep the doors open. Sales have picked up in the last six months, and everybody feels better."

She knew the figures for all of the GDD distilleries. Speyburn wasn't in the worst shape—thanks to Tom. "Leo wanted me to ask about the new blend, he's anxious to work on the artwork for the rollout."

Tom shook his head and chuckled. "Of course he is. I think we're on schedule. After we finish here, I'll send you down to talk to our master distiller. Liam is an artist, you know, can't rush him."

"And I wouldn't try. He has an excellent sense for the taste."

Liam did indeed have interesting news on the new blend. He'd found several local single malts of different ages, and after weeks, finally reached the balance he sought. He was ecstatic. Bryce could only smile. Although he had nothing for her to taste, he did write down a precise description to pass on to Leo. It would mean more to him anyway.

She followed the road back to Rothes and made a non-official stop at The Glenrothes Distillery to see if they were selling anything new. There was still time to meet Malcolm and enjoy a drink and dinner. As she parked, her phone dinged. *"Call from Reggie."*

"Hi, Reg. What's new?" She turned off the car and sat watching the sun play off the oxidized copper spire on the distillery. The aged sign in front read EST.1870. *Nice.*

"I finished up here and I'm going to stay in Oban tonight. Can you meet up tomorrow?" Reggie had music playing in the background. Was she in the car or a pub? Hard to tell.

"I just visited Speyburn and I'm heading to the Highlander to meet Malcolm. Do you want to meet me there? It's quicker to Inverness after. I can get you a room."

"Might as well. I've got enough to write up and send already. There are only a few others up north."

"How's your weather?"

"Pretty damn gusty. The sun is out but a storm looks to be moving in tonight. How about you?"

"Not bad. Foggy this morning, but I really like the dramatic changes. I'm even getting better at navigating these roads. Well, almost."

Reggie laughed. "What happened?"

"Oh, just one of those damn roundabouts. I made all the way to my exit and then hit the curb. More embarrassment than damage. Stop laughing."

"Maybe I should just stay with you so I can drive you around."

"Very funny. Maybe you should find the goose that lays the golden egg and Leo will be thrilled."

"All right, all right. Got to catch the ferry. I'll see

you sometime tomorrow. Bye."

"Take care."

The Glenrothes visit was fairly brief. She got a name from the sales clerk for a man from nearby Maggieknockater who recently began his own small start-up. He was a former employee and wanted more hands-on learning. Bryce wrote it down and called as soon as she got back to her room.

The man's name was Dan, and he regaled her with enthusiastic plans on how he was going to collect unique botanicals to add distinct flavor. When he took a breath, she asked him what he was distilling.

"Pure spirits right now, then I'll add the botanicals and create a new gin."

"Gin? Did you say gin?"

"Yes. It's the new thing, and it's already popular in the larger areas."

"I just thought, since you came from The Glenrothes, you'd be doing whisky."

"I was, at first. But when I started shopping for supplies and equipment, I changed my mind. This doesn't require years of aging."

"That's exciting. I hope you're a huge success. Thanks for your time."

She hung up and carefully wrote out "Gin with new botanicals. Check this out."

She added the small samples from Tom to the heavy box with dividers. Liam would send the new blend when it was ready. When they assembled all of them, she and Reggie would have the main office in Glasgow ship them to the States. The notes would stay with her and in her cloud file.

There was just enough time for her to change and catch a quick shower before heading downstairs.

Chapter Six

Malcolm was already at the bar when she came down. He stood when she came over.

She hugged him. "You are a sight for sore eyes, old friend."

"You, too, Bryce." He hugged her tight.

"Let me look at you." She held him by the shoulders. He was only a couple of inches taller, and stocky. Muscular and not flabby. His light brown hair was thinning, but his blue eyes twinkled with mischief above his always-pink cheeks. "I've missed you."

"Do you want a table, or the bar?" He asked.

"Let's sit down at the other end of the bar. It looks quiet."

The old wooden stools were worn and molded with age. The back bar and most of the wall space was filled with whisky bottles of every size and shape. Bryce could feel her jaw drop as she scanned the old labels.

"Four hundred thirty at last count." A deep smoky voice rumbled.

She turned and saw a large man with black curly hair that was grey at the sides, a handlebar moustache, green eyes, and dimples. "Billy?" She said incredulously.

"Well, you're a clever one. At your service m'lady." He grinned.

"I'm sorry. I'm shocked. I was here many years ago on my first visit to Scotland. And I remember you."

"Verra likely, as I've been here over fifteen years."

He set out beer mats with ale logos. "What'll it be?"

"Bryce, you order." Malcolm hung up his jacket.

The sheer number overwhelmed her. "Would you select something I might not get in the States?"

He rubbed his chin and nodded. "I think I know just the one. And you, sir?"

"I'll take Glenfiddich fifteen-year-old, neat." He unbuttoned his jacket and loosened his tie.

"This is so great. I'm sorry Reggie isn't here." It felt like no time had passed and they were all joining up after work for a drink. Good times. Then came the familiar pinch reminding her of the bad times.

"My gosh. How is the little tyrant?" Malcolm chuckled.

"Still the same. I have to keep an eye on her. She's over on the coast. She'll drive up tomorrow. Maybe we can figure something out."

Billy returned with two tasting glasses and a small pitcher of water. "Glenfiddich Fifteen for you, sir. And Balvenie Caribbean Cask for the lady. Slainté."

They added a few drops of water and performed the ritual tasting they always did.

Bryce let the first sip roll around, then swallowed. "Wow, I love this. It's definitely Balvenie, but what a different flavor. How's yours?"

Malcolm just grinned. "Lovely."

"Tell me about your growing family."

He set the glass down and tipped it slightly in a circle. "Emily is good. We had our third girl almost a year ago. So it's a good thing her mum lives so close. Rose and Daphne think the babe is a new doll for them."

Bryce smiled at the thought of his cherubic wife with three little angels. "And how are things at

Tamdhu? You happy?"

"I really am. It's a different group and a new philosophy for me to get used to, but I like the slower pace and having my opinion valued. I feel like part of the team." He sipped his whisky.

She understood what he meant. At their Glasgow facility he was a worker bee with no hope for advancement. He was smart, learned quickly, and was very soft spoken. She was sad when he left, but now felt it was the right move.

Billy came over and said, "How does that whisky do?"

She grinned. "This was quite a surprise, and very nice. What's the secret?"

He leaned over. "Distilled in rum barrels."

"No kidding?"

He reached back and handed her the bottle.

"I really like this one."

"I remember you!" Billy pointed.

Bryce stopped mid-sip.

Billy laughed and slapped his palm on the old oak bar. "You were here with an older fella, and he bribed me into giving you guys twenty different whisky samples." He clapped his hands and almost choked from laughing so hard. "A quiet weeknight turned into an epic whisky class. Old-timers are still talking about it."

"You remembered that?"

"Of course, we all do. Do you still work with him?"

"I sure do. I'm the west coast regional sales manager."

"Really. How come you're back here?"

"Speyburn is one of our holdings, and Leo sent us over to scout out some small-batch whisky distilleries."

"You don't say. Why'd you want to be looking for new whisky?"

"Its popularity is taking off in the States, just like the microbrews. We'd like to find some up-and-comers to represent in the States."

Billy smiled. "Well look around and tell me if you see something unusual you'd like to taste. Not twenty, you understand." He winked.

"Thanks."

"I was going to ask about your mission. Is it a new project?" Malcolm said.

"We're not sure yet. We all attended a craft spirit convention and found it really interesting. Scotch is getting even more popular—and so are the Japanese imports. Whisky is more global than ever. So why not check it out?" No need to mention Leo's concern about their market share. She took another swallow and smiled as it warmed her all the way down. Sweet on the lips, then leather and pepper. Interesting.

"Would you like a little something to nibble?"

Food. "Great idea. Go ahead and order something."

Malcolm waved at Billy. "Do you think we might have some oatcakes and cheddar?"

"Coming right up. You ready for another?"

"In a bit," Bryce said. "I'm not sure what to taste next." She waved at the vast collection.

When Billy returned with the cheese plate, Malcolm said, "I'd like to try the Benrinnes Fifteen."

"I think you'll like that. And you…?"

"I'm going with that Dailuaine Sixteen," Bryce said.

Both smiled when they tasted their second selections.

The aged cheddar cheese tasted nutty and rich,

the oatcakes a wonderful memory. "It's hard to get oatcakes at home. I forgot how much I like them."

He laughed. "I guess we were hungrier than imagined."

"We should probably start thinking about dinner."

Billy brought water glasses and cleared the plates away. "You know I've been thinking about your small-batch quest. Would you be up to a blind taste test to see what you might find out there?"

Bryce perked up for a challenge. "That sounds like fun. Do you have some unknowns?"

"Sure do. I'd be interested in how you'd rate them. And if you can identify the regions they're from."

"All right. I'll run upstairs while you set them up."

She hastened to her room. After she washed her hands, she grabbed a notepad and pen. She felt a little giddy and it wasn't just the whisky—she loved the challenge. More importantly, she could remember how green and inexperienced she was the last time she was here learning how to taste whisky for the first time. *I really want to tell Leo…but not yet.*

When she got back to the bar, five glasses were lined up with a small dram in each. Several of the staff and a few guests stood around talking. Somebody had blabbed. Oh well. It wasn't a contest, it was just a search. Scotland's got talent.

Billy stood, beaming. He'd lined them up from lightest to darkest, and had a scrap of paper behind each.

Bryce took a drink of water, then picked up the lightest. She sniffed, checked the color, sniffed, added water, then sipped. Sniffed and tasted.

The tasting proceeded from left to right in slow methodical order. The room was quiet except for whispers and the muted street noise that wafted in from outside. It took about twenty minutes.

Billy was bouncing on the balls of his feet.

"Okay. This was very interesting. Very different selections." She turned the page back. "Number one is delicate, fruity with a green apple nose. Taste was vanilla and smoke. It had an astringent end. Probably young, but I'd guess a Speyside." She put a number in the corner of notes.

"Number two was not as clear. Nose was smoky, toffee, and peaty. Taste was sharp, almost bitter spice with a sweet follow-up. Not sure, but this could be an Islay malt.

"Three was sweet grass, berries. The taste mixed fruit, floral, woody, smooth finish. I'd guess Lowland.

"Number four, rich color. Nose is garden flowers, fruity, woody. The taste is smooth, fresh apple, cinnamon, nutmeg. Ends with a nutty-sweet oiliness. Might be Speyside or Highland."

She scribbled another note, took a sniff, and held up number five, sniffed and looked at it. "Caramel, white oak, and lily. The taste is rounded with vanilla and spice, smooth, ends with a lingering smoke. I'd guess Highland."

"That was quite interesting. I hope you tell your boss that in the opinion of this old barkeeper, you've developed an excellent nose for our *Usighe Beatha*."

Malcolm grinned at her.

Bryce could feel the excitement growing. "Well, how did I do?"

Billy picked up the first slip of paper. "What region?"

"Speyside."

"Correct. Number two?"

She glanced at her notes. "Islay."

He paused. "Correct. Number three?"

"Lowland."

"Wrong. It's Highland."

Whispering and low groans of disappointment trickled through the onlookers.

Bryce swallowed. Her palms were damp.

"Number four?"

This time she paused to look at her notes. "Highland or Speyside."

"That's two, you'll need to pick."

She looked down at her notes and bit her lip. "Fresh apple" jumped out at her. "Speyside."

Billy looked down at the scrap paper. "Correct."

Several people clapped or cheered.

Bryce felt her face flush with embarrassment.

"Now, the last one, number five?"

"Highland."

"And you are…correct."

Malcolm high-fived her. "Damn, that was brilliant. I'm sure glad he didn't ask me, I'd have got more wrong. Good tasting notes. You really have a talent."

Billy shook her hand. "Next round is on me."

"Thanks, it was fun. Malcolm, I think we better eat. I'm starved."

❧ ❧ ❧ ❧

Dinner plates were removed and the server poured each some coffee. "Will there be anything else?"

"Not for me." Malcolm pushed back from the table.

"I'm finished, too. Please put this on my tab,

room four.”

“That’s not necessary…”

“Hey, this was a legitimate business expense. I was working up there,” Bryce said.

“I can’t argue with that. Say, what did you think of the samples?”

“I was impressed by a couple of them. The others were okay.”

She thought about them again. She might ask Billy if he’d repeat the test when Reggie arrived tomorrow with her newly acquired samples. “Before I go up, I’m going to ask for the names just in case.”

“It’s quite late,” Malcolm said. “I should get home before the missus gets worried.”

They walked through the lobby to the door.

Bryce hugged him. “This was like old times. I’m so glad we could get together.”

“It was. Give me a call before you leave, or if Reggie has some free time. Good night.”

Bryce watched him leave as the sun was setting. It had to be around ten. One more thing before bed.

“Excuse me, Billy? Do you think you could jot down the names for the five samples?”

He smiled. “I thought you might be askin’.” He pulled a note from his shirt pocket and handed it to her with a wink.

“Thanks, you’re the best. See you tomorrow.” As she turned to go up, she thought she heard him say something.

Chapter Seven

Bryce re-read the notes she'd just typed up for Leo as she sipped the aromatic Scottish breakfast tea. In recounting her effort for the past few days, she hoped he would be pleased. Not enough, of course.

She checked her most recent company list of Scottish export companies, and the two samples she liked were not listed. They must be small family operations and not registered companies.

Her phone beeped, indicating a text.

Reggie: Left Oban be there by noon. Ta.

It was sunny and warm, which meant she couldn't just sit around. She looked in the mirror. *Hmm. Jeans, company fleece, trainers. That's fine.* She grabbed her notebook and messenger bag, and trotted downstairs. She left her key and a note at the desk for Reggie.

On the way out, she spotted Billy wiping down the bar. "Good morning, Billy. Don't you ever sleep?"

His laugh boomed across the empty barroom. "How do you think we keep all these bottles dust-free?"

"You have a point. It's not a job I could do." She walked closer and opened her notebook. "I was writing up notes this morning and I had a question. Two of the whiskies I tasted weren't on my export list."

"Which two?"

"The anCnoc and The Highland Dew."

"Oh. The anCnoc is a retooled whisky from Knockdhu, but it should be available. The Highland Dew is out of production."

"Okay, thanks. See you later."

The sunshine dazzled her. Everything looked fresh and alive. She pulled her car out and felt grateful she'd gotten a midsize car. It was much more comfortable. She decided to go north and then west, because she had completely forgotten her plan to visit the Cardhu Distillery, one of the prettiest and most welcoming. It was one of the reasons its tour was rated so highly. In fact, Leo might want to consider renovating some of their older properties to add a more welcoming ambience and street appeal. Note to self: check web pages for ideas.

As she meandered through the countryside, she replayed the blind tasting. Interestingly, the two odd-ducks were the most unusual and attractive, especially that fresh apple one. It was unique and easy to like. On a whim, she tapped Cortana. "Highland Dew Whisky."

A list of Highland whiskies scrolled up. "Well, that's no help." She asked, "Closed Speyside distilleries."

She pulled off and read the list. It had dozens of entries. She tried the Malt Madness® website—no mention of Highland Dew. *Crap.*

The GPS alerted her Cardhu was 5.3 miles ahead. Truth be told, she liked Cardhu. Its unique flavor had become a sore point with Leo ever since he'd failed to sign them with GDD. Still, she thought it made a nice treat.

The visit took less time than planned since they had no new offerings. Didn't matter, and might get her back before Reggie. She'd go back via the A95, which would be faster. She followed the sign directing her to Marypark. Directly in front of her, a bus was turning the corner of the curve. Bryce gripped the steering and pulled as close to the shoulder as she dared. She held her breath and flinched as the bus passed within millimeters of her right side-view mirror.

"Damn. Will I ever get used to these nerve-wracking close calls?" She opened one eye as the diesel smoke cleared and did a double take.

The dilapidated white sign wobbled in the wind. "I'll be." It was the exact same place where she'd encountered the lumber-laden lorry.

The dark-haired woman flashed across her mind. "I wonder…" Without another thought she steered into the driveway of the not-abandoned farm.

She passed the orchard and made a U-turn behind the house, hoping to be seen. When she got out to look around, it was just her, the wind, and some apple blossom petals.

"Anyone about?" she called out, and looked around. No answer. The doors were closed up and the front garden was empty. Disappointment tugged at her shoulders. "It's no big deal, just thought it would be nice to visit," she said to no one.

It felt eerily quiet as she walked back to her car. The clock on the dashboard read 11:05. Might as well get back to the inn. She tracked back down the driveway and turned past the old sign and sighed. One of the legendary black Corbies sat on the post, ruffled his feathers, and cocked his head. The sleek black feathers glistened in the sun. He seemed to be looking at her. Intently.

Bryce felt her neck hairs tingle.

❧❧❧❧

Regina Ballard smiled when she secured her insulated sample case in the trunk. Confident with her selections, Reggie enjoyed a triumphant moment. Leo would surely choose at least one of hers and hopefully recognize her skill. Bryce had gotten all the glory for years. Time to share.

The morning had started out foggy, and she'd built in extra time because she wanted to stop in Ft. William at The Ben Nevis Distillery and check out their selection. If she remembered right, it was a favorite because of the fun staff.

Four years ago a trade magazine had written up their "McDonald's Glencoe 8-Year-Old Vatted Malt." She still remembered the "cereal, spice, and kick" description from Jim Murray and wanted to give it a try. Sadly, it turned out to be a disappointment.

Instead she chose a small sample bottle of their "Special Reserve" for comparison. It had potential, and they were exporting it to the U.S. She dictated a note.

The next roundabout indicated the way to the A82 and Reggie laughed as she passed McDonald's Golden Arches.

She put a mix CD in and opened her water bottle. The sun broke through and she steered northeast toward Craigellachie.

❧❧❧❧

Bryce pulled into the parking lot behind the Highlander Inn and stopped. Her stomach growled, and all she wanted was a hot meal. She grabbed her messenger bag and stood beside the car watching the

River Spey as it sparkled in the sun. The only sounds were the riffles over the rocks. The air smelled crisp, of pine and the mossy riverbanks. She took another deep breath and closed her eyes. The sun felt warm and comforting.

When was her last vacation? She couldn't remember. Maybe Leo would let her take a few days when they finished.

Once inside, she could smell lunch aromas and the wood fireplace. Her stomach gurgled. *Okay, time for food.*

She waved at Billy and trotted off to wash up. Her phone buzzed as she opened the door. "Hello?"

"It's Reggie. I just found the turnoff for the inn. Should be there shortly."

"Okay, I'll meet you downstairs at the entrance." She just had time to recharge her phone, scrub her hands and face, and jot an email to Leo. His last message had sounded impatient. Or angry.

Chapter Eight

"Murray, would you help me get Dad inside?" Fiona walked around the car to the passenger side.

"Here now, man, let me help." Murray put an arm around Gavin MacDougall and helped him navigate to the door. "What'd the doctor tell you?"

Fiona fumbled with the key. "The fall wasn't too serious. Nothing broke, but he injured some ribs and his hip. He needs to be watched."

Once Gavin was settled on the sofa, Fiona flopped into a chair. "Murray, I can't believe how bad everything has got around here. What's happened?"

Murray shoved his cap under his arm and shook his head. "It was all so sudden. He was just sad for missing his wife and then…well, he started getting belligerent with the boys till a couple left. We couldn't manage well with so few and the man wouldn't lift a finger." He leaned against the sofa. "He's daft more than he's not. I had to shut down any new batches, and there's been no shipments for a fortnight."

She leaned forward and pressed her hands against the side of her head. "Do you know where the books are? I need to figure out what's going on, or we're going to lose everything."

"I'll go out to the office straight away and get things in order."

Murray didn't wait for an answer and scurried

out the door. His dogged loyalty to her father since they both served together was the only reason he stayed on. He never did much to benefit the business except follow her father's directions.

"Fiona! When did you get home?" Her father smiled from the sofa.

❧❧❧❧

Bryce tugged her jacket closer and watched as Reggie turned into the parking lot behind the inn. The river now looked unsettled. Dark grey water mirrored the dark clouds that had rolled in. She waved.

"I made it." Reggie pulled her carry-on up the sloped drive. She offered a one-armed hug. "Boy, it's pretty up here."

"Good to see you." Bryce surprised herself with the sincerity. "Come on in, your room's all set." It was good to see her co-worker. She was used to seeing her on a daily basis at home.

"This is quaint." Reggie looked around the small registration area and into the bar. "How'd you find it?"

Bryce laughed. "I guess it was cellular memory. Leo brought me here ten years ago. I'll tell you the story over a drink. Let's get you settled." She steered Reggie to a room next to hers.

"All right, I'll be back down in a couple of minutes."

Billy waved as Bryce walked into the cozy bar area. Even though it was May and technically spring, the fragrant burning logs welcomed her. She walked to the end of the bar and sat down.

"What can I get you, miss?" Billy set a coaster in front of her.

"My co-worker just arrived and she'll be down

in a minute." She leaned a little closer. "I wondered if you'd be willing to try the taste test on her. I'd like to know if we have the same reactions. I'll certainly pay."

He smiled. "As you can see, I'm not overburdened with customers and I rather enjoyed the last tasting. Do you want the same samples or something different?"

She chewed her lip. "Hmm, could you keep the two I asked about and add a couple of different ones?"

He nodded. "Aye, that'd be the anCnoc and the Highland Dew. Sure thing." He moved down the bar and set out some glasses.

Reggie came in and looked around.

The old-world ambience of the room provided a perfect setting for a drink and conversation. Bryce smiled as Reggie walked around examining the game table and the antiques on the wall. When she turned toward the bar and saw the hundreds of whisky bottles, her jaw dropped.

"I thought you'd like this."

"No kidding. Have we died and gone to heaven? This is extraordinary." Her drawl deepened with her surprise.

"I thought you'd be impressed, and as a treat, I asked Billy to recreate a taste test like I had with Malcolm. Come sit down."

Five small tasting glasses were lined up in front of an empty chair. Reggie just grinned.

"Billy, this is Reggie Ballard, my co-conspirator. Reggie, say hi to the keeper of the spirits."

"Pleased to meet you, Billy." Reggie extended her hand. "This is a wonderful welcome."

He set out two water glasses and a plate with oatcakes and cheese. "Enjoy."

Bryce handed her a sheet of paper. "Here's the

deal, taste each one, jot down your first impression along with which region you think it's from. Then move on to the next. I'll do the same, and we'll compare with what Billy has noted."

Reggie grinned. "Game on."

Soft Celtic flute music drifted in from the hallway adding to the crackling of the fire. Bryce watched as Reggie practiced the ceremony of tasting—just the way Leo had taught them. She was careful and methodical, noting her impressions as she went without giving away any emotion. Bryce followed her and wrote her own comments.

The two she requested were more familiar, but Billy added some that were similar in nose and finish. She made her guesses.

Billy watched them as he carefully dried glasses, but his eyes twinkled with mischief.

Reggie finished the last one and wrote a few more notes while Bryce finished.

"Are these all small-batch? Because I'm impressed with several of them." Reggie picked up her water glass and drank.

Billy picked up the paper under each. He nodded to Reggie. "What were your guesses?"

"One: Highland, two: Highland, three: Islay, four: Speyside, and five: Highland."

"Not bad, except two was Islay and three was Speyside." Billy smiled.

"That's the same one I missed," Bryce said, "what is it?"

He produced a bottle labeled "Speyburn 10-Year."

Bryce and Reggie both groaned. "That's ours."

"Aye, right up the road a bit." He gestured over his shoulder.

Reggie began to laugh. "Leo would have our hides for missing that."

"Yeah, might be best to leave that out of our reports. Thanks a lot, Billy. Do you think we could look at a menu?" Bryce added.

Reggie broke off a piece of oat cake and added a bit of sharp cheddar. "That was fun. I liked the first one and the last two. Can we find out what they are?"

Not sure she wanted to share her pervious choices, Bryce asked, "Could you give us the distillery names?"

Billy handed her the list and cleared the glasses. "Your order should be up soon."

"You're kidding." Reggie laughed. "One of those I missed was a place I visited and tasted." She covered her eyes. "But I don't know the others."

"The last two were ones I liked, too. One of them, the anCnoc is available and comes out of the Knockdhu distillery. The other one is no longer made. Highland Dew."

"That's too bad. It was unique and stood out."

"Ladies." Billy set down two plates of fish and chips.

Bryce shook out her napkin. "So, tell me about your adventures in the Hebridean Islands."

✤✤✤✤✤

Fiona got her dad settled in bed, left his door ajar, and sat back down at the kitchen table to go through the sales and production numbers. More than likely she'd have to call David, their former bookkeeper.

She poured more tea and flipped through last-quarter earnings. Dismal. Only ten cases sold and two casks to the regional bottler for a blend.

"No wonder everything's gone to hell, that's not enough to cover expenses. Damn." She shoved back her chair and tiptoed into the parlor. Once around the corner she pulled out the phone and dialed her friend.

"Hello, Mary? It's Fiona. Sorry to bother you so late, but it looks like I'm going to be gone a bit longer. Could you look after my flat?"

She closed the phone and looked around the room that was once the center of their family. Suddenly it looked shabby and uncared for. Her mum had taken such pride in making curtains and chair covers. The wood always gleamed from the lemon oil. But now, stacks of newspapers covered the table, and dust covered the bookshelves and the china figurines her mum had loved.

This task was more than she could handle, and she began to cry.

Chapter Nine

Would you care for a bit more coffee, ma'am?" The server held a silver coffee pot.

"Yes, thank you. It's very good." Reggie smiled. "I'm surprised you're drinking tea," she said as the server left.

Bryce added cream to her cup. "I did it for a change when I arrived and found I really like it. Feels right." She finished stirring and took a sip. "I'm sorry you have to head out so soon."

"Me, too. But I only have a couple of sites on the north coast, and I want to spend a little time at Balblair with Tony. He owes me dinner. Then I'll come back so we can wrap things up."

Bryce took a bite of the warm scone slathered with blackcurrant jam. She wiped her mouth and gazed out the window. There was time. "I think I'll head down to Aberlour for a visit. They have some good local connections, and…the Walker shortbread is there." She winked. "It's Leo's favorite."

"Hey, it's mine, too."

"Yes, I will get you some as well. We may be able to ship it all back to the office."

"Good idea. Avoid the VAT if possible." Reggie folded her napkin and stood. "I'm going to run up and get my things. Will you walk me out?"

"Sure thing. I'll wait here." She lifted the bone china cup and sipped the tea. Oddly, the shortbread made her think of the dilapidated distillery and the mystery woman. What a shame that her business had withered. Bad economies hit everyone, but she always hated to see small distilleries close. They were always such an important part of local villages—like a heartbeat.

She watched the sunbeams dance across the white lace curtains of the dining room. During her career with GDD, she'd seen international corporations swallow up large and small distillers. It was business. She understood, but it felt like time was moving faster and she was missing something. *What? Time to smell the roses? Who knows?*

Bryce signed for the meal and headed for the lobby.

"All set." Reggie shifted her bag. "Is there anything you need me to do?"

Bryce held the door. "Be safe and find a gem."

They walked down to the lot and Reggie put her bag in the trunk of her leased car. "This was a nice break. Good choice."

Bryce gave her a quick hug. "Give me a call when you get settled some place."

She waved as Reggie pulled out, but something niggled in the back of her mind. Reggie had been holding something back. It wasn't like her not to brag about her exploits. She'd only briefly described her visits. It probably would have been a good idea to review her reports…too late now. Next time she'd be more careful.

❧❧❧❧

Aberlour was a short distance away on the A95.

It became familiar as she got closer. It was a cozy, attractive little village with tidy homes, flower baskets, and friendly shops. After a quick stop at the Walker Bakery for several cartons of shortbread—including a few samples—she continued to the distillery, just a few hundred feet farther. The Scottish distilleries were each as unique as their whiskies. Most were at least a century old with proud histories as well as some tasty rumors.

The sign on her left and the lovely gift shop welcomed her. She turned in and drove slowly back to the visitor area. It was a large complex with numerous buildings for malting, mashing, fermenting, distilling, bottling, and warehousing.

After she parked and retrieved her bag, Bryce stood looking around for someone to guide her to the right office. One of the brightly painted red doors opened and a pretty young woman trotted down the steps. "Excuse me, can you help me?"

"Yes, ma'am. Are you lost then?" Her dimples and wild curly hair were enchanting.

Bryce smiled. "Actually, I'm looking for someone in your marketing department. I'm with the Global Distillers and Distribution Company." She offered her card.

"Well then, why don't I take you over there." She gestured to a building behind them.

"Have you worked here long?"

"Not so long. This is my second summer. Last year I just ran errands and helped with the gift shop." She pulled open a door. "Frances, this lady would like to see someone about marketing. I wasn't sure..." She handed the card over.

"That's fine Brigid, thank you." The older woman

had a rather clipped brogue. Bryce wasn't familiar enough to recognize it.

Brigid smiled and backed out the door.

"I believe you'll need to see Mr. Marsh. Just a moment."

Bryce looked around the small office. The building looked to be newer—maybe ten years old—and rather Spartan. Still, the equipment was high tech.

"Ms. Andrews, I'm John Marsh. Would you like some tea?" He stood over six feet and was quite distinguished. He pointed to a large room that could have been meant for meetings or lounging.

"Tea would be lovely. I don't want to take up your time, especially without an appointment, but I just wanted to introduce myself and our company." She accepted the chair at a round table near the window.

He unbuttoned his jacket and sat across from her. He looked to be Leo's age, sixty or so. Comfortable in his skin, this man wasn't new to the business. He wore the look of experience. He tapped her card on his fingertips.

"Bryce Andrews. I believe our paths have crossed before. Can't recall just now, but I'm certainly familiar with Global. It's a fine organization. What brings you up here?" He leaned back and tipped his head to one side.

"Leo Edelman sent us on a mission to find some unusual small-batch whisky." She accepted the teacup.

He looked up. "Leo? My word, I haven't seen him in ages. How is the old rascal?"

She paused mid-sip. "You know Leo?"

"Oh, sure. We met about...I'd say fifteen or so years ago. We met at an International Whisky Symposium in Edinburgh. If I'm correct, we shared several cocktails and some good stories. So you work with him?"

"Yes, I started almost fifteen years ago in Chicago. When we opened a west coast office, Leo made me regional manager."

"I shouldn't think you're old enough. Must have started young." He smiled.

"As a matter of fact, I did. I worked in a vineyard part-time in high school. I majored in sales and marketing with a minor in chemistry. But, I had my eye on distribution. Leo hired me on a whim, I guess, because I sure was green."

"I suspect old Leo has some sixth sense about business—always has. So what can I do for you? I doubt you're here to purchase the distillery."

"Not that I wouldn't love to rep Aberlour, but I'm sure Pernod Ricard might object." They both laughed. "Actually, I hoped you might know of some new local brands that might benefit from wider distribution."

He rubbed his chin. "Are you looking for single malts?"

"Yes, but if you can think of anyone doing something new and different, it might be worth a visit for me."

He leaned forward and set down his cup. "There may be a couple of chaps... Will you be in the area long?"

"Maybe a week. I'm staying at the Highlander Inn over in Craigellachie. My cell number is on the card." She caught the look at his watch that meant she should leave. "I really appreciate your time." She stood.

"It was my pleasure. Please give Leo my regards, and I'll see what I can dig up for you."

Bryce shook his hand as he held the door.

"Thank you, John. I've enjoyed meeting you."

At the end of the driveway she paused and then turned left. The internal dialogue had continued in the twisty corridors of her mind for some time. Between Reggie's odd behavior and the eerie feeling she got from the spooky old distillery, Bryce felt driven to find at least one answer today.

The highway wandered through the scenic valley beside the River Spey. Wooded hillsides bordered the fields and a handful of farms. The air smelled like freshly tilled earth when she opened her windows. It was glorious.

On the left side, she spotted a large white sign for the Glenfarclas distillery. She might come back to that if she had time. For now, she needed to turn off on the side road at Marypark. That would take her across the Spey and up the B9102. The route actually seemed familiar now.

A text sounded through Bluetooth.

"Message from John Marsh. Read it or ignore."

"Read it."

"I found two names and will email their info. Have a good day."

Fist bump. Somehow, she knew he'd have something. Things were looking up. At least she was beginning to feel the time hadn't been wasted. If they could sign one or two, that might start things moving. It was a good guess that new entrepreneurs weren't thinking about global distribution right out of the gate. And so far, most were even surprised at the idea. That Leo…clever guy.

She slowed the car as she neared what she had lovingly nicknamed "dead man's curve." For sure, a ginormous vehicle would soon appear.

None did, so she steered into the long, weed-choked driveway past the orchard. The sound of machinery meant someone might be around. Near the house, she spotted the open front door and smiled.

She shut off the motor. *What the hell am I here for?* Her hands trembled a little and her mouth dried up. It seemed like a good idea.

"Hi there."

Bryce followed the sound to the side of the house and an overgrown garden. It was her. Same hair, same face.

She waved and opened the car door. "Hi. Since I was over in Aberlour, I thought I might swing by... and, well, see how things are going." Her cheeks felt warm and she felt silly. "I would've called, but I didn't have a number..."

"I'm glad. It's nice to have some company." Fiona pulled off her work gloves and shoved them in her back pocket. After she brushed her hands off on her jeans, she swiped her dark auburn hair from her forehead. "I was ready for a break and something cold to drink. Can you stay a bit and join me?" Her dimpled smile lit up her face.

Bryce gripped her keys a little tighter. "That sounds good."

Fiona pointed to some chairs on the small porch. "Great. Have a seat. Would you like water, tea, or beer? That's what I'm having."

"Water, I think." She sat in one of the old-fashioned, handmade wood chairs. It was comfortably worn.

"Be out in a minute."

The sun was filtered through the large oak branches and flowering pastel apple blossoms. The machine noise had stopped, and it was quiet.

She stretched her legs and crossed her ankles, then took a deep breath. *Nice.* From this vantage point, she could see beyond the orchard to the wooded hill beyond. Highland hills were numerous and majestic. Gently rounded, it was hard to determine their immense size unless there was a marker, like a stone fence or tree line.

Raised voices came from deep in the house. A man and woman, presumably Fiona and maybe her father. Bryce wondered if she should step away and not eavesdrop, but the screen door swung open.

"Sorry about that." Fiona handed her a glass. "My dad can be ornery and quite stubborn."

"I understand. My mother can be the same way."

Fiona sighed loudly and leaned back. "I think this is the first I've sat all day. When I came home from Edinburgh, it was to check on my dad, and now it looks like I may need to take a leave of absence to take care of things because he can't and there's no one else."

Bryce watched and thought she saw tears forming. "Is your father ill?"

"He's been depressed for some time since my mother died suddenly several years ago. But lately, Murray says he's been confused, forgetful, and unpredictable." She gulped her beer. "A few days ago he fell and we had to get him to the A & E for x-rays and some stitches." Her voice cracked. "I'm afraid to leave him unattended."

She swiped tears from her cheeks. "I'm sorry. I shouldn't be going on like this with a kind stranger. You'll be thinking we're all daft."

"Please, don't worry. I understand how frustrating it can be. Besides, you have an awful lot to deal with around here." She gestured around her. "Isn't there anyone who can help you?"

"I have cousins, but they don't live near and I'm not close with them. Sort of a black sheep, if you know what I mean."

Bryce thought she knew exactly what she meant and nodded. "Yeah, that makes it difficult."

Around the corner of the porch, a wiry, balding chap appeared. He seemed frail except for his small, almost-black eyes. He pulled off his worn wool cap. "Beggin' your pardon, but I got the generator running, so if you want me to watch himself while you run your errand…"

"Thanks, Murray, I almost forgot. Sorry, Bryce, this is Murray our foreman. Ms. Andrews is visiting from America."

He nodded. "Pleased to meet ya. Fiona, just let me know when you need to go." He turned and was gone like an apparition.

"I should probably let you get on with your errands…"

"Do you need to be someplace? I mean if you wanted to go with me, we could still talk."

Bryce replayed. *Did she just ask me to stay?* She looked up and saw Fiona looking at her expectantly.

"No, I don't have other plans." She smiled. "I'd enjoy that."

Chapter Ten

The market is just there." Fiona pointed and Bryce turned left into a small lot.

"Since we're here, I'd like to pick up some more tea," Bryce said.

"Shopping isn't convenient. This store in Archiestown is the closest, but if I need anything more, I have to go to Craigellachie or Aberlour." She picked up a plastic shopping basket and hurried down the single aisle.

Bryce stood looking around in fascination. So many strange names and brands. There was an occasional familiar product. And the produce looked good. The tea selection was vast and it took a minute to pick a couple of favorites. Lady Grey was a favorite but not always easy to find in the U.S.

"All set," Fiona said, her basket filled with items.

As the clerk added the total, Bryce cleared her throat. "Since you're off your leash, would you like to get a bite to eat?"

Fiona spun around. "That's brilliant. I haven't eaten and the hotel has a lovely restaurant."

Bryce paid for her tea. "I think since I barged in on you, the least I could do is buy you lunch."

"That really isn't necessary. After all, you offered to drive, so I should pay."

Bryce shook her head. "No."

Bryce unlocked the car and Fiona set her grocery

bag in the back seat. "The hotel is just down there, if you feel like walking?"

"Perfect. I've spent far too much time driving."

They walked along the tree-lined boulevard with neat stone cottages along the sides. A car passed and the driver waved. Fiona waved back. Two boys on bicycles rode past the Square monument to war heroes.

Bryce fiddled with the keys in her pants pocket. Good thing she dressed up a bit for her meeting. At least she looked presentable. Side by side, Fiona was several inches taller with long legs. It was a comfortable silence. They walked in step at a slow pace, just enjoying the afternoon sun.

"This hotel is two hundred years old."

Bryce looked up at the three-story building with dormers on two sides. The brown stone was greyed with age, but the royal blue door welcomed them. Whisky barrels holding planters filled with bright blue cornflowers marked off the patio and parking area.

"If you'd get us a table, I'll go wash up," Fiona whispered.

A delightful hostess showed her to a small table near the bar. Crisp white napkins proudly sprouted from the cobalt blue water glasses. The room was tastefully decorated with a modern flair. *This is nice.* Bryce couldn't remember the last time she had lunch with a woman that wasn't work-related. That was pitiful.

"I hope you like this. It's a favorite spot of mine." Fiona came up from behind and took her seat across from Bryce.

"It's really lovely." A ripple of sadness washed over her. "Americans don't seem to value older things. Every day wonderful old structures are bulldozed for huge modern buildings…Sorry."

"I understand. It happens in our larger cities, but not as frequently. Scots have a thing about our history." She grinned.

"As well you should. Scotland is often neglected for its contributions to history."

"Thank you for that." Fiona flipped open her menu.

The menu looked amazing. "These all look delicious. Do you have a favorite?"

Fiona smiled and her eyes twinkled. Much better than the tense teary look an hour earlier.

"I like the beef and venison meatballs and apple sage mashed potatoes with red onion sauce."

Bryce closed the menu. "Sounds awesome. Would you like something to drink? Wine, or beer?"

"You know, I think I'd like some whisky. It's been a long time."

"Good choice. You choose. Surprise me."

Fiona's laugh sounded almost joyful.

"Something to drink, ladies?"

"Yes, I believe I'll have the Balvenie Double Cask. Neat."

"And for you?"

"I'll have the same," Bryce said.

Fiona unfurled her napkin. "Perhaps you could tell me a little about you, since I forced you to listen to my saga."

Bryce would be perfectly happy to listen to the mellow brogue all afternoon. "First, you didn't force me. I'm the one who showed up unannounced."

The waiter set two tasters down along with a small crystal pitcher of water.

"Slainté."

They each added water and raised their glasses.
Fiona nodded. "To new surprises."
"Cheers."

⚜ ⚜ ⚜ ⚜

"…after graduating. I went to college at the University of Illinois." Bryce sipped her whisky. "My interest in the chemistry of fermented beverages started at a summer job in a small local vineyard, and then to production and distribution. With my business studies background, I got involved in sales."

"But now you're looking for new kinds of whisky?"

"Yes." Bryce smiled. "Our company represents several large and small distilleries for global distribution, but lately, there's been a new wave of young distillers changing things up. It's exciting to see their enthusiasm for trying new methods."

Fiona smiled. "I enjoy the excitement in your voice when you talk about this new challenge. It's certainly unlike my students."

Her eyes danced with merriment and she was delightful company.

"Have you had any luck finding some good candidates here?"

"Yes. I've gotten a few leads and tasted some remarkable whiskies. Sadly, some are already taken, some need more time to get into a groove, and others are no longer available."

Fiona swirled the mahogany colored liquid in her glass. "It's an interesting business."

"But you chose teaching?"

"My mother desperately wanted me to follow her

footsteps into music, but sadly as I got a bit older, I lost interest. Instead I devoted myself to a passion for literature. That's what I teach."

"Gave up on music?"

"Not really. I still play fiddle for relaxation." She covered her mouth. "Wow, I just remembered I left it at my flat in Edinburgh."

The meal was served and they both turned their attention to the food. Fiona was watching as Bryce tasted the meatball and mashed potatoes.

Bryce let out a satisfied groan, Fiona smiled.

"Oh, this is incredible."

"I'm glad you like it. It's a real comfort food for me."

The time passed quickly until Fiona said sadly, "I hate to leave this, but I think I should get back."

Bryce looked at her watch. "It has been a while." She quickly signed the credit slip and put her card and receipt in her pocket.

※ ※ ※ ※

It felt bittersweet. It had been a lovely afternoon, but Fiona had to get back to reality. Maybe it had been inappropriate to discuss her financial concerns, but Bryce was very familiar with the business, and her suggestions were good ones. An appraiser would be able to give her a better vision of the overall viability of the business.

She leaned her head against the car window as they drove through familiar countryside that she was seeing as a passenger on a new journey. The warm air felt good on her face. The scent of apple blossoms wafted through the air. A petal blew through and landed on Bryce's shoulder, she leaned over and pulled the petal off.

Bryce smiled

⁂

The ride was too short. "Here's my card with my cell number and email. If there's anything I can do to help you figure out your plan, let me know."

Fiona retrieved her grocery bag and stood by the driver's door. "This has been so enjoyable. Really. I can't thank you enough."

The sun seemed to reflect off the emerald green eyes like gemstones. "Fiona, this has been a perfect break from work. I enjoyed every minute." Her voice caught when she realized she might never see this woman again.

Fiona gently squeezed her wrist. "We'll keep in touch…"

"Take care." She steered the car down the drive and watched in her rearview mirror as Fiona stood and watched her leave. The tightness in her throat moved to her chest. She coughed and opened the window farther. Probably ate too much. She tried rubbing her chest, gave up, and turned on the CD player and selected one with some short pieces by Eric Satie. It had been a soothing favorite from college because of a roommate.

The ride back to the hotel seemed faster. It was after six when she parked at the Highlander Inn. She paused at the door and realized she wasn't hungry, and would instead opt for a hot bath and some tea. She'd no sooner settled in the warm water when her phone rang. *Fiona? Nope.* "Hi Reggie, what's up?'

"I couldn't wait to tell you. I think I found the hidden gem, the one in a million, the perfect small-batch whisky."

Bryce had to laugh. Reggie's excited drawl accosted her. "So happy to hear that." She grabbed the mug with the hot Lady Grey. "Can you describe it, or do I need to wait expectantly?"

Now Reggie laughed. "I should be back in a couple of days, but I'd say…the nose is like Oban, with some rich fruit and berry, then a smoky finish. I don't know. Never tasted anything like it."

"Where'd you find it?"

"It's down off the Cromarty Firth near The Dalmore. The guys bought an old rundown single-still site about five years ago. This was their first bottling. It's got time and room to grow, but I think they've found a good recipe."

"Are they interested in signing?"

"Yes."

"Great. I've got two new leads to check out tomorrow. But right now my bathwater is getting chilly."

"Got it. Take care."

Bryce turned the hot water back on and closed her eyes. An image formed of a laughing green-eyed woman. She groaned. Another image replaced it—her lying, cheating ex rearing its ugly head and sneering.

She shut off the water and slid down till her head submerged.

Chapter Eleven

Bryce hit send. Her report for Leo was brief and uninspired. Two new prospects and Reggie's news might soften the blow. After a restless night, her determination had flagged a little. She poured more tea and added cream and sugar. Breakfast had been a quick bite of toast and soft-cooked eggs, so a little shortbread might taste good.

The morning clouds faded, and she took her phone to the overstuffed chair by the window. The lounge pants and sweatshirt felt good as she curled up in the chair. The email note from Tom listed numbers for a Brian Townsend and a Kurt Morgan.

She dialed the first one.

"Hullo?"

"Hello, I'm calling for Brian Townsend."

"That'd be me."

"Hi, Brian. My name is Bryce Andrews and I'm with Global Distillers and Distribution. I was given your name by John Marsh, because I'm looking for some new small-batch distillers interested in expanding their reach in the market."

"You're from the States?"

"Yes, I am." She wrote his name and guessed his age to be mid-thirties.

"That sounds cool. Did you want to come see our setup?"

"That would be terrific. Would today be too

soon?"

"Fine. When could you be here?"

She smiled. "Well, I'd need an address…"

He laughed. "Duh, of course. We're near Dufftown…"

She crossed out mid-thirties and wrote early thirties. The address was clear. "All right, I can be there in about an hour."

Kurt Morgan wasn't available, but she left a message about meeting with him and added her number.

Fingers crossed these guys might have something. It wasn't so much competition with Reggie as it was giving Leo some solid choices. The notebook entries showed some solid leads but nothing that really jumped out and screamed winner. Well, except the mystery whisky called Highland Dew, and sadly, that was a non-starter. Even if they could find a few bottles, it wouldn't help. But, it might be nice just to have. Note: ask Billy to check around for her.

Even with a stop for petrol, Bryce was in Dufftown within fifteen minutes and took her time cruising through the quaint town. She had driven past the Balvenie and Glenfiddich distilleries and made a note to stop by later. The area's water had to be good— could be the River Fiddich.

Downtown Dufftown bustled with activity. She turned right and continued out of town until she saw the red and yellow sign.

The small distillery was nestled at the base of a hill. It looked old but solid. The grounds were well tended and the signage looked professional. All were indications they took their business seriously. She parked in front of what appeared to be an office. A small door sign read "Townsend & McClure, Ltd."

"Hello there." A voice called from behind her. She turned as a tall young man trotted toward her. His wild red hair and beard made him look like he should be running down a gorse-covered hill brandishing a broadsword.

"You must be Brian." She offered her hand.

"Yes, ma'am. Hope you weren't waiting." He took a deep breath and shook her hand.

"No, I just got here."

"Please come in." He opened the door and held it for her.

The office was larger than it appeared from the outside. Wooden barrels and barn-board planks made up most of the furniture and shelving. Bright yellow walls made the wood stand out. Chairs were covered with bright red fabric. A dozen small pin spots highlighted the bottles and awards.

"Please, have a seat. Would you like something to drink?" Brian sat in a barrel chair across from her.

"This is very attractive—and unusual." Bryce smiled. "No, I'm fine. Why don't you tell me a little about your vision?"

He crossed his foot over his knee and Bryce smiled at the Paddington socks poking out from under his worn jeans and trainers.

"My daughter…she's three." He blushed crimson.

"Very stylish. Please go ahead."

"Gary and I were friends long before we served in the RAF. We had no family history in whisky making, but loved the tradition, and, of course the product."

"This seems like a big endeavor to start."

"Och no, we started in Gary's basement years ago, just for sport. Our early starts were godawful, if you pardon me. But we found some old-timers willing to give us advice and taste the samples." He laughed and shook his head. "Since we had time, we tried so many methods and ingredients. Some were quite good. It was great luck that Henry Walker decided to merge his business with another. So this distillery was already registered when we leased it and were ready to start selling."

Derring-do was always a good start. "How much have you produced?"

"Just a few liters at a time to start. Since Henry offered to lease it to us, we've gone from liters to barrels and registered our product. And we've settled on two kinds, instead of continuously experimenting." He pointed at the shelf. "Wouldya like to taste a dram?"

"I would." Bryce smiled at the young entrepreneur. He'd done his homework.

He poured a dram into a whisky glass and set down a glass of water.

She carefully proceeded to look, sniff, and taste with and without some water added. The delicate balance surprised her. When this was aged it would be delightful. She sipped again and held it. Soft finish with a hint of oak.

"This is nice, Brian, very nice. How old is it?"

"Five years."

"Do you plan to continue aging?"

"Oh, aye. We're still not sure whether to use sherry casks—they're expensive."

She understood that that would be risky for new starts. "If it were me, I'd try one or two. That would round this out."

"Good to know. Here's the other, we tried a malt mix with a little rye."

It was darker with a strong cereal nose mixed with a caramel note. The flavor was complex but indistinct. The tail was lingering licorice. The color was slightly cloudy. She thought of how to describe it politely. "This might need some work." She shrugged apologetically. "Maybe less rye?"

He shrugged, too. "I appreciate your honesty."

"Brian, I like what you're doing and would like to recommend the pure malt for greater distribution. Are you interested in discussing it with my home office in Glasgow?"

"I'll talk to Gary, but I'm pretty sure he'd be interested."

"Great. Here's my card for now. I'm going to have the Glasgow office send you some material about our company and our long-term vision." She stood. "Would you be able to give me a sample to take back with me?"

He grinned. "Hell yeah." He grabbed a bottle off the shelf and thrust it toward her.

She laughed out loud at his enthusiasm. "Cleary you're a man who loves what he does. This has been great. We'll talk again, I'm sure."

Once in the car, she scribbled a note: Run financials on Townsend & McClure

As she turned north on the A941 through Dufftown, she spotted the restaurant and decided to stop. "A Taste of Speyside" sounded intriguing. A parking space opened up a few doors past it. She parked and looked back to the clock tower in the center of the roundabout. It had to be at least three stories tall and very elegant. The village looked so well maintained. Clearly, the people took a great deal of pride in their homes. It certainly wasn't like that in some of the

American small towns. She felt an odd wave of shame at what must look to others like a throwaway society. Why didn't they value things the way other countries did?

The small restaurant oozed warmth and comfort. Forest green walls showed off the wonderful red plaid carpet. Wallace, maybe? She chose the small window table and asked for water. The jacket wasn't necessary, so she took it off.

The phone beeped with two messages.

The first from Kurt Morgan. "Sorry I missed your call, I'd like to meet with you. I'll be here all afternoon. North of Dufftown on the A941, there's a curve, just look for the black and white signs. Turn right to Duff's Whisky."

She jotted down the name and hit next.

"Hi, it's Fiona. I wanted to thank you for dinner and quite a lovely afternoon. I'm sure you're tracking some wonderful new whiskies, but...I just wanted to say thanks."

Bryce hit replay. *No, thank you.*

The waitress interrupted her memory. "You ordered the Taste of Speyside platter?"

"Yes, thank you. It looks wonderful." A mouthwatering sample of local favorites circled the platter. There was even a small dollop of haggis with whisky sauce that was surprisingly good. Her appetite awakened with gusto.

❧ ❧ ❧ ❧

Fiona stretched the wet towels over the clothesline and clipped them so the spring breeze would dry them quickly. The apple blossoms glazed the newly cut grass and the smell was wonderful. It felt good to be outside doing something physical instead of going through hundreds of invoices and collection letters.

She turned toward the orchard and beyond to the road. This was the only home she'd ever known, and the thought of selling everything cut deep. It wasn't fair. Her father had always been there for her and supported her dreams. It wasn't his fault that some horrible disease robbed him of his life. She grabbed another towel.

From inside, she heard Murray and her father talking. Rather loudly.

"Gavin, you've got to help me find it. I've looked everywhere."

"I just don't remember, man. I keep trying, but there are just dark holes where my memory should be." He sobbed.

"There, there. I know, but things are bad and there's no money coming in and nothing to help us. Fiona is using her savings to pay off the bank loan. We have to find the envelope with the list you made."

"But where's Mary? She'll know. She's always kept the secret."

"Good lord, man, can you stay with me for ten minutes without going daft?"

"Murray. When did you get back from Stornoway?"

"Twenty-five years ago, man," Murray mumbled.

Fiona clipped up the last towel and hurried to the back door with the empty basket. Murray was halfway across the gravel parking area.

"Murray."

He stopped, but didn't turn. "Something you need, miss?"

She walked around to face him. "Yes. I'm sorry,

but I overheard you talking to my dad. Can you tell me what it is you're looking for?"

"It's nothing important, something your da' and me was working on. I just thought it might be one of his good days when he recollects things."

"Well, don't you think I might be interested if my father was involved?"

"Really, nothing. I need to get back to cleaning the equipment..." He turned toward the malting shed.

Nothing. I don't believe that for a minute. She watched him walk away, then grabbed her basket and returned to the house. The truth was her dad did have lucid moments, but she never thought to try to engage him. Maybe she should. This would all be easier if she had someone to talk to. He didn't even need to answer, simply nod his head. It was up to her now to make the hard decisions.

He was watching TV when she came in. She knelt next to his chair and put a hand on his arm. He still had strong arms and legs from years of backbreaking work. Side by side with his father, they'd doubled the size of the distillery. It took years and strengthened the MacDougall family. There was much to take pride in.

"Hi, Dad." She kissed his cheek. "I love you so much."

He turned his head and smiled. Something flashed behind his eyes. It was a look of recognition and he teared up...and then it was gone. He touched her face gently.

"Do you want me to make you a sandwich?"

"Thank you, Mary."

She swallowed hard and patted his arm.

Oh, Dad, where are you right now? Tears blurred her vision for a moment.

Chapter Twelve

The directions Kurt provided were surprisingly accurate. It was hard to miss the dramatic curve and signs. The wooded lane felt mysterious and primeval—a secret forest in the center of acres of fields. Visions of Alice and the White Rabbit teased her. Oddly, in her fantasy Alice looked a lot like Fiona. She replayed the phone message but thought Fiona sounded a little off. Worried or sad? She couldn't tell. Better call her later.

The large stone barn was whitewashed and highly visible. The driveway curved widely to the rear entrance. Smaller add-on buildings completed the complex. The office door was open and some lively Scottish pop lilted out into the spring afternoon. Fiddle, pipe, and drums never failed to make her smile.

"Hello?" She looked around the small, neat office. It was sparsely furnished with older furnishings that were simple and utilitarian, and not like other businesses she'd visited.

A bald head with an impressive beard popped up from under the desk.

"Oh, good afternoon. You must be Bryce Andrews." He wiped his hands on his jeans. "Just trying to hook up a new modem. We just got satellite coverage." He shook her hand. "Please, have a seat." He pointed to a sofa between two chairs and a coffee table.

"Thanks. And you must be Kurt Morgan." She sat and noticed the *Whisky* magazines carefully arranged in front of her.

"At your service." He took a seat on the other side of the coffee table.

"Pardon me, but you don't have much of an accent. In fact, I'd guess you were American." Bryce set down her bag.

"You'd be correct. Minnesota." He laughed. "I got interested in distilling about twenty years ago. It was just a hobby, but I got pretty good at making some decent bourbon and whisky. When the kids were grown, the wife and I took a trip to Scotland. And the rest is history."

"What a great story. How long have you been here?" This was a nice story; it would help promotion.

"About eight years. We started real small, but with some other locals who were interested, we formed kind of a co-op. We each contribute something to the process and share any profits."

That was a great idea. "Very unique. Where do you see yourself in five years?"

"If we could get wider distribution, we could get a loan to expand, and then produce more." He folded his hands and looked at her. "Can you tell me a little about your company?" He pointed to the new modem. "I haven't had time to do any background."

She laughed, and pulled a brochure from her bag. "Of course."

He took it and slid down the glasses from their perch on top of his head.

"Global Distillers and Distributors has been around for some time after starting in Glasgow. As you can see, we have several offices now."

"What would bring you out here looking for small batches?" He took off the glasses.

"Not too long ago, Leo Edelman, our CEO, took a couple of us to a trade show in Chicago. The American Craft Spirits Association. Some of the new artisanal whiskies were remarkable. Leo wanted to see if we could reach out to similar interests in Scotland, where we already have a network in place."

Kurt stood. "How about a wee dram while we talk?"

"Sounds good. I'm anxious to see what you've got." Bryce unbuttoned her jacket and pulled out the leather binder with her whisky notes.

He returned from another room with a tray holding two glasses, two bottles, water and crackers. "When we're finished, we can go back and taste some of the new batch." He poured a small amount in both glasses and handed her the water pitcher. "This is the very first we made here. It's the eight-year-old single malt. The majority of it's now in wine barrels for a few more years."

She took her time, knowing it had more aging to go. Still, the nose was strong and the color pale. After a couple of sips, she said, "This is quite good and different."

He beamed. "I dried the malt a little different—something we talked about for a long time."

"You and the co-op members?"

"Yup. The first thing I worked to get started was some gin. A bit of that grain got into the barley malt and made a difference in the taste. We liked it."

"That would be unique."

He opened the other bottle. "This was the last bottling before I left Minnesota. I left several barrels aging in sherry casks for a couple more years. I brought a few bottles with me just for pleasure." He poured each of them a sample.

This was much darker and smelled lush with fruit and vanilla. The taste added some smoke and fresh grass. "This is also quite good—a little sweeter." She jotted notes. "Kurt, I think you have a good handle on what you want to do. Can you tell me a little more about how your co-op works? I mean, is the business run by committee?"

"Okay. There are only four of us. One fella is a cooper who can do wonders with wood and makes our barrels. Our oldest is in farming, and can get the best barley around. The third is a lady from a long line of distillers. She knows her whisky and has been a big help teaching me the tricks of the trade." He laughed loudly. "And it is *she* who must be obeyed."

"Is this full-time for them?"

"No. We get together once a week to talk about stuff. When there's something ready to bottle and sell, we each get some of the profit. But my name is on all the papers."

It was an unusual setup, but logical for someone starting out. She had a hunch Leo would like this guy. "Why don't you give me a quick peek and I'll get out of your hair."

He did a double take and snickered. "Yeah, good one. Right this way."

The cask room was small and utilitarian, but had the distinct musty whiskied-oak essence from what was lovingly called "the angels share." Alcohol evaporation from the wooden barrels accounted for a small percent of loss.

Kurt set two glasses on an upright barrel and

removed a wooden plug.

"That's a beautiful whisky thief." Bryce pointed to the two-foot long copper tube that looked like a large ballpoint pen.

"Thanks. My dad bought this for me when I finished my first batch of decent whisky. I consider it good luck." He slid the tube into the barrel in put his thumb over the hole on top. When extracted, the amount captured in the tube provided a sample for each glass.

It was a lighter color with a very complex nose and taste. Strong, astringent, and citrus.

"This is different," Bryce said.

"A new recipe. We'll have to see how it ages."

The door opened and a woman stuck her head in. "Kurt, I don't want to interrupt, but your shipper is here."

"Katie, this is Bryce Andrews, from Global. This is my lovely bride, Katie. Would you excuse me for just a minute?"

"Sure. I should probably be going."

"No need to rush," Katie said. "He won't take long."

No mistaking this woman's origin. Average height and looking every inch Scandinavian. Her light brown hair was pulled back in a long braid. Her pink cheeks and blue eyes shined in the dimly lit room.

"I've just taken some cookies out of the oven. Won't you come in and have some coffee?"

Homemade cookies? "That sounds wonderful. A bit of home."

"Kurt was so excited to get your call. It's kinda serendipitous since they were talking about finding new markets. This has been a dream of ours forever, and it's thrilling to see it unfolding." Katie pointed to the house and waved to Kurt, who was talking to the truck driver.

Two hours later, Bryce pointed her car north toward her hotel with a signed representation authorization and a bag of cookies. She wanted to call Reggie with the news, but hesitated for some reason. The recent lapse in communication raised some concern about the normally loquacious southern belle. Maybe she was busy…or maybe she'd had another night of drinking.

Chapter Thirteen

Reggie pulled in to the Station Bar Hotel in Alness and parked. The small village was nestled between the hills along the Cromarty Firth partway between Inverness and John O'Groats on the northernmost tip of the mainland. The Dalmore Distillery, one of her favorites, was very near.

Her last visit netted a contract for representation, and Joe, the younger partner, insisted on buying her dinner and she had only twenty minutes to get changed. The suit and heels had to go. This was her second visit to the small distiller and Joe wanted her to talk with the banker holding a note. Happily, Leo was willing to make a quick call to the Glasgow office and approve a preliminary contract based on the one quarter of earnings the boys had posted. She ran up to her room and changed into jeans and a cashmere V-neck sweater. A spray of perfume and she hurried down to the lounge.

"What can I get you?" the bartender asked. His curly silver hair and dark turtleneck gave him a nautical look.

"I think I'll have McEwan's on tap." Reggie offered her most authentic Charleston drawl and smile.

His hardened face softened. "You must be one of the Southern ladies from the U.S. I've heard about."

She blushed. "Why yes, however did you know?"

He placed the beer glass on a mat. "I guess it's

the delicate way you talk. Don't sound like a Scot's lass, t'all."

"That's very kind of you. Are you from around here?" His deep guttural brogue required careful attention.

"Up the coast toward Brora."

Joe walked in at that moment and pulled a seat closer to her. "Hope I'm not late." He'd clearly changed and showered. His dark wavy hair glistened.

"Not at all, I was just talking to…"

"Murch—well, that's what folks call me."

"Sure, we're all familiar with the randy old sailor. I'll have a beer as well." Joe smiled.

Reggie leaned back and watched the interaction. Joe had been flirting with her since they met and she used it to get the deal. Hopefully, dinner would be a fitting reward for his help. His brother wasn't all that keen, but Joe convinced him to give it a try.

Leo would be happy to pick up this tab. The small distillery had a long family history.

※ ※ ※ ※

Leo coughed. "I'm pleased with the success both you and Reggie have had. I'd rather have a few too many in case some don't pan out."

"I feel the same way, although, I have been impressed by the earnest and enthusiastic attitude of these entrepreneurs." Bryce propped her feet on the window seat and slouched down in the chair. She was tired from yesterday's calls, but very encouraged.

"Do you think there might be more in other regions?"

When she considered her luck in just the Speyside

region, she knew that the concentrated searches were more helpful. But, she dreaded the thought of more searching in new areas. She needed a break.

"Not sure, I think we've figured out how to scout these small local areas more efficiently…"

"I hear a 'but'…"

She let out the breath she was holding. "But, I'm really tired, Leo."

There was a pause and she heard keys tapping. "Let me see, looks like your last real vacation was over two years ago. How did we let that happen?"

She closed her eyes. "Because we've been so busy with new offices…"

"Bryce, I apologize for not paying more attention. You're a valuable employee and I don't want you to burn out."

I hope it's not too late, she thought. "It's my fault for not asking."

"What would you like to do to remedy this?"

"I'm not sure. I'd like to wrap things up before I think about that." The sun moved out from behind a tree and the river reflected the dancing beams of light. A wave of calm washed over her. "I might spend a few more days here."

"Just let me know. Before you wrap up, I'd like a conference call with you both at Ian's office in Glasgow."

"We planned on it. Thanks, Leo."

"Take care."

The cookie bag was calling her name. Resistance was futile. The cinnamon sugar pastry melted in her mouth. The cozy warm room felt even more comfortable, probably because she let go of the guilt about being tired. Two years? Hell, she deserved a vacation.

She grabbed her phone and dialed. After all, since she was taking the day off... Voicemail. "Hi Fiona, it's Bryce Andrews, I have the day off and wondered if you wanted to get an early supper? I'll be doing a couple of errands, but I have my cell phone."

By four o'clock, she'd finished the nonessential time-wasting errands and was near Archiestown. She turned into the hotel lot where they had eaten before.

"I could have a beer or walk around. It's a nice village." She leaned over to switch off the ignition and stopped. Instead she shifted to Drive and got back on the road west to upper Knockando.

Bryce, you're being ridiculous. If you want to see Fiona, go see her.

She turned up the music and opened all the windows. Many of the fields were lush with a green carpet of new life. Others were newly tilled dark soil waiting for a new crop. Bryce smiled at the redolent smell of spring, as if she'd somehow never seen farm fields. "Hello. You grew up in the Midwest."

As she slowed for curves, she remembered a Christmas when her grandparents had visited from Pennsylvania. Her grandfather had retired from the ministry and then spent time as headmaster of a fancy girls' school. He was an imperious-looking man with a thick shock of white hair, wiry black eyebrows, and rimless glasses. But, boy could he tell a story.

The one that came suddenly to her mind described the arrival of her ancestors from Scotland in 1650. They split into two groups to find land to settle. When a suitable property was found, one man returned to Philadelphia for the rest of the group. When they returned to the new settlement, all they found were the remains of their kin.

She slowed the car and pulled off to the shoulder. The stone cottages came into stark relief and with that, a strong sense of déjà vu. The stone fences, fields, and the hills. The endless hills. Did her own heritage lead back to this part of Scotland? Who knows. Had some farmer with her DNA actually worked these fields in the past, and now she had returned to the exact same spot?

The irony wasn't lost. She'd worked for almost fifteen years selling products from the country where a majority of her forebears had lived. No wonder it felt so familiar. She started to laugh. The sound of wind seemed to be answering her.

She opened the car door and got out. A steel field gate was open and perched on top was a shiny black Corbie. Was he following her? He bobbed his head as she passed him and walked into the wheat field. The sun ducked in and out of the clouds while she ambled through the narrow rows and raised her arms over her head. "This is where I want to be," she said loudly to no one.

A lorry loaded high with feed sacks rumbled by and she waved. The driver waved back and she grinned. Mind made up that she wanted to talk to Fiona, she hurried back to the car and continued her journey.

The dangling, faded MacDougall & Son Distillers sign hung just as she'd last seen it. She navigated up the driveway and circled around the house looking for signs of life. The car was gone and she called out, "Anyone here?" She got out to look around. "Murray?"

The office door was closed and so was the back door of the house. She listened for some sound and heard nothing. "Well, this is disappointing."

The various buildings once held dreams and promise. Now, the neglect made them empty vessels. Ghost ships, of sort.

An old truck sat parked near a loading dock at the end of the row of buildings.

It was eerily quiet, and she called out Fiona's name as she approached the partially raised loading door. No answer. She ducked under and called out again. It was silent except for the sound of water dripping. Sunlight through dusty skylights partially illuminated an empty warehouse with stacks of wooden pallets.

When her eyes adjusted to the dark dank space, she saw a dim light down a wide sloping corridor. *That's odd.*

"Fiona? Is anyone here?"

What are you thinking? Get out of here you're trespassing—again. You know this is the part of the movie where the audience screams "Don't go down there!"

But the faint smell of whisky was irresistible. Near the bottom she used the flashlight app on her phone to see past the narrow gap in the metal door. She opened the heavy door a little farther and stepped into a damp, cool room with rows of ghostly looking barrels.

"This must've been the storeroom."

Scurrying feet startled her and she almost ran, but her flashlight strobed across the stencil on the nearest barrel.

MacDougall & Son #1892 Highland Dew 1998

She rubbed the cobwebs and dust off the surface of the cask and gasped. And read it again. *Highland*

Dew…isn't that the same…? The rest of the room was dim and shadowy. Her flashlight barely penetrated the darkness.

She backed toward the door, pulled it closed, and ran up the ramp. After ducking under the heavy door, she stopped to catch her breath. No one around, mercifully, so she wouldn't be prosecuted. But if that was really…

Where was Fiona? She had to talk to her. The back door might be open, and she trotted toward the house.

"Hello? Is anyone home?" Bryce knocked louder.

The wind rattled the door on the loading dock and she spun around. No one there.

"I wished I had asked for the home phone number."

The phone.

She pulled out her cell and asked, "What's the phone number for MacDougall & Son distillers?"

The waiting logo circled around and around.

"That information is not available."

Bryce took a deep breath. "Crap. Okay, I'll leave a note." She scribbled her request on the back of her business card and stuck it in the door. The wind whistled through the trees and scattered more of the fragrant petals.

"This is unreal." She looked around again. Was this really the distillery that she'd been looking for? Billy! She needed to talk to him. She started the car and sped down the driveway.

Chapter Fourteen

"Hi, Bryce. It's Reggie. Are you busy?"

She hit the Bluetooth. "Hey, Reggie, glad you called. I'm just heading back to the hotel, but have I got news."

"Must be good. You never talk this fast."

"Very funny. Yes, it might be great news. Remember when we did the tasting?"

"Sure."

Bryce checked her speed and slowed down. "There were two samples we both really liked and one of them was no longer being produced. Remember?"

"I've tasted so many…wait, the apple flavor?"

"Exactly. Well, I just stopped in at the old distillery I found the other day. The one I thought was abandoned."

"The one with a pretty teacher?"

Had she really said that? "Yes, but no one was there. I snooped around and found a storeroom in the creepy old building. Inside I found a barrel with that name—Highland Dew."

"One barrel?"

She flushed with embarrassment. "I don't know. I freaked out and ran out of the building. No one was there so I had to leave a note."

"I don't know what to tell you. I'm not sure one barrel is proof of anything. Maybe your bartender friend might be able to shed some light. But listen, you remember the two guys I was trying to get to up near Dalmore?"

Bryce shook her head. Why was Reggie changing the subject? This could be a huge find. "Yeah, I think so."

"Well, I had dinner with Joe last night and he signed the Request for Representation. I called Leo and he's thrilled."

Had dinner? "Why… Never mind, that's great. What do you have planned now?"

There was a long pause. "Um… I'm not sure. I have a couple of ideas. Let me know what the bartender says. Gotta go."

The conversation felt off. Reggie had never been so vague or cagey. Hopefully Leo would tell her if he suspected a problem. But, she might be right—getting excited about the printing on one barrel was hardly earth-shattering evidence. Her buoyant mood withered like a birthday balloon. She'd still talk to Billy, but first, it would be a hot meal and a hot bath.

The bar area at the inn was nearly empty except for an older couple enjoying tea. There was a new face tending bar. An attractive young woman in her late twenties maybe.

"Good afternoon, my name is Ann. What can I offer you?"

Bryce scanned the immense whisky selection. "I think I'd like the Glenfiddich nineteen-year-old 'Age of Discovery,' neat. I'd also like a menu, Thanks."

The warm whisky opened as she savored the first swallow. "That's nice. Wish they exported this bottling to the States." She smiled.

"Oh, they will some day. Have you decided on something to eat?"

Her bright blue eyes and curly hair made her appear younger.

"I think I'll try the venison burger. Bet that's less expensive."

"Good choice." Ann set off for the kitchen.

Bryce checked her phone for the hundredth time. No messages. She needed to finish the notes from yesterday, but didn't feel like it. On impulse she typed in her mom's email address.

Hi Mom, I'm enjoying Scotland more than ever. We've had a successful trip and contacted some interesting local distillers who're promising. We'll probably wrap up pretty soon, but I may stay on for a few days. The Speyside region is lovely and I really need a break. Hey, has Dad ever mentioned where the Andrews clan came from? It'd be fun to know if we have relations over here. Love, Ellen

She sipped the whisky. *I hate my first name. And I'm sure that's why she insists on using it. As many times as I've asked her not to.* Their relationship had soured as soon as she met Gretchen. When they moved in together…well, that was it. The final nail. Her sister wasn't much better, but at least they could talk.

She picked up the phone and took another drink. At least her dad and brother were really supportive.

The phone chimed with an email.

Ellen dear, thank you for finally sending a such a brief note. We've been quite worried since we hear from you so seldom. Even if you do not wish to correspond with me, think of your father. It just breaks his heart

Bryce put down the phone. Even thousands of miles couldn't prevent the stinging slap. Taking vacation was no longer optional. Even with her many successes, her mother could cut the legs out from under her with very little effort. Yes, she'd definitely be staying in this place that made her feel happy, safe, and more like an adult professional. Staying in the Speyside area was a great idea. Edinburgh had a strong appeal, too. Maybe she'd take a couple of brief holidays.

"Excuse me, Ann?" The young woman came over.

"Ready for another?"

"Not just yet. I wonder, do you know much about the local whiskies?"

She shrugged. "I'm afraid not much. I'm at University in animal science."

Bryce smiled. "I guess that's not your field. I was curious about a sample Billy gave me." She pointed. "Highland Dew. He said it was no longer produced and I wondered if there was any other information."

Ann retrieved the partially full bottle. "I don't know if the label will help, but have a look."

Bryce held up the green and white label. It looked almost identical to the sign at the site, but above it read: *Highland Dew, Single Malt Scotch Whisky, Distilled and Matured in Moray. 10 years old.*

The cook appeared carrying a plate. "Heilan' venison burger?"

"Yes ma'am." Bryce unrolled the napkin.

It looked wonderful. Venison could be tricky, but the kitchen knew how to cook their food. Of course, the bacon, Scottish cheddar, and thick potato wedges didn't hurt. The first bite was mild and flavorful. Not beef, but a tasty, mild, gamey flavor.

The whisky complemented the meat perfectly. For a short time, she forgot about her roller-coaster day and enjoyed a leisurely meal. The idea of some down time was more and more appealing.

The lavender bath salts filled the room with the light scent. Bryce slipped into the tub and allowed the warm water to melt any remaining tension. It was only then she realized the stiff shoulder and neck that had tortured her daily for a couple of years seemed to be gone. She couldn't remember when it disappeared or even when it started to abate, but the relief softened all the adjacent muscles. The silky water glistened on her skin and beaded until she swiped her hand across.

The sensation brought back some of the tender moments she had shared with Gretchen. It hadn't always been bad. The first heady days after they met in Chicago, she felt like she was perpetually high. Never in her life had she felt that kind of euphoria. It lasted for a few years until they started to take things for granted and drift apart.

Then on Valentine's Day a year ago, she found the letter in Gretchen's briefcase. She hoped to sneak in a card that Gretchen would find when she got to work. Instead, on two pages of a yellow legal pad was a love letter…from Tina.

Her throat tightened and a sob escaped. "Damn you."

The tears flowed uninterrupted until the bath water cooled. Bryce got out, dried off, and slipped between the soft sheets. But before she switched off the light, she checked her email. Force of habit. There was a message.

"Hi, Bryce, I'm sorry I didn't get your message

sooner. I had to take Dad for a doctor appointment. Call if it's not too late."

Bryce looked at the time. It was nine-thirty. Was that too late? Did she want to start a conversation about the warehouse?

She hit call. One ring.

"Hello?"

"Hi, it's Bryce. I hope it's not too late."

"Let me go in the living room."

Bryce pulled another fluffy pillow behind her and felt a funny sensation in her stomach.

"There. Dad's in bed so I need to be quiet. I'm glad you called. I wish I'd seen your message earlier, but I left my mobile at home."

"It's not a problem. I just wanted to come by since I had no appointments." Bryce tried hard for chipper.

"That would have been nice. You're always welcome to come by. Normally I'm here—as you know." She laughed.

"Well actually…I did. No one was there and I…"

"That's odd. Murray didn't mention it."

Bryce sat up straighter. Odd, indeed. He must have watched her. "Oh. Maybe he was busy, so I left a note in the back doorjamb."

Silence. "I didn't see it. It might have fallen. I'll look tomorrow. Say, do you think you might have time tomorrow?"

Bryce took a breath. *I will make time.* "Sure, maybe we could have lunch?"

"Great idea, I'll fix you something. Would that be all right?"

"I'd like that. Eleven work for you?"

"Perfect. I'll see you then." Her voice was like

music.

"Good night, Fiona."

Bryce plugged the phone in the charger and switched off the light. Sleepiness swept over her along with a niggling thought. Murray was there? Why didn't he say something?

Chapter Fifteen

Before breakfast, Bryce wanted to take a walk and get her thoughts in order. She didn't want to rush in without testing the waters. She zipped up her windbreaker and tightened the hood. The morning mist was heavier than usual. In fact, in California they'd call it rain. The trail behind the inn ran through a heavily wooded area that provided some protection.

The walk was brisk, mainly to warm her, but the analytical part of her brain ran in the background and calculated several scenarios that might answer her questions.

First, was the Highland Dew barrel in the warehouse full, and was it their whisky? Was there more? If so, could they reopen, and what would it take to do so? Was Fiona even interested in the business? Would Murray be a help or a hindrance?

After twenty minutes, she turned around, thoroughly soaked, and started back. Could she find enough of the whisky to convince Leo to invest in the product? It could be a big project, but if she was right, they could all benefit from the investment.

Once dry and dressed, Bryce went down for breakfast. Since she was going for lunch in a few hours, Bryce decided on something lighter than the yummy Scottish breakfast.

"I'll have the soft-cooked eggs and toast."

"More tea?"

"Thank you." Bryce looked over the notes she'd made after her walk. This meeting was important for several reasons, not the least of which was she believed it was the perfect small-batch whisky. The best she'd ever tasted. And, what would that mean for her, her company, and most of all, Fiona and her family?

⁂

"Can I have a bit more parritch?"

Fiona turned and looked at her dad, surprised by the request. "Certainly. I'm happy you like it." She brought the pot from the stove and spooned more oatmeal into his empty bowl, to which he added cream and brown sugar.

She sat across from him and sipped her coffee. The doctor had started him on a new medication and it seemed to help with his concentration. On the ride home, he had told her the family legend of how his great-great-grandfather began making whisky back when it wasn't permitted. After being caught illegally distilling several different times, it came out that it really was his very proper wife who'd been making the whisky from her family recipe.

The tradition had continued with the next generation. The woman who married their youngest son followed her mother-in-law's teachings to continue the business.

"Dad, did you ever want me to go into the family business?"

He blinked. "Och, no. Your mother, rest her soul, wanted you to get an education."

"But, what did you want?"

"I wanted to make the best whisky in the valley and give your mother reason to be proud." His voiced cracked and his eyes teared up.

She went for the coffee pot and refilled his cup. When he looked up again—he was gone. Fiona could see the blankness.

He said nothing.

It was exhausting trying to find him, even if just for a few minutes. At least he had more energy with the new medicine. She could take him out in the car or for a walk.

"Miss Fiona?" Murray stood at the back door.

"Come in. Would you like some coffee?"

He nodded. "Thank ye. Good morning, Gavin." Murray sat.

The blank eyes showed no recognition.

"He was pretty good earlier." She handed him the steaming cup and took her chair. "Can I ask you something?"

He nodded. "Yes."

"Do you remember my dad ever talking about teaching me the business?"

He removed his cap and scratched his balding head. "Well, 'course he was all excited when we first put up the sign. Then your ma brought a wee baby girl instead of the boy." He sipped the coffee and glanced at her dad like it might help him remember.

Murray actually chuckled. "Once he held you for the first time, he was smitten. After that, you couldna do a wrong thing." He leaned forward on the table and moved the cup around. "I may be wrong, but if your ma wasn't so set on sending you to school...I think your da would have enjoyed teaching you what he knew and what he loved."

Her throat tightened and tears formed.

Murray stood and took his cup to the sink. "I'd best be getting's those files sorted."

"Thank you…"

He was gone and her dad was watching her very carefully. Did he understand all that?

"Dad?"

"I need the bathroom." He pushed back his chair and left—remembering his walking stick. That was a first.

"Crap." *I completely forgot to ask about Bryce's visit.*

❧❧❧❧

Bryce ran back to her room when she remembered the gift she wanted to take. Because of the rain, she'd planned some extra time. The car hummed to life and she turned the heat up. Even though the temps had been mild, the rain brought a chill that was hard to control—especially for a Californian.

Reggie had been right about buying the hand-knit wool sweater in Glasgow. It felt good. She'd always loved the look of the beautiful knit wear that was so prevalent. On her last trip she'd brought home a thick blue St. Andrew's tartan throw, which had been a great comfort in the many of the rough spots she'd weathered.

The two-lane road curved through the farms and woodlands. Cattle roamed in large pastures. All the earthy scents formed a rich medley of smells that, to her, evoked Scotland and whisky. Things that were basic and essential.

When had she drifted away into the tempestuous

realm of business and numbers? Being in the rural areas where life is at its most basic seemed to be a wake-up call. Bryce needed to slow down.

There it was, the dangling sign. She smiled. Then came the tingle she vaguely remembered as a pleasant sensation often associated with happiness. A genuine laugh rumbled up and surprised her.

The ground around the house was littered with pink and white petals. It almost looked like snow. The old stone farmhouse looked like a painting. The rain glistened off the slate-tiled roof and dripped relentlessly from rusted gutters on the flowerbeds below the windows.

Bryce turned off the car and picked up her gift. *Let this whisky be the one.*

"Fáilte, please come in." Fiona held the back door and soon aromas wafted from the kitchen.

"Thanks. It smells wonderful in here." Bryce unzipped her jacket and Fiona pointed to pegs on the wall. "I brought you some shortbread. I imagine it's nothing new."

"Oh, I love this, and so does Dad. I never think to buy it. Thank you."

The small bright kitchen felt homey and welcoming. Plaster walls painted yellow and worn oak floors were accented by exposed beams. On either side of the kitchen were large-paned windows.

Fiona walked to the stove on the back wall and opened a black stew pot.

"I started some stew yesterday, so I'm just adding a bit more." She turned to look. "Please, have a seat. I'll get you something to drink. Oh, before you sit, would you hand me the cookbook above you on the shelf?"

"Which is…?"

"The old leather book. The family cookbook for generations."

Bryce plucked the worn collection of recipes from the shelf and then chose a chair by the window at the long wood table. Above were several bunches of drying herbs, and over the sink hung other pots. "This is a wonderfully homey kitchen."

Fiona chuckled and said, "It's had quite a lot of practice. The farm's about a hundred and six years old. It's had some modernizing. My dad put in the electric." She read over a recipe, added some mystery spice, covered the pot, and turned down the temp. "I can show you the rest after we eat."

Bryce liked Fiona's casual appearance with a pair of worn jeans, a soft cotton shirt untucked, and some short brown boots. Her auburn hair was tied back at her neck and her face flushed from the cook stove. She had trouble seeing her as a teacher.

"Tea, coffee, or water?"

"Water is fine."

"Dad is still resting. I thought I'd let him." She set down two glasses and took a seat across from Bryce. "I'm so happy you could come over."

"I'm glad you asked. I really feel bad about just popping in without an invitation."

"Please don't worry, I'm just surprised Murray didn't come out to greet you. It's not like folks wander around here all the time." She shook her head. "And then when he was here yesterday, I completely forgot to ask him. I'm just sorry you made the trip for nothing."

Bryce set her glass down. "Well, that's what I wanted to talk to you about." She swallowed hard. "I was walking around hollering hello, then I saw the loading dock door open back there." She pointed to the last building. "I thought someone might be in there."

Fiona chuckled. "No one's been in there for ages—no real need."

Bryce leaned forward. "Really? Huh. The warehouse did look empty, but there was a dim light coming from a corridor...so I went to check...and the metal door was cracked open, but no one around."

Fiona's face tightened and got serious.

"When I peeked in, there were rows of barrels and the stamp on one said it was Highland Dew."

Her breath caught. "Well, yes...but I'm sure they must have been empty barrels."

"So, MacDougall is the maker of Highland Dew?" She tried to be calm, but her mouth had dried up.

Fiona slowly shook her head back and forth. "That was our signature brand, but I'm sure there's some mistake..."

From the parlor just past the door came the sound of a walking stick and, "Time to eat, lass?"

"It is." Fiona stood and pulled out a chair with a covered cushion at the end of the table. "Dad, this is Bryce Andrews, my American friend. You remember, I told you about her job with the distributor?"

He stared. Then there was a brief flash of recognition. "Oh, aye, lookin' at small distillers."

Fiona looked over with raised eyebrows. "Yes, that's right."

He was tall and unsteady. But beneath his bushy eyebrows, his eyes twinkled just like Fiona's. Thick mussed up grey hair came almost to his collar and matched a well-loved grey cardigan sweater.

"Pleased to meet you, Mr. MacDougall." Bryce extended her hand when he got settled.

"Mister was me dad. I'm just Gavin." He shook

her hand with a strong grip and looked at his daughter. "I smelt that stew in my sleep. Woke my hunger."

"Coming right up." Fiona pushed back from the table. "Bryce was just asking about our whisky. Maybe you could tell her." She put down napkins and spoons, then started filling bowls.

"Ah yes, the Dew." His eyes looked hazy and unfocused. "The MacDougall family legacy for over three generations, until…" He looked at Fiona as she put his bowl in front of him. "Until when, Fi?"

"Just a few years ago. Let's eat now." She stroked his hair.

Bryce saw the pain change Fiona's expression.

"This stew is delicious," Bryce said. She buttered a thick piece of bread. "You teach and cook?"

Fiona smiled. "True modern-day woman. I can do it all."

I wouldn't be a bit surprised.

After dinner, Bryce dried while Fiona rinsed the dishes. Gavin faced the fire and lit his pipe. It smelled good, but it was an unusual tobacco.

"I'm thinking you'll want to go explore the warehouse," Fiona said. She glanced over at her father. "I wonder if it might be good to take Dad. He seems pretty sharp today, and I'd love to get some answers. Murray seems to have forgotten quite a lot."

"It would be great if he could solve the mystery." Fingers crossed. This could be the hidden treasure she sought.

Chapter Sixteen

The rain let up and the sun tried to peek through the grey clouds. Fiona held her dad's elbow as the three of them slogged across the yard to the warehouse. Curiosity chewed at her ever since Bryce had told her what she found. Any other time she would have felt annoyed with the typical American cheekiness. In this case, she might never have known.

"Watch your step, Dad." The muddy ramp looked slippery.

"I'm fine. You worry too much."

Bryce pushed the rolling door up higher, which allowed more light.

"Where's the switch?" Fiona asked.

"There, to the left." He pointed with his walking stick.

"I'll get it." Bryce walked a few steps and hit the switch, which lit four industrial fixtures hanging from the tall ceiling.

The large gymnasium-sized room was indeed empty. Peeling paint, cobwebs, and a few dusty pieces of equipment perfectly depicted the status of MacDougall & Son Distillers. She was heartbroken when she glanced at her dad's face. He was stunned. His dream lay in ruins.

Bryce spoke up. "Over there is where I saw the light." She pointed to the far end.

They walked down the ramp to the metal door,

which was still ajar. "Do you remember what's in here, Dad?"

He shook his head. The expression was unreadable. "Why is the door unlocked?"

"Do you know where the light is?"

He pointed to the wall behind Fiona. It looked like a fuse box.

"This?" She opened the door and saw several switches. They had tags that read: Fan, Cooler, Row 1 lights, Row 2 lights. She looked at Bryce, who shrugged. She flipped the Row 1 light and Bryce pushed open the door. The back half of the room glowed with the light from half the overhead fixtures.

Dust and shadows obscured their view, but Fiona saw three tiered rows on both sides of the aisle holding the large casks. The front panel paint was faded and hard to read.

"Dad, what is this? Are these full?"

He took a few steps to the nearest row and touched the plug. His eyes widened. "1989."

"Turn on the other row," Bryce said.

The lights above went on.

"Unbelievable. Dad…?"

He turned and smiled. "I think this might be the Distiller's Edition. It was to have been bottled a couple of years ago…"

Fiona reached for the nearest wood rail to steady herself. She looked around and saw several racks full, but not all. "How many are there?"

Bryce walked down the row counting.

"Dad, why is this still here?"

"I…I don't remember. Murray said two fellas quit." His face clouded over.

"Oh, Dad." Fiona felt her knees weaken. What

had happened after her mom died and why hadn't she paid closer attention?

Bryce grabbed her arm when she stumbled back. "You okay?"

"I don't understand what's happened."

"Let's go back to the house. I think your dad is done for today."

Fiona looked up to see her dad walking along the row staring at the casks. "Oh, Dad… Come on, let's go." She took his arm and steered him toward the door.

"I'll get the lights. Go on," Bryce said.

"Thanks." She shrugged and guided her dad toward the door.

❧❧❧❧❧

Bryce sagged against the nearest cask. "Whoa." Her head spun as the ramifications of this discovery unfolded like petals. The casks filled several racks and counted at least one hundred thirty. If they were all full, that would be…Hell, she couldn't do the math. It was astonishing.

She pulled the door closed behind her and saw the dangling padlock. She switched off the lights in the storeroom. This would need to be navigated carefully. Fiona looked shell-shocked. Clearly, this whole project had lost its captain. Who could possibly take over?

As she walked through the empty warehouse, she imagined a hive of activity with forklifts moving barrels to trucks. It was easy to imagine the next stage with those casks going to the U.S. and elsewhere. This could be a huge success. Or not.

Grey clouds swirled above, and the wind picked up. More rain blew toward her. She picked her way across the yard to the house, holding her jacket closed. *And what about Fiona?*

She knocked. "Hello?"

Fiona opened the door. "Come in. My gosh, you're soaked." Fiona took Bryce's jacket. "Come sit in the parlor. I've lit a fire and I'll bring some tea."

Like the kitchen, the living area was long and narrow. A stone fireplace covered the wall joining the kitchen. The wood floor had two large area rugs, and near the fireplace was a comfortable old couch and two overstuffed armchairs. Everything had patterned slipcovers.

Wood smoke and pipe tobacco filled the air, and the soft aroma of the stew hung with it.

Bryce took a seat in an armchair. Her pant legs were damp and the fire felt good. She noticed family photos on the mantle next to two award plaques.

"Do you take lemon, or milk and sugar?" Fiona asked from the kitchen.

"Milk and sugar."

Fiona set a tray on the coffee table and retrieved a whisky bottle from the sideboard behind the couch. "I think a wee dram might help with the chill."

Bryce took the teacup and sipped. "This is good."

Fiona sat with her cup and didn't look up.

"Are you okay?"

"No!" Her voice cracked. "I don't know what in the hell is going on here." She took a swallow and put the cup down. "You must think we're all daft, or liars. Evidently, I've been so absent that I have no idea what's going on around here. I called and left a message for Murray but he hasn't called back."

"I can sure understand why you're confused. There's certainly enough whisky that the bills could have been paid, unless your dad wanted to keep the stuff longer." It was a treasure trove of fine whisky.

"He doesn't know. By the time we got back here, there was no talking to him. He's napping now." She sipped from her cup.

"It looked like he was pretty lucid for a while." And very proud.

"Yes, I'm glad he went with us. Just being there must have been familiar. It was probably a mistake to keep him close to the house." She poured a little more whisky into her cup. "I wanted to keep him safe. Damn."

"Maybe I should go." She put her empty cup on the table.

"Oh no, that's not necessary. I'm sorry I feel so confused. I just need to figure out what to do now."

"I do know a little about the business, if I could assist?" She wasn't sure how that sounded, but she truly wanted to help. "Not to intrude."

Fiona looked up. "You know it might help to have someone to talk to who's not addled."

"I don't have any magic power, but I do sell a fair amount of whisky."

"Right." Fiona stood and walked out to the kitchen. She returned with a tablet of paper and a pen. She flipped a few pages. "I've been writing down questions and problems and…oh, damn."

"What?"

"I should've counted how many casks there were."

"I did." She pulled an envelope from her pocket. "There were one hundred thirty barrels, and three larger barrels. I'm pretty sure they were all full, but I didn't check closely."

Fiona squinted. "That might be two hundred plus bottles per barrel. That would really help us out. Of course, we'd have the added expense of hiring the men back, bottling, shipping…"

"May I ask a question?"

"Of course."

"Do you want to reopen the distillery, or just sell the stock on hand?"

The second hand on the wooden clock behind her clicked rhythmically while sheets of rain whooshed against the windows.

Fiona shook her head. "What would you do if you were in my place?

That caught her off guard. "I really don't know how to answer that. If it was hypothetical…I'd quit my job, take out a loan, and reinvent the brand." Bryce laughed, knowing she hadn't the first clue about running a business—in Scotland. "Like I said, fantasy."

Fiona smiled again. "You make it sound like fun."

"But I don't know the reality. I'm sure there's more involved."

"Suppose I would just sell the whisky we have. Do you think anyone would buy the distillery?"

Bryce felt her business brain bristle with possibility, but resisted. "I could make some phone calls."

"Of course, nothing has to be done today. I still need to see how much Murray knows about this. And I still haven't sorted out the papers." She put her cup on the tray.

"I really should go. But, I will make the calls and will help any way I can." The flutter in her chest started.

Fiona took the tray to the kitchen table and handed Bryce her jacket. "I'm so glad you happened by and found the whisky. I think that wasn't a coincidence. You've been wonderfully supportive." She placed her hand on Bryce's arm and pulled her into a quick hug.

"I'm glad, too." *Leave before you say any more.*

"Drive safely, and…" She waved.

Bryce backed the car up and waved through the foggy windshield. The tingling continued on her arm and throughout her body as if she'd gotten an electric shock. Only this was more pleasant. Much more pleasant.

The wet, slippery drive back to the Highlander Inn went quickly, and Bryce found herself in the parking lot staring at the sign. She needed to get it together. Still, the day's events blurred together like an old black-and-white movie. Fiona and Gavin, whisky barrels and cobwebs, warm fire and beef stew.

She hurried in and up to her room. It took two attempts to get the door open and she dropped her bag. "Okay, settle down."

The room felt cool so she adjusted the thermostat, then chose a pair of sweats and thick wool socks that provided instant comfort. With the teakettle hissing, she dumped her bag on the bed and gathered the notes and cards together in piles. That calmed her and provided a nice grounding activity.

"Okay. Plug in the phone and fix some tea." Talking to herself out loud became more frequent whenever she felt overwhelmed. And trying to focus on business while thinking about Fiona defined stress. It was so hard to avoid those gorgeous green eyes.

It was five-thirty in the evening, so it must have been around 11:30 a.m. in Chicago. She punched Leo's name on her cell phone and waited. When it went to voicemail, she called the office number. What she wanted right now was Leo's sage counsel.

"Mr. Edelman's office, how may I help you?"

"Hi Margaret, it's Bryce. Can I talk to Leo?"

"Oh, Bryce, I'm glad you called. I have a message for you."

Her heart began to pound. "What do you mean a message?"

"Mr. Edelman had a possible stroke and was admitted to the hospital last night. He's having tests this morning, but gave me instructions to send you a message."

"You're scaring me. Is he all right?" Her throat tightened.

"He was quite alert, but had some weakness in his left side. He was insistent that you be told that the project in Scotland was now yours. Whatever you decide will be approved from this office."

Bryce fell back on the bed struggling for a deep breath. *I can't do this. I need Leo.* "Margaret...I'm not sure I'm up to this."

She chuckled. "He told me you'd say that, but he was confident in your judgment. He trusts you, Bryce."

"Will you call me with any news, please?"

"Of course. Don't worry so, you'll be fine."

"Thanks." She hung up. The chilly room was suddenly stifling and airless prompting her to get up and open a window. The window seat gave her a cozy perch as the cool rainy air blew in.

"God, please watch over Leo. I need him." Tears filled her eyes, and for the first time in ages, she felt very alone.

Chapter Seventeen

M urray, it's Fiona. Please call me, I need your help." She hung up and watched the morning sun creep over the peaked roof on the malt shed. The pages from the ancient ledger and stacks of invoices were strewn across the desk. The past years were thoroughly documented right up to three years ago, when things became spottier. Her dad's neat script deteriorated, and entries were more sporadic. It was clear that the actual distilling business slowed and there were no new orders for barley. The last shipments went out almost a year ago.

She cradled her head. Accounting was not one of her strengths. David Bascomb used to handle the monthly billings. When did David leave? Or did he? She remembered him as an attractive young man with a ready smile, boyish charm, and quick sense of humor. Had she shown the slightest interest, she'd likely be Mrs. Bascomb today. Alas, she'd followed her heart to her university roommate instead. It lasted until shortly after graduation when Magritte returned to Heidelberg. Alone.

"Dad," she called from the kitchen. "Where's David Bascomb?"

The newspaper rustled. "Huh, what's that?"

She pushed her chair back and walked to the parlor. "I'm trying hard to sort out the books, but I need some help." She sat on the other end of the couch.

"Didn't David used to do the books?"

He pushed his glasses up on top of his head and scratched his whiskered cheek. "David, aye, fine lad. Haven't seen him for a bit. Hope he's not ill."

"Do we have a phone number for him?"

"Course. The list'd be under the blotter." He smiled and returned to the paper.

Fiona sighed. "Thanks, Dad." She patted his arm. His curly hair and ruddy skin reminded her of the man who bragged about his beautiful daughter. It seemed so long ago.

Might just as well check. She grabbed her woollen jacket from the peg by the door and walked across the yard to the office. The morning sun glinted off the damp leaves and cobblestones. The sweet smell of apple blossoms filled the air.

The nearest large tree still held the tire swing her dad hung for her as a child. Happy memories from those early days often brought her comfort while she was at school in Edinburgh. Today all she could think about was the mind-boggling mess that lay before her.

The office door creaked open. Not locked. She shook her head and looked at the cluttered desk covered with papers. The rest of the office wasn't any better. Boxes and sample bottles filled one corner. A muddy path through the rubble led to the entryway of the distillery. She wanted to scream.

Instead, she sat down and pushed piles of paper back to find the blotter. Under it were several pieces of paper with prices, addresses, business contacts, and phone numbers. She pulled all of them together. "Well, it's a start."

Bascomb was on one sheet with a number. She dialed it from the desk phone.

"Hello?"

"Hi, is this David?"

"Speaking."

"Hello, David. This is Fiona MacDougall. Do you have a minute?"

"Hi, Fiona. Of course. What's up?"

She described the current state of the business and asked for his input. "David, I could really use your help."

"I'm sure sorry things have got so bad. I always liked your dad, but he got sort of…unpredictable. He'd change my schedule every time I came in. Then he'd forget to do payroll. Well, I needed a steady income, ya know."

"I understand. I just don't know who else to ask."

"There are two projects I need to finish for a local business. That shouldn't take more than a few days. I'm setting up a new system for them."

"Any help will be appreciated. Would you call me when you can?"

"Sure. There's one thing…"

"You'll be paid, I promise."

❧❧❧❧

The sunlight reflecting off the river didn't erase the cobwebs. Bryce slept fitfully and did not feel rested. Nor had she come up with any solutions for herself, or for Fiona. In fact, the situation with MacDougall Distillers was even more tenuous.

The fragrant tea helped a little. But she needed to make some decisions soon. She picked up her phone and it suddenly rang, startling her. *Leo?* No, it was Reggie.

"Hi, Reg. What's up?"

"Hi. I finished with my list and planned to head over your way. I thought we could get all the samples and reports boxed up."

What should I tell her? And how much? "That sounds good. I may have to run down to Glasgow to check in with Ian. I'm not sure when."

"How come? Is there a problem?" Her voice quavered with worry.

"No problem. In fact, maybe good news. I had a serendipitous discovery at the MacDougall place. Turns out there may still be some magical whisky ready to be signed."

"No kidding! You mean the mystery stuff you thought was unavailable?"

"The very same. They produced the Highland Dew until they closed up, but there are still some barrels that were forgotten." Bryce thought that was enough for now. She didn't want to share Leo's news until she knew more.

"That would be huge. Have they agreed to sell?"

"Not yet. His daughter, Fiona, has to make the decision. Her dad is no longer able. I'll tell you more when I see you. I have to make some calls."

"Sounds good. I'll leave tomorrow. Could you get me a room?"

"Sure. Drive carefully." Bryce hung up. Hearing Reggie's enthusiasm reassured her a little. Maybe it would work out. But, before she approached Fiona, she needed a solid plan to bottle, distribute, and hopefully reopen the distillery. Ian could help.

An idea struck and she jumped up and got dressed. Breakfast and Billy.

She hurried downstairs with her notebook,

stopped at the desk to make Reggie's reservation, and walked into the lounge area.

"Good morning," Billy said.

"Good morning. Can I still get some breakfast?" She pulled out the barstool on the end.

"Oh, I think we can manage that." His grin lit up his rugged face. "Care for some tea or coffee?"

"Coffee, I think, and some oatmeal."

He brought a mug and a small carafe of coffee with additional cream and sugar.

"I haven't seen much of you. Are you finding what you're looking for?"

"You know I've been pleased with the places I've visited." She opened her notebook. "Mind I ask about some names?"

He grabbed his own coffee mug. "I'd like to know who's selling new whisky. Might be worth a call."

"My first stop was outside Stirling, the Braehead Distillery. The man's name was Dusty Hamilton. Ever hear of Braehead?"

He squinted out the window. "I don't recognize the name. Is it new?"

"He told me he started after the war, but it's a pretty small operation." She added cream and brown sugar to the steaming porridge he set in front of her. "This smells wonderful." Steel-cut oats cooked to perfection.

"Enjoy. I need to run down to the cellar."

Bryce looked over her notes as she ate. Braehead, Townsend & McClure, Duff's Whisky, MacDougall & Son…Her throat tightened. She sipped her coffee and relaxed her shoulders.

How could she make this work?

❧ ❧ ❧ ❧

Fiona gripped the pen tighter. "Okay, Murray. I understand the confusion, but try to remember just when everything went off the rails."

Murray shuffled back and forth by the door. "It's all fuzzy, you know. When the missus got so sick, everything slowed down."

"Can you at least tell me what my dad meant about the whisky barrels still in the cask room? He told me he saved that for a Distiller's Edition." She tapped the end of the pen against the desk.

"Oh ya, I remember something about that…but then he changed his mind and wanted to add another batch. I think."

"Did you know there are one hundred and thirty barrels sitting in the cask room?" She shouted.

He looked startled and quickly hung his head. "I forgot. After your mum died, I had to do everything. You weren't here and nobody wanted to stay without getting paid. If you think you know better, do it." He yanked the door open and stomped out, slamming it hard.

She clenched her fists and pounded the desk. "Dammit to hell!" The inbox tipped over, spilling unopened bills across the desk.

"I can't do this!" She swept her arm across the desk sending everything flying to the floor, and began to sob.

When there were no more tears, she got up and walked into the empty heart of the distillery where the ancient copper stills reflected a modest amount of light through small skylights. All was quiet. She had never been in here when there wasn't commotion, talking, and laughter. For over a hundred and fifty years, this family had produced whisky. Workers had come and gone, but there was always a MacDougall at the helm, including two of the first MacDougall women. Her great-great-grandmother had kept the process going when others were failing.

She touched the copper still and closed her eyes. It was cold. She couldn't remember a time when the pot stills weren't in use. Old Timmy. He was a well-known local character her dad hired once in a while to come and polish the copper. It took him a long time, but they glistened when he was done.

Fiona continued through the various rooms holding the mash tun, the grinding area, drying room, and then outside. In spite of neglect, the equipment seemed to be in good condition—so were the buildings. The credit belonged to Murray.

What would it take to get everything going, and how much would it cost?

❧ ❧ ❧ ❧

Bryce refolded the map on the bar and pointed to a spot near Glenrinnes. "This is where the Townsend & McClure Distillery is located. It's quite new and very modern." She laughed. "Brian Townsend is a real character, but very serious about his whisky. It's quite good, actually."

Billy jotted down the name. "I'll remember in case he pops in."

"This one is really interesting. Kurt Morgan and his wife are American. They started experimenting twenty years ago in Minnesota after a trip to Scotland."

"Minnesota?"

"One of the northern states between Wisconsin and North Dakota."

He nodded. "Of course."

"Anyway, when the kids were grown, they came back to Scotland to try to have a go of making whisky. They've really worked hard. With some help from a group of locals, they formed a co-op."

"I should get out more." Billy laughed.

"They'll have some good stuff in a few years. Meanwhile, we'll try to help."

"Excuse me."

Billy walked over to an older couple just sitting down at the bar. He poured two beers and served them.

She folded her map and debated the wisdom of discussing Fiona and the lost treasure.

"Any other prospects?"

"Reggie has lined up a few and…can I confide in you?"

"That's what bartenders are famous for—tight lips."

"Remember how interested I was in the Highland Dew?"

"Sure, both you and your friend."

"Well, quite by accident I stumbled in to what I thought was an abandoned farm a while ago. Turns out it wasn't completely empty, and I spoke to the owner's daughter. They recently shut down the distillery because of his illness." She took a swallow of water.

Billy watched her.

"Long story, but I went over when no one was around and stumbled into a cask room in an empty warehouse. The barrels were stamped with Highland Dew."

"Really?"

"Really. Somehow they had been overlooked, and now the daughter is trying to decide what to do."

"Well, I'll be. That's kind of a coincidence isn't it?" He shook his head. "That would be great if they got back to making whisky. It's very popular around here."

"So can I ask a favor?"

He raised one eyebrow. "And what might that be?"

"Do you have any more of it in stock?"

"I'm not sure, but I can check. What are you looking for?"

"To help me put together a marketing plan, I'll need something for the District manager to taste. I'll be happy to pay you."

He rubbed his chin and stood there. Finally, he said, "Let me go see."

She let out the breath she'd been holding. "Thanks."

If she had something for Ian to taste, she was sure he would agree with her idea. It was a risk, but it was a win-win for everyone. If only she could call Fiona and tell her…but not yet. It wasn't worth the risk if the plan did not get approved.

After what seemed like forever, Billy returned with two bottles. "If you hadn't asked, I wouldn't have looked in the back of the storeroom. We've got a couple more."

He set one in front of her. "Put it on your tab?" He winked

"You're a prince." She folded her napkin. "I believe I'll be spending some time in Glasgow. I probably won't get back until tomorrow. Thanks, Billy."

After she packed a small bag and wrote a note to Reggie, Bryce hurried out to her car. Now that she had something to show Ian, as well as the approval and backing from Leo, it was time for a plan.

It was past nine when Bryce pulled out on the A95. Midweek traffic permitting, she'd be in Airdrie by one o'clock.

Chapter Eighteen

Reggie Ballard took her time over breakfast. She'd decided to stay in Inverness for the night, and since she was in no hurry, she decided she'd drive the northern road along the coast to Craigellachie.

"More coffee?"

"Thanks." Reggie smiled at the young woman who must still be in high school. The notes in her folio outlined miniature marketing suggestions for each brand she'd selected. Why waste time waiting for approval? Her business sense was every bit as good as Bryce's, and she had far more enthusiasm for the project. In fact, she might just send the samples off first. And what was up with Bryce? Enthusiasm, hell. She could hardly muster a smile.

The sweet, hot coffee tasted good, and she leaned back to look around at the other diners. Some were clearly tourists by their conversations and guide books. A few local men read newspapers while they drank their tea. One man in particular reminded her of their former employee, Malcolm Harris. Had Bryce connected with him? She couldn't remember, but thought he'd be interesting to talk to.

Her list of contacts didn't include his number. She punched Bryce's speed dial. Voicemail. "Hey, Bry. Could you text me Malcolm's phone number? I may try to meet him for lunch. Thanks."

The original plot she had recently hatched now

germinated without much help.

Reggie waved at the waitress and pulled a couple of Scottish pounds from her coin purse.

A few miles east of Inverness, she saw the sign for the National Trust for Scotland site for Culloden battlefield. She had visited the site on her second trip. The desolate moor was, again, shrouded with fog and the wind whistled just as it might have almost three hundred years ago when so many gave their lives in their quest for freedom.

Her phone beeped with a text. Malcolm's number. Reggie smiled and steered into the site's parking lot. Once parked, she called the number.

"This is Malcolm." The voice was familiar. Very.

"Hi there. It's your long-lost friend from Georgia."

There was a long pause. "Reggie?"

"The one and only. I'm on my way to meet up with Bryce in Craigellachie and wondered if you had plans for dinner?"

"I think that would work. Let me—"

She heard pages flipping and shook her head.

"Good, the meeting is tomorrow. What time and where?" He sounded cheery.

"I'll be at the same place as Bryce, the Highlander Inn. Say, six?"

"Perfect. I can't wait to see you."

I'll bet you can't, you old fox.

She steered out to the highway and smiled as she remembered the last trip. Leo arranged for them to gather for a big meeting in Edinburgh. He had chosen a weekend when almost all the employees could be present. It was to unveil a new product, distribute new policies, and hand out awards.

The fog obscured some of the highway and she

slowed.

Malcolm Harris had bought her drinks until the bar closed and then suggested a nightcap in his room. He was a little too drunk for anything to happen, but seemed satisfied with some harmless titillation.

They corresponded for a while, but his guilt sent him back to his happy marriage. One of several times, she reminded herself, to watch her drinking.

The sign ahead indicated a roundabout and the A941 south to Craigellachie. The afternoon plan was a quick nap, a shower, and hopefully, a chat with Billy, the knowledgeable bartender.

❧❧❧❧

Bryce opened the windows in her car. The Vauxhall felt more familiar and comfortable to drive. She smiled. "And no more curb injuries." The air smelled of young buds and turned fields. Young and hopeful. Bryce loved spring.

Ahead, a sign indicated a side road leading to the town Dalwhinnie, home of the famed whisky, which she also liked. Sad, she didn't visit the distillery earlier. After signaling her turn, she waited for one car, then pulled right into the turn lane. The highway slid between the wooded hillside with railway tracks and the River Truim.

The only sound came from the river surging along the rocks. The hillsides thickened with forests. Bryce slowed and felt her lungs swell with the fresh scents. Why had she spent so much of her life in big cities racing from one job to the next? Forty years nearly passed her by, and what did she have? Tears blurred her eyes. "What am I doing?"

An odd sadness washed over her, and she gave

in to it.

The tiny hamlet flashed by. Ahead lay a splendid sight. Bright white buildings spread wide with peaked roofs and twin copper towers with their greenish tint high above. A distinctive distillery. She knew it was a big operation, but wow. Very tempting, but she had an appointment, so she turned around in the parking lot and paused a moment to look at it.

MacDougall & Son Distillers of Fine Whisky. The comparison unavoidable. Fiona's small family operation would never achieve this kind of standing in the global arena of premium whisky. Did she even want that? Bryce felt certain the urgency of debt would drive Fiona to just sell the whisky on hand.

But her gut told her this Highland Dew might be something very special and worth investment.

If only Ian would go along with her idea. She had samples and a tentative proposal to either bottle and distribute the existing stock, or advance money to cover start-up of the business and share the profits with Fiona and her dad. She patted the leather bag on the seat next to her. The spreadsheets contained columns of figures for each scenario. Most important, she had a bottle of the product.

Her phone rang.

Glad she'd thought to finally pair her phone to the car system, she hit the button on the steering column. "Hello?"

"Bryce, it's Leo."

"How are you? God, I've been so worried." Her throat tightened.

She heard the familiar chuckle. "I knew you'd worry. That's why I'm calling, so listen. If they catch me with this phone there'll be trouble." He coughed.

"I had a bit of a stroke. It's not bad, but I have a fair amount of weakness on my left side…and I drool."

Bryce laughed with relief. He still had his sense of humor. "Okay."

"I can't go back to the office until I'm more mobile. Might be a little while. I hope you got my message. I want to know how the project is going. Have you two found anything?"

"Yes, we have. Reggie and I each have samples and reports that we'll send off from Glasgow. I'm on my way there to meet with Ian." Did she want to tell him her plan? Probably not yet, not until they had something solid.

"Good. I've had a few glowing progress reports from Reggie. She seems very excited about some of her prospects."

What? Bryce hadn't seen any of those glowing reports. "Right, we've both been pretty lucky. I think you'll be pleased." Her shoulders bunched and her jaw tightened.

"Oops, doctor's coming. I trust you, Bryce. You know what I'm looking for. I'll be in touch." He disconnected.

Her hands trembled slightly and she hit the disconnect. Red flags had popped up periodically, but she'd ignored them. Why? Reggie had been a friend for over ten years, but her recent behavior was odd. She'd always been competitive, but forthright.

She looked twice when she saw that the sign for Stirling indicated a turn to the left. Clearly she'd been fixating on Reggie's behavior, which distracted her. Shortly after that she'd need to look for her turnoff to Airdrie. Time for some new music. From the six CDs she preloaded, she selected an Ella Fitzgerald Favorites.

"Bewitched, Bothered, and Bewildered" seemed timely.

⁂

Fiona sat behind the desk in the company office. Five folders lay in the middle of the blotter on the clean desk. David Bascomb had spent most of the day sorting and explaining. He made a spreadsheet for her expenses, inventory, and overdue bills.

She felt a new sense of calm she'd not experienced since she arrived home to this mess. Nothing was solved, but she had hope and the beginnings of a plan. If only Bryce hadn't needed to go to Glasgow…She wanted her advice. That could wait until tomorrow afternoon. She pushed her chair back and walked across the yard to the warehouse, carrying the folders and a notepad. A list of what was in the cask room would be necessary. In the morning she'd sit down with her dad and find out what he had in mind for these barrels. God willing, he'd be lucid enough to tell her where to start, and maybe even what his wishes were.

⁂

The afternoon sun shone on the unusual handmade quilt covering Reggie's bed at the inn. The nap and shower had refreshed her, and she anticipated a fun evening with Malcolm, as well as a little research. The pegged pants were perfect with her red silk blouse. A spritz of perfume completed the ensemble, and she grabbed her phone.

The quaint bar, surrounded by hundreds of whisky bottles, was lit with some soft light from half a dozen wall sconces and an intricately carved chandelier. The smell of wood smoke wafted toward the door and Scottish flute music welcomed her. Best of all, Billy stood behind the bar.

Reggie adjusted her collar for more exposure and slid onto a barstool. "Well, hi there. Billy, right?'

He flipped a bar towel over his shoulder and walked over. "That's me." He squinted. "And you'd be Bryce Andrews's friend?"

She giggled. "You sure have a good memory."

"What can I get for you?"

"I'll try the anCnoc. I haven't had one for ever so long." Reggie reviewed her plan to get some information before she met with Malcolm. If she could convince him that she was working closely with Bryce, he might be willing to collaborate with her.

It took an hour, but the bar emptied enough for Reggie to call Billy over. She tossed back the remainder of her glass and waved.

"Would you be ready for another?" Billy reached for her glass.

"Sure. I still have some time before my dinner… appointment."

He poured. "This one's on the house."

"You're sweet. Thank you." She held up the glass and sipped. "I wondered if you could help me?"

"If I can, I will." He folded the towel and leaned against the back bar.

"Bryce needed to get the samples down to Glasgow and I told her I could get some papers ready for Fiona. You know, if she wants some information from us."

"Hmm, think she'll want to sell?"

"Bryce is trying to help her by finding some solutions for her dilemma, poor woman. Her dad being so sick and all."

His eyes narrowed and he shook his head. "Aye, bad business."

"Are you familiar with the family?" *Be careful.*

"Seems my father might have worked for the family for a short time. He was a cooper, but picked up work with some of the locals in the summer."

"So the distillery is around here?"

"No. We came from over near Knockando. Excuse me." He walked down the bar where two men had sat.

She opened her map app on her phone. Why was that name so familiar? Ballindalloc... Knockando. Bingo. That was the location of Tamdhu Distillery and Malcolm Harris! It couldn't be more than ten miles.

She typed into her search: Distilleries near Knockando.

Cardhu, Tamdhu, Glenfarclas. Tormore was nearby. She hoped Malcolm might have an idea.

❦ ❦ ❦ ❦

"Come in and have a seat," Ian Smith said. "It's so good to see you again, Bryce."

"Thanks, Ian. It didn't take near as long as I thought." She set a box on the table and her messenger bag on the chair next to hers. His office was small and utilitarian. It didn't surprise her. Ian was fastidious and efficient. The office looked tidy, but without decoration.

"May I offer some refreshment?"

"No, thank you. I stopped for a bite on the way. Did you have time to look at the reports?"

"Yes, and I was looking forward to tasting what you found." He walked over to the credenza and returned carrying a tray with glasses, a carafe of water.

Bryce pulled corked sample bottles from the box. "Let me set these up in chronological order." They wore hand-printed labels: Braehead, Townsend & McClure, Duff's Whisky, MacDougall & Son.

"Yes, I read your tasting notes." He picked up each in turn, held them to the light, poured a small amount, rolled and sniffed, then tasted.

Bryce watched with her fists clenched. Her body vibrated with nervous energy. *Please agree with some of my notes...*

Five minutes of expectation felt like waiting for a firing squad. Her right knee began to bounce. He poured the Highland Dew, and she held her breath.

Unlike the others, he smiled and turned to face her. "My, my." He looked at all four. "I think you're right—these are unusual and have great potential... but, this one..." He held up the last one. "Is utterly remarkable. Please tell me about it."

She let out a breath and spots danced before her eyes. She grabbed the edge of the table.

"Are you quite all right?" Ian's normal calm momentarily evaporated.

"Yes, I'm fine. I guess I was a little nervous." She laughed and took a deep breath.

"Why on earth would you be nervous? You are, by far, the most experienced taster in the ranks, and Mr. Edelman trusts you implicitly."

Her cheeks warmed. "You're very kind. I was, well, I hoped you'd agree because I'd like your help with an idea."

"Regarding?" Ian leaned, back giving her his full attention.

"The last sample, the Highland Dew."

He smiled. "Let's hear what you've in mind."

Chapter Nineteen

Here's more tea, Dad." Fiona poured for both of them. "I'm glad you're feeling much better, because I could use your help."

"Of course, as much as I can. What are all them papers about?" He adjusted his glasses.

"David Bascomb—you remember, the accountant—came over to help me understand what needs to be done." No need to give much detail. "This paper shows how much we've got in the bank, and how much we owe to people."

He looked closely. "Not so good."

She smiled. "That's right. I think we need to sell some of the whisky we found yesterday." She held her breath.

Gavin looked at her with a blank stare.

Damn.

"The Distiller's Special. Aye. That should be ready soon. It's gonna be a winner, Fi." He pulled out his pipe.

"Dad, do you think we should just bottle and sell it? Or should we use some of the money to try and reopen the distillery?"

"Of course we should keep the place runnin'...I don't know. I want everything back to normal, but I can't make my brain work right. I'm sorry. I'm just no help." He teared up, and Fiona took his hand.

"I know. We don't have to decide right now.

Either way, I need to make some calls and buy us some time. You rest. I'm going to see to the dishes, then take care of those calls." She took his arm and handed him his walking stick.

"You know I love ya," he said.

She covered her mouth, and her throat tightened as she watched him walk into the parlor. *I can't remember the last time he said that.* She took the dishes to the sink and washed them. The urge to run back to her quiet life teaching in Edinburgh felt overpowering.

Predictable semesters, class schedules, and a new syllabus for each class. She would even enjoy grading papers compared to this interminable purgatory at home. It felt like treading water every single day.

She wiped the table and hung up the towel. "Dad, I'm going over to the office for a bit." No response. Probably snoozing.

With the papers in hand, Fiona opened the back door and heard a car coming up the lane. Maybe Bryce had come back early. She hurried to the driveway and saw a similar car, but the driver was blond.

"Can I help you?" Fiona asked as the car pulled up and stopped.

An attractive young woman got out and smiled at her. "I'm Reggie Ballard. You might have heard Bryce mention me. You must be Fiona" She extended her hand.

Her clothes and makeup looked expensive. Her coquettish drawl was surprising.

"She didn't mention you'd be coming here." Fiona stepped back.

"Oh, she was so busy trying to get everything ready for a meeting in the home office, it might have slipped her mind." She looked around. "You have a lovely spot up here with all these trees. I love apple blossoms, don't you?"

"Yes. The MacDougalls have been here for over a hundred years, but I'm guessing you already know that."

Reggie turned quickly. "Well, Bryce and I discuss everything, you know. It's important for business partners, don't you think?"

"Indeed." Fiona folded her arms, covering the papers to her chest. "I guess that's why I was surprised that Bryce didn't come herself."

The flinch barely showed. "I was sure she would have talked about our luck finding new customers. Why, these new distillers are popping up everywhere." She turned to face Fiona. "Of course, yours is very important, and that's why she asked me to check in with you to see if you wanted to sign a Right to Represent form, so we could help you with the sales of the whisky…when you're ready to sell."

Fiona gasped. "What?" A slap in the face would have felt the same.

"I'm sorry. I thought she had already mentioned it. Don't you fret." She patted Fiona's shoulder. "I know she was worried about your dad and the bills."

Fiona trembled. *Why would Bryce send someone over here? Why wouldn't she come herself?*

"And what is it she wants me to sign?" This felt wrong.

"It's not a big deal. It just says that if you sell your product, you want Global Distillers and Distribution to handle the arrangements. It's not like a sale form."

"I don't understand. I'll have to think about it and talk to my father." She turned toward the office. "I need to go." She hurried to the office, leaving the young woman standing by her car.

Once inside, she watched the petite charmer's face morph into a dark mask. The car revved, circled around, and sped off.

Fiona plopped down in the chair. Her breath came in brief gasps. Heat flushed her neck and face. "What the holy hell is going on?" She slammed the papers down. A million thoughts flooded her brain.

She'd believed that Bryce was truly concerned with her family's plight. It had seemed genuine, but then why wasn't she here herself to make this proposal? And speaking of, when had selling the distillery become the best-case scenario? Bryce had laid out a few options, and hadn't seemed to be leaning in this direction. But maybe she had been all along. Maybe, for gain of her own, she was just trying to finagle a way to gain her trust because of the whisky she thought was so valuable.

Angry tears covered her cheeks and deep sobs filled her chest. "Dammit to hell! I can't trust anyone."

⚜ ⚜ ⚜ ⚜

The conference room felt close. Bryce fidgeted in her chair watching Ian Smith sign the bank forms with the trustee from the Bank of Scotland. She checked her watch for the third time, anxiously wanting to call Fiona.

"Thanks for coming over, Charlie." Ian stood and shook hands. "We'll get Joan to make some copies and you can be on your way."

Bryce stood. "I appreciate your suggestions, thank you." She shook his hand.

"You're quite a forward thinker, Ms. Andrews. It

was a pleasure working with you."

Both men left the room and Bryce collapsed in her chair. This was going to work out for everyone. She could hardly sit still. All she wanted to do was hurry back to the inn and celebrate the new plan. Maybe she could call Leo. Better not, at least until all the ducks were in a row.

Ian returned after a while with a legal-sized manila envelope. "Nice work, Bryce. I'm sure Leo will be glad when this falls into place. It's a good plan. Take it slow, and make sure the details are clear to everyone."

"I couldn't have done it without your help." She wanted to hug him, but shook his hand instead. "I hope I'll be back early enough to tell the MacDougall's, but I might have to wait for morning. Gavin is more alert early in the day."

Ian leaned over. "So am I."

They both laughed.

"I'll make sure your samples get packed and shipped to Chicago with the reports. You can send the final contracts whenever you're ready."

"Thanks again."

"Drive safe, hear?"

⁂

Bryce studied the map as she filled up the car with petrol. As much as she enjoyed the breathtaking views of the back roads, she chose the M80 major throughway toward Edinburgh, then the M9 to the A9. The four-lane roadway would be faster and more direct. There'd be time for touring when her project finished.

The purchase paid, she turned toward the

entrance to the highway. Bryce smiled. "I can't wait." She punched in Fiona's number on her cell phone. As it rang, she checked her watch. There would be plenty of time to stop and tell her in person.

Voicemail. "Damn."

"Hey, Fiona, it's Bryce, hoping to find you. I'll try as I get closer. Bye"

As soon as she navigated herself into traffic, she set the cruise control and let her imagination work.

This would be a big project for her and for GDD. If Fiona and her dad were interested, she could lay out a phased program for international distribution. It would require some time because whisky changed as it aged and needed to be checked and tasted by a knowledgeable distiller along the way. Gavin couldn't do it.

The distillery might need a major overhaul. Who could make that determination? If Highland Dew became part of their represented product line, it would need new branding and consistency. And what about the Distiller's Special? If they led with the top of the line…they'd have to wait years for another batch.

She reached over and jotted a note on the large envelope to check the dates on the casks. There might be some newer batches. Anything newer than 2003 could work for future release.

As the signs for Perth appeared, she watched for the roundabout for the A9. Once through, she tried Fiona's number again. No answer.

"Me again. I hope everything is okay. I'm worried. Would you give me a call when you get this?" She disconnected.

Her effervescent joy leaked like air from her famous bruised tires.

☙ ☙ ❧ ❧

Reggie slammed her car door and stomped into the inn. She stopped inside the door. The bar for a drink, or upstairs to regroup? She took the stairs two at a time, nearly colliding with the hall maid.

"Sorry." She fumbled the key and kicked the doorjamb. The maid scurried down the stairs.

"Sonofabitch!" She threw her things on the bed. "The plan was perfect. Shit." She kicked off her shoes and stripped off her Yves Saint Laurent slacks. "I have to think of something, and I don't have much time."

Once she'd gotten into jeans and a GSU T-shirt, she pulled out her folder and files. If there was a way, she'd find it. All the information she'd been able to find on the MacDougall family and the Highland Dew whisky lay spread out on the bed. There wasn't much. "Connect the damn dots, Ballard."

All her life she'd found the right corners to cut and the best wheels to grease. Her rapid rise through the ranks at Global were directly related to her close relationship with Bryce. Most of the time, one or the other of them had been single and took the part of Sancho Panza to the questing Don Quixote.

Bryce rewarded Reggie's support with perks many others did not get. While she basked in the shared limelight of Bryce Andrews's meteoric rise, it cost her the trust of her co-workers and clients. Normally, a small price to pay.

Her cell phone rang, and she jumped. "Bryce, what a surprise." Her heart thudded against her chest.

"Hey, Reg. I'm on the way back and I wanted to check in. I have some really great news about the whisky I took in, specifically the Highland Dew."

"That's great! Did Ian say anything about mine?"

"He did. He liked what you got, especially the one south of Glasgow."

"Good. I did, too. What time will you be back?" Reggie tried for enthusiastic.

"Not sure, an hour and a half or two. Why?"

"I thought I'd wait to eat with you." *Sounds nice.*

"Great, then we can catch up. I may try to stop and see Fiona. She isn't answering her phone and I want to be sure they're okay."

Reggie froze. "Probably just busy. I can't wait to hear what you and Ian talked about."

"You're probably right. Well, see you later." *Click.*

She flopped back on the bed. "What the hell do I do now? Do I have time to get over there to apologize and would she even talk to me?" Her pulse was racing and her palms were damp. She didn't get Fiona's phone number. Not that it would do any good. That bridge was burned.

"Ballard's aren't quitters." She jumped up and slipped her shoes on. She tucked her sketch pad under her arm along with the pencil case. "Plan B."

Downstairs, she found a small table near the window where she set her materials.

"Could I have some Macallan, neat? Wait, make that a double."

Billy nodded. "Rough day?"

"Maybe, maybe not." She smiled.

He set down a glass and poured, generously. "That should help."

"Thanks." She returned to the table and flipped open her sketch pad. She knew Leo appreciated her initiative in other areas, particularly visual concepts. If Bryce wanted to fast-track the Highland Dew, it might be good to have some marketing and branding ideas ready. If Leo approved…Bryce would need to play nice.

The whisky helped move her into the present, and in the next hour she sketched out some new logo ideas and a label. Since she'd seen the outside of the MacDougall distillery, she could sketch the building framed by blooming apple trees. Nice. She turned the page and tried a few sales slogans.

❧ ❧ ❧ ❧

The Cairngorm mountains loomed on the horizon, still capped with some snow and only a few scattered clouds. This area felt more and more familiar to her. She checked her phone. Still no response to her three messages. There certainly wasn't any solid reason to be concerned, but…she really wanted to talk to Fiona.

Truth was she might explode from the excitement about the new deal. Reggie would understand what a big deal this was for the company. They'd never done anything like this.

Throughout the long drive, Bryce mentally compiled a list of pros and cons on how this might impact her own life. It was a huge undertaking. At thirty-eight, she had accumulated an impressive amount and variety of business expertise. It was time to put it to use. What was the cliché? Time to fish or cut bait.

The roundabout ahead veered off to Grantown-on-Spey, Knockando, and the turnoff for the farm. She steered round to the exit and the nerves set in. How would she explain the plan? It was nearly four. It might be too late in the day. Maybe she could just check and set up a time for tomorrow.

A light rain began as she entered the town. The buildings were tidy and the streets orderly. A broad boulevard ran through a large town square with parallel front streets. The rain released the scent of wet stone and grass.

Bryce relaxed and embraced the slower speed of the two-lane road and the rhythm of life in a small community. It had taken a couple of weeks to partially undo the American hustle she normally lived by. The hillsides sloped up with forest and farmland until it narrowed to a path-like ribbon through the woods. Rain and sun skittered between overhanging branches.

Below and on the right, she could hear the riffles of the river over the rocks. She flashed on a vision of Fiona when she first appeared to Bryce coming out of the house. The image reminded Bryce of this environment—fresh, enchanting, and redolent with life. Truly a remarkable woman. She radiated confidence.

The fluttery sensation grew in her chest. It had been so long since she'd felt anything...anything pleasurable, certainly. Fiona MacDougall was a breath of fresh air. Sitting across from her in the kitchen or watching as she prepared their food. Now she knew that the indescribable feeling of that moment was contentment, which had been missing from her busy life.

Bryce turned the wipers on high as she focused on the fields and fences, searching for the dangling white sign. It was easy to miss, and she slowed. *There.* The drive slicked with mud, she cautiously steered to the blurred outline of the farmhouse. Her senses sharpened and her pulse pounded.

The car and the old truck were parked in back, so she pulled close to the back door and shut off the engine. As she opened the door, she saw Fiona standing at the office door in the rain.

Bryce smiled and got out. "Fiona, I'm glad to see you—"

"I can't believe you'd have the gall to show up here!" Fiona's face darkened and her voice sounded tight and threatening.

"What? I wanted to tell you the good news."

"I got the message. I trusted you, and you used me."

Her head spun uncontrollably in this bizarre universe that was nothing like the one she left when she exited the car. "I don't understand. There must be an explanation...I really have good news for you and your dad."

"Get out!" Fiona shouted. "I don't want anything from you." She stormed past the car and into the house.

Bryce stood in shock. Rain coursed down her face. She couldn't move. She stared at the back door as if it would magically open and the real Fiona would come out and welcome her.

It didn't. Soaked to the skin, she got back in the car. Torrents of rain blurred the windshield, obscuring everything including her own tears.

Chapter Twenty

Reggie heard the thunder and watched as sheets of rain splashed the front windows. It had driven several hillwalkers indoors to dry off and enjoy a drink. The flute and fiddle music got louder as the voices around her increased. Warming spirits created happy spirits. One couple began to dance as others clapped along.

She checked her watch. Bryce should have been back by now. Maybe the weather had slowed her down. She shook the ice in her glass. After her double whisky, she'd switched to cola and kept sketching, but now she was hungry.

"Hey."

Reggie looked up at a drenched woman with a few familiar features. "Bryce?"

"Yeah. Order me a drink while I change into dry clothes." She turned and squished toward the door.

Reggie hardly recognized her. *Something must have happened. I hope it wasn't an accident.* She waved at the waitress. "Would you bring two of the Macallan?"

"Would you like water for both?"

"Yes, please, and could we get one of the cheese and biscuit plates?"

Reggie could barely remember when Bryce Andrews had looked so…what? Out of sorts? Dazed? It seemed out of character for the rock-steady, controlled manager she was used to. Even though it worried her,

Reggie looked over her sketches and hoped they might cheer her friend a little.

"Shall I set these here?" The waitress held a plate with the sliced cheese, biscuits, and jam.

"Oh, yes." Reggie moved her sketch pad over.

As she set down the two drinks and water, Bryce reappeared—somewhat more composed, but her hair was still wet. The jeans and long-sleeved shirt suggested she might still be cold.

"That looks good. Thanks." Bryce sat across from her.

Reggie signed the check. "You look better. Is everything okay?"

Bryce took a large swallow of her drink and held it for a minute. "No, actually. Something has gone terribly wrong." She swallowed another mouthful and set the glass down. "I did stop at the farm. Fiona ripped me a new one. I've never seen a woman that pissed. She wouldn't even let me tell her about the deal. Do you have any idea what the hell is going on?" She growled in a low, ominous whisper.

Reggie felt her stomach drop. *Oh shit. This is not going to be good.* A thousand ideas vied for attention. "Did she say what she was mad about?" She swallowed hard and tried to keep her voice even.

"She said she got the message. Then said, 'I trusted you and you used me.' What the hell does that mean?"

"I'm not really sure. But, after I got your message about striking a deal with Ian...well, I thought it would be wise to be...proactive so we wouldn't lose the sale."

Bryce put her glass down and her eyes narrowed. "Reggie, what did you do?"

"Nothing really. I just suggested she might need

some help from us and I offered her a Request for Representation—"

"You what?" Bryce leaned forward.

Reggie's throat tightened and she felt cornered. "It wasn't a big deal. I thought you had already discussed it after you discovered the whisky. I think she was just upset because she didn't really know me."

"Did you actually go over there? Without calling or asking me?"

"Yes, but—"

"How the hell did you know where they lived?"

Reggie shoved her glass forward. "Bryce, you're shouting. Here, drink this."

In a low, measured voice, Bryce whispered, "How in the hell did you find the farm?"

"I had some notes. Then I had a drink with Malcolm, and he mentioned something about a distillery near Tamdhu, and I just asked if he'd ever heard of MacDougall, so I just took a chance I could find it."

Bryce clenched her fists and put them in her lap. She closed her eyes and took a deep breath.

Reggie had never—ever—seen Bryce this angry, and didn't know what to do. "I'm sorry if you think I overstepped. I'll certainly apologize."

"No. Don't do anything. I need to think about this. We'll talk in the morning. I repeat, do not do anything." She shoved back her chair and hurried out of the bar.

Reggie watched her leave and looked around to see if anyone had heard the exchange. The music and conversation continued in the crowded bar. Her hands trembled and she reached over for the drink she'd offered.

She leaned back and sipped the whisky. *Well, that sure didn't go as well as it should have.* In all likelihood, Bryce would be her old self in the morning. It was probably a rough day and Fiona just set her off. She took another swallow. *I hope.*

The cheese tasted good, and now she wanted to eat. When the waitress walked by, Reggie asked for another drink.

Might as well enjoy myself since Bryce doesn't seem interested in the sketches. Maybe I'll just send them to Leo. She opened the sketch book and tried to focus on the blurred logos. The room moved slightly and the music sounded distorted.

❧❧❧❧

The rain had let up, and Bryce opened her patio door. A crescent moon was rising over the trees along the river. She felt drained. Two more phone messages to Fiona were left unanswered, and the waste basket was half filled with tissues.

Traffic diminished as it got darker, so she could hear the river as she sat with her feet propped on the balcony rail. Her brain felt muddled by the whole Fiona-Reggie ordeal. She desperately wanted to talk to Leo or Ian—someone to advise her. And Fiona. God, she was angry. Her eyes teared up again when she thought about not ever seeing her again. "Why did this have to happen?" she cried out to no one.

The sound of a car horn jarred her. She glanced at her watch: ten fifteen. *Wow, must've fallen asleep. No wonder my feet are numb.*

But that time had allowed her some clarity. She went in and switched on the lamp. Her phone sat on the nightstand charging, and she grabbed it and texted:

Bryce: Fiona. I got the story from Reggie. She was wrong. I'm coming over in the morning to explain. Please don't let her mistake affect our relationship.

She dialed Leo's phone, no answer. "Leo. It's Bryce, and we have a little problem I want to run past you. It's after ten here, so I'll call again tomorrow. Hope you're feeling better." She sat on the bed and debated whether or not to call Reggie. Her room was directly above and quiet. Probably asleep.

"Okay, tomorrow then." She hung up her clothes, brushed her teeth, and slipped between the sheets. The moon shone on the balcony railing and she watched the tree shadows until her eyelids began to droop. Her last thought was Fiona and apple blossoms.

Morning seemed to come too soon, but Bryce had slept hard and felt a bit more rested. "Yes, good morning. Could I have some tea and scones for two? Andrews, room four." She hung up and texted Reggie.

Bryce: I've ordered something to eat. Would you come on down when you're up?

With the envelope from Ian, she sat in the rocker and waited. Sleep had provided some much-needed clarity, and the shower had solidified it. Now was time to try and familiarize herself with the detailed plans for MacDougall & Son. And have the talk with Reggie.

She was re-reading the loan document when there was a knock at the door. "Come in."

A tall red-headed young man carried the tray over to the table. "Your order ma'am." He set down the tray and uncovered the scones.

Bryce handed him a tip. "Thank you."

As he walked out, Reggie walked in. She looked rode-hard, as she often described it.

"Hey, Bryce. I guess I didn't know how late it was." She pulled out a chair from the small café table.

Bryce smiled. "Yeah, I was up much earlier, but decided to let you sleep in." She poured tea for both and sat down.

Reggie cleared her throat. "You know, I didn't mean to muck things up, I just wanted to help."

"I don't know what to believe anymore. I've known you for a lot of years and thought we were friends—"

"But, we—"

Bryce put up her hand. "Just let me finish. This is hard enough without interruptions. This trip has been strained and uncomfortable for a long time. I don't know what's going on, but I figured it was personal or you would have told me." She fidgeted with her napkin.

"This assignment is important for both of us. Leo sent us to see how well we would manage on our own. And while I appreciate the work you did and the contacts you made, you've been unpredictable and... you may have screwed up a really important project."

"I told you I was sorry. Mistakes happen. I know I can fix it," Reggie said.

Bryce shook her head and sighed. This was not easy. "Reg, I don't have time to argue. What I'd like is for you to pack and go home."

Reggie nearly dropped the cup she was holding. "What? You must be kidding."

"No. I'm not. Take your reports to Ian and have him arrange a flight for you."

Reggie spoke up. "You can't just dismiss me like that. Leo sent us both."

"Listen to me. Leo had a stroke and isn't back at work yet. He left instructions with Margaret that I'm in charge of the project until he's back."

Reggie laughed. "No, you aren't. We both are."

Bryce rubbed her forehead and stifled a remark. "You can check with Margaret or Ian, I don't care. But, when I get back from trying to make peace with Fiona, I want you gone. Understand?"

Reggie jumped up, shaking with rage. "You can't do this to me. You'll find out, missy, you messed with the wrong person." She stormed out the door and slammed it.

Bryce could hear her upstairs, stomping around cursing. This was not the friend she'd known for ten years. What the hell had happened?

She picked up her phone, hesitated, and dialed Ian Smith.

"Good morning, Ms. Andrews. A pleasure as always."

"Not this time, I'm afraid. We've hit a rather large bump in the road with the MacDougalls."

"I'm not sure I understand. You had such a good rapport set up and such an innovative idea—"

"It's a long story, but I need to go over there and try to reason with them. The problem is Reggie took it upon herself to draft a Request for Representation and to take it over and ask Fiona to sign it. Of course, Fiona had no idea who she was or what she was talking about, and assumed it was me manipulating her into something shady."

Ian groaned. "Oh dear, this is not good. What are you going to do?"

"Go over there and try to explain this mess. But I wanted you to know because I told Reggie to take her stuff to you and ask you to get her a flight home. She's probably going to be nasty, because she doesn't believe I can do that."

"Naturally. I think I can handle it. Don't worry." Ian sounded calm. "I'll put in a call to Chicago. You go fix this deal."

"Thanks. I hope it's not too late or I'll be on the way home, too." She gripped the phone. "Thanks, Ian."

If she wanted to get to the farm, she'd better get moving. It was almost nine.

❧❧❧❧

"Who is it?" Gavin called when the doorbell rang.

"It's okay, Dad, it's just David." Fiona dried her hands on the way to the front door.

"Who's that?"

"David Bascomb. The accountant." She whispered and opened the door. "Hi, come on in. You remember my dad."

"Indeed. Good to see you, sir." He walked over and shook hands. "It's been awhile, aye?"

"It has. Good to see you, lad. You're dressed up fine. Working at a bank, are you?" He leaned back in the recliner and took a draw on his pipe. The fragrant smoke circled around him.

David laughed. "No, not a bank. I've some accounts in town, you know. I need to look presentable."

"Dad, David is helping me sort through the bills." Fiona steered David toward the kitchen. "I'll bring some tea in a bit."

David took a seat at the kitchen table where some

ledgers sat. He opened a leather case, and took out some forms and a calculator. "You sounded so frantic on the phone, I was a bit worried."

"I appreciate you coming over on short notice. I need some guidance and Murray has been AWOL—or not listening." She hung up the dish towel. "Can I get you anything?"

"No. I'm fine. Why don't you tell me what you need?" David folded his hands and waited.

Fiona released the breath she'd been holding since yesterday morning when that woman showed up with the papers. She sat across from him. "When you were here the last time, we'd discovered a large cache of unrecorded whisky. My dad remembered it had been set aside for a Distiller's Edition."

"Yes, that was a great find. Were you able to sell it?" David smiled and looked so hopeful.

"That's why I called. I met a representative from an international distribution company, quite by accident. We got on quite well, and she offered to help if I wanted."

"That's great. We don't often get anybody interested in the small offerings from our community." He laughed. "Remember when I tried to get your dad interested in making gin?"

She just nodded. "I do. It didn't go over well."

"Yeah. It's even more popular now." He shrugged.

"Okay. I wanted to ask her for some advice, but yesterday some other woman I didn't know showed up here and asked me to sign some kind of contract." Tears welled and she swiped at them. "David, I don't want to sign something I don't understand, but I need some money soon. The bank is frustrated, and I don't want to lose everything."

"Show me what you've got. I need to see the balances in arrears," David said. "We can figure this out."

Fiona opened the ledger and slid it around to David.

He adjusted his glasses and ran a finger along the column of figures. After several minutes, he said, "Now, how many barrels have you got on hand?"

"One hundred thirty."

"All right. Last figure I saw was about £1,500 per barrel, if it's in bourbon barrels." He looked up. "That'd be about two hundred thousand pounds. Especially if it's as old as you say."

Fiona flopped back in her chair. "You're serious?"

David's face remained stoic. "Well, of course I am."

"That's a great deal of money." Her brain felt short-circuited. "That would cover our debt?"

He barked a loud laugh. "Oh yes, it certainly would."

A warm sensation started in her chest and bubbled up as a smile, then a big grin. "Oh David…I had no idea."

"Yes, you did seem surprised." He smiled.

The doorbell interrupted the merriment. "Fi, there's someone at the door."

She laughed and got up. "Yes, Dad, I heard it." She hurried to the door and swung it open.

Chapter Twenty-one

Bryce spotted a newer-model 4-door car parked next to Fiona's car near the back door and slowed down as she looked around. Her nervous anticipation momentarily sidelined her curiosity. Had Fiona been so angry that she'd immediately called someone to sell the whisky for her? *Quit manufacturing problems.*

She glanced in the mirror. Aside from bags under her tired eyes, she was presentable. With her messenger bag over her shoulder, and a box of Walkers Shortbread, Bryce rang the front doorbell. Gavin hollered, and she heard Fiona.

When the door swung open, they both stood like deer in headlights. Bryce thrust the cookies forward, and Fiona's quick smile drooped.

"What can I do for you, Bryce?"

"Please let me apologize and explain. Please?"

Fiona wavered, then said, "David, I'll be right with you." She stepped out and closed the door behind her. "Be quick, I have company."

"I did not send Reggie over here. She went behind my back in an effort to gain some kind of recognition." It was hard to catch her breath.

Fiona just listened.

"She knew I went to Glasgow to try and arrange a way to support you and your dad, and thought she could muscle in and get credit." No reaction.

Bryce looked her in the eye. "I am so sorry. I would never do anything to hurt you or your father." Her voice cracked. "If you could just listen to my offer, I think you and your father would be pleased."

Fiona sagged onto the wooden chair beside her and shook her head. "This is so hard and so confusing. Dammit, Bryce. I want to believe you, but that woman said you sent her because you were too busy."

Bryce crouched in front of her and touched her hand. "Fiona, when I told you I wanted to be here for you, I meant it. I've brokered a deal with the main office to help MacDougall Distillery get back on its feet...if that is what you want. And I'm willing to take a leave to help you...if you—"

"Are you serious?" Her face clouded with confusion.

"Yes. I believe this is a worthwhile investment."

Fiona leaned back and took a breath. "If that's so, then it's serendipitous that our accountant, David Bascomb, is here waiting in the kitchen."

The sun filtered through the apple tree branches and lit up Fiona's green eyes. Why hadn't she noticed the dimple in her left cheek? "Can I show you what I have?"

Fiona invited her in and called David from the kitchen. "Let's sit in here with Dad, so he can hear what you've got." She sat next to him. "Dad, you remember David. I've been talking to him in the kitchen."

"Of course, I do. He's been here for awhile now." He nodded at him.

Bryce sat next to David on the couch and smiled.

"And this is Bryce, the woman who went with us to look at the Distiller's Edition in the cask room the other day. Do you remember her?"

He squinted then smiled. "Aye. Switched the lights and counted up the barrels."

Fiona let out a relieved sigh. "Yes, you're right. She's come to talk to us about a proposal to reopen the distillery, if we want to." She turned to Bryce. "Could you give just the outline version, and then we can discuss it with David?"

Bryce opened her bag and pulled out some folders with the Global logo and picture. She handed one to Fiona and one to her dad. "David, I'll share this one with you."

Gavin smiled. "This looks pretty fancy, miss."

"As I mentioned earlier, our company is interested in distributing Highland Dew internationally. I believe it will be very popular, so if you are both interested in restarting production, I am willing to help provide a low-interest loan for renovation and training of staff. Global will help with bottling and promotional material to roll out the new Distiller's Edition. We'll pay you cash up front to restore your credit based on the anticipated sales of the whisky." She looked at Fiona, who seemed to be following. David was reading through the numbers, and Gavin nodded and looked pleased.

"It's still my distillery?"

"Yes, sir, it is. You may have people you want for the different jobs, and might offer Fiona a position."

He squeezed Fiona's hand. "Indeed, I would. First thing, though, we'll need to change the sign out front, since it's the daughter, not the son."

They all laughed.

He stood. "You folks work out the details. I need a little rest." Then grabbed his stick and navigated back to the bedroom.

Fiona sat, biting her lip. "I think this sounds

good—a little too good. Let's get some tea and talk about this in the kitchen."

Bryce anticipated her hesitancy. "I'm sure you have questions, and I think you might have a few for David. If it's okay with you, I'd like to check the dates on the barrels so we know what we're dealing with. If that's okay?"

Fiona set the kettle on the stove and turned. She looked at David, paused, then said, "Okay."

Bryce slipped her bag over her shoulder. "I'll be back shortly."

The yard was dry and quiet, but the bay door was closed. She pulled a notebook and flashlight from her bag and stuck them in her pants pocket.

She pulled on the dented door handle until the metal door creaked up about five feet, enough to get under. Her flashlight helped find the light switch and everything looked and smelled the same: dank and musty. The ramp to the cask room was damp, and she looked for the fuse box and flipped the two switches, which startled a bat that flew out when she opened the door.

"Geez." It felt creepier than the last time. There wasn't a lot of time, so she started on one end and wrote down the label on each row, rack, number, and letter. She used an old piece of newspaper to wipe the lettering on each. With better light, she could see the label more clearly. Distillery on top, name of whisky, year, and serial number.

The rack held eight barrels on three tiers. She copied each one, and after an hour, her feet were cold and she felt dizzy from the whisky fumes. But, it was an amazing collection of whisky. Three different batches from 1989 and 1998. She'd hoped to find a way to taste one, but until the ink on the deal dried, she dared not.

Lights off and the cask room door shut, she looked around the large room. She'd need some measurements of the warehouse itself, and jotted a note. Another metal door marked "Keep Door Closed" was in the far corner. That was tempting.

It wasn't locked, and opened easily. Inside, was a huge two-story room with two copper stills. She climbed a ladder to the elevated platform. The old stills were gorgeous and oxidized from neglect. She touched the side of one that was cool to her touch, and solid. Six skylights lit the space and tools of the trade like thermometers, funnels, mallets, and spreadsheets lay on scattered barrels used as desks.

A slow drip of water caught her attention. It came from the bent edge of the metal roof. This place would take some work to get up and running, and she'd need some expert help to evaluate it for recommendations. Malcolm maybe? He had started in production.

She returned to the farmhouse, closing doors as she went.

❧ ❧ ❧ ❧

Fiona poured another cup for David. "So you think this deal is good?"

"I'm not an expert. You'd need Owen from the bank to evaluate it. But I will do some research on this company." He pointed to the brochure. "If they're as stable as they look, this would be a wonderful opportunity." He sipped the tea and looked at her. "Fiona, you know this person better than I do, but it seems she has a serious interest in getting the business up and running, which tells me they really like the 'Dew.'"

"That would be wonderful. But there is so much

involved in running this business, and I'm not sure I'm up to it."

"Where's Murray? He certainly knows this stuff like the back of his hand."

"That's a good question. He slips in and out says nothing. He's done chores and checked on things, but he's acting so strange. I don't know if I can depend on him."

"I suppose that can be sorted out, but just know it would be a good idea to sell some of the whisky to get some bills paid."

"You're right. I can do that without deciding about the distillery." She stirred sugar into her tea and looked at the brochure for Global Distillers and Distribution. They certainly did have offices all over the world and represented a number of different brands, including several she recognized. "Would you be able to help me decipher the initial deals?"

"Of course. I don't think you should worry too much. This company looks pretty legitimate."

"Yoo hoo?"

Fiona responded, "Come in."

Bryce set her bag down. "Would it be okay if I wash my hands?"

"Sure. Right over there." Fiona pointed over the counter. "Would you like some tea?"

"That'd be perfect."

When they were all seated, Bryce opened her notebook. "Sorry, that took a bit longer than I expected. But, it's good news. Everything is clearly marked, and there are sixty barrels labeled Highland Dew 1998. Seventy-two are marked 1989 Special Ed. Six are marked Highland Dew Sherry 1989."

David whistled. "That's more than a little leftover

whisky."

Fiona couldn't make her mouth work. Without a lot of sales experience, it seemed like a great deal of whisky. She knew even with back-debt, that would definitely cover the expenses. She looked at Bryce. "Thank you for doing all that. Can you break down what you propose in small steps I can understand?"

"Let's see. If I were you, I'd want to get an idea of the costs to bottle and ship some of the whisky—enough for immediate expenses. Then I'd like a reliable third party to plan out subsequent releases for the most benefit, while deciding whether or not it's worth reopening the business."

David spoke up. "Do you know anyone who's qualified?"

Bryce tapped her pen. "I think so. There are a couple of savvy people in the area that I trust."

"Can we arrange another meeting with them before I have to sign anything?"

"Sure," Bryce said. "One question. Do you think there's a way I can taste what's in those barrels?" She smiled. "Wouldn't do much good if they'd gone bad."

Fiona smiled. "I don't think that's unreasonable."

"I've got an appointment this afternoon. But I'll be in touch." David picked up the folder. "Can I keep this?"

"Sure. Thanks for your help."

"Let me walk you out." Fiona showed him through the living room and out the door. "Thank you for being here. It really helped a lot."

She closed the door and took a breath. She had to face Bryce alone, and she was more confused than ever. Reggie probably was acting on her own, but that still didn't say much for Bryce's employees. On the other hand, it would be wonderful if that was true—the immediate problems would be solved. It might be possible to return to Edinburgh and her own life, she thought as she headed back into the kitchen. Bryce sat huddled over her notes, chewing on the pencil while her bangs, sprinkled with grey, fell over half her face. Her shoulders rounded, but they were broader than Fiona first thought. A streak of dust covered the side of her dark slacks. This did not look like a person working a scam.

"Still crunching numbers?" Fiona sat across from her.

When Bryce looked up, a reddish blush covered her neck and cheeks, beneath a smear of rust. "I have to be honest with you. I've worked in the business end for almost fifteen years, but always in sales." She laughed. "I did spend my summers working in a vineyard, so I know how to get my hands dirty."

Fiona smiled. "Yes, I can see that." She pointed to Bryce's face.

"Oh yeah." She wiped her cheek with her hand. "The problem I'm having is trying to give you a dollars-and-cents idea of what you have here. I can only speculate on the barrel price, but then there are fees, taxes, shipping, bottling." Bryce swept her hair back. "After we get that, I can work my magic."

Her smile was radiant.

"I understand. I'm not sure who used to bottle for us. It might be on one of the invoices."

Bryce gazed into space for a moment, then said, "Just a thought. The bottle of Highland Dew I had at the Inn said it was a ten-year-old, and the most recent barrels you have here are at least twelve years old."

"That's good, isn't it?"

"Yes, but what I'm thinking is new labeling because this will be a new product. And the other barrels contain what will probably be a twenty-one-year-old, in sherry casks." Bryce jotted some notes. "If I can suggest an idea."

"Certainly, why not?"

"This is the part I know." She grinned again. "If I was responsible for getting the word out, I'd do a new marketing campaign for the MacDougall Family Distillery. A new brand to show the long history and new thinking."

Fiona leaned back. That had never occurred to her. Since it hadn't been available for some time, there might be people who had never heard of it. "That makes sense, but it's beginning to confuse me."

Bryce set down the pencil. "I'm getting carried away. Let me toss out an idea." She slung her arm across the back of the chair. "I don't know if I mentioned it, but when I first arrived, I met with an old friend and former employee, Malcolm. He started with us in production at our Airdrie distillery and worked his way up to administration, then left to work for Tamdhu."

"That's right over in Knockando."

"Yes. He was the one who did the original testing with me when I discovered Highland Dew. I'll bet he'd be able to explain the steps to get the whisky to market."

Fiona smiled. "That would help." She walked over to get the kettle when she heard the back door, and turned.

"Afternoon, miss. I didn't mean to barge in when you had company, but it was warm outside and I thought Gavin might enjoy a bit of a walk."

"Murray, I'm glad to see you. You remember Bryce Andrews? She's interested in getting the business back on its feet."

"How do." His expression darkened.

"Nice to see you, Murray."

"He might be up now, why don't you ask him?"

She poured a little more tea.

"Fiona, do you think Murray has ever tasted the whisky during the process?"

❧❧❧❧

Reggie finished packing and walked downstairs to check out.

"Sorry you have to leave us," the young desk clerk said. "I hope you enjoyed your stay."

"The staff was wonderful and everything very comfortable." Reggie handed her the key and her business card. "Ms. Andrews and I are here for a business trip, so she asked that I put my charges on her account so she can submit them to the main office."

"Of course, we can do that. Would you just sign here?"

Reggie smiled, and picked up her bag. "Have a nice day." The idea of running back to Alness and seeing Joe tempted her, but there'd be too many questions. Better to use the drive time to figure out the next step. Her advantage would be arriving home first and inventing her version of the wildly successful trip. First task: Ian Smith. She needed him on her side.

The sign showed the entrance to the A95 and she merged onto the highway, opened her windows, and turned up the radio. Even though she was still pissed at Bryce and that damn Fiona MacDougall for screwing up an opportunity, it was a relief to be done with all this wasting time driving around farmland looking for a magical whisky. It would be good to get back to San

Francisco and her social life.

Chapter Twenty-two

Bryce had left several six-ounce sample bottles in hopes that Murray or Gavin could help Fiona get the whisky samples they'd need. The water swirled around the sink as she washed her hands and face, half-amused by the dust and dirt she'd attracted in the old cask room. Fiona had shown great restraint by not laughing out loud.

Bryce hung up her towel, and dug for a clean shirt. Her jeans needed washing, and so did most of her things. Might be a good idea to ask about a laundry soon.

What next? She flopped on the bed and recounted the day's events so far. It could have gone so much worse. In fact, she honestly expected an angrier response from Fiona. Maybe her dad and David had talked her down, but either way, plans were moving forward. Fiona agreed to have dinner with her. Now, who to get to help?

She rolled over and grabbed her notebook, happy that she'd made a contact list from day one. *First, check with Ian.* She picked up her cell phone.

"Ian Smith, may I help you?"

"It's Bryce, do you have a minute?"

He chuckled. "Certainly, it's good timing. I just hung up with Margaret in Chicago and Reggie phoned to say she'd be here in an hour."

"Did Margaret have any news about Leo?"

"Actually, she did. They thought he'd be discharged in a day or two. He's done very well in physical therapy and is becoming somewhat cantankerous."

Bryce laughed. "Of course he is. He's not good at taking orders."

"He's apparently not the only one."

"Oh, no. Reggie?"

"Yes, she wants a phone meeting with the home office to discuss her treatment."

Bryce clenched her teeth to keep from saying something impulsive. "I'm sorry to dump this on you. Just send her home to cool off. I may have smoothed the stormy sea for now. I'll be meeting Fiona later, and hopefully she'll have the samples we need."

"That is good news. Don't worry about Reggie."

"Good. Here's what I need to know. If Fiona and her dad want to proceed, and if the whisky samples are as good as I expect, I need someone with distilling experience to help decide what should be done with the whisky. We need to think about a new brand because none of this whisky is the ten-year-old, like their last offering. There are some barrels that are twenty-one years old."

"We do have a couple of still-men that could help. It depends on how much they trust us. Of course, if that's the case, we can arrange to have the whisky transported, bottled, and shipped." Ian sounded pleased.

"I thought I'd ask Tom Hobart to come over and offer his impression—just as a neutral voice. His master distiller, Liam, is the one working on the new blend." Bryce offered.

"That's an excellent idea. No need to rush them.

If they just want to start with one barrel, I think we could try that."

Bryce let the breath out she'd been holding. "You're right. I don't want to push, not now. But, I could offer some money up front to keep the wolf from the door."

"That's up to you, if you think it will reassure them."

"Thanks for being there, Ian. You've been a good resource." She jotted a note in her notebook, "tread carefully" and underlined it.

"Don't forget, this is a competitive business. Be kind but be professional."

She smiled. "Good thing to remember. I'll keep in touch."

❧ ❧ ❧ ❧

"Dad, do you know where Murray went?" Fiona asked her dozing father.

He stirred and cracked one eye. "I believe he was going back to the office... Oh, I'm not sure."

Fiona bent over in front of him. "Dad, I need to get some samples from the cask room. Can you help me?"

He appeared to perk up a little. He opened both eyes and they actually twinkled. "Oh, that, I can. Been a while, but it's a lot like riding a bike, you know."

"I suppose it is." She helped him up. "What do you need?"

He grabbed his walking stick then scratched his stubbly chin. "Hmm, mallet, gloves, some bottles, and the whisky thief. They'll be in the office, I think."

Fiona offered her arm as they negotiated the

gravel between the kitchen door and the office. It was only about twenty meters, but the stones had worn a bit more from the years of foot traffic. Had her great-grandmother walked this path, and the generations before her? These old buildings had seen so many changes, and now maybe the most dramatic. Twenty-first century business was a far cry from the way her dad had been making and selling whisky. Was he up to the challenge? She smiled and looked at him. Heck, was she up to it?

The office looked much like the way she left it, except for the newspaper, beer bottle, and a full ashtray. Her dad didn't seem to notice; he walked to the cupboard near the still room door.

"Here we are." He stuck gloves in his back pocket, grabbed a wooden mallet, and carefully picked up the antique copper whisky thief.

Fiona remembered him showing her when she was still a little girl. He had proudly polished it to a shine and showed her the faint etching of Archibald MacDougall's name.

"Have you the bottles?"

Fiona held up the portioned cardboard box Bryce had given her. "All set."

She followed him through the eerily quiet, dark distillery. He moved quickly as he had for almost seventy years. How many MacDougalls had walked through this building carrying on a tradition? Her eyes teared up. *I can't let this die.*

Once they reached the cask room and she'd flipped on the lights, her dad grinned.

"Dad, why wasn't this room locked? I see the padlock. Aren't there rules about this?"

His face clouded over. "Oh, indeed there are. It

should always be locked. I'm certain Murray has a key and there's another on a nail by the mantel."

She pushed open the heavy door. "I'll see to it, then."

"Which ones do you need?" Gavin said as they stood between the rows of barrels.

She opened the box. Bryce had written a list with the locations for each of the three different samples and had labeled two bottles for each.

"Let's start over here." She watched the rows until she saw one marked 1998.

He slipped on his reading glasses and checked the barrels on the row end for one with a bung. "Here we go." He grinned, pulled off his glasses, and twisted the wooden plug on the top side.

Fiona opened the box and grabbed two bottles marked HD 2003. She uncapped them and watched him carefully slip the long copper tube into the barrel and cover the end with his thumb. "Ready?"

She held one bottle out as he withdrew the whisky thief and angled it toward the bottle. "Hold 'er still." He moved his thumb and the dark amber liquid filled half the bottle. It was beautiful, even in the dim light.

Her dad slid the copper thief back in for one more, which then filled the sample bottle.

Fiona capped one bottle and opened the second so he could repeat the process. Once the samples were back in the box, her dad withdrew another small amount and placed it in the small tasting glass he got from his shirt pocket.

"You don't think I'd let anyone taste this first, do ya?" He lifted the glass to the light, sniffed a couple of times, closed his eyes, and took a sip. His smile said it all.

"What's next on your list?" He downed the small amount left, put the glass in his pocket, and replaced the wooden plug, using the mallet to secure it.

Fiona felt nervous and excited. Her dad seemed like his old self. "This way." She steered them back two aisles until she spotted the older barrels marked Distiller's Edition 1989. "I can't believe these are still here."

Her dad patted the first one. "This was to be a special anniversary bottling." He looked for the wooden plug and meticulously repeated the procedure.

Fiona watched him with a quiet reverence she'd never held before. When he dipped the thief for the sample he'd taste, she said, "Do you think I could taste it as well?"

His eyes twinkled. "I've waited so long to hear you say that. 'Course you can." When he finished, he handed her the glass and watched her.

She repeated the same steps he had, and then she sipped the aged whisky. Her lips got the sweetness first, then a complex assortment of flavors combined in a strong taste. Her eyes watered. "Wow, that's much stronger that I expected."

He laughed. "That's cask strength, probably a hundred and twenty proof. It'll be diluted a bit in order to sell."

"It's good. Very different than I expected."

"Aye, that's the idea, lass. Did you say there's another?" He returned the plug and pounded it into the barrel. "I'm not sure I remember the other."

She walked down to the last aisle and spotted six barrels that were slightly larger. "Here, Highland Dew-Sherry 1989."

He walked closer and put his glasses back on. "I'll

be..." He wiped his hand across the front of the barrel. "I said I wanted to experiment with sherry casks, but I kept thinking I'd just dreamt that."

Once he found the plug, he proceeded with the ritual, muttering occasionally. He pulled out his glass a dipped one more sample. "Sláinte." He sipped slowly, twice, and then opened his teary eyes. "It's even better than I imagined, Fi."

She took the glass, suddenly feeling like she was a part of the MacDougall family distillery. "Oh, I like this. It's still quite strong, but lovely. Why did you only do a few in the sherry casks?"

He put his things in his pocket and wrapped an arm around her shoulders. "At the time it was too expensive because there weren't many available. I'm done for the day. I'll need to rest a bit."

She hugged him. "Thank you so much."

❧❦❧❦❧

"I certainly understand your disappointment, Ms. Ballard. This has been a challenging task." Ian leaned back from the table.

Reggie felt as though she might explode. Why were these people so damn calm? She took a breath. "I'm sure that must be what it looks like, but I assure you, I believe I have been discriminated against and mistreated. Bryce Andrews is only interested in her pet project and wants all the credit. On the other hand, I was trying to be a team player. This is unfair, and I expect Mr. Edelman to be advised."

She felt her face flush and took another deep breath. It was not her intent to screech at Ian. It wasn't his fault. *Damn.*

Ian finished writing some notes in a leather notebook. He put down his pen. "These are serious accusations and I will, of course, submit them. But you must be aware that Ms. Andrews will also have her report." He stood and pushed his chair in. "As I mentioned, Mr. Edelman is still too ill to be involved with personnel matters, but I will report your concerns. Meanwhile, I have taken the liberty of selecting a flight to Chicago departing at seven forty-five tomorrow morning. You'll transfer at Heathrow and arrive in Chicago at three-fifteen in the afternoon." He handed her the ticket folder and itinerary.

"Are you seriously dismissing me?"

"Certainly not. I thought you might wish to return your leased car and enjoy the evening." He smiled warmly.

Reggie bit back the sarcasm. "Ian, I thought you, more than anyone, would be understanding." She sniffed and tilted her chin for effect.

"Trust me, I do understand and will take your concerns directly to the top." He held out his hand. "Have a safe journey."

Chapter Twenty-three

Bryce looked at her watch. There might be time to catch Tom Hobart in his office, but not enough to meet. After she located her cell phone under the clean laundry on the bed, she dialed Speyburn.

"Good afternoon, Speyburn Distillery, may I help you?"

"Yes, this is Bryce Andrews. I'd like to speak to Tom Hobart."

One ring. "Hello, Bryce."

"Hi, Tom. I hope I'm not interrupting. I just need a minute." She'd had the conversation a dozen times in her head.

"No problem. I'm clear."

She heard him close the door.

"I need to ask you a favor about a potential client."

"Sure."

"Have you ever run across Highland Dew whisky?"

He repeated the name a few times. "I'm pretty sure I have, but I can't recall where."

"The MacDougall Distillery produced it for many years, but it's a small operation. Long story short, there were some family problems, and they haven't produced any whisky for a few years and all but closed it down. It's a very unique product, in my humble opinion." She wiped perspiration from her temple. "However, it turns out they have discovered a large quantity in an old cask room that looks very promising."

Tom laughed. "This sounds like the plot to a movie."

Bryce hadn't thought of it that way, but it was rather melodramatic. "You're right, but here's where we are stuck. The family needs to sell some of it to pay creditors, but they're not sure how to do it or whether they want to reopen the business."

"I can understand that, but don't they know you and Global can do that for them?"

"Well...yes and no." The perspiration trickled down both sides. "I thought we had reached a sort of agreement, but there was a glitch. Anyway, I called Ian Smith and he suggested you and Liam might be able to offer some good advice after you tasted the products." She closed her eyes and held her breath. The vacuum went on in the hall, so she hurried out on the balcony.

"That sounds reasonable and practical. How would you like to set it up?"

She jabbed her fist in the air. *Yes!* "Great. They live over near Knockando, so I thought halfway might be a meeting here at my hotel. Maybe dinner?"

"You're staying in Craigellachie?"

"Yes, the Highlander Inn. Can we try tomorrow night around six? Of course I need to clear this with them."

"It works for me, but I have to check to see if Liam can make it."

"Wonderful. Let's plan on that—barring complications."

"See you then."

She collapsed in the plastic deck chair. "Thank you!" One more call...

Fiona had all six sample bottles on the kitchen table. They looked lovely lined up in a row with the sunlight behind them. Each label was meticulously written out with all the information on each. She rested her chin in her hands and thought about what these little bottles could mean for her and her dad... and possibly the business.

Her dad seemed excited earlier, but she didn't trust that to last. Still, for a while, she felt closer to him than she had since she was little. It was evident that, at one time, making whisky was a real passion. She wished, now, she'd paid closer attention and had learned more about the operation. And what the hell was wrong with Murray? This disappearing act was getting old fast.

The living room clock chimed five and she needed to plan supper. At the same moment her phone rang.

"Hello?"

"Hi, Fiona. It's Bryce Andrews. Is this a bad time?"

"Bryce?"

"Yes, I didn't want to interrupt, but I wondered if you and your dad would like to join me for dinner tomorrow night?"

She sat back down. "That's very nice, but why would you want us to come over?"

"I've thought a lot about your dilemma and what I would do in your place. Since you may feel like you don't have enough information to make a decision, and right now you don't exactly trust me...I wanted to provide some unbiased opinions."

Fiona listened carefully. "It sounds logical, but why would you do that?"

"Because I still feel horrible about what Reggie

did. It may not help, now, but I asked her to go back to the States."

"Oh. How would you want to do this?"

"I would like you and your father to come over to the Highlander Inn tomorrow evening, bring the whisky samples…did you get them?"

Fiona laughed, surprised Bryce hadn't asked sooner. "Yes, my dad and I got them all, and he seemed to really enjoy doing it."

Bryce sighed audibly. "That's great. I invited Tom Hobart, the general manager at the Speyburn Distillery, and his Master Distiller, Liam. My hope is that they can give you a fair evaluation of your product and your options."

She never thought of having more than one option. "You know my dad is unpredictable. He may not be any help at all."

"Or…he may enjoy the conversation immensely. Either way, you'll have a nice meal and conversation. There's no obligation."

"That's true. What time would you like us to come over?"

"I told Tom six, but why don't you come at five thirty so your dad can get comfortable?"

"That's very considerate. I'll say yes, but things can change in a day."

"And we can reschedule, if necessary."

⁂

Bryce ended the call and let all the tension drain. This meeting could mean so much to so many, and especially for her. For the last couple of weeks, she felt driven by some other force outside of her business. But being in Scotland and being a part of the life here felt so grounding and hopeful. It was hard to describe, but it felt right.

She jumped up and looked for her shoes. With her phone and notepad, she hurried downstairs. The desk clerk waved hello, and she waved back. The bar area was empty except for a young woman lighting candles on each table. It was still light out—and would be for hours, but it provided more ambiance to the rustic-modern atmosphere. Dark green walls provided a nice background for the whisky bottles and the rough-hewn ceiling timbers held brass and copper light fixtures.

As she wandered to the end of the long oak bar, she smelled the faint hint of smoke from the large fireplace and the tinge of whisky in the air.

She smiled. It felt like home after all the time she'd used the place as home base.

"Good afternoon," Billy boomed.

It startled her, and she laughed. "Where'd you come from?"

"Cleaning out this lower cupboard. I don't believe it's been done since before the war."

"What war?"

"WWI." He laughed. "What can I get you?"

"I believe I'll have some Highland Dew, if you have any."

"Did you finish the bottle you bought?"

"Nope. I'm saving that, for now."

He poured her a generous dram and handed her a small pitcher of water. "Enjoy."

She sipped the whisky and smiled, then looked around. "I may need some advice."

He put down his bar towel. "Sure."

"Tomorrow night I've invited two fellas from

Speyburn to meet with me and the MacDougalls."

His eyebrows shot up. "You don't say. There's a man I'd like to meet."

"Well, here's what I'm wondering. Do you have a semi-private area where we can talk business without distraction?"

He pointed. "Behind that fireplace is a small dining room for wee parties and such."

"Perfect. I asked Fiona and her dad to come early to meet you, so they'll understand how I first discovered Highland Dew. I thought you might tell them how much folks enjoy it."

"Aren't you a clever one? Of course I will."

Bryce sipped her whisky. "They'll bring some samples from the whisky we discovered. I want them to understand what kind of options they have for that whisky, and maybe for the distillery."

Billy smiled and nodded. "Wouldn't that be grand for them. Do us all proud to see that up and running again."

She felt a twinge of pride and just as quickly, discarded it. "I hope so. We have other distillers interested in going with Global, and I want this one to be a collaborative effort to restore a part of history. How many whisky stills are currently owned by the founding families?"

"Good point. I don't think many. Most have partnered with giant corporations." He cocked his head. "But, I've a question. What would you be getting out of this?"

Good question. "I'm not sure anything. They still don't know which way they want to go. I think Fiona would just like to sell the whisky and get on with her life. And her dad…well, I'm not sure."

Chapter Twenty-four

Fiona waved as the truck pulled into the yard. "Murray, can I talk to you for a minute?"

He parked and walked to meet her. "Aye. What's up, miss?"

"Tonight I'm going to take dad into Craigellachie to meet with some men about selling the whisky."

He shoved his hands in his pockets. "Does he want to sell the Special?"

"Yes, I think so. Why wouldn't he?"

"Don't know for sure…just thought he had something special he was saving it for. Wanted to wait twenty years before unveiling it."

"He's never mentioned it." Fiona worried that it might be important. "His memory is so patchy now. Are you sure you don't know what it was? It would really help."

"Suppose I could look back through log entries to see if he wrote anything…"

"You know, we both want the best for him and I could really use your help. You and dad have been a team for so long…and he needs you now."

He backed up a step. "I'll go see what I can find, miss."

She watched as he scurried to the office. Why hadn't she asked more questions about him before she moved to Edinburgh? Her father trusted him, and he probably knew everything about the damn business.

She grabbed the basket from the back steps and walked around the house to retrieve the laundry. The wind gusted and the clothes snapped. She suddenly remembered the overheard conversation between Murray and her dad. What was it he wanted her dad to remember? Something about an envelope.

A sheet pulled loose and she had to grab it before it blew out to the driveway. The fresh, clean smell assaulted her senses and vague memories. This time was about her mother, who graciously allowed Fiona to help fold the dried linens. She smiled when she remembered how honored she felt…until she got a little older and figured it out. Her mum had been a teacher before she married, and felt strongly that girls be educated. It felt like torture then, but now, she felt grateful.

Her throat tightened. *Oh mum, I love you and still miss you so much. So does Dad. I wish you were here to help us decide what to do, because I feel so lost.*

"Fi, where are you?" her dad called from the house.

"I'm coming, just have to get the laundry."

⁂

The corporate office for Global Distillers and Distribution sat in downtown Chicago on lower Michigan Avenue. Reggie Ballard had barely checked in to her hotel before she made an appointment with HR. There didn't seem to be much point in trying to talk to Leo. Besides, she knew he'd take Bryce's side anyway.

The long flight gave her time to stew and added fuel to her complaint. She'd worked too hard for this to give up. After all, more contacts signed with her, because she wasn't wasting time on that broken-down distillery. How dare Bryce send her home? Ridiculous.

The cab stopped in front of the building with the large brass sign for Global Distillers and Distribution, and she paid and got out. The traffic noise deafened her. After a couple of weeks in the quiet hills of Scotland, this was sensory overload. Just then, the legendary wind off the lake whipped around the Art Institute and almost flattened her.

"Shit."

Grateful to squeeze into the elevator, Reggie moved behind a woman with a bad cough. She straightened the jacket on the only clean outfit she had left. It would be vital to appear calm and professional.

"Excuse me." She moved out to the carpeted hallway in front of the illuminated logo for GDD. Most of the executives were up on the next floor, and she didn't want to be seen up there. The Human Resources office door was open.

"Good afternoon. I'm Regina Ballard, and I have an appointment."

"Hello, Ms. Ballard. Please have a seat and Nora will be right with you."

Reggie chose the small settee by the coffee table and picked up the latest issue of the company quarterly report.

Only moments later she heard, "Ms. Ballard, please come in."

Reggie followed the tall, blond, Viking woman into her tasteful small office.

"How was your flight from Scotland?"

No secrets in this company. "Rather long, as you might expect, but it's always good to be home."

Nora opened a folder. "I received a report from Mr. Smith in the Glasgow office, and knew you might want to talk. He felt there might have been some misunderstanding. Would you like to talk about it a little?"

Misunderstanding? "That might have been his take, but I'm a little more concerned that we may be talking about a case of discrimination."

❧❧❧❧

Bryce changed clothes three times. Would casual make Fiona and her dad more comfortable? Or maybe they would think she wasn't very serious. And what about Tom and Liam? They would think this was a business meeting.

Happily, her khaki slacks and company polo shirt were clean. She dried her hair and tried to comb it into some order. It was past time for a haircut, and she felt a bit shaggy.

Tom had sent a text they would be on time. Fiona had left a message they were leaving soon. All she had to bring down were the forms she might need, the tasting glasses she had Ian send her, and the bottle of Highland Dew for them to taste.

One last look and she headed downstairs. She hoped the small dining room would be comfortable. She had them set the table for six, in case Billy could stay for dinner. He waved as she walked into the bar.

"All set, are we?"

"I think so." She held up crossed fingers and took her things back to the dining room. It looked lovely. Two sets of windows with sheer white curtains lightened the room. It felt a little stuffy, so she opened two windows slightly.

She'd sit at the head and have Tom and Liam sit across from Fiona and her dad. She put the glasses in the center of the table next to the water pitcher and napkins. The bottle of whisky tempted her, but she'd better wait. Her watch read 5:25.

Laughter sounded from the bar.

"Aye, she'll be about somewheres," Billy boomed.

"My cue." Bryce hurried out. "I'm here. Fiona, Gavin, so nice to see you again. I'm glad you could join me. Have you met Billy?"

Fiona had on a cotton sundress with a faint olive and blue pattern, her auburn waves hanging past her shoulders. Bryce stopped. She was utterly stunning.

Gavin turned to her, cocked his head, then smiled. "Hullo."

"Good to see you, Gavin. And Fiona you look… lovely."

Fiona looked over her shoulder. "Thank you."

"I, um, wanted you to come a little early and meet Billy."

"And so they did," he said. "Pleased to make your acquaintance."

Bryce moved closer to the bar and Fiona. "It was Billy who set me up with a blind taste test, and it was the Highland Dew that caught my attention and continued to haunt me. Then, when I stumbled onto the distillery, I had no idea it was the same origin."

Gavin laughed. "I'm surprised you could even see the drive or the sign."

"It is tricky. Would you like something to drink?"

"Nothing for me, just yet. Dad?"

"D'ya still have some of the Dew?"

Billy pulled the bottle from the back bar. "Yes,

sir, I do."

Gavin started talking about who knew who, and Fiona stepped away, nodding to Bryce.

"I wasn't sure earlier, but once we got here, dad brightened up. Seems he and Murray used to come to town to play cards with some locals."

"That's wonderful. He sure looks dapper in his tweed jacket."

She smiled. "He used to be a real looker back in the day. Coal-black hair and bright blue eyes."

"I can see whose looks you inherited."

"I don't know if that's true. My mum was a fair beauty, herself."

"I'm really glad you decided to give me another chance."

Fiona's cheeks reddened. "I'm not sure yet what I'm doing, but it would be crazy not to listen and find out."

"That's all I ask. I want to help you in whatever way I can, and I won't push."

"Bryce." Tom and Liam walked in and waved.

She slowly introduced everyone and made sure that Gavin was accorded deference as the Master Distiller from MacDougall Distillery.

"Why don't we go back to the private dining room and talk about some whisky." She could feel her heart thudding against her ribs, and sent up a silent prayer.

Chapter Twenty-five

Bryce steered everyone to a seat and nervously explained what she hoped they could achieve.

"Fiona and Gavin were kind enough to provide some samples for Tom and Liam to evaluate." She looked at Fiona.

"Oh, yes, I have them here." She lifted her tote bag and pulled out the sample box.

"Thank you." Bryce carefully removed one of each and smiled as she checked the labels. "I personally catalogued each barrel by name and date. These represent the three types available—at cask strength." She set them down next to Tom. "Would you do the honors?"

He checked each and put them in order of year. "Who'd like to join us?"

Everyone nodded, and he poured a half an ounce in each glass and passed them around.

Billy walked in. "I've got a few minutes and wanted to see how it was going."

Tom poured another. "The card in front of you lists each one if you'd like to make your own notes."

Bryce waited and watched the reactions. Fiona sniffed hers and waited for the water pitcher to come round. "Thank you."

Fiona watched the men across from her.

So did her dad. He sipped from his glass and watched the men as if they were jurors.

Tom and Liam had done this thousands of times, and shared a shorthand of descriptions which they jotted down. Once finished, they dumped any residual in a small bowl and moved to the next one.

Bryce reached for the sample, poured a small amount, and offered it to Fiona and Gavin. They both shook their heads but passed it to Billy, who scribbled some notes and then poured a small amount. She watched his face as he tasted it. His eyes lit up.

She added some water and tasted it. It warmed her, and she didn't want to even swallow it. This was the whisky she had originally noticed with more maturity and softness. It was divine. What a lucky twist of fate had brought them there.

Gavin grinned broadly. He must know how good this was.

Tom and Liam finished the sample and wrote more notes as they nodded and commented. Tom picked up the third and final, poured, and passed.

This time everyone took a sample. It felt like an hour passed without any conversation. The faint sounds of music and laughter broke in when a server opened the door and nodded to Billy.

"Excuse me." He finished his sample, smiled at Bryce, and left the room.

She let out a breath and sipped the sherry-aged whisky. Heaven.

Gavin whispered something to Fiona and she smiled.

"Sorry, this feels like a prayer meeting," Tom said.

Relieved snickers and comments erupted from around the table.

"I'm used to working in a small tasting room at the distillery because I get distracted easily. So, thank you for your patience." Tom looked at his glass one more time and set it down. "If I understand the situation, Gavin and Fiona are looking for some honest recommendations for these new samples."

"Yes, please. It is quite a surprise, and we understand the market may have changed in the last few years," Fiona said and looked over at Gavin.

"Of course. I can tell you up front, these are three fine whiskies." Tom smiled.

There was an audible sigh from Fiona.

He picked up the second sample. "The Distiller's Edition is ready now, but holding it a little longer wouldn't hurt, as a twenty-three-year-old sells better. Same with the sherry cask." He picked up the first sample. "I like this, but I'd love to compare it to the original."

Bryce jumped. "Oh, shoot, I'm sorry." She looked around and spotted the bottle on the window sill. "I was opening the windows." She pushed her chair back and grabbed the bottle. "We should have had this first."

The tension was broken when everyone laughed.

Tom took the bottle and poured a bit for both himself and Liam. They tasted and re-tasted the original Highland Dew.

"Mr. MacDougall. This is a happy accident. Two more years in the barrel added a nice richness and balanced the fruit with the oak. I'd say this is ready to go."

Liam picked up his notes. "Well, sir, I'm honored to be tasting this wonderful old brand. As a Master Distiller, I work hard to find just the right taste. I don't know how much you've changed your original recipe, but it's clear this is a heritage product developed over decades with great passion."

Bryce glanced over to see Gavin push himself up. With tears in his eyes, he reached across the table and shook hands with Liam and then Tom. "You've made me very proud, and I thank you for your time and experience."

Bryce swiped her eyes and Fiona dug out a tissue.

"Tom, if this were your product"—she held up the first sample—"and you needed to decide what course you'd take, what would you offer?" Bryce said.

"Judging by what I've tasted, the storage has been good and there doesn't seem to be any problem. You could begin slowly by bottling and selling one or two barrels at a time until you have enough capital to ship more." He looked at the other two samples. "You can sell the whisky to someone else through a good broker and let them worry about the details. Or you could hire a reputable company, like GDD." He winked at Bryce. "I have to say that. Let them set up a rollout plan that includes branding and marketing. Either way, you can expect around £2,000 per barrel, and get a yield of about 350 bottles."

Gavin looked dazed, and Fiona was scribbling madly.

"All right. If there's nothing else, let's get some dinner," Bryce said. She leaned over to Fiona. "Is there anything else you want to ask them?"

She looked up with surprise. Her eyes glistened and her cheeks were flushed. "I don't know. But that's a lot of money. Just a few barrels would cover all the bills."

"Why not go out on the patio while the staff prepare for dinner?" Bryce ushered them to the patio door past the fireplace.

Liam moved to Gavin and began asking some

questions. Gavin sat on one of the benches and pulled out his pipe. Bryce watched them and imagined what Gavin was like as a young distiller.

Fiona returned from the restroom and sat next to Tom. "Would you mind if I ask some questions?"

"Of course not. I sensed you might have a few." He smiled.

Bryce slipped back inside and went to check on dinner. Her phone vibrated and she stepped into the now-empty back dining room

"Bryce, it's Leo. Am I interrupting?"

"We just finished our meeting between the MacDougalls and Tom Hobart."

"About the new samples?"

How did he know? Oh, Ian. Of course. "He was very complimentary. Both he and Liam were impressed. I'm glad." She sat on the window seat near her chair.

"That's great. I'll give him a call tomorrow."

"Are you back to work already?" She thought he sounded pretty chipper.

"Not exactly. I got a call from Nora in HR. We have a little problem."

Her heart jumped into overdrive. That was never a good comment.

"For whatever reason, Ms. Ballard has decided that her disagreement may be a discrimination case. Do you have any idea what she's talking about?"

Spots danced in front of her eyes and her breathing ramped up. *What the...Discrimination?* "I...I have no clue."

"Ian didn't know either. I guess I'll have to go in and meet with her so I can nip this nonsense in the bud. Just wanted to check with you. Don't worry about it, I'll handle it and let you know." He hung up.

Her hands began to shake and her chest tightened. This couldn't be happening. The room began to spin. Blackness crept in from the sides.

❧❧❧❧

"Bryce? Bryce can you hear me?" Fiona replaced the cool towel and Bryce moaned. "You're all right, just lie still."

"Can I get her anything?" Billy said.

"Let's just wait a bit. Maybe you could close the door." She turned the towel and wiped Bryce's face. Some color edged into her cheeks.

"What happened?" Bryce whispered.

"I think you just fainted, but you're fine. No damage done." Fiona sat back on her heels and breathed a sigh of relief. Being a teacher didn't qualify her to treat the unconscious.

Bryce covered her face and took a deep breath. Perspiration dotted her forehead and she wiped it with the towel. She started to sit up.

"Here, let me help." Fiona put an arm under her shoulders while Bryce sat and tipped to one side. "Easy there." Her damp polo shirt clung to her back, and the color in her face started to drain again.

"I'm okay, just disoriented. What time is it?"

"Almost seven thirty. It's only been a few minutes. I heard a noise and came in to find you out cold." Fiona brushed the damp hair from Bryce's forehead. Her dark brown eyes focused a little better. "Do you want some water?"

"Yes. My mouth is really dry." She took the bottle and sipped it.

Fiona kept a hand on her shoulder, and noticed

surprising muscles. She remembered something about playing sports.

"What about dinner? Did I mess everything up?" She started to get up.

"Whoa. Not so fast. They're holding it for a few minutes and Billy is talking with Dad, Tom, and Liam. Everything is fine."

Bryce looked at her shirt. "I'd like to go up and change and splash some water on my face."

"If you're sure, but I think I'd better help."

"You don't have to—"

"I think it would be wise." Fiona stood and put her hand out. Bryce took it and pulled herself up, where she wobbled again.

"Okay. You were right. My room is just at the top of the stairs."

They slipped out through the lobby and made it upstairs. Bryce found her key and opened the door. "You can come in. I won't be a minute."

Fiona sat on the foot of the bed. "This is a lovely room." The homey appointments like the quilted bedspread and curtains provided cheery color to the rustic furniture.

Bryce stood at the bathroom sink, splashing water around her head and neck. Fiona watched with a surprising fascination. When Bryce pulled her shirt off and threw it over the shower rod, a warm flush rose up Fiona's chest and neck. Clearly an athlete. She swallowed.

"I'm so embarrassed. I don't remember fainting since the state finals in high school. Anxiety, I guess." Bryce dried her face and shoulders, then ran a comb through her feathery short hair. "Did anyone come in except you?" She opened the closet door and pulled out another shirt and started buttoning it from the bottom.

Fiona felt her mouth dry up. She just asked a question. "Um…no. Well, Billy followed me and got the towel and water."

Bryce sat down on a nearby bench. "Fiona, I wanted this whole evening to go smoothly for you and your dad because it's so important."

"But it was perfect. Really." She put her hand on Bryce's wrist and quickly pulled back. "The whole tasting went well, and Dad was so touched. He lost some of his confidence when Mum died and he couldn't help her. Tonight, he got that back." She felt the truth of what she had just said, and the gratitude. "You gave me back my dad."

Chapter Twenty-six

Reggie had been cooling her heels waiting for Leo Edelman. The call came late last night from Margaret. "Mr. Edelman would like to see you at nine tomorrow morning." She glanced at her watch for the tenth time.

Leo Edelman was a bit of a legend in the import-export business, just like his father before him. Employees worked hard to earn his respect, but he worked just as hard if not harder. The same went for his darling mentee, Bryce Andrews, even though she got no special favors.

Maybe the wild idea of a discrimination case would bite her in the ass. It seemed like such a clever idea. She picked at some rogue nail polish she'd slapped on hurriedly. The dress looked good and accented her best feature with a deep V-neck. *Here's hoping he isn't too old to notice.*

Margaret's phone rang. "Yes, sir, I'll tell her."

That sounded ominous.

"Mr. Edelman is on the way up."

It was too late to run to the bathroom. Deep breath. She heard the private elevator ding.

"Good morning, ladies." He walked in with a cane and a notable limp.

Reggie almost gasped out loud. He'd lost so much weight and looked so…frail.

"It was good of you to come on such short notice.

Come on in." He moved slowly into his office and sat carefully in the big leather chair behind his enormous cherry desk. A banker's lamp, desk pad, and double pen holder were the only items on his desk. A large-screen computer and desk phone were directly behind him on his credenza.

"Please." He indicated a chair. "Would you like coffee, or something else to drink?"

"No, thank you." She looked around at the spacious, sparse space. A few modern canvases hung on two walls. Built-in shelves held numerous awards. And a wall of windows faced east over Lake Michigan.

Margaret came in carrying a tray with a teapot, and cup and saucer.

"Thank you, I'll take it." He lifted the top and set it back down. "No more coffee for a while." He smiled.

"I heard about…well, I'm sorry you were laid up awhile." *Lame.*

"It's quite all right. A minor stroke and I'm getting back to normal. It will take some time." He poured the pale tea. "Why don't you tell me about this discrimination problem?"

Smack! No more polite conversation. Her rehearsed speech flew right out of her head. A bubble of anxiety popped open in her chest. "I'm not sure where to start."

He sipped the tea and smiled. "Just take your time. I want to understand what happened that upset you so."

"The trip went well, and I think we both—Bryce and I—had some wonderful contacts. But it took time and a lot of driving around, in and out of hotels. Even though we talked daily, it was a bit lonely."

"I understand."

"When I finished up at Balblair, I had some time and decided to accept a dinner invitation from my last client, Joe. As a rule, I never do that. But he was a nice kid and very enthusiastic about the business he and his brother were building." She smoothed her skirt and wished she'd asked for water.

"Anyway, we had dinner at my hotel and… several drinks. He had so many questions and it was so fun to just be able to talk and laugh with someone." She sniffed and wiped her eye. After she dug a tissue out of her purse, she took a deep breath. "I know now it was the wrong thing to do. It wasn't a message I wanted to convey, but sometimes things just happen." She wiped her nose and looked down at her lap.

"Yes, I can see how that might happen. You're a very attractive woman and I'm sure many men would agree, especially those unfamiliar with a Southern belle such as yourself."

Was he mocking her?

"I should have been more careful. In retrospect, I realize I was too tired to be meeting with a client."

"Unfortunate. But I'm curious about where the …discrimination is coming from."

"Oh. This is so difficult."

"Take your time. Are you sure you wouldn't like some water?"

"Yes, that would be good."

He tapped a button on the phone. "Margaret, may we have some water?"

Within a minute she was back with two water bottles.

"Thank you."

Reggie took several long swallows and recapped the bottle. "Much better." She pushed her shoulders back and lifted her chin.

"I'm sure it comes as no surprise to you that Bryce is a lesbian." She paused.

He nodded solemnly.

"Well, we've been good friends for many years, but...there was a time when we were, shall I say, closer?"

"Go on."

"It didn't last because our working relationship was so much more important." Leo's face gave nothing away. She opened her water bottle and sipped. "Well, when I drove over to meet her in Craigellachie with my reports and samples, we talked about the people I'd met. I mentioned Joe and the evening we shared. Bryce actually scolded me."

"About your relationship with Joe?"

"Yes. I agreed and apologized. Then she told me all about the MacDougalls and how important their business might be. I wasn't sure it was worth all the time she was spending, but I wanted to help. She decided to go to Airdrie to talk to Ian and take the samples with her.

"I thought about what she'd said, and thought I could help by talking to them about how we could help them and offering a Request for Representation. But, apparently, Bryce hadn't even gotten that far. I barely got a chance to explain when Fiona MacDougall yelled and threw me out."

"I still don't quite understand." Leo sipped more tea. He looked confused.

"I guess Ian and Bryce came up with some hair-brained idea to gradually convince Fiona. So, when I told her what happened, she got really mad. I've never seen her like that." She looked up. "Leo, I was actually scared. She screamed and told me she was in charge and I had to go home. I didn't believe her, but I had no choice." She sniffed and wiped her nose again. "I had hoped Ian might be able to reason with her, but she'd already called him and said he booked my flight." Tears flowed easily.

"I can certainly see why you'd be upset. I'd like to help, but I still don't understand where the discrimination case comes from." Leo leaned forward.

"I didn't either, at first. But I figured it out while I flew home. Bryce is interested in that woman, Fiona, and was mad that I butted in. Then wanted to punish *me* for an innocent mistake with Joe. She was fine when she thought I was playing for her team, but not when I switched sides." *Point. Game. Set.*

Leo nodded. "Now I see. And of course, you know our company policy on discrimination. I'll need to think about this. These are serious accusations." He stood. "I hope you will do me a favor and sit on this information for a little while before you do anything rash. I think we can work this out."

She smiled. "Thank you so much for listening. You have no idea how hard this has been."

"I think I do. Why don't you take another day before you fly back to San Francisco. If I hear anything, I will contact you. And nice work on the project."

"Thanks, Leo. I will." She practically bounced down the hall to the elevator. Time for a little celebrating.

❦❦❦❦

The bar was hopping when Bryce and Fiona returned. A small group had gathered near the fireplace with flutes and fiddles, and entertained with some local favorites. Song and laughter filled the air.

"This is fun." Fiona leaned close and tried to be heard.

"Is this a holiday?" Bryce dodged a young man juggling five pints.

"I've no idea. Could be a graduation or something."

They made it to the bar and waved at Billy. He looked busy, but nodded at them.

Fiona scanned the room. "Where do you suppose the gentlemen have got to?"

"No idea," Bryce shouted.

"Outside, last I saw them. I'll have a look since Dad might be smoking his pipe."

Bryce watched the celebration. In this chaos, no one would likely know what happened to her. Still, she felt uncomfortable for Fiona to see her like that. Although it might have been worse if Tom or Liam had.

Billy interrupted her thoughts. "How're you feeling?"

"Embarrassed, but otherwise fine. Thanks for your help."

"It wasn't a problem, believe me. Can I get you something?"

"Have you seen any of the guests we had?"

"Oh, yeah. Tom got a phone call and they had to leave in a hurry, but said he'd call."

"Okay. Did you see where Gavin went?"

He looked around. "Last I saw he was talkin' with some lads by the patio door."

"Thanks, we'll look for him. I'm sorry about dinner." She pushed off toward the door. "Excuse me." She steered around two dancers. No sign of Gavin or Fiona.

Once outside, she took a breath. The cool evening

air wafted up from the river. The sky glowed pinkish as the sun dipped close to the horizon. Three or four people stood around chatting, so Bryce moved out to the rear parking area.

"Bryce." Fiona called. "I've walked all the way down to the river...no one has seen Dad. Now I'm scared."

Chapter Twenty-seven

They walked around to the front, and Fiona spotted flashing lights farther up Victoria Street and her heart began to race as she ran. "Oh no, please not Dad."

As they got closer, she could see a group of people in the parking lot on the south side of the hotel. In the dim light she couldn't see who lay on the ground, but the constable was talking. She jumped when a small ambulance sounded a siren and turned in before her.

"Bryce, is it him? Can you see?"

"No. Look over here. Excuse me." They moved between some on-lookers.

"That hurts!" Gavin called out.

"Dad, what happened?" His face was hard to recognize because of the blood. A paramedic held a large bandage to his forehead, as he sat against a stone wall.

"Oh, my God." She covered her mouth and stared. Bryce grabbed her elbow to steady her.

"Let them help him," Bryce whispered.

The constable approached her. "Pardon me, miss, do you know the gentleman?"

"Yes, he's my dad. What happened?"

"It appears he may have tripped and fallen over that ledge. He can't really give much information, but he cracked his head pretty good and will likely need some stitches and an x-ray."

"Yes, of course, if you think that's best." She started shaking. "Can I talk to him?"

"Be quick."

"Are you all right?" She took his hand. It was scraped by dirt and gravel.

His eyes searched her face. "I dunno, think I took a spill. My head hurts, Mary."

"I know. We're going to get you to hospital right away." She looked at the medic. "Does he need to go in the ambulance?"

"Afraid so. Head injuries can be serious, so we'll run him up to Dr. Gray's in Elgin. You're welcome to follow."

"He has dementia, just so you know. But he's been all right on his feet up to now." She watched as he wrapped a large roll of gauze around her father's head.

"We'll take care, don't you worry. Let's move him."

Another paramedic lowered a stretcher, and they moved him onto it and covered him with a blanket. Once the straps were buckled, they hurried to the waiting ambulance.

"I'll be right behind you, Dad." She turned to Bryce. "We have to hurry and get to Elgin."

"I know. We will, but you need to focus. Please take a breath."

Fiona sagged against her and took a breath. "My God, I've never seen him like that. It's frightening."

They jogged back toward the inn. "Let's take my car," Bryce said. "You can pick yours up later."

Fiona simply nodded.

❧❧❧❧

The moon peered over the ridge as Bryce steered the car back on the A941. They had been in the waiting room at the Accident & Emergency department for over two hours before the doctor spoke with them. She glanced over at Fiona, who still looked dazed.

"Do you want me to take you straight home?" She touched her arm.

"What?"

"I thought you could get your car tomorrow, if you want."

"I don't know. Can you tell me again what the doctor said?" Fiona sounded tired.

"He said there were no broken bones. The laceration was dirty and they were worried about infection, but they irrigated it before closing it," Bryce said slowly.

"Yes, it did look bad...go on."

"The x-ray showed a possible injury on the front of his head, so they want to keep him for a day or two for neurology checks."

"I shouldn't have let him out of my sight."

Bryce cringed. *She wouldn't have if she hadn't been trying to help me.* "He was busy talking to Tom and Liam. We couldn't know they'd leave in a hurry."

Fiona squeezed her arm. "Oh, I'm not blaming you. I just feel guilty. I'm glad you're here, and thank you. Most of my friends are in Edinburgh and have no idea what my family does. Good idea. I suppose it would be better to go home and worry about the car later."

They drove in silence for a while, but Fiona kept her hand on Bryce's arm like some kind of tether. She didn't move it. The dark night surrounded them except for the sliver of moon and a blanket of stars. Bryce felt relieved they had made the trip to Elgin while it was still light out.

After about twenty minutes, Fiona pointed. "You'll need to turn off just before the Craigellachie exit. See the sign for Archiestown?"

Bryce slowed and took the turnoff.

"Where is your family from?" Fiona asked.

"Central Illinois, just south of Chicago. Are you familiar?"

"Vaguely. I know where some of the states are because I teach Twentieth Century literature, so I'm familiar with Carl Sandberg."

Bryce wracked her brain. "Wait… 'Hog Butcher for the World/ Tool Maker, Stacker of Wheat/ Player with Railroads and the Nation's Freight Handler,/ Stormy, Husky, Brawling, City of the Big Shoulders.'"

Fiona laughed. "Yes. In poetry, 1914."

"You do know your stuff."

"I really liked that image. Is it really that…raw?"

"I guess it was back in the beginning. At one time it was frontier and a major hub for trade, which is how it grew so big."

"Is it really so big?"

Bryce smiled. "With the adjacent suburbs, it's around ten million people."

"What? Really?" Fiona asked. "The whole of Scotland is probably not more than five million." She covered her mouth. "That's utterly mind-boggling to me. Someday, I should like to see that."

"It's an amazing city with lots of character…and great food."

"What's your favorite?"

Bryce had to think. "I know. Deep dish Chicago-style pizza."

"What makes it so different?" Fiona shifted in her seat to face her.

"Where to begin? Each piece is like a whole meal. It's about two inches thick with lots of rich tomato sauce, chunks of Italian sausage or pepperoni, and gobs of mozzarella cheese. You sometimes need to eat it with a knife and fork." Bryce felt her stomach rumble.

Fiona laughed. "We didn't ever eat, did we? Are they going to be angry at the inn?"

"I hope not. Billy will have told them, I think."

"There's a tight curve ahead and the drive is just beyond, easy to miss." Fiona said.

"Well, I know that curve." She slowed and switched on her high beams to look for the sign.

"I know it's quite late, but I'm famished and still a little wound up. Would you like to come in for a bite?"

Bryce felt her cheeks warm, happy it was dark in the car. "That does sound good." She pulled alongside the house and stopped. As she got out, Fiona asked something about ham, but Bryce noticed a light in the office.

"Does Murray often work this late?"

Fiona came around the car. "Fire! That's not a light." She ran to the office and pushed the door open.

Bryce came in right behind and saw flames licking up from the wastebasket beside the desk that Murray was slumped over. "Grab the back of the chair."

They both held his jacket and the chair, and rolled him out.

"I'll get water." Fiona ran to the house.

Bryce looked around and spotted the heavy doormat, which she dragged in and draped over the flames. By the time Fiona returned, the blaze seemed to be dying.

"Let's wait a second before pulling off the mat."

Fiona put down the bucket. "My God, what happened?"

Bryce moved to the other side of the desk. "There's a half empty bottle of whisky and a full ashtray. I'd guess he fell asleep and dropped a cigarette in the basket." It seemed peculiar. "Has he done anything like this before?"

Fiona shook her head. "Not that I know of, but it's one more thing I don't understand."

Bryce carefully lifted the corner of the mat and the flames were gone; just smoke remained. She grabbed the bucket and slowly poured the water on the smoldering paper. "When the metal cools, I'll take it out of here."

"Thanks. We better check on Murray."

He snored quietly, draped in the chair in the middle of the driveway.

"I've a good mind to leave him there," Fiona said.

"Where does he live?"

"He's one of the two cottages just behind the building." She nudged his shoulder. "Time to go home, Murray."

After another poke, he cracked one bleary eye. He sat up when he recognized Fiona. "Oh. Miss Fiona… Where is. Yes, I'll be on my way." He pushed up and teetered.

"I'll steer him round back if you can get the trash can outside."

Bryce watched her push and pull the man down the driveway. The idea of a quiet pleasant meal together faded with the smell of the smoky wet papers and the grey smoke stain on the back wall and ceiling. She used the mat to pull the basket out the door, and went back to check the desk, wall, and file cabinet to be sure they were cool.

Fiona returned just as she put the chair back and turned off the light. "Might be a good idea to leave the door open to air the place out, if you think that's safe."

"Sure. Let's go in, I'm still hungry."

Chapter Twenty-eight

Old smoke. Fiona sniffed again. It was on her shirt. She opened her eyes and saw the back of the sofa. Slowly her mind's eye tape rewound to the fire in the office, then making sandwiches… drinking wine…listening to old music from the forties. She rolled over and looked across the room to see Bryce sound asleep in the recliner looking so relaxed and…what? Attractive. Her dark hair hung across her forehead and her lips were barely parted. She looked so young and peaceful, not at all like the worried business woman.

Fiona sat up and folded the small knit blanket. They had talked about everything long into the night and early morning. Their family, friends, and not surprisingly, their last girlfriends. Who was Bryce talking about? Gayle? No, Gretchen. It must've been painful since she still seemed so raw. How could anyone cheat on this woman?

She quietly slipped out to the kitchen and started some coffee. The refrigerator held nothing wonderful, but there were some scones and jam.

Dad. The scones brought back the whole evening and tears blurred her eyes. It was still too early to call. Yesterday felt like it was so long ago, but it hadn't even been twenty-four hours. She set out two cups and sat at the table where the sun warmed the room. It felt overwhelming to think about all that had happened in the past few weeks.

She wiped her nose and sighed. Solving all the problems loomed even larger with no real solutions in sight…or too many. What she did know for sure, was that she had been wrong about Bryce. Her offer to help was genuine and generous.

"Hi."

Fiona looked up and saw Bryce standing in the kitchen doorway. "Hi. Did I wake you?"

"No. My hand fell asleep and hurt."

"Would you like some coffee?"

"That sounds great." She came over to the counter. "I guess we faded quickly last night. Last thing I remember was hearing Ella Fitzgerald."

Fiona laughed. "I don't think I made it that far." She set the table and brought over the scones and jam, milk and sugar. "Please sit, here's your coffee."

"Thanks. Have you called the hospital yet?"

"No, I didn't want to wake you. I will. Sorry I don't have a proper breakfast."

Bryce touched her hand. "It was a long day and a longer night. I probably should have left sooner, but I really enjoyed myself. It was nice to relax, drink wine, and laugh with someone. It's been awhile."

"Yes, it was nice for me as well. I'm glad you were here. I would have been a wreck if I'd had to juggle everything by myself. You were a life saver."

"Speaking of…any word from Murray?"

"No. I don't expect him to show his face any time soon."

"I was going to go check the office."

Conversation stopped, and they both sipped their coffee in companionable silence.

When they finished cleaning up the kitchen,

Fiona called the hospital and Bryce washed up.

Then they'd check the property. Fiona realized Bryce had only seen the warehouse, cask room, and office but none of the back buildings. Since she was determined to learn and help, she might as well.

"All set?" Bryce's hair was damp but combed, and she looked happy. She extended her hand.

Fiona took it and they walked out into the morning sun. Everything looked new and fresh except for the blackened wastebasket.

"I'm glad you thought to leave the door open to air it out." Fiona stepped in and looked around. "It needed painting anyway." The desk had dozens of small slips of paper lined up. Rings from a wet glass were splotched over several. The old adding machine had a long column of figures. "What do you suppose he was doing?"

Bryce leaned over her shoulder. "Think he had bills to add up?"

"I doubt it. We went through all the receipts last week."

"Hey, what did the hospital have to say?" Bryce picked up several slips of paper and sifted through them.

"Dad slept well and ate breakfast. The doctor hadn't been in yet."

"Very reassuring."

The closeness and quiet felt awkward, and Fiona said, "I want to check on Murray, and I want to show you more of the property."

❦❦❦❦

Reggie used the extra day to meet with an old friend from school who worked for a large law firm specializing in discrimination. The restaurant he'd chosen looked expensive and noisy. The tables were set to allow some privacy, but there was no sign of Curtis Lee.

She had dated him briefly sophomore year. Frat boy, old money, and a total misogynist. He'd be interested if her story was lurid enough. After all, she wasn't looking for a big win…just a payoff and some payback. As she rehearsed her story, a small cloud of nostalgia and guilt passed over. Bryce had been a good friend for a long time, and truth be told, she felt more jealous than angry. The MacDougall product would be a big coup, not to mention the attractive daughter.

Her phone dinged. Text.

"Running late, be there in twenty minutes."

Arrogant asshole. But, she did promise to make a call if she got to Chicago. "Yes, may I speak to Mr. Takata? Just tell him it's Ms. Ballard from our meeting on Islay."

❧❧❧❧

"I figured Murray would disappear for a bit." Fiona closed the cottage door. "And I should probably get my car. I have a few errands to run before Dad gets home."

"Right. When we get to the inn I can give you a check in advance for the two barrels you want to sell immediately."

Fiona stopped at the back door. "Are you sure you can do that?"

Bryce pulled her keys. "Grab your stuff and I'll explain on the way."

"Okay. Oh, would you close the office door…and lock it?"

Smoke still lingered, but not nearly as bad. Bryce looked at the scraps of paper again. "Never heard of Ladbrokes." The figures looked like times or amounts of something. She heard the back door of the house slam, and turned to leave. The door locked as she pulled it closed.

"All set." Fiona got in and Bryce started the car. "You wanted to explain?"

"Yes." She lowered the windows. "When I drove down to Glasgow to meet with Ian, we talked about taking a small loan, if you and your dad decided to reopen the distillery."

"Why would you want to do that?" Fiona snapped.

"Hear me out. After we inventoried what you had and figured out what expenses you'd have to get the whisky bottled and sold, I added in a guess at the amount still owed—about five thousand pounds more. Ian agreed, and the bank was willing to open a line of credit for twenty thousand against future sales." Perspiration dampened her forehead, and she gripped the steering wheel in case Fiona went off.

Silence. More silence.

"I'm not sure I understand why a big company like yours would be willing to loan money to a small enterprise run by…no one. It doesn't seem to be a very sound business plan."

Her voice sounded measured.

"You'd be right. However, regardless of how the details are worked out, we do know, for sure, that you are in possession of whisky that is worth approximately two hundred and fifty thousand pounds."

"Really?"

"Yes. If you should decide—and it doesn't need to be in a hurry—to reopen and start making more, you can parse out the release of the current stock for a while until you're on solid ground with staff you trust."

Bryce slowed through Archiestown, where they'd had lunch.

"This seems a little too good to be true. The banks I've dealt with aren't so generous, and I'd expect that international corporations wouldn't be, either."

Bryce laughed. "Right again. This deal was done through our Global Distillers and Distribution main office in Airdrie. They might be able to do the bottling and distribute it."

"What if something happened to mess things up? If Dad doesn't get better or we can't find help, or…if I decide I don't want to shoulder this?"

"That's why it's a line of credit and…I cosigned the first draw."

"What? Are you crazy?"

Bryce pulled off the road and parked. "No, I'm not. I believe in this product, and I believe in your family. Regardless of which way you decide to go, I promise I will be here to help. Whatever you need."

Fiona opened her mouth and stopped. "What about your job?"

"I've been doing a lot of thinking—trust me, a whole lot. I'm going to take a leave to work and live here." She sucked in a deep breath. "I love being here and I don't know exactly why, but some of it has to do with you and some to do with the challenge of being involved in the production end of the business. That's the part I enjoy."

"I'm flattered but, I still don't understand." Fiona's eyes crinkled with worry.

She unbuckled her seatbelt and twisted sideways. "Do you remember the day David came out and I went to count the barrels?"

Fiona nodded.

"When I finished, I saw the door leading to the still room. I went in and looked around. I wanted an idea of how much it would take to get things up to speed. When I looked at those beautiful old copper stills, something inside me opened up, I guess. I wanted to be a part of something with pride and tradition. I wanted to do something that required skill and passion, not just selling."

Fiona took her hand. "This really is that important to you."

Bryce wiped her teary eyes. "Yeah, I guess it is. I didn't mean to go all mushy on you."

"Don't apologize. I actually do understand. I've had similar feelings lately about pride in the heritage of what my family built. It's just I was also overwhelmed with how to take care of it. I still am."

"Would you promise me to just think about it?"

"Of course. In the meantime, let's sell a little whisky and get the bills paid."

Bryce grinned and buckled up. "Great!"

Few words were spoken for the rest of the ride. Bryce felt a huge sense of relief just being able to verbalize her desire. Now, it felt like an actual plan—and a good one at that. The next hurdle would be telling Leo. But for right now, she took Fiona's thoughtful silence as a good thing. She hadn't balked or laughed. With any luck she'd see the wisdom of this partnership. Is that what she was proposing?

As they neared the inn, Fiona said, "I parked around back."

Bryce parked next to her car. "Can you come in, or shall I run up and get the check?"

"I'll come with you." She unbuckled her seat belt and got out. "I love this view of the river. Do you ever leave the slider open to hear the sounds?"

"Yes. When it's not a rowdy night in the lobby."

They walked around to the front entrance and upstairs. "What I need you to sign is a loan agreement that the money will be repaid with the sale of the Highland Dew whisky, minus expenses or a contract with GDD for sales and distribution with MacDougall Distillery."

Fiona read the form and took the pen. "Tell me honestly, if this was your decision to make and your family…would you do it?"

Bryce touched her shoulder. "I wrote this for that exact purpose. This form is between you and me, not the company. If you get the bills paid and decide you want to do something else, you're free to do it."

Fiona shook her head and smiled. "Where did you come from? Your kindness is…so, unexpected."

"Sorry to hear that. I must have inherited some Midwestern values."

Fiona signed the form and Bryce signed the check.

"Here's to the MacDougalls." Bryce put out her hand, but Fiona threw her arms around her neck instead.

"I can't thank you enough for believing in us."

Bryce didn't move or breathe. She wanted to remember this moment and the woman in her arms. It'd been a long time since she'd enjoyed the comfort of belonging. Too long.

Chapter Twenty-nine

Fiona followed the A95 down to Charlestown where the family had always banked. She hoped she could slip in and deposit the check in the company account without running into the bank manager. He was just doing his job two weeks earlier, but she'd felt so foolish begging him for a loan. Of course, at that time she didn't know about the whisky in the cask room. That certainly would have provided collateral.

The coast was clear, and she filled out a deposit slip hurriedly while watching the office door on her left.

"May I help you?" A very young woman smiled at the open teller counter.

"Yes, thank you. I'd like to deposit this check in the MacDougall Distillery account." She signed her name and wrote the company name on the back.

"Right away, then. Oh, did you want any cash withdrawn?"

"No. Just the deposit, thanks." She glanced around casually. It would not do her well to attract suspicion from the security guard. She smiled. *As if.*

"All set. Will there be anything else?"

"Not today." She took the deposit receipt and stared at it. There was a great deal of money in the account. She felt almost giddy. *I can't wait to tell Dad and write checks for those overdue bills.*

She pulled out on High street and her phone rang. "Hello?" She stopped.

"Ms. MacDougall, this is the nurse from the Doctor Gray Hospital calling about your father."

"Yes, is he all right?" Her stomach tightened.

"Oh yes, but the doctor wants to speak with you. Could you come by?"

She glanced at her watch. "I can be there in half an hour. Will that work?"

"That'll be fine. I'll let him know. Goodbye."

So much for shopping.

With a few minutes to spare, she passed the old hospital building and parked near the new addition. She hurried up to her dad's room and let the nurse know she was here to see his doctor.

Behind the curtain, her dad dozed. The gash on his forehead was bandaged over and he now had a black eye. "Hi, Dad." She kissed his cheek.

He blinked a couple of times. "Fi, I'm so glad to see you. Can you take me home now?"

"Let's see what Doctor Evans has to say, shall we?" She pulled a chair closer. "How're you feeling?"

He shrugged. "Mostly fine, but they won't let me have my pipe."

"Do you remember what happened the other night?"

He offered a blank stare and shook his head.

She heard a knock.

"Ms. MacDougall? I'm Karl Evans." He walked to the bed. "How are you feeling, Gavin?"

"Better'n yesterday."

He used a small flashlight to check his eyes. "I'm going to chat with your daughter for a minute. Shall we?" He gestured to the hall.

"I think the bleeding we saw on the x-ray is resolving without treatment, and his wound is healing. I'm not sure if his cognition or balance are satisfactory, so we've had the physical therapist come up a couple of times. Gavin is still quite unsteady."

"I'm surprised. He's used a walking stick for a year or so, he only had one fall...that I know of. My only concern is that he wanders sometimes."

"Since his physical condition is quite good for his age, safety is the major concern. I'm reluctant to send him home just yet and would advise some aftercare for rehabilitation."

Fiona leaned back against the wall. "Oh. I didn't realize...how long would he need that?"

"Of course that depends on his progress. Some folks move quickly in order to get home. On the other hand, some have trouble with orientation and focus, and it's more difficult. Our local source is managed by a geriatric specialist with excellent credentials. I have great faith in him."

Her head spun with "what-ifs" and worst-case scenarios. "Can I think about this a little?"

"Of course. He'll need a bit more therapy, and I'd like an occupational therapist to work with him as well."

She walked the hall for a few minutes and gathered her thoughts. There were so many questions she needed to ask whenever he was in a good space. She hoped today was one of those.

❧❧❧❧

"Please come in, Reggie." Leo stood in his office doorway looking frail. "I know you need to get to the airport, so I'll be quick."

"I'm all packed, and the flight doesn't depart for three hours." She sat across from him and fidgeted with the tabs on her jacket. After talking to Curtis, she'd jotted down a few quotes that sounded reasonable, and composed a letter to corporate headquarters. She hoped it sounded contrite and humble. Curtis had convinced her that she'd never get a lawyer to take the case. Her best bet was to negotiate a deal and try to get some kind of compensation.

"I've reviewed your letter with Ari. You know how much my people are family to me and that I hate to see anyone unhappy. Since I haven't had an opportunity to sit down with Bryce, and my doctor won't allow me to travel yet, I've asked her to come home and discuss this."

Reggie looked up. *This isn't good.* She definitely did not want to meet with them both. "I see." She swallowed the last moisture in her throat.

"In the meantime, I'd like you to return to San Francisco and see who you'd recommend for your current position there—"

"What? Are you…?"

He smiled. "No. I'm looking at a promotion to another level. There are still some details I need to work out, but it shouldn't take more than a week or two. In that time, I'd like you to carefully look at what we may need in the west coast office that would prepare it for the additional business I hope to sign from Scotland." He stood.

Reggie got to her feet. "That sounds great, I suppose a promotion would include a change in benefits." She wasn't naïve enough to let go for just that.

"Of course, it'll be a whole new contract. Thanks for bringing this to me. I appreciate your trust." He walked around and shook her hand. "Have a safe trip."

So much for her counter offer…

❧❧❧❧

Bryce dried her hair and hung up the towel. She'd spent the past two hours walking around Craigellachie looking at cottages, yards, and small businesses. It might not be exactly where she would want to stay, but it was convenient and familiar.

With nothing on her schedule, she might as well stay casual. She pulled on a clean T-shirt and shorts, and stretched out on the bed. The past twenty-four hours had been a crazy roller-coaster. Weeks of driving and researching had suddenly become very frenetic. It had filled her with both anticipation and hope, but nothing was guaranteed. Not yet. Anything could happen with Fiona and her dad, not to mention Murray.

But even if they didn't want to deal with GDD or restart the distillery, she felt determined to take at least three months to try life in Scotland.

Her eyes were heavy and the breeze from the river tickled her still-damp legs when her phone rang.

She jerked up and grabbed it. "Hello?"

"Good afternoon, Bryce." *Leo.* "Am I interrupting?"

She pushed up against the headboard. "Nope, perfect timing. I was thinking about writing to you."

He laughed. "I guess I saved you a letter."

"It's good to hear your voice. How are you feeling?"

"Much better, but I'm only back part-time and

I still can't drive or fly, otherwise I'd be there to visit you."

Despite the hierarchy of the corporation, Leo was fun to travel with. "I wish you could."

"There's a dozen things I'm interested in asking you, but I also want you to review some business ideas. I'm not sure when you planned on returning, but if you'd be willing to fly back for a couple of days, I'd be grateful."

Her brain clicked in and ran through her list of projects. Nothing urgent except Fiona…and that was personal. "I think I can do that. There are a few things pending, but not urgently. Let me check in with Ian and make some arrangements."

"Thank you, Bryce. I hope you know I wouldn't ask if it wasn't very important."

"Yes, sir, I know. I'll let Margaret know as soon as I have a reservation."

"Good. Safe travels." He hung up.

She stared at the phone. The only thing she could imagine as urgent would have to do with Reggie. Dammit. What the hell had she done?

She needed to call Ian first, then Fiona. What would she tell her?

Chapter Thirty

Her dad was sitting in a chair by the window and a nurse tucked a blanket around his legs. A lunch tray sat on the over-bed table in front of him.

"That looks good." Fiona pulled a chair next to him. The tray held a bowl of thick soup with vegetables and beef. A piece of wheat bread and a bowl of applesauce completed the meal.

He leaned toward her and whispered, "You know, the food's not half bad." He winked.

"I'm glad. Can we talk a bit whilst you eat?" She turned the chair to face him.

He nodded.

"First, some good news. Bryce…you remember the American? Well, after the meeting we had the other night—"

"Aye, the lads from Speyside."

She blinked. "Er…yes, exactly. They were so pleased with the samples of the Dew, that Bryce got us a loan to cover the outstanding debt."

He looked up, paused, then smiled. "That is good news!"

"We will arrange to ship two barrels of the 1998 for bottling and sale, and decide what we want to do next. Dad, what would you like to do?"

He wiped his chin and then sipped some tea. "First, I want the sign changed. MacDougall Family—

Distillers of Fine Whisky. Then I want David to see if he can get you put in charge legally. We can't risk any more accidents."

She took his hand. "Dad, you're doing much better, we don't need—"

"I know. But let's do it my way anyway."

"All right. What do you think about reopening the distillery? Would you rather just sell what we have?"

He gazed out the window for several moments, and she worried that the lucidity was fading. Instead he scrubbed his face with both hands and turned to her.

"Right now, I'd like to get things back to running the way they were, but I'm not sure I didn't scare off some of the boys by acting daft. And I worry that I might get worse. There are so many details."

"Well, what about Murray?"

"What about him?" His face got pale.

"I thought he was your foreman, right-hand man. Don't you think he could help?" She decided not to mention the fire just yet. It wouldn't help to upset him.

"I've known the man for many a year, but I'm afraid it was more me helping him. Poor Murray had some war injuries that made him a little off in his own way. I took him in when he couldn't get decent work."

Fiona sat up straighter. Was she hearing correctly?

"But I thought all this time since Mum died, he was taking care of you."

"He was…some. I felt so lost without Mary, and Murray made sure I'd get something to eat or get something to help me sleep. Just good company, you know?"

Something niggled in the back of her mind. "I didn't know you had trouble sleeping. It seemed to me, you dropped off quite easily—even in the middle of a sentence."

He chuckled. "Well, sometimes I do. But mostly it's because of the sleeping tonic. I'll say I've missed that being stuck in here."

"Dad, where do you get the, uh, tonic?"

He shook his head and put the tea cup down. "Long story, but after the Falklands we both had some shell shock, and we set about looking for something to help. You remember the lad so keen on the herbs and botanicals? He suggested a few that helped a little, but we added some whisky. That did the trick."

"What herbs?"

"It's in a dropper bottle either with Murray or in the kitchen. I think there's some melatonin and Valerian and some others I can't remember. But when he mixed it with a little of the cask strength we put in a couple of bottles, it worked great."

I'll bet, but how do those things react in alcohol?

She stood and paced a bit. That would answer some of her questions about his mental state and why he seemed more alert after being in the hospital with a head injury. *Wait.* The whisky bottle on the desk after the fire…it had no label.

"Dad, I need to run and do some errands, but I'll be back. Do the exercises and get stronger. I need you." She kissed his cheek and hurried out.

⁂

Reggie took a nonstop flight to San Francisco. First class. *Challenge that expense.* The flight attendant brought her second cocktail as she looked over the list of potential replacements for her position. None were as versatile or attractive, but a few of the younger ones could be trained. She sipped the vodka tonic and tapped her pen. A promotion, Leo had said. That certainly must mean he believed she had a case and wanted to placate her. *Good.*

In truth, she'd had some remorse over her character assassination of a good friend, and she felt guilty about going behind her back. Fiona MacDougall was attractive, but not necessarily available. Certainly not worth losing a commission over.

The tops of those fluffy white clouds reminded her of a commercial for bathroom tissue. She snickered. The vodka soothed the rough edges nicely. She took another sip and scribbled a note on top of her list. *Note to self: check out flying lessons.*

Inspired, she started a new list of goals. With a new position, she might as well set her sights on the next plateau. And her promise to keep in touch with Matt Takata.

"Would you care for another drink, ma'am?"

"Yes, please. And do you have anything to nosh on?"

Reggie pushed her seat back farther. She thought about poor Joe, her Highland fling. He did wonders for her ego and libido. She might need to dip in that pool again.

⁂

Bryce scratched the last thing off her list and reviewed her progress. Secured the next four days at the inn, arranged the rental car stay in Airdrie, confirmed a flight reservation for Thursday afternoon, and packed. After she got to Chicago, she'd call her folks and maybe run down for a quick visit.

The phone lay still beside her. She wanted to explain her trip in person, but wasn't sure how Fiona might react to her plan. Still, it was foolish to wait. Leo would never have asked if it wasn't important, and besides, it would only be a few days.

"Hello, Fiona? It's Bryce, I wondered if you had time—"

"Hi, you. I just walked in."

"Great, could I swing by for a few minutes?"

"Yes, I'm glad you can, because I wanted to ask you something."

She pulled on her shoes, grabbed her bag, and hurried out. The drive would give her about fifteen minutes to arrange her thoughts. The sun poked through and made spots in the fields glow bright green between the shadowed areas. Spring birdsong floated on the breeze and made her smile. Why had she never noticed these things normally? Too much racing around, she surmised.

The speed of traffic slowed as she entered Archiestown. The hotel where they'd had lunch sat across from the main square. As she passed, she spotted a young girl—no more than seven or eight— with a wagon full of spring flower bouquets.

She pulled close to her. "Hello. May I buy some of your flowers?"

"I was taking them to the market, but I suppose you could." She picked up two bunches, one a mix of several colors, and the other just yellow and white.

"I really like the mixed colors. They're so pretty. How much?'

The girl handed over the flowers and began to count on her fingers as she chewed her lip.

Bryce handed her a five-pound note. "Will this be enough?"

Her eyes lit up. "I can't give you any change…"

"That's okay, you have a fun day. What's your name?"

"Helen."

"Thanks, Helen. I'm Bryce. See you."

She drove on, occasionally glancing at the large bouquet of fresh flowers. *I should do this every day.*

Fiona's car was near the back door, and Bryce parked next to it. She stuck her phone in her pocket, grabbed the flowers, and trotted up the back steps.

"Hello?"

"Come in."

Fiona was drying her hands in the kitchen, and smiled when she saw the flowers. "Where on earth did you find those?"

"Helen sold them to me on her way to market. I couldn't resist her red braids and dimples."

Fiona laughed and took the flowers to the sink. "I had no idea the regional sales manager had such a soft spot."

Bryce followed her to the sink and watched her arrange the flowers in a tall, green, glass jar. Her hands were gentle and delicate as they pushed and pulled each bloom to the correct spot. Fiona stepped back to assess her handiwork.

"I think that spot has been dormant for too long to remember." Bryce had whispered the thought, but Fiona heard her.

"Why would you say that? I was joking."

"I'm not sure. Probably just fatigue." She pointed

to the arrangement. "They look gorgeous. You might have missed your calling."

"I don't think it would be flower arranging. Come sit and have some iced tea."

They sat at the kitchen table across from each other. "Have you heard anything about your dad?"

"Yes, I went up there right after I left you. He's doing well and they're not worried about the shadow on the x-ray, but the doctor wants him to stay a few days for some therapy. After that, he may want him to do some aftercare rehabilitation because of the falls."

"Mostly good news, I guess." Fiona had a worried look about something. "What else?"

"It may be nothing, but Dad was quite lucid the whole time, but when I asked him about having Murray help get the business back on its feet, he surprised me. It seems they both had a rough time when they were discharged from service—he describes it as shell shock. Anyway, the two of them concocted some herbal sedative mixed with whisky that he claims took the edge off and let him sleep." She put her glass down and looked across the table. "I think that might be what was in the bottle Murray left on the desk, and I think it might have something to do with his mental state."

"Wow. That's a little scary. If they're both using it, it might explain why the business fell apart."

"I know. I haven't had time to look around, but I wanted to let you know that this morning Dad told me he wanted the sign fixed and a legal document to give me control of the business. He was pleased about getting the bills paid, your loan, and the whisky sale."

"That is great news! I'm really happy for you...if you're sure you want to take this on."

"I'm not sure I would have, but your encouragement and support along with Dad's interest have given me some courage."

"I'm glad. I wanted to let you know I'll be out of town for a few days, but when I get back, I'm all in."

Her face darkened, and Bryce grabbed her hand before she could jump up. "Don't go there. Listen to me. Leo summoned me home for some big corporate problem since he can't fly over yet. I'm afraid it may have to do with Reggie."

She relaxed. "What more would she have done?"

"I don't know, and neither does Ian. But I'll fly out tomorrow and hopefully be back by Monday."

"You scare me."

"I know, that's why I wanted to come over and tell you in person. I want you to trust me, and I know that it will take time."

Fiona squeezed her hand and nodded.

"Since your dad is safe, what say we go over to the hotel in Archiestown and grab a bite?" Bryce smiled.

"Is that so you can see Helen?" Fiona sneered.

"Well…yeah."

Chapter Thirty-one

Bryce awoke to silence, sunshine, and crown moldings. She blinked several times before it all came back to her, the time adjustment, hordes of travelers at Heathrow and O'Hare, and the soundproof black limo Leo had sent for her.

The city of big shoulders. Chicago.

From the window, the rising sun reflected off the bright blue sky and Lake Michigan water. Below lay Monroe Harbor, Millennium Park, and the Buckingham Fountain. Leave it to Leo to pick the grand Blackstone Hotel, an elegant old building.

The clock on the desk read seven fifteen, so she had time to eat before walking to the office.

Showered and dressed, Bryce opted for a small table by the window overlooking Michigan Avenue. It was unexpectedly thrilling to be in the heart of Chicago after weeks of country living. The traffic, the people exhilarated her.

"Yes, thanks, I'll have the full American breakfast." Bryce smiled and felt her stomach growl.

"Oh, are you visiting from elsewhere?" The waiter poured coffee in the china cup.

"I guess I am. I've been working in Scotland for weeks, and I'm only back for a business meeting." How odd to be visiting her hometown.

"I hope you enjoy your stay."

She read his nametag. "Thank you, Scott." *Irony?*

The coffee tasted strong and rich. Many of the other diners looked like Chicago business types with dark suits or stunning haute couture. There were tourists as well. It felt so different than meals in Scotland, which seemed so much more laid back. There was a palpable energy in the room.

The traffic outside was endless. Cars, buses, cabs, trucks, bicycles. Even though their main office was nearby, she had seldom spent much time there. It was so much more efficient to communicate via phone, text, computer, and teleconference. Still, it was nice that Leo still had some old-fashioned style, and visitors always noticed his gracious hospitality.

The waiter reappeared with her entrée. "More coffee?"

"Yes, please. This looks wonderful." Fluffy scrambled eggs, hash brown potatoes, bacon, and toast. Same kind of ingredients, and a completely different taste. She groaned with pleasure, then looked around to see if she'd been heard.

❧ ❧ ❧ ❧

"Hi, Dad." Fiona smiled at him, now dressed and up in his chair.

"Hullo." He waved her over. "I'm glad you're here. I'm bored."

"I have just the news to entertain you." She pulled a chair close and opened the manila folder. "Here are the two Powers of Attorney to look over. We'll need to sign them with a notary present. And here's a list of accounts that are now paid."

He took the papers. "I don't suppose you've my glasses?"

They both laughed. "Darn, I knew I'd forget something. How's the therapy going?"

"Good, I guess. They want me to use that damn walker. I don't want to. I'm not a damn invalid."

Stubborn, as usual. "Just keep trying. Please?"

He nodded. The blue-purple coloration below his eye had paled a bit.

"Dad, I wanted to ask you another question. When you and Murray were talking a while back, he kept asking you about an envelope. Do you remember that?"

"Hmm, I remember you asking me about that, but I'm not sure what he meant. I can ask him when he comes to see me."

Surprised, she said, "Has he come to see you?"

"Sure, he's been up a time or two."

"Odd, I haven't seen him at all. What did he have to say?"

He looked out the window and scratched below his chin, a habit when he wanted to avoid something. "Let me see, he mentioned a couple of the lads that meet up for horseshoes..."

"Dad, why can't you tell me what's going on?"

He looked at his lap. "It's nothin' for you to fret about."

"Fine. I have to get back. There'll be two fellas coming to pick up the whisky barrels and I have to meet them." She stood and put the chair back. "Please do what they ask so you can come home." She kissed his cheek and he patted her hand.

"I will."

At the reception desk, Fiona stopped to see if the doctor had visited yet. He hadn't. "Will you ask him to phone me when he has a chance?"

"Of course. Might be later this afternoon."

Dark clouds rolled in as she left the hospital. As she turned toward home and set the cruise control, she thought about the email from Ian Smith containing proofs for the new MacDougall labels. Since she had no idea where the previous work had been done, she told Bryce to use the information she had from the existing bottle.

Bryce. It'd only been a day, but she realized that she'd gotten used to being able to call any time just to talk. It was a mistake to lose touch with old friends. When she had gotten involved with another teacher, they both cut off ties with friends to spend more time together. They ignored warnings from wiser women who encouraged them to socialize more. Even now, the scar from that breakup stung, and the growing attraction to Bryce set off red flags.

❧❧❧❧

The west coast regional sales office seemed so small after her visit to Chicago's main office. Reggie booted up her computer and looked around her small office with a partial view of north 101—Van Ness Boulevard. From the roof, there was a distant view of Alcatraz. Inspiring.

The morning had been devoted to reviewing records in HR. It'd taken hours to come up with three names from the department sales team that she considered able enough to replace her. Her standards were high, but certainly not unreasonable. When Leo called, she wanted to be able to give him a concise recommendation.

When she heard the knock on the door, she said, "Come in."

"Ms. Ballard? HR said you wanted to see me." The tall, thin, attractive young man stood in the doorway.

"Yes, come in and have a seat. Eduardo Morales, right?"

"Yes, but most people call me Ted."

"Great. Ted, it will be. I'm glad to finally meet you. It says you've been here for three years." She scrolled through his personnel information. "You started in receivables and transferred to sales a year ago. It sounds like you were looking for advancement… or just a change?"

"At first it was for more customer contact, but since we had a new baby…"

"Congratulations."

"Thank you. It's a little girl, three months." Instantly Ted produced his phone with a picture.

"She's beautiful." Reggie smiled at the proud father.

He blushed. "Thanks. So, Maria—she's my wife— and I talked about it, and since she won't be working for a while, I need to pick up more hours." He shifted in the chair.

"You've done well so far. Your numbers are good, and evaluations are positive." She turned to face him. "Since business is growing, we're looking at changes. And since Ms. Andrews is still in Scotland, I was asked to review some names for Mr. Edelman. I'm not exactly sure what he has in mind, but I'll keep you in the loop." She pulled out her best debutante smile and swept her hair back.

Ted blushed, and he blinked several times. "Yes… uh…thank you." He stumbled standing up.

"One more thing. Since I have to talk to a couple of other people, I'd like you to keep this to yourself."

He nodded and closed the door behind him.

She tapped a nail on keyboard. Good possibility. Smart, overachiever, polite, and not cocky.

She gazed out the window to the low clouds crawling across the bay. As anxious as she was to finally be promoted, she regretted her actions with Bryce. They had been good friends for a long time, and without her, she wouldn't have this job.

Was it too late to make amends?

Chapter Thirty-two

G ood to see you again, Bryce." Leo pushed out of his chair to stand. He looked bright-eyed, but quite frail.

"Not as glad as I am to see you." She leaned across his tidy desk to shake his bony hand, which could still grip.

"Would you like coffee?"

"No, thanks. I'm coffee-ed out from a great breakfast. The Blackstone provides wonderful food and is still an elegant hotel. Thank you." Bryce sat in the club chair in front of him. For a very successful CEO, Leo's office had always felt comfortable to her.

"I'm glad you're enjoying it. I figured the long plane trip might drain you." He winked. "And I wanted you well rested. First, tell me how things are going."

She wanted to ask for a leave of absence immediately, but that might have to wait a bit. "I think we accomplished what we set out to do. The samples we collected and interest in our company seemed authentic. Plus, I must say, I learned a great deal about distilling whisky. It's another world from sales."

"Was there anything in particular you liked?" He shifted in his chair and leaned forward.

Fiona's smile jumped into her head, and she quickly refocused. "I think spending some time in an actual distillery and experiencing the amount of work involved was the most educational—and fun. The roasting, the mash, and the slow distilling in the huge copper stills…it seemed so old-fashioned. Probably the same as it was a hundred years ago, but the lengthy process achieves the incredible tastes."

Leo smiled. "You're sounding like a master distiller."

She laughed. "Far from it, but in spite of the variety in personalities and philosophies, the product has a wonderful uniformity."

"Good for you! That wasn't my original intent, but I'm pleased that you learned so much."

Margaret knocked and stuck her head in the door. "Excuse me. You asked that I remind you of the meeting in thirty minutes."

"Thanks. Before we go down there, I wanted some ideas from you about the west coast office. I told Reggie that we were looking at a promotion, and I wanted her to suggest some replacements for her position."

This subject hung over their heads since she walked in. "Did you say 'promotion'?"

His eyes twinkled. "Yes. I didn't mention to her it would be overseas—Thailand."

"I'm confused. Didn't you tell me she had a discrimination case?" She bristled. Why in the world would he reward her?

"She didn't have a case, and she knew it. But I also didn't want to fire her and give her cause. I think she was blowing off steam, but it still wasn't appropriate. And wasted our time."

A trickle of perspiration slid down the back of her neck. *Just tell him.* "Before we talk to the board, I wanted to ask you something."

"Of course, what is it?" Leo looked worried.

"Remember when we talked about my last

vacation?"

He smiled and shook his head. "Yes, sorry I was negligent, or rather…HR was."

"Well, I thought about it and how much I've enjoyed the slower pace in Scotland…I…I'd like to take a leave for a few months." She exhaled.

He cocked his head. "I see. What's a few months?"

"Three to six…"

"You've certainly earned it. Let's see what the team thinks, shall we?"

Another knock, and Ari Gellman, the company's general counsel, appeared with a wheelchair. "Your chariot, my lord. Hi, Bryce."

Leo groaned. "Did Margaret put you up to this?"

"I volunteered. Come on, enjoy it while you can." Ari locked the chair and deployed the footrests. Leo reluctantly lowered himself onto his wheelchair.

Bryce could feel his sense of defeat.

They walked the length of the hall to a large, airy conference room with a wall of windows overlooking the lake. Three men and a woman were seated at one end of the table. She recognized all of them as longtime employees and a generally cohesive group. Each nodded or waved as she went around the table and sat next to Kathleen Grayson, head of international marketing.

"It's so nice to see you in person, Bryce." She patted her hand.

"You, too," she whispered as Ari moved Leo to the head of the table.

"I'm glad you could all make it on such short notice." Leo opened a folder. Margaret appeared with a notepad. "I want this to be brief, so unless there is urgent business, I want to focus on some changes to the west coast office."

"In addition, I wanted to let Ms. Andrews know how excited we are with the new contacts in Scotland. Ian Smith briefed us on a conference call. Thanks, Bryce."

"Thanks. I enjoyed it more than I thought I would and the people we contacted were wonderful to work with."

"That's a perfect segue," Leo said. "I think Ari briefed all of you on the personnel problem that precipitated this meeting. We negotiated a solution to avoid further problems by offering Ms. Ballard a promotion to another division. I asked her for some names of a replacement, which she provided." He held up a list. "But I'd like to consider another shift. Ms. Andrews has asked for temporary leave to spend more time in Scotland. Selfishly, I think this might be advantageous because of her connections with the new partners."

Bryce swallowed hard. She knew Leo had his own reason for bringing this to the table, but she suddenly felt spotlighted. Her heart jackhammered in her chest, and she slid her sweaty hands into her lap and out of sight.

The other members glanced at each other, but Leo continued.

"We need to consider another experienced individual to fill in for her as West Coast Sales Manager, as well as choosing Ms. Ballard's replacement. We don't want this transition to cause an upheaval that creates anxiety."

One by one, they offered comments and suggestions, but Bryce withdrew into her own thoughts about how this would affect her team when they found both Bryce and Reggie gone. It never occurred to her that this might upset the balance she'd worked so hard to achieve. Maybe a leave right now was not a good idea. Should she wait until she could choose Reggie's replacement?

⁂

Reggie deleted the note she'd typed, and started over. Damn. This was harder than she thought. She swallowed more of her whisky and took a breath.

Dear Bryce,
I'm sure this is too little, too late, but I feel awful about stirring up such a shit-storm over nothing. I'll be writing a note to Leo as well. I probably won't send this until I get settled wherever they're sending me. That's selfish, I know. But I am a good employee and you've always said so.
We had a good friendship and shouldn't have pushed it. That was my fault, too…

⁂

Fiona steered into their driveway and her dad put his hand on her arm.
"Can you stop?"
"Of course. What's wrong?"
He chuckled. "Nothing, I just wanted a quick look at the sign."
It looked the same, dangling on one hook, the paint chipped and fading. Even the weeds around the posts echoed the neglect and sadness.
"Mary and I had the new sign made when she told me she was pregnant. It's always said that same thing

for five generations." He cleared his throat. "Looks like it needs a facelift."

"We'll get it fixed, and we don't have to change it if you don't want." She drove on to the house. "Let's get you settled and fed." She saw the faraway look in his eyes. He seldom shared the soft side with her.

Their truck sat next to the loading dock in the shade of a broad tree. She wondered if Murray would come over now that her dad was home.

"I need the loo," he said, leaving his walker by the kitchen door. She shook her head and pushed it into the living room, and set his duffel bag on the table.

The room looked clean and tidy. It smelled like spring. She'd used his absence to do some cleaning and reorganizing. Hopefully, he'd not notice some things missing—like the stack of magazines, the soiled tea towels from the armrests of his chair, and the collection of pipe cleaners in an old cup. All of the windows sparkled, and the house smelled fresh.

"I'm going to fix some lunch. Why don't you, and your walker, join me in the kitchen?" She snickered.

What was Bryce doing in the Windy City of Chicago? She looked at the clock and realized it was too early to be working. Again she was tempted to call her…but always felt silly and childish.

As she sliced the ham, she recalled the night they spent drinking wine, sharing stories, and laughing. It was probably the most fun she'd had in a year. Probably more than a year since her painful breakup.

From the window sill she picked up a bright red tomato, perfectly ripe and juicy. The perfect topper for their sandwiches.

"Dad, are you ready to eat?"

"Aye," he called, and pushed the walker in front

of him, grumbling. "I'm more apt to fall over this damn thing."

She turned to hide her smile. "Let's try to avoid falls and hospitals for awhile."

"This looks good. They tried to starve me at that place. Gruel and weak tea. Bah." He picked up the sandwich and took a large bite.

"I thought you said you liked the food in the hospital."

"Aye, the hospital, not that rehab place."

They ate in companionable silence. It was a relief to have him safely home.

When he popped the last bite in his mouth, Fiona tested the waters for a serious conversation. "Does Murray know you were coming home today?"

"Sure. I told him last night when he called."

"Good. Can I ask you a favor?" She refilled his water glass.

"Of course, darlin'. This is a good sandwich."

"Would you tell me more about how you and Murray got to be friends?"

He cocked his head and wiped his mouth with the napkin. "That was an awful long time ago." He squinted a bit.

"Murray was from up near Elgin. We met in training for the Royal Navy. In eighty-two we were working maintenance on the HMS Hermes when it got shipped to the Falklands to fight the Argentines. Messy business. Never did understand why they wanted that island so far from home." He leaned back and got out his pipe.

"You never mentioned you went to the Falklands. Why not?"

He shrugged. "I wanted to get away from here

and see more of the world. Your granddad wasn't an easy fella to get on with." He puffed his pipe.

"When did you come back?"

"When my mother finally wrote and said Dad needed help, but didn't want to ask. Stubborn old goat."

She patted his hand. "Guess that apple didn't fall far from the tree."

"Hmpf. Well…Murray had no place to go and I thought he might get a job helping out here. I'll bet we weren't back a month when I ran into little Mary MacCray, prettiest girl in our school."

Was he actually blushing? "Let me guess."

He chuckled. "Two months and I asked her to marry me. And she did."

Fiona cleared the table and wiped it with a damp cloth. "Do you feel like sitting out on the front porch? It's so lovely out."

He eventually settled in his favorite rocker by the window. "I'da been out here five minutes sooner without that contraption." He shoved the walker aside.

"Or I might have been picking you up off the floor," she mumbled, and pulled a chair close. "Do you remember the night you fell and needed to go to the hospital?"

"I'm not likely to forget that for a while. I still have this lovely shiner."

"True." She softened her voice and began slowly. "Well, when Bryce brought me home from the hospital that night…there'd been an accident in the office."

Chapter Thirty-three

They were sitting in Leo's office around a stained-glass table near the windows. Outside, angry clouds roiled over the choppy, gunmetal-grey waves on the lake. A spring storm in the making.

Leo asked her and Ari to come back to talk after the board meeting. The others had left for lunch. Leo wanted to order gyros from his favorite Greek shop on the corner. At one time, Stavros—the owner—worked in delivery for the Global warehouse, but his long-range dream was to buy his own restaurant. Leo made it happen.

"I know it's a bit early, but I'd like a dram of that Old Pulteney. Ari, would you do the honors?"

"Sure thing." He unfolded the doors on a mirrored wall unit that displayed at least twenty bottles of whisky. Tasting glasses lined the bottom shelf.

Bryce watched the ritual as it had been performed many times before, and remembered all the little tips Leo had given her over the years. He'd been so patient and kind. How could she take time off when he was just recovering?

Ari handed each of them a glass, and sat down. "*L'chaim.*"

Maybe for the first time, Bryce felt like an integral member of the company and not just Leo's pet. She relished the smooth, warm taste as it filled her mouth.

"I feel like this might be the wrong time for my leave—"

Leo put his hand up. "No. It's the perfect time. You need a break, and I want you in Scotland. Remember, it's a paid leave, and I'd appreciate your wise counsel as we move forward with some of these new accounts. Not full-time, you understand."

"I'm not sure I do. Take a leave but be on-call?" It suddenly felt weird.

"Do you trust me, Bryce?"

"Of course."

Leo smiled. "Go on back and decide where you want to live and what you'll be doing. It will take some time to get these new people on board. I want you to take a real break and relax. I mean it."

She took another sip as Ari asked Leo about another matter.

The wind had picked up and the clouds were buffeted wildly across the sky. She felt the same way. *Remember he has invested a lot of time and money in you.*

"Hey Leo!" A booming voice introduced a large dark-haired man with a prodigious black moustache carrying a box. "How's my old friend. I miss you too much lately."

"Stavros! It's wonderful to see you, too." He stood and hugged the man. "I had to take a little sick time, but I'm back."

"Wonderful. Here, I brought your favorite with some extra tzatziki sauce. I know how much you like it."

Leo slipped a large bill into his apron.

Stavros pushed his hand back. "No, no, my friend. This is for you." He hurried out the door.

The sandwiches were huge and hot, and smelled wonderful. Warm pita with spicy sliced gyro meat was stacked with a generous portion of the white sauce, tomato, and onion.

"Good choice," said Ari, mouth half-full.

She groaned with the deliciousness. "I can't remember the last time I had one of these. Do you think Stavros could ship to Scotland?"

Leo smiled. "With overnight delivery, my dear, anything is possible."

She listened as the two talked about business, but her mind was already in Scotland and hoping to settle someplace where she could wander the countryside at leisure and still help the MacDougalls make whisky... if they'd have her.

Just thinking about physical work and not doing "deals" made her smile. After all her years of sedentary work, she wondered about her physical stamina. Better start some reconditioning soon. That meant running, and probably some free weights if she thought she'd be able to move those barrels. And that storeroom would need to be organized...maybe some new shelving, better lighting...

She looked up, and both men were smiling.

"Was...I talking out loud?"

"Muttering is more like it, but clearly you weren't here. Why don't you go back to the hotel and start planning your new adventure? I'll call you later with some replacement names."

"I will, thank you. I'd like to take the rest of this with me, if you don't mind."

"Of course! I would, too, but I'm going to finish mine. Thanks, Bryce."

The cold, damp wind hit her when she exited

the building. She wished Fiona could be right here, experiencing the dramatic changes in the city on the big lake. It was pretty majestic. She loved the smell before a storm, but decided to run to beat the rain.

She needed to make some phone calls—soon.

⚶⚶⚶⚶

"What do you mean, 'a fire'?" Gavin shouted.

"Everything is all right. But we think Murray fell asleep at the desk and must've dropped a cigarette in the trash bin. Bryce and I were able to pull him to safety and put out the fire."

"What the hell got into him?" His face flushed with anger.

"I don't know. But it's why I wanted to ask you." She took a breath. "There was a half-empty bottle on the desk, but no label. I have no idea what he was drinking."

"Well, what did he tell you?"

"Nothing. I steered him back to his cottage and he stumbled into bed. I haven't seen hide nor hair since."

He rubbed his chin and looked up in the tree.

"Dad, I don't know if we can trust him to help run the business. And I don't think we can do it alone."

"Maybe it was a foolish dream," he whispered.

"What's happening here that I'm not being told?"

"These apple trees were the first things your great-great-grandmother planted when they had to rebuild the house. There was a terrible fire. It nearly took all the buildings, the story goes. An awful lot of work and dreams are part of this place." He tapped out his pipe on the railing and dug his tobacco pouch from his vest.

The ritual was always the same, and soon Fiona could smell the same familiar tobacco smoke she had as a toddler. She remembered the old brown-and-white tin of the St. Bruno's Flake tobacco on the mantel shelf as one of her earliest memories. When he kissed her good night, she smelled it.

"All these years…I thought sometime we'd have a chance to talk to you." He crossed his ankle over his knee. "The short of it is this: while we were at sea, Murray lost his family—mother, father and two sisters—in a horrible fire. A lorry filled with fuel oil went over the rail and ran into the house. Neighbors described it as a great fireball. He didn't get word for days."

"Oh, my God." Fiona felt her stomach drop. It was unimaginable to lose everyone like that and not be able to get there. It explained so much of Murray's odd behavior. And then he almost…

Silence enveloped both of them.

"I was the only one he had, so I took him in. The lad was a mess. Started drinking and betting. I covered for him as best I could, but he piled up some serious debt."

"That's what the little receipts were on the desk. Offsite betting." It made sense now. "He must've been worried about his debt…"

He nodded. "I would hold those for him till payday and give him a money order to cover the debt. The less cash he had, the better. Your mother never understood why I did it." He looked up with teary eyes. "What else could I do? He was my mate for all those years."

"I guess we'll have to keep a better eye on him."

Her quick trip home to check on her dad had become something much more complicated.

The thought of submitting a resignation from her teaching career felt heavy, like a mantle of chainmail that seemed to increase daily. There were no options. This was her home and her family.

"I'm going to get some water. I'll be right back." The tears wouldn't wait as she dashed to her room and closed the door. With her face in her pillow, she let the sobs come from her deepest soul. She'd never felt more alone. She cried for her lost dreams and her hopes.

⁂

Reggie held her head in both hands and stared at the flashing cursor on the laptop.

We had a special friendship, and I shouldn't have pushed it. That was my fault, too…

And I do understand what you were trying to do with the MacDougalls. They have a great whisky and it was wrong to butt in. It's exactly what Leo was looking for and you found it. I don't know why I got so pissed. Embarrassed, I guess. And jealous of you—again.

Leo reacted so calmly and was kind. More so than I would have been. He was vague about the promotion, but I don't feel I deserve it.

This is so fucked up and I don't know how to fix it.

I'm sorry.

Reggie stared at the message she'd typed to Bryce. For several hours, she'd agonized about sending it, hoping to mend fences, but unsure about the timing. It didn't much matter: she had a conference call with Leo and Ari in an hour.

She took a deep breath and hit Send. There was no way back now.

She pushed back from her desk and walked to the window. The hazy sun sank a bit lower over the ocean and reflected a warm glow on the windows of the tall buildings around her office. Now that the energy from all that anger and antagonism leaked out, she had little left. Might as well go back to her apartment.

Chapter Thirty-four

By the end of the day, Bryce had talked with her California landlord about subletting her condo, sent her wonderful neighbor a list of items she'd need from her closet, and promised a shipping address in a few days.

The list looked less daunting. There were still some casual clothes she'd need. In the past ten years she'd rarely needed anything more casual than slacks and a polo shirt. The shorts and three T-shirts she'd taken to Scotland were essentially for sleeping or travel. Maybe heavy-duty shoes or boots? No sense in getting those in the U.S. It made more sense to stop in Glasgow and shop when she knew for sure what she'd be doing.

She flopped on the bed and picked up her cell phone. One message:

From Brian Townsend:
Ms. Andrews, wondered if we could meet up sometime. I have a few questions.
Thanks, Brian

She replied that she'd call Wednesday when she returned from the States, then checked the time. Nearly two—that meant nine at Fiona's. Might be a good time.

It rang three times before Fiona picked up.
"Hello?"

"Hi, Fiona. It's Bryce. Can you hear me okay?"

"Yes. What a wonderful surprise. I'm delighted you've called."

Her lilting voice and soft burr sent a shiver through Bryce. "I wasn't sure if it was too late. I didn't want to disturb you, but I was curious about your dad." *More curious about you.*

"How nice. He's been released and is home. It's strange, but he seems to be a bit better since the conk on his head."

Bryce grinned just hearing any news. Fiona sounded pleased. Hopefully, it was the call. "That's great news. I have some, too. I finished my business in Chicago and my boss very happily granted my leave."

"He did? You mean you are coming back here?"

She really sounded incredulous.

"Well...yes. Didn't I say that I wanted to return to help you?"

Fiona paused and then took a loud breath. "You did, but...I guess I've heard that before and I wasn't sure. It's been so difficult...well...I'm glad. Really."

It surprised her that Fiona wasn't happier to have the support. Had she really been that vague? "I want this new venture to succeed for you and your dad. I want to be there for you, as I promised." Her heart pounded when she thought she'd read the signal wrong. "But, if you don't want to restart the business, that's okay, too. I want to spend some downtime in Scotland anyway, and I—"

"I do want you to come back. It's just...things are confused right now. Nothing bad. We can talk about it when you get here. When will you leave?"

"I'll leave tomorrow, so I'll probably be back in Craigellachie sometime Tuesday."

"Wonderful. Are you going to stay at the inn?"

"For now. I looked at a couple of cottages in the area. I'll see what's available. No rush—I have time to decide." Bryce smiled, thinking about having that much time off no matter what she chose to do. Travel, sleep late, hang out in the pub, walk the hills…

Fiona laughed. "It really is good news. I've missed talking to you."

"I have, too." That was it—the connection she hoped would be there. They both had danced around that special night they spent talking. Something had happened, but she couldn't quite name it. "Listen, is there anything you'd like from the States?"

"Really? Wow, I never thought about it."

"No hurry. Text me if you think of something."

"I will. Have a safe trip, and will you let me know when you land?" She sounded worried.

"I will. I'll see you very soon."

"Good night."

Bryce kept the phone on her chest and closed her eyes. It was true. There was indeed a spark, and she could feel it. All this time they were focused on the distillery and her dad. Underneath, an electric current ran between them, and it wasn't until she left for the States that Bryce had felt the disconnection.

For so many months, she'd kept a singular focus on work and nothing else. The pain of Gretchen's betrayal still burned, and she couldn't risk a distraction. She sat up.

Was her laser focus damaging her other relationships? Did Reggie rebel because her feelings were hurt? She may very well have permanently burnt an important bridge, one that could adversely affect the company. She could call Reggie…but, probably not until Leo completed the changes in the San Francisco office.

Right now, there was one more task to complete. A call home. Since it was still early, she decided to call her dad at work. Yes, she was chicken. Her mother would pitch a fit about her going back to Scotland for months without coming home. Her dad would be more understanding and supportive.

"Make the damn call, and you can go down to the gift shop and buy the beautiful coffee table book about Chicago for Fiona. Maybe even some of those Marshall Fields' Frango Mints."

Fiona heard the birds before she opened her eyes. A spring breeze brought earthy scents overlaid with flowers. She stretched and enjoyed the totally relaxed sensation from a solid night's sleep. Letting go of her grief and anxiety, along with the wonderful news about Bryce's return, turned everything around. The whole tangled web of loose strings surrounding Murray and her dad were pulled together. The weight of her responsibility lightened—especially since Bryce was willing to share the burden. In the morning light, clarity reigned, and she felt more confident. Plus, the damn bills were paid.

A hot shower, lighter clothes, and the smell of coffee and eggs got her singing and smiling. She set the table and poured some juice.

"Dad, it's ready."

"Coming." She heard the clump of the aluminum walker on the wood floor. He'd finally quit complaining about it, and had only forgotten to use it once or twice.

The bruising under his eye faded and the laceration healed. Best of all, his mental state continued to improve. The doctor correctly guessed the "sleep tonic" had caused a cumulative toxicity. Since she dumped the bottle from the office, she'd seen no more of it.

Her dad appeared at the same time as a knock at the back door. "Murray. Come in and eat with us."

"Morning. I don't want to intrude. I just wanted to ask a question." He came barely to the end of the table.

"Have a seat. I'll get you a plate." Fiona set down two cups of coffee. *This might be the perfect time to sort things out.*

"Thank you. It's good to have you home, Gavin."

Conversation focused on the weather, a leak in the office roof, and the recent passing of one-hundred-year-old WWII veteran from Dufftown. Fiona listened and watched the two men interact, something she'd never bothered to do before. They certainly had a camaraderie that seemed a little guarded on Murray's part. His comments were measured, and he was watchful.

She gathered the plates and then poured more coffee. "Dad, have you talked to Murray about restarting the business?"

Gavin brightened. "I haven't. You've not been about much, so I guess I forgot."

He winked at Fiona and started with his pipe. The look suggested that she busy herself with something.

"I'll leave you to it while I wash up." She picked up the remaining dishes and condiments, and ran some hot water in the sink.

"Some good news. All that whisky I forgot about is still good and will soon be sold and sent out. Fiona worked out an arrangement, and even got enough to pay off the creditors."

"That is good news," Murray said.

"I guess I need to know what you think about getting everything back up to working again."

The question sounded harmless, but Murray's hesitation suggested some concern. Fiona shut off the water and started the slow process of washing each item very carefully.

"Well, you know, I'd always want to help you anyway I can…but, we're both getting on in years, and none of the lads are around to help."

"That's true enough. What if we could find a crew that knew what they were doing? Is the equipment working?"

"I think so. I could check everything, if that's what you want."

Murray sounded less than enthusiastic.

"It's a big decision."

She turned as her dad leaned heavily on the table and sighed loudly.

"This has been a family-run distillery for five generations, and I hate to be the one that let it die, but I'm not sure I have the stamina, either. Fiona has offered to take over, but there's an awful lot to learn. She'd need our help."

The few dishes were dry and stacked. She brought a towel to wipe the table, and took the opportunity to speak up. "I know how important this is, Dad, and believe it or not, I want this legend to continue. Proudly." She sat down. "Right now, the folks at the Speyburn Distillery are bottling two barrels for us. There'll be money coming in regular as long as we have whisky to sell. But in order to get back to makin' the whisky, we'll need to fix things up a bit, and that won't be easy or cheap."

"That's the truth," Murray said.

"I think we might need to start making a list of repairs and such. Can you do that?" Her dad sounded committed to the idea.

"Oh, I think I could."

"Murray, I have to ask you a question. Seems there was a fire in the office, and you coulda burned up. What aren't you telling me?"

The color drained from Murray's face, and Fiona sat very still.

"You know things was getting bad, and you were acting a bit daft sometimes…I didn't know what to do when everyone had left." His voice caught. "I'll admit I was scared and probably had too many drinks now and then…but that night, well, I don't know what happened. I woke up in me cottage, sick and stinkin' of smoke."

"You nearly burned down the place if Fiona and the American lass hadn't come back just then. That's not the man I knew and trusted with my life."

Murray just hung his head. "I'll leave if you want me to."

"I don't want you to, eejit."

"I'll just excuse myself for now." He stood. "Thanks for the meal, Miss Fiona."

The back door latched, and she looked at her dad. His eyes welled with tears.

Chapter Thirty-five

The flight back seemed faster, although Bryce knew it wasn't. Maybe the later flight made a difference, but she wanted to arrive the next morning in order to avoid a motel stop. The hour layover at Heathrow got her in at a reasonable time.

The plane braked hard on the landing, and she braced herself on the seat in front of her. A balding man shot her an irritated glance.

"Sorry."

The woman next to her smiled and mouthed the word "ass." Bryce nodded. She stretched her legs and pulled up her messenger bag. Once her phone booted up, she saw a message from Ian.

Ian Smith: Would appreciate it if you had some time to talk when Larry drops you to pick up your car.

I hope there's no problem. She stepped out as the aisle cleared and headed for the exit. Her imagination filled her with anticipation and excitement about her leave. On the one hand, she'd daydreamed about a small cottage of her own where she could cook and have some real privacy. The inn had been comfortable, but often quite noisy.

As she cleared the Jetway, she moved quickly to the crowded concourse and exit. Now that she knew about the special pickup area, she didn't want to keep

Larry waiting.

The messenger bag was heavy on her shoulder with not only her laptop but also a thick photo history of Chicago she bought for Fiona. She couldn't prevent the smile when she felt a small flutter in her chest. It'd been a long time since she'd enjoyed the first rush of infatuation, and she liked it.

Larry waved his arm as she approached. If she remembered correctly, he'd started in the mailroom a couple of years ago. The bright blue GDD windbreaker identified him easily.

"Welcome, Ms. Andrews. Let me take that bag and stow it." He easily pushed the roll-aboard bag into the van and helped her in.

"Thanks. I'm sorry I'm late. We had to go around a storm." She unzipped her jacket and tucked the messenger bag next to her.

"It's no problem. It was quite jammed earlier." He buckled up and steered them out into a dark, rain-soaked Glasgow motorway.

The rain made the view a watercolor of angular shapes on a blurred background. As soon as they neared the exit for the office, she experienced an odd sensation in the center of her chest…almost a release or opening. Not unpleasant, but it still startled her. The pressure from her hand soothed it, and she inhaled deeply.

This was a new start. A new chapter. She wanted to make the most of it.

"Larry, would you mind going through the employee parking and I'll drop off my bag?" She rifled through her messenger bag for the ring of keys she'd hooked in a compartment, then remembered leaving the car key with Ian.

"Oops, I don't have the key—"

"I've got the one you left. Where did you leave the car?"

"Over there. The Vauxhall Insignia." He handed her the key as she climbed out of the van into the downpour. "Thanks."

Ian greeted her at the front door with a towel. "Oh, dear. I'm afraid your welcome was a bit damp. Come in and we'll have some tea."

"Thanks." She stamped her wet trainers and used the towel on her hair. "Tea sounds great."

They moved into his office, and he hung up her jacket.

"I hoped this would clear up earlier." He poured two cups and handed her one. "Milk and sugar?"

"Yes, thanks." The steaming Earl Grey smelled wonderful. It warmed her soul more than anything. Fiona loved Earl Grey. She glanced at her watch. Nearly ten o'clock. She could be back in Craigellachie around two. That would give her time to unpack and change.

Ian sat across from her and unbuttoned his tweed jacket. "The reason I wanted to speak with you is about the MacDougall whisky."

"Is there a problem?" She put her cup down as a ripple of adrenaline coursed through her body.

"Nothing serious. We had an interruption over here at the Airdrie plant, and it would have backed things up. When I mentioned it to Tom Hobart, and he said he could run it at Speyburn, and they'd really like to work with the MacDougalls. Seems he and Liam were impressed with what they tasted. We sent the information to them and notified Fiona."

Bryce slumped back and smiled. "You're right, that's not a problem. I certainly trust Tom, and they've all met."

A wave of dread washed over her as she remembered that night. Her collapsing, Gavin disappearing, and the night they spent after leaving him at the hospital…it felt so long ago, but it really wasn't. So much had happened. With Leo and Reggie…

"…then you could offer that as the distribution point…"

"I'm sorry?"

"I said that if they decide to sign a contract, Tom and Liam would manage the final product."

"Oh. Yes, that would be great. They all got along well. I'll certainly offer that." She finished her tea. "I think I'll be working more in a consultant role for a while. I don't know if Leo mentioned it, but I'm on a working leave for a few months. I'll still be in touch with the new contacts, but I want to do a little touring and relaxing."

"That sounds grand. He did mention some changes, but said he'd fill me in. I hope you enjoy your time." He stood. "I'm sure you're anxious to get to it. It looks like the rain has let up."

She grabbed her jacket. "Thanks for everything, and I'm sure we'll be talking."

⁂

"Hello, Leo? It's Reggie Ballard." She set the phone on speaker after she closed her office door.

"Thanks for calling back. It looks like the new replacement selections for the San Francisco office were approved by all parties. The change should go into effect in two weeks. In the meantime, I'd like you to look at the Hong Kong office."

She dropped her pen. "I thought you said

everything was set for Thailand?"

"It was, but we just got word about a problem with the distribution of our Scotch imports. The demand is much higher than the supply. You are in a much better position to rectify that. I want you to trust me, Reggie. It's a better fit, and you're going to love Hong Kong. Let Margaret set you up for a quick visit. If you agree with me, we'll sign a contract. Agreed?"

Her head was spinning. When he told her about the Far East transfer, she'd had a complete meltdown. But, after she did some research, she thought it sounded like a good move. There was nothing holding her on the west coast, and she'd have a lot more autonomy. Maybe Hong Kong would be interesting.

"You always know what's best, Leo. I'll trust your instincts." She oozed southern charm.

"Good. I think you'll be glad you took this. Have a good trip, and let me know what you think."

❧❧❧❧

The skies cleared as Bryce drove through Pitlochry.

The recent shower wiped the landscape clear of dust and dirt. The bright green leaves sprouting on the trees, the black slate on the roofs, and the color of spring flowers—everything seemed to sparkle.

The clock read eleven thirty. She'd be back at the Highlander Inn soon. She flipped on the music and began to sing along with Adele.

Another sharp curve, and Bryce smiled at her improved driving skills—no more curb adventures. Beyond the white fence on her side were dozens of sheep scattered across the broad hillside enjoying the

 Barrett Magill

new grass. She slowed as several of them took turns hopping on and off a large bale near the fence. They watched her for approval or appreciation of their skill, she was quite sure. So, she waved.

Fatigue crept in as she turned off on Victoria street. Suddenly, a nap on the soft bed sounded appealing. The parking lot looked empty, and she parked near the rear door.

The room looked tidy and smelled fresh. The Inn staff had been very obliging about her quick trip back to the U.S. After kicking off her shoes and dropping her bags, she flopped on the bed with her phone. Hard as it was, she opted for a quick text to Fiona. Otherwise if she heard her voice, she knew she get right back in the car and drive over.

Bryce: Hi Fiona, I just got back to the inn and wanted to let you know. I guess we can talk whenever it's convenient. See ya.

That sounded dorky, but her eyelids were drooping. Fiona MacDougall…

❧ ❧ ❧ ❧

"Tom, I really appreciate your time," Fiona said. "This whole distribution has overwhelmed me. Bryce tried to explain, but had to go back to the States."

He set out two sets of papers. "We want this to be a good experience, and a profitable one. I've outlined the steps we'll follow to get the whisky sold and your money deposited. Here is a draft of the new label for you and your dad to approve. We tried to make it look like the original. If we consider any changes, we can always rebrand the product."

"Oh, I like that very much. Looks clean and crisp." She tapped the print. "I think I mentioned my dad gave me power of attorney and asked that we change our brand name to MacDougall Family Distillers. But that can wait for the next run."

"That's nice. I'm glad the two of you will be working together on this. When Bryce gets back, you'll want to decide how you want to write up the agreement." He laughed. "I'm sorry. I'm assuming you want to sign with Global Distributing."

She held the papers and straightened the edges. Had she? Was there another option? The amount of money was staggering, but she'd never even looked at another company. Shouldn't she at least ask around some? "Yes, of course. I'm sure we'll be talking when she gets back."

"Fiona, there's no rush. It's important that you feel comfortable with us."

"I understand. It's just there are so many things to decide on for the future." She stood and walked to the large window overlooking the wooded hillside. Tom had given her a tour of the large facility. Thinking about the small capability of their modest operation, she felt overwhelmed. She turned.

"Tom, do you think we should sell off the whisky and close our little operation?"

He rubbed his chin and thought. "Hard to say. I don't know how much work it might be to retool to get back up to working. Be glad to come down and look, if you want. Or I can send Liam."

She leaned against the sill. "Maybe that's a good idea. We really would like to preserve the legacy, but I'd hate to get in over my head, you know with Dad's health."

"As I said, you needn't hurry your decision. There are many more barrels to move. You may want to consider letting Liam blend some of it."

"You've given me some wonderful information. I should let you get on with your day." The papers fit nicely in her folder. "Thank you."

"My pleasure." He stood and shook her hand. "I'm sure we'll speak again."

A bright white cloud moved off the sun and a breeze picked up. The scent from the malting shed made her smile. Speyburn Distillery wasn't large by most standards, but it was far larger and more modern than MacDougall's.

Fiona followed the road south to home. The bucolic scenery freed her mind and allowed her imagination to fly free. What would it take to bring the place into the twenty-first century? Could she find qualified workers?

She'd probably need a manager and more room. Offices. A wider drive and car park. More facilities for people. Would they have tours?

After all, she was still in her thirties…for another year. She had a good education and physical strength. They had plenty of time while the finished whisky went into distribution.

The sign for the Archiestown turnoff appeared and she turned right onto the side road and glanced at the clock. It was noon and Bryce would be back sometime this afternoon. The emails she'd received the past couple of days sounded promising. Bryce had been granted her leave and would be available to help. And not a minute too soon.

It felt good to have a friend to talk things over and

problem-solve. The past couple of weeks challenged her limits and forced her out of her comfort zone. Taking care of someone else pushed a lot of buttons for her. Her time in Edinburgh consisted of teaching and solitary pursuits.

She thought back to the grad school romance with her then-roommate. Their love had burned bright and burned out in a scant seven years. A hot flame burns brighter. The heartache lasted much longer. Fiona withdrew and refused her friends' entreaties to start dating. It was too painful. Her job fulfilled her need to be with people, and she'd begun to crave her solitude right up to the minute that car showed up with the American.

Who would have imagined an attractive, single woman would just show up at her door? And still she'd fought those feelings for weeks until Bryce left for the US. Then, of course, she suddenly remembered what this kind of attraction could feel like. *Damn.*

As she pulled her car up to the back door, she saw Murray and her dad standing in front of the office talking. When they spotted her, Murray took off like a scalded cat. What kind of mischief were they up to?

Chapter Thirty-six

Reggie closed her eyes as the hotel limo navigated to the Marco Polo Hong Kong on the harbor. The driver had estimated forty-five minutes because of the traffic. Even through the tinted windows, she gaped at the amazing skyline. Having spent a month in Scotland with desolate and wild highlands spotted with quaint villages, this looked totally alien. Every building looked like a skyscraper. The traffic was unimaginable, and the air pollution looked like heavy fog. Her brain couldn't quite absorb the radical difference twenty hours in a plane could create.

Too tired and too overstimulated, Reggie closed her eyes and tried to relax. Leo had given her a week to acclimate and talk with the local staff. Hopefully some real sleep would open up some neural pathways soon.

Mercifully, the uniformed bellman helped her through a painless registration. They moved through the long narrow marble lobby to the elevator and into her lush, quiet room overlooking the harbor. Across the bay sat Hong Kong island. The sun had set, and a swath of lighted towers took on a motion picture quality—like a film sequence at the beginning of a movie.

She stood barefoot and mesmerized at the window, holding a miniature bottle of vodka.

Bryce walked out on her deck at the Highlander Inn and re-read Fiona's text—the one she apparently missed while enjoying her brief coma.

Fiona: So glad you've arrived safely! Would be happy to offer you dinner if you're not too tired out.

She smiled and replied.

Bryce: I would really enjoy that. See you around six?

There was time for a quick shower. Fortunately, she had made time to stop at a mall outside Airdrie and picked up some casual and work duds. New shorts, trainers, and a couple of camp shirts. The other unpacking could wait.

She undressed and turned on the water. "Don't forget the souvenirs." Her messenger bag lay open on the bed, and she pulled out the wrapped book and candy. The book she'd chosen had a whole section on Sandberg. Fiona had seemed so excited about his work about the city. Maybe, someday, she'd want to visit the Windy City.

Don't get ahead of yourself, tiger. Business first.

The cold water made her jump and squeal. "Shit."

She fumbled for the adjustment and twisted it more to hot. Her own squealing made her laugh. Why on earth would Fiona give her a second look?

Light clouds gradually became a velvet grey drape over the area. The air stilled and even the birds took cover. It didn't look like a storm, but Bryce wasn't familiar with weather patterns after such a short time. The air did have that fresh ozone smell. Could be rain nearby.

She slowed as she neared "dead man's curve" and then saw the white posts, but no sign. Panic faded as she remembered they planned to change the sign. One deep breath and she turned up the driveway. As she neared the stone cottage, her pulse revved up and her palms began to perspire. Classical music drifted out the door. A violin piece.

"Hello?"

Fiona appeared and pushed open the back door. "Welcome back."

Bryce jogged up the steps and gratefully accepted a warm embrace when Fiona encircled her shoulders with strong arms. Her hair smelled of lavender.

"Thank you. I'm happy to be back." *Really happy.*

"Please come in. I just opened a nice bottle of pinot noir, and dinner will be ready shortly." They moved into the living room and Fiona poured the wine.

"Things look a little different in here..." Bryce noted a lemon oil scent.

"I did some spring cleaning while Dad was in hospital and got rid of some of the clutter he's so fond of," she whispered.

"I like the new arrangement and the new slipcovers." The couch and two chairs had matching grey-and-blue-checked covers that were more fitted. They picked up the blue in the oriental carpet.

She sat on the couch and Fiona joined her with two glasses of wine. "Thanks. Since it seemed pretty clear I wouldn't be returning to Edinburgh and university, I had to make some tough decisions and phone calls." She sipped her wine. "Whatever we decide to do with the business, I'm going to need to be here."

"That must have been a hard decision. You told me how much you enjoyed teaching. And you probably have good friends there."

"It's bittersweet for sure, but I had to face up to the fact that the administrative part of teaching sapped my enthusiasm more than I realized." She turned and tucked one leg under her. "These past few weeks—with the ups and downs—have been challenging, in a good way. Mostly. Running the business will be a steep learning curve, but I'm hoping you meant what you said about helping, because I'm sure going to need you."

Bryce felt the quivering in her chest as heat flushed up her neck. "I'm glad you're thinking about restarting, and yes, absolutely. I'm here."

The bang-step-repeat came from the hallway, and she looked at Fiona.

"Dad and his walker," she whispered. "Hey Dad, remember Bryce? She's joining us for dinner. Would you like some wine?" She helped him settle in the recliner next to his pipes and tobacco.

"Don't think so. I'll wait for dinner. Good to see you, Miss Andrews." He began puttering with filling his pipe. "Heard you had to pop over the pond for a bit." He laughed.

"Yes, a quick business trip to arrange some time off. I wanted to be able to help out, if you'd like the help." Bryce figured it might be a touchy subject for a proud man and his legacy.

"Since you're both here," Fiona said. "I thought I'd brief you on the conversation I recently had with Tom up at Speyburn."

"He the fella I met with Liam?"

Fiona smiled. "Yes. I'm so glad you recalled our meeting. They were very impressed with the Highland Dew, and are doing the bottling for us." She picked up a folder from the coffee table, slid out the drawing of the new label, and leaned over to hand it to him. "This is a preliminary drawing. I told them we'd be changing the name slightly to MacDougall Family Distillers of Fine Whisky in the next run."

He held it up near the light and smiled. "I like it. Looks snazzy." Fiona and Bryce both laughed.

Bryce leaned back as Fiona replayed her conversation at Speyburn. Tom was the perfect guide to help them. With his knowledge and experience, she felt certain that Fiona's dad would feel like he had an ally. It seemed important to consider Gavin's pride and heritage if they were going to make changes.

"I guess we'd better eat before it gets too late." Fiona winked at Bryce.

❧❧❧❧

Fiona returned to the kitchen after settling her dad and found Bryce drying the dishes. "You didn't need to do that."

"No problem. I wanted to be sure I remembered how to do it if I'm going to be on my own." She grinned.

Fiona felt a shiver looking at that smile. "I think you'd say it's like falling off a bike."

Bryce's laugh echoed through the kitchen.

"What's so funny?"

"I think you meant riding a bike. The other phrase is falling off a log."

Fiona covered her face. "I feel so stupid. Of course. Must be too much wine."

Bryce carefully folded the towel and hung it up. "Would you like to walk a bit? Dinner was wonderful, and I'm stuffed."

"That's a grand idea." She noticed Bryce had taken second helpings and felt proud of her chicken dish. "Dad's sound asleep."

The threat of a storm had vanished and left a pink and lavender sky. Fiona led Bryce out around the office to a narrow path through the orchard toward some woods.

"I had no idea there was anything back here," Bryce said. "How much land do you own?"

"I'd have to check with Dad to be sure, but I think there's about fifteen or sixteen hectares in front down to the road. The area back here is probably about the same, but we've never used them. The original plan was to start growing our own barley, but there have never been enough hands on deck."

"You certainly have plenty of room to expand if you want to." Bryce ducked under some low-hanging branches and held them. "It's really lovely back here. You'd never know there was a working distillery this close."

Fiona laughed. "If it was working, you'd certainly hear it. Believe me." She stopped and pointed back to where the warehouse was. "It's funny you mention that. I've actually been doing some daydreaming about what we might need to expand. Of course, I have no particulars like the cost of repairs or buying new equipment, but I was thinking about extending the driveway some and creating more parking. We might even have a visitor center one day."

Bryce was staring and rubbing her chin slowly. "You know, if I allow my imagination to take over, I can see room to expand and enhance this place."

"It sounds a little overwhelming…but it's also pretty exciting. I feel much better knowing that you and Tom are going to be helping."

Bryce nodded at a circular bench on a large oak. "Think that's safe?"

"Sure." She pulled Bryce by the hand. She released it as soon as they sat, feeling a little embarrassed by the gesture. The tree bark was still warm from the sun, and felt good on her back.

"Oh, I almost forgot. When I got back to the inn there was a message from a leasing agent I contacted. They found a small place south of here, in Black-something-or-other. I'm going to take a look tomorrow."

"That's fantastic. I'll bet it's Blacksboat, near Mary Park. That's really close. I know you like the inn, but this might be less driving." She twisted to face Bryce. "I wish I could offer you a place, but you saw the two cottages…I'm not even sure how Murray manages."

"Oh, please don't worry. I certainly want to be closer, but I'm kind of a recluse sometimes. Besides, I don't want your dad to think I'm too pushy. Best I be respectful of this huge change."

Fiona swallowed a lump. "That's quite considerate. I guess I didn't think that far. I just wanted some help. But, you're right, this will be hard for Dad."

Bryce took Fiona's hand in both of hers. "I'm so sorry. I wasn't trying to make any kind of judgment. You are making an enormous life change. It's amazing what all you've had to do in just a few weeks. You really are a remarkable woman." Her voice cracked.

Fiona couldn't speak. Her eyes were locked on Bryce's, and she couldn't take a breath. For the first time—maybe ever—someone actually saw her soul. It felt wonderful and terrifying. Bryce continued to look deep into her eyes, and squeezed her hand.

Nothing moved. The breeze stopped and the birds were still.

Fiona leaned in, closed her eyes, and willed the trembling to stop. She waited. Very lightly, Bryce kissed her lips. Fiona released the breath she had been holding. She put her hand on Bryce's cheek and kissed her. Seconds ticked by and Fiona pulled Bryce into an embrace. Bryce groaned softly when Fiona stroked the back of her neck.

Neither spoke. Fiona absorbed every molecule of warmth and strength. It coursed through her like an infusion of new hope. She inhaled deeply of Bryce and her warm skin, clean hair, and new shirt. Softly, she whispered, "I am so grateful you are here with me."

Chapter Thirty-seven

The whitewashed holiday cottage looked like so many others in the area. The flower boxes, picket fence, and gravel drive. A sign at the road was the only giveaway she'd arrived at the right place.

"Good day," a tall, youngish woman answered the knock. "Ya must be Ms. Andrews, aye? Please, come in."

"Thank you. Yes. I'm Bryce. Thank you for showing me your cottage." The small living room looked comfortable and homey.

"Happy to give you a look-see. I'm Kathleen and my husband is Daniel. He's at work," she said, and walked straight through the kitchen and out the back door. "Works days at the distillery over yonder." She waved her hand toward the east. "We just recently decided to fix up the little place to let."

They followed a winding path several yards toward some trees.

"We lived here after we got married until my mom passed last year."

"I'm so sorry," Bryce said.

"Cancer, you know. Can be beastly." She pointed to a wooden chalet-type building. "Here 'tis."

A few steps led to a nice deck with a great view of the fields beyond. The interior had the same chalet feel. More like a Northwood's cabin. Two small bedrooms—furnished. A galley kitchen with appliances, table, and chairs. There was even a door out to a small back deck.

Bryce smiled as Kathleen described other features. When she paused, Bryce said, "This is perfect. When will it be available?"

The stunned woman shook her head and laughed. "I think probably by the weekend. I'll have to call you when Daniel gets home."

Bryce waved as she backed out of the driveway. She checked the odometer. Already the plans were percolating. Probably use the store in Archiestown. Might have to travel to Inverness or Aberdeen for any large purchases. She opened her window and smiled. Even now she could imagine her days. An early walk behind the cottage. Looked like a creek or stream ran through the property. Then she'd make tea and some breakfast. Might even make her lunch. After a short drive…Wait. "I wonder what the roads are like in the winter?"

In contrast, a warm breeze made her shiver, remembering the kiss. Wow. That sure wasn't planned…but, it felt so natural and so good. Fiona's soft skin flushed pink and the dark desire in her eyes… Could it be real, or was it wishful thinking? Didn't matter right now. It became the missing keystone of the whole adventure. That moment held together the stones randomly placed by the other players. For now, the disparate parts of this effort consolidated. She and Fiona could make this work.

"Woo hoo!" she shouted out the window at a half dozen shaggy heilan' coo's.

She passed the empty white sign posts and the apple orchard, since Fiona said she'd be taking her dad for a follow-up with his doctor. The odometer showed 2.4 miles. *Only five minutes to get to work. Terrific.* The breeze and sweet smell of the blossoms evoked a quiver in her chest and sheen across her forehead and neck. *Fiona McDougall, what have you done?*

Her cell phone rang. She punched the answer button on the steering wheel. "Hello?"

"Ms. Andrews, it's Brian Townsend from Dufftown. I wondered if you might have a few minutes to talk."

"Well, I'm in the car heading back to the inn. Is there a problem?"

After a pause he said, "Well, we may have hit a snag. I'd really feel better talking to you in person."

What the… "Okay. Can you meet me in a half an hour at the Highlander Inn?"

"I'll be there." She disconnected

"Shit."

⚘ ⚘ ⚘ ⚘

Reggie kicked off her shoes and flopped back on the bed. For a slow and easy southern girl, these representatives of the Far East Division worked hard to get ten hours' worth of work done in an eight-hour day. These guys did not waste time on small talk or any part of her normal, relaxed sales regimen. It was exhausting.

She reached for her laptop and pushed back against the pillows. When the message from Bryce had arrived last week, she'd ruminated over the contents and Bryce's surprisingly kind reply. It was unexpected considering how reprehensibly Reggie had acted. Even more surprising that Leo hadn't fired her.

It might be foolish, but maybe she and Bryce could repair the damage. Reggie swiped at the tears for a lost friendship she'd taken for granted. If she were honest with herself, she'd recognize how happy Bryce had become in the past month or so. Maybe Fiona had helped heal the broken heart…Bitch.

The clock radio indicated 18:30, but she was too tired to do the math. Maybe an email tomorrow.

The knock at the door startled her; then she remembered her room service order.

⁂

Fiona pulled the car up to the house and parked. The doctor had seemed very pleased with the improvement in her dad's physical and mental health. She was, as well.

"Wait, let me help." Fiona hurried around the car.

"I'm fine. No need to baby me." He pulled his cane out. "Not sorry about losing that damn walker." He laughed.

"Oh, it's not lost, just retired for awhile."

"After I change into something more comfortable, I'd like to do some inspecting in the main building." He climbed the steps easily. Fiona smiled.

"Good plan. I'll join you for some instruction."

At the back door, he smiled and held it open.

Fiona shrugged off her jumper and quickly donned some old jeans and a long-sleeved shirt. Her father's steady improvement made her very hopeful. Maybe everything did happen for a reason. Tom had already sent her a check for their first sales. It seemed reasonable to begin cleaning and renovating the distillery.

"Dad?"

"I'm out here. Bring a notebook and some extra light."

Evidently, he was anxious to get going. She grabbed a clamp-on flood light and an extension cord, and hurried to catch up with him.

"Before we do that, I want to look at the warehouse. I think it might be good to have a spot to put the barrels going out in order so there's no mistakin' which ones go first. That might mean some cleaning and better light."

"Do you remember any of the lads from around here to help?"

He scratched the back of his neck. "Not offhand. Let me look through the payroll books. I might be able to put a name with a face."

"Okay, I'll bring them up to the house after supper." She stopped and looked around. "Have you seen Murray lately?"

❧ ❧ ❧ ❧

"Brian, it's good to see you." Bryce shook his hand. "Why don't we go in here and talk." She chose a table by the window in the bar and smiled at Billy. "I haven't eaten. Would you like something to eat?"

"I don't want to take up a lot of your time..." He pulled out a chair and sat down. He ran his fingers through his thick red hair and clasped his hands tight. He seemed to be perspiring.

"Brian, it's fine. You look worried. How about a beer?"

"Thanks. That'd be great."

Bryce waved, and Billy came over.

"We'd like a couple of draft beers. And I'd like you to meet Brian Townsend, one of our enterprising new distillers."

Billy shook his hand. "Glad to meet you. I'll get those beers."

"Oh, and a menu." Bryce leaned back and smiled. "So, what would you like to talk about."

"I sent off the papers you gave me to the fella in Airdrie. I'll bet it wasn't a week later me and Gary got a letter from a solicitor representing the old fella we lease from."

Billy set the beers down along with the menus. "Give me a call when you want to order."

"Thanks, we will." Bryce looked over as Brian quaffed about half his beer and wiped his beard. "Go on."

"Seems the old fella passed and his niece and nephew want to sell to a developer for some upscale housing." He rubbed his chin and took another swallow. "We tried to see if we could buy it, but the property is quite large—well, you know that. We can't afford it." His voice cracked.

Bryce put her hand on his wrist. "I'm so sorry. I wish I could think of something."

"It's no worry of yours. I just wanted to let you know because you seemed fond of our whisky and we've only got what we've stored. They gave us three months. It ain't much, but we will be able to finish this last run." He scrubbed his face with both hands and finished off his beer.

Her mind raced with a dozen different thoughts. "This is heartbreaking news. You still have some time and there's maybe a solution." She waved at Billy and pointed at the empty mug in front of Brian. *I wish Leo was here. He'd know what to suggest.* They might be able to buy what he had...but there was no guarantee how it might age out. Neither Airdrie or Speyburn had large enough storage areas.

"Thanks for listening, I didn't mean to go all soft on you. Just wanted to tell you in person that we wouldn't be able to keep to the agreement."

"Brian, that's not a worry. You just agreed to let us represent you. We can put that on hold, if you like."

Her cell phone chimed a text. "Excuse me a sec."

Fiona: Hi. We spent most of the afternoon working on the warehouse and listing more projects. Whipped. Can we talk tomorrow?

Bryce: Sure. I'll call.

"Sorry. Would you like to order something?"

Brian pushed his chair back. "I think I've taken too much of your time. If you don't mind, I ought to get home to the family." He stood. "Thanks for your time…and the beer."

"I understand. Please keep in touch. Okay?"

"I will."

He hurried out as Billy brought the beer. "Somethin' wrong?"

"Yes and no. Poor guy lost his lease at the distillery they were hoping to build."

"Do you want this?" He held up the pint.

"Might as well. I'm done for the night and it will go great with a venison burger—if I may."

Billy set the beer down and nodded. "I'll put in your order."

Wonder if I'll miss the food and company of this place? It's not like another continent—you'll only be a few miles away. I'm surprised I haven't heard anything from Reggie.

Chapter Thirty-eight

"Hello?"

"Ms. Andrews, this is Daniel calling back about letting the cottage."

Bryce sat up and dropped her book on the floor. Evidently, she'd dozed off. "Hello, Daniel Thanks for calling back." The clock read eight thirty.

"Kathleen told me about your visit and was quite excited that you were interested in a long-term lease. We could offer a month-to-month lease for £575, or £500 for six months. Of course, we'd need a deposit. Do you know when you'd want the place?"

Bryce grabbed her notebook and checked the calendar. She'd paid up through next week. "Could we say end of next week?"

"Sure. That will give us some time to get the place spiffed up a bit. I'll leave the lease here, and you can stop by anytime to sign and leave a deposit."

"Sounds perfect. Thanks, Daniel. If you don't mind my asking, where do you work? Your wife mentioned a nearby distillery"

"Down at Tormore. Been there for three years. Was there a reason you're asking?"

"Sorry, yes. I'm in the same business doing sales and distribution. I'm always curious."

"Makes sense. We'll see you then."

The room at the inn felt so cozy. What would she need to buy for the cottage to make it more comfortable?

She flipped to a blank page in her notebook and wrote down "household items" and underlined it. The walkthrough with Kathleen had given her a good visual. After jotting a few notes, she decided to shop at the Filling Station store in Craigellachie.

The phone surprised her. "Hello?"

"Bryce. Hope I'm not bothering you."

"Hi, Leo. I'm really glad you called. How are you feeling?" Relief washed over her hearing his strong voice. The frailness was gone.

"Getting better every day. I'm back to work, but shorter days. How are things with the MacDougalls?"

"Amazingly good. Gavin had a fall and was hospitalized then rehabbed. Since then, he seems to be getting more alert and remembers more. He has a newfound interest in the whisky business, as well as teaching it to Fiona."

"That is good news. Have you decided on a place to live?"

How does he always know exactly what's happening? "Matter of fact, I looked at a cottage about five minutes south of the distillery. It will be easy to help out whenever I'm needed."

"Sounds good. Have you heard anything from Reggie?"

Bryce grimaced. "Not exactly. An email a while ago where she apologized for making a stink. I've let it go."

"Good. She needed to do that. What she did was unprofessional and uncalled for. On another topic, I had a note from Ian says he hasn't heard much news from the recent clients lately. Everything moving along?"

She sat up and took a breath. "Well, I'm not sure,

but we may not keep the Townsend-McClure fellas. Brian came over today to tell me they will be losing their lease in a few months. The owner died, and the heirs want to sell."

"Wow. That's hard, especially for youngsters just getting started. Do they have stock we can sell for them?"

"I'm quite sure, but it still needs a few years." It made her feel good knowing Leo treated everyone with consideration. Most in the business would probably just cut their losses and move on. "I'll give him a few days, then ask him if we can help."

There was a long pause. "Let me talk to Ian and see if we can figure something out. I'm sure this isn't the first time that young start-ups have hit a block. I'll let you know. And I don't want you to worry—I want you to get some rest."

"Thanks, Leo. I promise I will. Please take care of yourself." She ended the call.

Bryce flopped back on the bed and remembered she'd promised to call Fiona back…maybe a text would be okay.

Bryce: Sorry I didn't get back to you sooner. Crazy day. Can we get together tomorrow?
Fiona: No problem. After lunch ok?
Bryce: See you then. Sleep well.

She rolled over and remembered the apple blossoms, the sunset, and the sweetest kiss she'd ever had. *Sweet dreams.*

Fiona continued to stir the soup while her dad sat at the table scribbling furiously. He was very engaged, which was wonderful, but she worried he wasn't getting enough rest.

"The equipment seems to be working, but I'm afraid there's a bit of maintenance to be done for loose parts, a bit of oil, and a good cleaning. I'll make a list."

A knock at the back door surprised her.

"I'll get it. Come in, Murray. We were just going to have some homemade Cullen Skink, why don't you join us?" She cleared a spot at the table.

"I got the note you left on my door. Sorry I haven't been around. I had some business to tend up in Elgin. But I'm ready to help with whatever you need." He hung his cap on a peg by the door.

"Murray, we're gonna have some work ahead of us. Me and Fiona went through the place today. There's a few loose spots and some leaky hoses." He looked up and squinted. "Who was the lad had that power washer?"

"Do you mean Amos? John's boy." Murray pulled out the chair and sat.

"'At's him. Think you might get him to come help us out? Course we'll pay him for sure."

"I'll try to find him tomorrow. Anything else?" Murray sipped the hot tea.

"We're going to need to get some fellas who can just help clean stuff. I can't be climbing ladders, and neither should you." They both laughed. "Fiona, do you think Tom and Liam might be willing to come by and make some suggestions for improvements?"

"I'll ring him up and ask if he can come over tomorrow." Fiona shook her head and smiled at the two old mates talking. It helped knowing their history better. "Make some room." She set down a wooden cutting board with a fresh loaf of bread and some butter, then went for the soup. Both men dug in like they hadn't eaten in days. It pleased her that she'd taken the time. And thank heaven for the old cookbook. She crossed her fingers. Let this be a good beginning.

Chapter Thirty-nine

Fiona stood at the top of the driveway, waving. She looked beautiful. Her jeans looked new and fit perfectly. The loose-cut cotton shirt was a jewel-tone blue. Bryce stopped the car next to her and reached over to open the door. "You look lovely, but too dressed up to be puttering in an old cottage."

"Thanks, but the truth is simply I haven't done a wash." She buckled her seatbelt and smiled. "I'm excited to see the place you found. I'm sure I've passed it a hundred times but never noticed."

"It's small but I really like the way it feels — kind a woodsy and comfortable. I just picked up a few things at the Craigellachie Filling Station this morning to make the place more personal."

Fiona looked over her shoulder at the number of bags filling the back seat. "I can see you had no difficulty finding a few things." And then she giggled.

Bryce followed the road south just a couple of miles and turned into a gravel drive and past the pretty white cottage. "Kathleen said I could come over and leave whatever I needed, and she'd bring over the lease."

"I see what you mean." Fiona got out of the car and walked around the front of the cottage. "It's really secluded, but you have a great view."

The door was unlocked. "Do you want to look around or unload?"

Fiona trotted up the steps. "I want to see."

They were a foot apart and Bryce really wanted to pull her closer, but Fiona slid past into the house.

"This is quite nice." She walked from one room to the next opening cupboards and testing cushions and mattresses. "And very tidy."

Bryce covered a smile, but appreciated how much Fiona cared to be so discerning. "Thanks."

"It'll do quite well, I suspect." Fiona grinned.

"Hello?" A voice came from outside. Bryce went to the door.

"Kathleen, hi. We just got here."

"I heard the car and brought over the lease and some housekeeping rules." She handed over a folder. When she noticed Fiona, she stuck out her hand. "I'm Kathleen Grant. My husband Daniel and I are letting the cottage."

Fiona took her hand. "I'm so happy to meet you. You have a lovely spot here. I live just up the road a bit, so I guess we're kind of neighbors."

"Fiona and her dad own the MacDougall Distillery, and I'm fortunate to be helping them refurbish the business." Bryce took the folder to the kitchen counter and read through the lease while Kathleen and Fiona visited. Pretty standard lease. She signed one copy to leave with Kathleen and took the other copy for her files, and pulled a check from her pocket for the rent and deposit. "I know it's a bit early, but I just brought a few household items I needed. Do you mind if I bring them in?"

"Please go ahead. We finished up in here last night. Daniel is just getting copies of new keys made for you. Nice meeting you, Fiona. Daniel will be thrilled to find out you folks are right up the road."

"Thank you." Bryce waved as Kathleen walked

back up the driveway to the main house that was barely visible from the cottage.

"She seems nice," Fiona said. "Let's bring in your stuff."

It took about an hour to put everything away, and after she washed up Bryce brought two water bottles to the small rear deck where Fiona was sitting. A wooden bench was built into the railing and Fiona sat with her legs stretched out.

"You look relaxed. Here." And handed her a bottle.

"Thanks." She cracked open the cap. "I don't know if I mentioned it, but I'm awfully glad you decided to stay on. It's been such a weight off my shoulders knowing you'd be here to help me." She smiled. "I'm even sleeping better."

"I'm glad, too. I needed a break, and already it feels like the right decision." She put her arm across the rail behind Fiona. "I wish I could say I was sleeping better." She cleared her throat.

Fiona's face flushed. She rested her head on Bryce's arm and put her hand on her knee. "You know, I was quite smitten when you first stumbled into my driveway...or out, but never considered it might be mutual."

"Really? I'm surprised because I felt that I was doing a lot of stumbling." She stroked some hair back from Fiona's forehead. "You took my breath away." Bryce set down her water bottle. "With all the frenzy of my job and Reggie's screw-up, I just couldn't let myself 'feel.' You know what I mean?"

Fiona nodded. "Oh, yes. I know exactly what you mean. I've felt like I was running a race for months with no end in sight. And I feel terrible about the whole row with Reggie. Something about her showing up just felt off. I should have trusted you, but I—"

Bryce stopped her with a kiss. A deep, passionate message. Fiona moved into her arms and clutched the back of her neck. Bryce felt her center collapse as ripples of electricity raced through every cell in her body.

She pulled back and held Fiona's face in her hands for just a moment to look into her incredible green eyes that reflected the same desire. She kissed her again deeply.

The wind came up from the east and brought the smell of the river and freshly mown grass. Bryce caressed Fiona's hair and relaxed into a soft embrace and the silence between them. Her heart swelled with a newfound joy that might never have come again. The vibration against her hip made them both start.

"Sorry, my phone." Fiona sat up and pulled it from her pocket. "Hello? Hi, Tom…really…? That's perfect."

"Was that Tom Hobart?"

Fiona stood. "Yes. I left a message asking if he could come by and give us some advice." She smiled. "And he's on his way over with Liam."

"Guess we better move." Bryce took the water bottles with her and picked up the empty Filling Station bags. She wanted a chance to talk to Tom about selling some of Brian's whisky. Might as well see about storing it somewhere. If Brian would be interested. It would be a shame if they both got discouraged by this misfortune.

Ten minutes later, they parked in the driveway next to Tom's Speyburn Ltd. vehicle. The warehouse door was up, and Liam was standing with Gavin at the office door.

Fiona looked over and shrugged.

Chapter Forty

All six of them were crowded around the kitchen table with spreadsheets and card files scattered about. Fiona took the pitcher to make more lemonade. Much of the conversation was lost on her, but she guessed by her father's interest and enthusiasm he felt very comfortable. Even Murray provided something to their problem-solving.

They had arrived at the point where a budget needed to be made.

Bryce pulled out her phone and scrolled through it. "With the next round of bottling and sales, all past expenses will be paid and there is still a loan for renovating and salaries."

Murray looked surprised. Fiona knew he hadn't ever received an actual check. *Could they trust him, now?*

"I think you have a good schedule for modernizing the still room and upgrading the plumbing and wiring. For now, you might want to use Liam to blend some of your stock, but keep putting out the original." Tom jotted some notes. "If you only send us one or two barrels a month, maximum, it will be time enough for the distilling to start up and age a bit. With over one hundred barrels to bottle, you'd have a decent start." He leaned back.

Gavin lit his pipe and no one said anything for a few minutes. This was really happening. They might actually save MacDougall's. Fiona leaned against the counter and Bryce turned to wink at her.

"Fi, think you could find a bottle of the Dew?" Her dad grinned.

"I sure do."

Tom stood. "I don't think we can stay. It's getting late for us."

Liam moved out from his spot behind the table. "Mr. MacDougall, I'm really looking forward to working with you on this blend."

"Och, Liam, I'm just Gavin. I'm glad we'll be doing something different. Should be tasty." They shook hands.

Fiona and Bryce followed them out to the car.

"I can't tell you how much I appreciate you helping us out." Fiona shook both their hands.

"Thanks, fellas. We'll catch up soon." Bryce waved as they pulled out. "Fiona, could we go look at the warehouse for a minute?"

Fiona shrugged. "Sure, why?"

"I have an idea, and I'd like to run it past you and your dad."

They crossed the yard and up the ramp. "Is it secret? Or do you just want to get me alone?"

Bryce laughed. "Now that you mention it, maybe kill two birds—so to speak." Once inside Bryce found the light switch. "Were you in here when it was actively in use?"

"A long time ago. Not in the past few years when I was in Edinburgh." This certainly was mysterious. "Why?"

"Just an idea right now." Bryce wandered in wide circles. "One of my contacts from Dufftown lost his lease at a small distillery. He has a good product, but it needs more time to age." She stopped. "After listening to the guys talk, I wondered if your dad might consider renting him some space."

"It's certainly worth discussing. Do you think he'd come over to meet with us?" Fiona liked the idea, but wasn't sure about her dad. He'd been awfully agreeable since he got home from the hospital, but the new plan was gradually moving into his long-held realm.

Bryce joined her. "I haven't spoken to him since he stopped by a few days ago. They may have figured out something or found a place. But it's worth a call. Your dad might enjoy talking to a young fella on the way up."

Fiona looked around and slid her arms around Bryce. "Can you guess what his daughter might enjoy?"

"Hmm…don't tell me. Would it be dinner? Ouch! Why'd you pinch me?"

Fiona pulled her closer. "Too much talk about business. I feel left out."

Bryce caressed her cheek gently then kissed her. The sweet lingering taste of lemonade and fragrant scent on her skin caused a shiver. Her knees felt like jelly, and she was a little short of breath. Being held so close helped, and their lips fit together perfectly as if they always had. Her lips parted, and Bryce took the invitation.

The screen door on the kitchen banged shut, and they both pulled back.

Fiona laughed. "I guess this is the pattern now: catch and release."

"I'll get the lights." Bryce jogged over to the spot near the door. "At least I'll be in my own place in a few days…" She waggled her eyebrows.

"Right. Let's go in."

"Okay. You talk to your dad and I'll call Brian when I get home to see if they want to meet." She pulled the creaky overhead door and Fiona helped.

As they walked toward the house, Fiona asked, "Do you think this is really going to work out? Are we really going to get the place back to being profitable?"

Bryce stopped and looked at her seriously as the sun moved toward the horizon. "I do. With everyone's cooperation, I believe it will. Plus, I think Leo is invested enough in the product that he's willing to allow Tom and Liam some leeway."

When they got to the kitchen, it was empty. "I guess the old guys are tired from all this work."

Bryce laughed. "Let me grab my stuff and I'll get going. I want to call Brian and Leo, if I have time."

Fiona walked with her to the car. "Do you ever talk to Reggie?"

"I haven't and probably should make the effort. After all, she was exiled to Hong Kong and they called it a promotion."

Fiona leaned in the window and brushed Bryce's lips. "Drive carefully."

"Good night."

❧❧❧❧

"Thank you, gentlemen. I'm happy that Global Distillers and Distribution could provide you with a new resource. Our offices in Scotland will begin processing your orders as soon as the papers are filed." Reggie smiled and disconnected the conference call with the local buyers' group.

This deal had been simmering ever since she had arrived in Hong Kong. Leo warned her that frustrations ran high since sales outlets were unable to maintain supplies of Scottish whisky imports. Even though she had explained limited production due to the worldwide economic downturn, demand was through the roof. It was hard to believe their regional offices in Scotland were so cooperative. Either Leo had a hand in this, or the South was gonna rise again. This might be a good time to see what she could work out with Matt Takata.

Either way, tonight would be dinner at Petrus compliments of GDD. "May, would you make a reservation at Petrus tonight for three at eight o'clock? Thanks. And please let Jack and Howard know."

None of this would have happened without her local team. Both had been with the company for years and had earned Leo's respect. Everything had worked out perfectly, and yet it somehow lost some luster since she had no one to share the news with. She thought about calling Bryce...but would she even care?

The lights were coming on across the harbor and the sound from the boats ricocheted amongst the tall buildings growing fainter as they reached the sky. Hong Kong turned out to be a remarkable city filled with excitement, sophistication, and mystery. Her initial apprehensions had gradually faded. Leo's sense that a young, blond, southern belle would impact male-dominated sales teams had turned prophetic.

From the small display bar, she poured a small amount of a new blend from one of the lowland distillers into a tasting glass. "Let happy hour commence."

Her phone app showed the times across the globe, and it indicated Scotland at 9:30 a.m. After a brief pause she dialed Bryce.

She almost lost her nerve when Bryce answered.

"Hi, Bryce. Hope it's not too early..."

"No. What a nice surprise. What time is it there?'

"Five thirty, quitting time. I was celebrating a new deal and wanted to share the news. I mean other than with the folks here who know. I'm taking the team out for dinner later…well…I just wanted to touch base with you."

"I'm glad you did. Leo mentioned some problem they had over there with availability that he wanted you to work on. Guess you did. That's great."

An uncomfortable pause prompted Reggie to speak. "Bryce, I'm so sorry."

"I know you are. Why don't we put that behind us and move on?"

Reggie put down the glass and relaxed. "Thanks. How're things going with the MacDougall project? Leo seemed really pleased."

"I'm cautiously optimistic. They've agreed to let us help them and we've already sent a couple of barrels up to Speyburn to bottle and distribute locally. Gavin seems much more involved, and so is Fiona. I think they want to rebuild."

Surprising information. Reggie wondered what caused the turnaround, but wouldn't push it right now. "That's terrific. Along with the other leads, Leo must be excited. Are you staying long, or returning?"

Another pause. "I asked Leo for some time off, and he agreed as long as I could still keep an eye on the new accounts. I've leased a small holiday cottage in the general area so I can be available."

I'll bet. Don't push it. "Well, you certainly deserve some time off. I can't remember the last time you had a vacation." She laughed. "I'll bet your mom does, though."

Bryce groaned. "She's not happy about this.

I called Dad to let him know. Safer move. Listen, I hate to cut this short, but I have a meeting with the Townsend-McClure guys, but congratulations on the deal."

"Thanks. Keep in touch." Reggie felt relief, and a little bit of melancholy. She missed the camaraderie they had developed over ten years. What she really wanted to know about was the relationship with Fiona. Next time. She tipped the taster and finished her drink.

Chapter Forty-one

A week before, Bryce had talked with both Brian and Gary about the prospect of helping out the MacDougalls in return for storing their whisky. They wanted to talk to their respective families, but were keen on a chance to save what they'd done. They were all scheduled to meet at the distillery at ten. Fiona wanted it to be early because her dad functioned better.

Her first few nights in the cottage had taken some adjustment, as the farmland around Blacksboat was still as a churchyard, but now it felt like home.

She finished drying her hands, hung up the dish towel, and looked out through the trees. The privacy really helped her to unwind. She even had food in the fridge and had invited Fiona over for dinner. Everything in order, she grabbed her bag and keys, and set off for the distillery.

When she pulled in, Gavin had two young men following him toward the warehouse. Fiona waved as she parked.

"Am I late?"

"No, the lads were a bit early, and Dad was so excited to show off the place he's been talking their ears off. Hope he doesn't frighten them off." She gave Bryce a quick hug.

Fiona looked happy to see her. The now-familiar shiver shot through her. "Might be a good thing. Let them form their own opinions and then we can discuss possibilities."

"Would you help me bring a couple more chairs out on the front porch? I thought it might be easier than crowding around the kitchen table."

They moved three kitchen chairs out and arranged them on the porch. Fiona stood next to the railing, chewing her lip. Bryce moved closer and took her hand. "Are you worried about this?"

"Not really. It's just…everything seems to be moving so quickly all of a sudden." She put her arm around Bryce's waist. "Ever since I came home from Edinburgh, it's been chaos and worry and fear. Then things settled, but I keep thinking the other shoe is going to drop. Do you know what I mean?"

"I do. It has been a crazy few months in so many ways." She put her arm around Fiona's shoulders. "Certainly not what I imagined when I left San Francisco. The whole hassle with Reggie, Leo's stroke, your dad's fall and hospitalization…"

"Don't forget the fire."

"How could I? Guess we've had some hurdles. But finding this place was pure divine intervention in so many ways." She kissed Fiona's forehead. "And I'm sure there's a lot more to come. Together, there's no doubt in my mind we can figure it out."

"We'd better catch up with the tour or my dad will have those poor lads working."

They found all three crowded around the still. Brian was grinning. "This is a thing of beauty! I can't believe you still have it working."

"This design's been in my family for generations. Remember me telling you about the women holding onto the process to keep the excise men from finding out? Well, they also kept a good eye on everything that went on out here."

"They did a fine job. When did ya say was the last time you fired this up?"

Bryce noticed Gavin working a rag around the whisky safe. He looked wistfully at the copper still covered with dust. "Been over a year or two, I expect. Too long."

Brian hopped down off the platform. "I understand. It's a hard thing to let go. When me and Gary shut down after the last run it was like a knife in the heart. Ain't that right?"

Gary McClure looked completely different than Brian. Short, stocky, with thick dark hair and glasses, he spoke in low measured tones. "Aye. It hurt. When we first started up we had to set up everything. From my basement to a real distillery took a leap, and losing it, well…"

"Gentlemen, if you're done with the tour, we could all retire to the front porch for something to drink." Fiona took her dad's arm.

❧❧❧❧

Once she had everyone comfortable with something to drink. Fiona sat down with them.

Gavin filled his pipe. "I gave the lads a taste of the Dew and the Special Reserve just so they have an idea what we do here." He winked at Fiona.

"We're so glad we had a chance to come over and meet you and see your place," Brian said.

"And it's a relief we'll have a place to let our whisky age in a perfect environment," Gary added.

"Dad, I'm not sure I follow. Did I miss something?"

"We've got empty rows in the back that can be used. Plus, the lads will help move our whisky up front for shipping to Speyburn. Shouldn't be hard to get the barrels lined up to load."

Bryce smiled. "So, you guys are willing to barter a little work for getting your whisky aged?"

Brian winked at Gavin. "We're talking about a kind of partnership. If we help get the place renovated and up to speed, your Dad offered to share his experience and let us help get back to distilling the Highland Dew, as well as maybe some of our own brand." He grinned. "He even hinted at creating a blend."

"We'll have to wait and see how well you learn before I start giving my secrets away," Gavin grumbled.

Bryce looked at both men and said, "I'll be. Here I was hoping to find a place for you guys to store your product. And pow! You're working partners."

All three men laughed.

Fiona cleared her throat. "I may be the only one here who thinks this sounds amazingly simple. Isn't there more to arrange?"

Gavin patted her arm. "Of course there is, darlin'. That's what you and the business woman are here to take care of. We'll work on the whisky and you can figure out the details. See that's where the 'MacDougall Family Distillery' comes in." He winked.

Bryce looked at her and smiled. "I guess we have some work to do."

Gary stood up. "I think we better head back. We have a lot of packing to do, and don't forget the meeting with Revenue and Customs. Let us know when you want us back."

Brian shook Gavin's hand. "I'm looking forward to working with all of you. This is such a blessing for me and my family."

"Let me walk you out," Bryce said.

She looked back as they got to the cars. "I'm really pleased that everything worked out so well. Do you have any questions I can answer?"

Gary nodded, and Brian stepped closer. "Thanks for setting this up. Gavin is a treasure house of fine information. But I guess I'm not really sure how this will work day-to-day, or what it means for our deal with you."

"I think we're still good. We can use your whisky when you think it's aged enough, and have it shipped wherever we agree there's demand. It will still be separate from the Highland Dew. Same goes for their stock." She leaned back against their car. "I guess I'd like to know how much you're willing to help and whether you know anyone who can pitch in on the clean-up and renovation. Storing your product won't be a fair trade for all that needs to be done. Any other work should be compensated, and we'll get you contracts so you don't need to worry."

Brian and Gary both smiled. "That would be grand! I mean, we both have families to feed, and our whisky can't last forever."

"And don't forget those important Paddington socks."

Gary looked confused, but Brian laughed. "Can we check around for helpers and get back to you? The sooner we get things right, the sooner we can get to making whisky."

"Of course. In the meantime, I'll talk to Tom Hobart at Speyburn and let him know they can combine deliveries when the time comes. Plus, Liam might be a big help when it comes to blending—he's a pro."

"Thanks for all your help." They both shook her hand and waved as they drove off.

She typed a couple of reminders into her phone and smiled. A great agreement and beneficial for all. Leo should definitely approve. When she got back to the porch, she found Fiona relaxed with her feet on the railing and her eyes closed. Bryce cleared her throat and Fiona cracked open one eye.

"You look deserted." Bryce sat next to her.

"Dad headed in for a nap. He's exhausted, but very happy. Who could have imagined this serendipity?"

"I hoped to help the boys with their whisky and thought they'd enjoy meeting your dad...but this partnership sounds great." She paused. "Fi, are you okay with this?"

"Sure. Why wouldn't I be?"

"Well, you and your dad seemed to be on a path for him to teach you the business. I hope this won't affect that. I didn't mean to butt in."

Fiona put her hand out and Bryce took it. "There will be a lot of work and details to be handled before a single drop of whisky comes out of that grand old still. I'm happy to let the young men handle it. When it comes to the family secrets, I'll be right there at his side soaking them up."

"How did you become so wise?"

Fiona laughed her happy lilt. "Good Lord! I think it's more resignation. I'm tired of pushing the river. Thanks to you, my dear, our whisky is selling, the bills are paid, and we have new partners to help us."

Bryce smiled. It actually seemed like it could all work out even better than she planned. But, there were still phone calls to be made. She stood. "I think I'd better head back to Andrews Manor for a while and get some work done."

Fiona laughed. "Is this you taking it easy?"

Bryce squeezed her shoulder. "I think that may come quite soon, but I need to let Ian, Tom, and Leo know the new game plan."

Fiona walked her out to the car. "If you can carve out some time, I'd like to ask a favor."

"Of course, what do you need?"

"Not now." She kissed her sweetly. "I'll let you know."

⁂

"Hi Margaret, is Leo available?" Bryce had changed into a T-shirt and shorts, and took a can of soda out to the small deck near the kitchen. While the temps stayed in the upper 60s and lower 70s, it was still humid, and mostly cloudy. Comfortable, but a bit sticky.

"Oh, hi, Bryce. It's nice to hear from you. Sorry, the boss is in a meeting with the lawyers. How're you enjoying your overdue holiday?"

Bryce laughed and spilled the soda on her shorts. "Oddly enough, it's been crazy busy since I got back, but I think I have some good news about both the Townsend-McClure deal and the MacDougalls. They seem to have teamed up a bit. Could be a win-win."

"Sounds like it. I'll give him the message. I'm sure he'll call when he can."

"Since I have you, how do you think he's doing?" Bryce didn't want to add to his worries.

"He's doing remarkably well. Even the doctor is surprised. It helped his mood that the quarterlies came in from the San Francisco Regional office and they're doing well."

"I'm sure that's a relief. Good to catch up, Margaret. Thanks."

"You get some rest, Bryce."

She flipped off the phone and stuck it in her pocket. Since her unrelenting hunger spasms hadn't abated, she went back into the kitchen to dig out the baked ham and hard rolls she bought from the market. While she reheated some soup, she sliced the ham and made a sandwich. As she stirred the warming vegetable soup, the memory of Fiona's kiss teased her. Happily, their relationship had grown closer every day since she'd returned. Friendship had morphed into fondness, and now a physical familiarity that simmered fiercely.

The past few months had been so consumed by the project that she deliberately refused to indulge the fantasies that monopolized her dreams. The majority of time she believed that eventually she would return to her west coast home and Fiona would go back to teaching. Recently, however, those ideas had reversed. And now with more time to share, they each had the opportunity to explore this wonderful new relationship.

The bubbling splatters of the soup brought her back to reality. She wiped off the stove, then took her soup and sandwich to the table. The only question that remained was which one of them was going to make the move. She looked around her new home and smiled. "Let it be."

Chapter Forty-two

Dad, where are you?" Fiona called from the back door.

He poked his head out the door of the warehouse. "Just here. I wanted to find space for Brian and Gary." He was spending more time out there since young Amos came by and did a very thorough power wash of warehouse and loading dock.

She crossed the yard, chuckling. The past couple of weeks flew by in a flurry of planning, phone calls, estimates and bids. Evidently, her dad liked having new pals to hang out with...and bossing them around. "When did they call?"

"While you were at the store. Brian called and asked if they could make a few trips with some of their whisky. He has some friends with a bigger truck. They don't have one of those great lorries like Tom does." He wiped his face with his shirt sleeve.

"You're not overdoing it are you?"

He laughed. "No, I'm just walking around trying to figure where to put a dozen barrels."

"That's quite a few for being so new." She joined him at the door.

"That's about what we did on average when we started. 'Course, we slowed quite a bit."

"Do you miss it, Dad?"

"Aye, I do. Not so much the hard work, but getting the final taste just right. That's pure joy."

"How do you know when you have it?" She followed him back to the damp storeroom with rows of whisky barrels standing proudly. The sheer number stunned her. How could they have forgotten?

"The original recipe from your great-great-grandmother spelled out exactly what the final test should be and what was needed to adjust it. Over the years, it's just got ingrained that I know by the look, smell, and taste just how to create that exactly."

Fiona put her arm around him. "Will you know if you lose that ability?"

"I certainly hope so." He laughed again.

"Do you think it something you need to write down?"

"It got written down a long time ago." He tapped the side of his head. "I have it committed right here."

"That's the part I'm worried about." She winked at him. "I think it's time for supper, so why don't we go in." They shut off lights and started up the ramp. "Is Murray back yet?"

"I expect he'll be back tomorrow. He's taking care of his debts. I told him he needed to square up for the things he's done." He held the door until she was out, then lowered it.

Fiona washed her hands and pulled several bags from the refrigerator. *What else had the man done?*

"Brian said he'd bring along a bottle of his whisky tomorrow with his first batch of barrels."

He'd washed up and changed his shirt, and even combed his hair some. Once settled in his chair at the end of the table, he started his pipe ritual. Fiona brought a pitcher of water and two glasses and sat across from him.

"Dad, I think this might be a good time for you

to let me know just what Murray has been doing all this time."

Her cell phone rang on the counter and she glanced over.

"You'd better get that, it might be important."

She checked the Caller ID. It was Bryce. "Hello?"

"Hi. Is this a good time?"

"Uh…I was just talking to my dad. Can I call you back in a bit?"

"Sure, no rush. Just wanted to catch up." Bryce sounded chipper.

"Okay, I'll call after we eat." She hated to put her off, but she felt it important to get more information about Murray's shenanigans. She returned to her chair. "It was Bryce checking in. Tell me more about Murray. I think I need a better understanding before we get too deep in this new venture."

He scowled a little and finished lighting his pipe. Again, the sweet smell transported her to an earlier time in this house. Her pretty, idyllic childhood.

"I told you about his rough beginning and losing his people and all. Well, one of the few pleasures and distractions for him while we were at sea got to be some cards or other games of chance. Worked fine when we were getting a check regular, but once we got home it wasn't so easy." He tapped off some ash and tamped his pipe a bit. "When we started here, the work kept us busy and the other lads were good company for a beer or game of quoits, but the past few years since Mary's gone…" He took a swallow of water and looked out at the trees.

Fiona squeezed his hand. "I understand."

"He took to disappearing, and then I found out he was piling up debts around town. I tried to help, but we just weren't making enough to spare." He looked up and there were tears in his eyes. "Just after the new year, I found a small barrel in the office. He'd been siphoning off whisky from some of the barrels, taking bottles, and selling it. He used some for the sleep tonic. I was furious and kicked him out. But after a few days, I had to find him because I needed help and most of the guys had quit."

Fiona sighed. What a mess. "I see. You had no choice, and neither did he. I wish you'd let me know. Still, this is not a great start to a new business. How do we know he can be trusted?"

"I guess you don't. That's why he had to go get the debt cleared up. I don't want them coming after us."

"That cannot happen. I'll need to think about this, but right now let's eat. You'll need to rest up if the boys are going to start reorganizing the warehouse tomorrow."

Once the dishes were done and the kitchen tidied, Fiona took her phone to the front porch and dialed Bryce.

"Hello?"

Hearing her voice caused a shiver. "Hi. I hope it's not too late."

"No, I was just doing some non-work-related reading for a change. After checking online, I realized how many bestsellers have come and gone in the past few years."

Fiona laughed. "Boy, you really do take your work seriously. What was the last film you saw?"

"Wow. I think that was *The Hurt Locker* at a hotel stay in Tokyo."

"You are seriously behind the times. Good thing

you're taking some leave."

"I'm beginning to enjoy it. What's happening with you?"

"Dad told Brian he could start bringing their whisky barrels over. I have no idea what they have in mind, but it's keeping him busy and engaged. We even had a good talk about the complex problems with Murray. I'll fill you in some other time, but it seems resolved."

"How are repairs going?"

Fiona propped her feet on the porch railing and gazed through the apple trees toward the road south to Bryce's cottage. It was only a few miles. "Brian found a team of guys who specialized in major renovations. They gave us their assessment and have been making great progress."

"That sounds great." There was a pause. "More importantly, how are you?"

Fiona felt herself blushing. "I'm well and busy and missing the *manager* of our project. It's weird that you're so close by…and, well, I'm thinking about you."

"You could come over if you'd like…"

The temptation pulled her, but she didn't trust herself when she felt so weak. "Not tonight, but I'd like a rain check. Do you think you'll be by tomorrow?"

"Count on it. I have got some errands to run over to Dufftown and need see Kurt, then I'll be over."

"Sleep well, Bry."

"Not sure I will, but I'll try. G'night."

Fiona stared at the phone and smiled. Bryce Andrews came into her life like a new-age wizard and made everything better. The fantasy of finding someone so wonderful had shriveled up years ago. And after her mum died and her dad disappeared, Fiona had grown resolved to her spinster life as a teacher. Not her dream. That was supposed to be a successful life as a professional musician. Now even that had changed. The summer holiday had begun, so her year was over. She called her superior to explain the circumstances and that she would not be back next semester. Now all that she needed to do was pick up her few belongings from the small flat, sign her resignation paper work, and say goodbye to her friends.

It had grown quite dark, so she went back in, closed the door, and switched off the light. The busy days trying to clean up the distillery were making for early nights. With all the new help, maybe she could entrust her dad to Bryce and Murray so she could run down to Edinburgh?

Chapter Forty-three

Thanks, Ian. I knew you'd have a solution. I'm not used to being on the managing end." Bryce scribbled a couple of notes on a legal pad. "So we need contracts signed from Townsend-McClure that they will sell and distribute their product with us within five years, or provide a new plan that allows for six months' notice to GDD. We also need an agreement between them and the MacDougalls about their work/storage exchange. Is that right?"

"Yes. Unless they have someone who can do that. And while it's not imperative right now, you need to talk to them about your responsibility to them and to GDD. Right now you're being compensated by the company, but if you become…more invested in the distillery, that will change things."

"I understand. I suppose you've had a similar conversation with Tom?"

Ian chuckled. "I believe Mr. Edelman has already done that."

"Great. I appreciate your valuable input. Would you email the documents?"

"Certainly. And Bryce, be sure you get some rest."

Bryce laughed out loud. "I've heard that somewhere before. Now that we've navigated this deal plus the other clients, I will take some time off."

After putting her notepad in her bag, Bryce paused and walked over to the small mirror by the door.

Do I look tired? Everyone seems to comment about it. A few more grey hairs and a few laugh lines…not so bad.

As she drew closer to the distillery, she slowed the car. No mistake. There was a young red-headed lad riding a tractor much larger than he was, dragging a mowing blade. He'd already cleared the south side of the driveway and was starting on the north side. It looked good. She waved as she passed him. He flipped off his cap in response.

Several cars and trucks crowded the space near the warehouse and office, so she pulled over under an apple tree near the front porch. With gloves in hand, she walked toward the office.

Fiona met her at the door. "Good morning."

"Hi. Busy place." She motioned to the road. "That kid's doing a great job."

"That's Gary's oldest, Robbie, aged twelve. His kids are out of school, so he asked if we'd let him help out a little."

Bryce's business brain clanged *Liability*. "Nothing dangerous, I hope."

Fiona laughed and pulled her into the office. "Worry-wart. Nope, just errands and tasks he's familiar with. Let me show you something."

Behind the desk on a newly painted wall, Fiona had installed two large whiteboards. One listed daily tasks with names after each. The other had a schedule for every day and who was working. Next to that was a list of weekly and monthly goals, as well as some shipping and receiving plans. "This is what I've been doing when I can't sleep." Fiona grinned proudly.

Bryce stood with her mouth open. "This is amazing."

Fiona sat behind the desk and straightened some

papers. "My dad had a rather loose system of doing things that relied on his memory." Her facial expression clearly explained her distaste for that method.

Good thing to know. "I'm sure this will save hours of worry. It looks great." Bryce moved around the desk to get a better look. "Where're you putting me, Boss?"

Fiona cocked her head. "I know where I'd like to put you..."

Bryce flushed hot and looked around. "Maybe we could take a long walk later?"

Fiona winked. "Certainly. Should I pencil that in?"

"No."

"Actually, when you are here and have checked what's going on, you can write in what you think needs to be done. I want both of us to manage this, not just me. I'm pretty good at organizing, but have no clue about the business."

"That sounds like a great plan." Bryce liked Fiona's initiative.

"I also asked Dad, Brian, and Gary to join us for Friday meetings." She tapped the papers together and looked up with a very self-satisfied and endearing grin.

It took some willpower not to lean over for a kiss her. Fiona must have had a similar thought, because the pause was too long and they both looked flushed.

Bryce moved closer to the door and smiled. "Gee, doesn't seem like there's much for me to do, maybe—"

"Not so fast. I need a favor." Fiona put down the papers. "I need to go to Edinburgh to close up my apartment and sign some papers at university. It will be quick, but still most of the day. I wondered if you'd be willing to watch over things, especially Dad. The boys are too new, and I can't trust Murray."

"No problem. I'd be around anyway. Just leave

some written instructions." She winked. "When do you want to go?"

"Wednesday okay?"

"Fine. Shall we go check things out?" Bryce pointed to the warehouse.

※ ※ ※ ※

Fiona washed her hands and started making sandwiches. So much had happened with the Townsend-McClure guys helping. It had only taken a few days for everyone to develop a routine. Before hauling over their barrels, Amos spent two full days with a power washer on the inside and out. It showed exactly where paint or varnish needed to be replaced. After they rearranged the racks to accommodate more, they moved their barrels into the cellar. They built shelves in the warehouse and installed new lights. When new equipment arrived, they'd have a place to put it. All this made her trip to Edinburgh a little less painful.

She set plates on the table for her dad, Bryce, and Murray. This had been invigorating for her dad and Murray, but they couldn't keep up with the younger crew and faded early in the afternoon. Fiona suspected the boys got more done after they left.

She brought some water over and sat looking out the window. It was exciting, and she felt good about the time and money they were spending from Bryce's loan. Sales profits helped defray some of the daily expenses. This never would have been possible without Bryce: her connections, her money, her ideas, and her personal support. She swiped at a tear. To think she had almost ruined everything with her temper.

Voices sounded from the yard, and she jumped up to get glasses for everyone.

Chapter Forty-four

I t looks like the equipment is all working, so what would you say to a trial run next week?" Brian sipped his beer.

Her dad fussed with his pipe a little too long. "Dad, what do you think about Brian's idea? I think it's time."

"Those motors haven't hummed so sweet for a long time. It's music to my ears," Murray said.

"What'd you have in mind to run?" Gavin asked.

Brian and Gary looked at each other. "Maybe just some pure spirits. We can sell that to the fellas workin' on their new gin creations." They both laughed.

"There's at least four of them around here," Gary added.

Gavin shrugged. "May as well. See if anything is off. Where do you fellas get your grain?"

"We have two sources we use near Dufftown for the barley, but there's some dealers that offer wheat as well. Do you have someone you prefer?"

Gavin chewed on his pipe stem. He glanced at Murray. "Where's the last we ordered from?"

Murray shook his head. "Uh, I'm not sure. I'd need to look at the invoices."

Bryce sat forward. "I think for the trial whatever's cheaper would work. Did you fellas decide which one you want to distill first?"

"I think that should be Gavin's choice. We both

have whisky aging in the barrels. Ours won't be ready for a few years…maybe you'd like to start with the Dew?"

Gavin looked around. "Let me sleep on that will you? I'll need to dredge up the recipe. I haven't used it in so long."

Fiona stood. "I think that should be our final question. Anything we missed?"

Brian and Gary, in turn, stood. "This has been great. Thanks again for giving us a chance to save our tiny enterprise."

Fiona and Bryce watched as the guys left. Murray and her dad wasted no time getting out of the crowded office. Fiona carefully put each file folder in its assigned space while Bryce took the glasses back to the house. When she returned, Fiona flipped off the lights and said, "Are you up for a leisurely walk in the orchard?"

✥ ✥ ✥ ✥

The intermittent rain and clouds had mostly quit, but left enough in the air to create a beautiful sky. Bryce smiled, thinking about the surprise she had waiting. Once clear of the cottages, Fiona had taken her arm as they walked. When they got to the small clearing with the large oak and bench, she let go and gasped. "Look at our bench. It's beautiful, did you do that?"

Bryce chuckled. "Not exactly. Robbie looked a little bored earlier this week so I found him some sandpaper and paint. Mercifully, it survived the rain."

Fiona's embrace and kiss were exactly the response she'd imagined. It sent a power surge that short-circuited her brain and flooded her senses with molten joy. She took Fiona's face in both hands gently and pulled her closer as she responded with a groan.

Suddenly, Fiona pulled back and put both hands on Bryce's chest. "Wait."

"What's wrong? Are you okay?" Bryce steered her to the bench. Maybe she was dizzy.

Fiona looked up with tears in her eyes. "Yes, I'm just…scared."

Bryce felt her heart pounding in her chest. "My God, tell me what's wrong."

Fiona stroked her face with her fingertips. "Very clearly we've passed the point of some casual affection. At least, I have. But we've never talked about it. About us. If there really is an us." She hesitated and took a deep breath.

"What are you scared of? I'm a little confused. Of course we can talk. About anything." The pleasurable sensations chilled instantly.

"Bryce. Together we've created a plan to salvage the business, and without you it never would have happened. Who knows if we'd ever have found the cache in the cellar." Fiona took her hand. "We'd likely be foreclosed, Dad would be in a care unit, and I would go back to teaching."

"I don't understand. I thought everything was going smoothly. What's upset you so?" This wasn't making any sense. Fiona was anxious, but it was hard to figure out why.

"When you got back from the States, you told me you were given an extended leave that would be a working holiday. And I was thrilled. But I didn't foresee this. This attraction growing…and so fast." She sat up and took a breath. Her face was still flushed but her eyes were dark forest green and focused. "Don't you see? Damn. I've fallen for you. Hard. And we've never discussed the relationship because it's happened so fast. And I'm not even sure how you feel, but we should have, and now we're at this awkward…I don't know what, and—"

Bryce took her by the shoulders. "Fiona, stop. You're not alone in this. We're partners. Remember? I told you the day I drove up your driveway and you stepped out of the house…at that moment, you took my breath away—it still does. I'm crazy about you. That's why I came back."

Fiona smiled a little. "I remember. What I guess I'm scared about is you leaving. When your leave is up, your company is going to send you somewhere else, and I don't want this to go any further and end up here without you." The tears brimmed over.

Bryce pulled her closer and held her. She felt terrible. She'd been just as self-absorbed as Reggie. Maybe worse because she'd hurt Fiona.

※ ※ ※ ※

The wind changed to the east and brought a chill. It was dark and still except for the hoot of a nearby owl. Fiona felt warm snuggled against Bryce, but they were both exhausted. They'd talked about a number of options and plans, and she felt slightly better about their mutual feelings, but the future was no more solid.

"We'd better head back. We both need rest." Fiona tugged Bryce to her feet.

"Good thing tomorrow is Saturday." Bryce put an arm around Fiona's shoulders.

Fiona pulled closer. "It might be safer for you to stay and sleep here."

Bryce kissed her forehead. "That's the good news, I live five minutes away. No long hauls on mystery roads. But…you could come with me."

"You're a wretched tease. I just can't leave Dad alone or have him asking where I was." Fiona felt an ache that had been long forgotten. "We have a lot to figure out, but it helps that we at least know this crazy attraction is real."

Bryce stopped and pulled her into an embrace and passionate kiss that took her breath away. "My feelings are genuine and heartfelt. I love you, Fiona, and I will find a way to make this work. I promise."

Fiona held tight to the magical moment. She was almost afraid to hold too tight for fear it might vanish. It helped to see Bryce's earnest expression. Her eyes were dark and her cheeks flushed. Even her voice sounded surprisingly hoarse. It surprised her.

So much of their relationship had been focused and businesslike. The softer side of Bryce Andrews held a different kind of passion and power. Fiona felt captured in a force field. A lovely one, to be sure. She smiled.

"I'm so very glad you came into my life." She caressed the side of Bryce's face and hair. "Sometimes I just have to pinch myself."

"I'd be happy to help you with that." Her hands slid across Fiona's hips as she nuzzled behind her ear.

Fiona gasped as she felt her knees weaken. Another kiss revived her. "We really should head back or I won't be able to."

Bryce smiled lasciviously and nodded toward the bench.

Fiona shoved her shoulder. "Come on, you evil temptress."

⚜ ⚜ ⚜ ⚜

Bryce opened all the windows in the car. The rain had left the air thick with moisture and although the temperature was cool, she mopped perspiration from her head and neck. Clearly the damn hormones were again asserting power over her. That started before she left California, but it had been irregular and mild. Her older sister had the same problem years ago.

Once home, she tossed her keys on the counter and made a beeline to the shower. Happily, she wasn't paying for water.

Thoroughly chilled, she donned a clean T-shirt and gulped a bottle of cold water. Once she's adjusted the ceiling fan, she stretched out on top of the bed and wondered if Fiona had needed a shower. She nodded off, smiling.

Chapter Forty-five

Fiona refilled her dad's coffee cup and glanced at her watch. "I have to run a couple of errands. Will you be okay here for a bit?"

"Och, ya worry too much. If it'll give you peace, I'll sit and read the papers until the lads get here."

She kissed his cheek. "I'll have my phone if you need me."

He chuckled and waved her goodbye.

At the bottom of the driveway, rather than turn right toward town, she turned left and accelerated. Her fingers were tight on the steering wheel. "Just take a breath. There is nothing to be nervous about. Bryce may be surprised, but she'll be fine." She had no sooner relaxed her grip when the small sign for the cottage appeared. Edging the car carefully down the driveway past the landlord's house, Fiona looked for any sign of activity. The guest house looked quiet. Maybe Bryce was still sleeping.

She parked the car near the steps and approached the front door quietly. After listening, she tapped on the door. When Bryce open the door, Fiona let out a breath she was holding. "Good morning, I hope it's not too early—"

"What a lovely surprise; please come in."

Fiona closed the door behind her and leaned against it. "I didn't sleep well last night. I just kept thinking about our conversation and how frustrated I was."

"I felt the same way. I even took a walk before I went to bed and it didn't help."

The air was heavy and the silence was oppressive. Fiona couldn't speak. Bryce stood before her in a well-worn T-shirt and boxer shorts. Her hair was rumpled with sleep, but her eyes were dark and her dry lips parted. Fiona stepped forward and slid both hands around her waist. She took a deep breath and slipped the T-shirt over Bryce's head. When it fell to the floor, she carefully touched the warm skin on a surprisingly muscular shoulder. Weeks of watching Bryce work side-by-side with Brian and Gary should have prepared her, but it didn't. "Could you...er...slip off the shorts. Please?"

Bryce's face reddened. With a loud gulp she obliged. "Fiona, I'm feeling a little embarrassed—"

"And turn around." Fiona could not believe what she was asking...or seeing. "Oh, mercy." Her body was perfect. Strong, toned, tan, and exquisite. "Were you a swimmer?"

Bryce spun back. "What?"

"A swimmer. Did you swim? You have that physique."

"Soccer."

Bryce put both hands up and pulled Fiona so close she could feel her warm breath. "Is it time for the kissing, or do you have another strange Celtic ritual?"

Fiona just shook her head.

"Then if you don't mind, I'm a little overstimulated right now."

Her kiss was soft, but quickly became hungrier. "I am, too." Kissing and tugging at her clothes made Bryce stop and laugh.

"Easy, tiger. I think we have time to do this right."

Fiona pulled back and kicked off her shoes. "YOU may have time, but I'm about ready to explode!"

Bryce pushed her toward the bedroom on the right. "Yes ma'am. Let's do it!"

⁂

Bryce followed her back to the house grinning like the Cheshire cat. Exhausted but temporarily sated. There was something to be said about being a little older: transcendent sex.

Fiona straightened her top when she got out of the car, and glanced at Bryce. Her coy smile and red cheeks said it all.

Chapter Forty-six

The next few weeks were chaotic and swift. Fiona's quick trip to Edinburgh resulted in cartons, bags, and a few pieces of furniture occupying a corner of the living room. She had no time to organize anything, and it made her feel crazy.

It seemed like lorries from somewhere arrived nearly every day delivering or retrieving something related to whisky. For the most part, Brian and Gary seemed to have a handle on the traffic.

The first run of the old still was successful and they quickly started another, since they had several orders for spirits.

Tom Hobart had made room in his schedule to take more of the Highland Dew for bottling. Once word got out that it was once again available, inquiries poured in.

Fiona was thrilled with the regular checks because she could start paying off some of Bryce's loan as well as paying for the work being done on the place. Even old Murray got a small salary—as long as he remained sober and debt-free. His sobriety had greatly enhanced his crusty personality.

Fiona laughed and unloaded the extra groceries. While it wasn't always necessary, she did enjoy offering some sandwiches or beverages to the hard workers making her father's dream come true.

When she wasn't checking on GDD's new

clients, Bryce had even asked to be involved in the process so she could learn each step. She helped unload the barley, set up the malting process, and played gopher whenever something was needed. She never complained, and by the end of the second week in the trenches had grudgingly earned a great deal of respect from the men.

Truth be told, that physical labor had done quite a bit for her physique. Her office-worker appearance had disappeared. She now looked strong, relaxed, and tanned. Most of all, happy. Hard work agreed with her. And the relaxed happy Bryce made Fiona happy.

Fiona put the last of the sliced meat away and went to wash her hands. Physical labor had never really held any appeal for her. Music and teaching were more her style.

From her window view of the yard, she could see Bryce and young Robbie pushing a heavy barrel toward the loading dock. A small thrill zinged through her. The growing intensity of their relationship seemed to parallel the intensity of the workload. She sighed and turned to her next chore.

❧❧❧❧

Bryce steered her car off the A9, onto the highway, and followed the signs to the Old Bridge Inn, where she had stopped on the start of her trip a few months earlier. She took the day to recoup and clear her head. Between her new chores in the distillery, checking in on Kurt and Dusty Hamilton, not to mention the distracting and tantalizing thoughts of Fiona, she needed a little perspective. Her solution: a road trip. It occurred to her that it might be a good plan to reintroduce a couple of her favorite barmen to the new release of Highland Dew.

She parked near the door to the inn and retrieved the two bottles of the Dew in a gift box with a note for Jamie Meigle. Happily, he was behind the bar.

"What can I do for you, miss?"

"Well, Jamie, I've got something for you." She set the box on the bar. "I wanted to report back to you about our search for a small, boutique whisky. Turns out it's been around over a hundred years, but recently disappeared. We're very proud to usher it back into circulation."

He opened the box and removed one of the bottles. After turning it and holding it up to the light, his expression changed to a big smile. "I think I remember this one! Verra popular." He opened the bottle and poured a sample into a tasting glass.

Bryce smiled at his joy. These old barmen knew their whisky.

"Oh, this is grand. Is it available now?"

"I left a card with the information. Currently, Speyburn is doing the bottling."

"Well, this is a verra fine gift. I appreciate it. Glad you stopped by again."

Bryce waved and headed out to her car. She drove south to Loch Alvie and followed the road to the small peninsula and the lovely Alvie Church.

After she parked, she pulled a water bottle from the cooler and hiked down to the loch. The morning clouds had dissipated, and the sun warmed the ground and made the water shimmer like jewels. The majestic hills surrounding the area made all the features around her seem smaller and protected.

Bryce sat near the water's edge and removed her

shoes. She relaxed her shoulders and inhaled as deeply as possible. The damp soil, the memorable lake smells, and the soft scent of pine trees filled the summer air.

Scotland truly was magical. It'd been so busy in the past few weeks, she'd forgotten her resolve to appreciate the land and the people. She smiled. *Well...I DO appreciate one of the people.*

Just the thought of Fiona made her blush. She'd have never believed her passion could be resurrected so easily. Working so closely the last few weeks just felt natural and easy—like they could read each others' mind. It was hard with her dad...or any number of people that were around all the time. Fiona did sneak down to her cottage some early mornings. They talked about getting away for a few days, but there was never a good time. Hopefully, the guys would be able to take charge of the production soon. Gavin permitting.

Chapter Forty-seven

Gavin had just finished his lunch and disappeared for a nap when Fiona heard a rap on the back door. "Come in." Fiona hung up the dishtowel and Brian stuck his head in.

"Hope I'm not interrupting."

"Nonsense, you're a part of the family now. Would you like something to drink?"

"Water would be great." He pulled the chair out from the table and used his sleeve to wipe his face.

She handed him the glass and took a seat. "How are things going?"

"Actually, we're a bit ahead of schedule. Gary and I thought Gavin might like to get started on a batch of the Highland Dew. We've got everything ready, we just need his recipe. I want to be sure where he gets his barley and malting." He had trouble hiding his excitement.

"That's wonderful. I can ask him as soon as he wakes up, and I'll let you know. That should make him and Murray very proud."

Brian finished the water and headed for the door. "Thanks again. Gary and I will be heading out in a bit, but you can call."

Fiona smiled. It was hard to believe it was finally going to happen. The family legacy was intact. She suddenly remembered her mum and how proud she was of their contributions. "Oh, Mum, I wish you were here to see this." Tears filled her eyes and she reached up to the shelf near the door for her mum's—and grandmother's—cookbook. Sometimes, just seeing her mum's handwriting made her feel the presence. The leather notebook was ancient and fragile. Pages of old recipes—some barely readable—dated back at least two or three generations. Scraps of envelopes, yellowed paper, and index cards marked favorites.

"Hello? Anybody here?" Bryce came in carrying a large bundle of wildflowers.

"Hi, you. What beautiful flowers."

"I got them especially for you," Bryce said and kissed her cheek.

Fiona crooked one eyebrow. "Should I be suspicious? Wait, these aren't from your other girlfriend, Helen, are they?"

Bryce laughed. "Caught me. I guess I have to confess. I stopped to see Billy at the Highlander and give him some of the Highland Dew. After all, he did introduce me to it. Then, of course, I had to drive through Archiestown to get here...and...well, Helen was in the square with way too many flowers to sell this late in the day, so..."

They both cracked up and Fiona hugged Bryce. "You're incorrigible."

Bryce held her at arms' length. "What's wrong? You've been crying."

"Nothing. I just got a little melancholy. Brian told me they're ready for a run of the Highland Dew and he needed the recipe from Dad. Just made me wish Mum was here to see this. She'd be so proud."

Bryce hugged her. "I'll bet she would. It's very exciting. Did Gavin remember what was in it?"

"Dunno. He's still napping."

Bryce grinned. "You know, when that batch is done, we should plan a celebration."

Fiona perked up. "That would be fantastic! We haven't done anything fun here in ages. We could get a tent…and music…"

"Hold on, missy. We have a lot to do yet."

"But there's no harm in jotting down a few ideas." Fiona took the flowers to the sink and began arranging the unwieldy bouquet. "These really are quite lovely. How was your trip?"

Bryce pulled out a chair and sat by the window. "You know, it was rejuvenating."

Fiona turned and simply shook her head.

"Really. I went to Aviemore to see Jamie Meigle at the Old Bridge Inn, and afterward I drove to the Cairngorms National Park and sat awhile by Loch Alvie. I was all alone and it was beautiful. It reminded me why I love being in Scotland." She stood and walked over to Fiona. "And I love working here with the guys. Making whisky is what I want to do…and I want to do it with you."

Fiona circled Bryce's waist with her arms. "That makes me so happy."

The moment was broken by the sound of Gavin whistling.

"Fi, what time will supper be?"

Fiona pulled back and went to the kitchen door. "I thought six, but I can give you something to tide you over if you like. Come sit down. I have some news."

Bryce remained at the sink arranging the flowers in the vase. "Afternoon, Gavin."

He waved. "Bryce."

Fiona concealed a smile. "Brian came by while you were napping, and said they were ready to run the Highland Dew. All he needed was your notes and recipe. I told him I'd ask."

Gavin cleared his throat and gazed out the window with an odd look on his face. It almost looked like fear.

"Dad? Are you all right?"

"Aye. Here's the thing, Fi. It was such a long time since we were putting out the barrels. Once the last shipment went out, things started coming undone. I wracked my brain trying to remember how we did those things and I can't. I've begged Murray to see if he can. But, it's all a blur."

"Gavin, are you saying you don't know how you got the special effect that made your whisky unique?" Bryce looked incredulous. She pulled out a chair next to him.

"I've really tried. I know it was on the original piece of paper along with the changes, but I don't remember where we kept it."

Fiona felt her heart in her throat. She covered her mouth to keep from shouting. This wasn't happening. Everything they'd recreated, all the work, the new agreement with Brian and Gary, the contract she'd signed. What were they going to do? She looked at Bryce, who had started pacing around the kitchen.

"Okay." Bryce took a deep breath. "There must be a solution. If the piece of paper is around, can you think where you might have needed it to reference. In the office, the malting floor, the office safe?"

Gavin wiped his mouth and tried to speak. "I…I just don't remember."

"Okay. Why don't we walk over and take a look around? How would that be?" Bryce sounded marginally calm.

❧❧❧❧

All three marched across the yard as though walking to the gallows. Bryce knew her heart rate had doubled. In all her planning and troubleshooting, of all the "what-ifs" she'd planned for, she never dreamed they'd be unable to produce the magical whisky. Her career would be over. *Patience.* They could figure this out. "Fiona, why don't you go get Murray to help. I'll start the search with Gavin."

For the next two hours, the four of them went through every drawer, cupboard, shelf, crevice, ledger, and file. They found a number of production notes which might help a little. But not the one they needed.

"Miss, do you remember you asked me what the arguing was about between me and your da?" Murray said meekly.

"Yes! Out in the yard. You wanted to know where he put the envelope." Fiona seemed revived and excited.

"That's what I was asking himself. Where he put the envelope with the recipe." Murray shook his head. "I'm awful sorry I don't know how to help. I never worked on that part of the job. It's too complicated, you know."

Fiona patted his shoulder. "It's all right, Murray. You tried. But, if you think of anything, I want you to come get me immediately."

He simply nodded and headed back to his cottage.

"There's nothing more we can do today. Let's try another tack tomorrow," Bryce said.

Gavin moved toward the driveway. "I think I'll sit on the front porch awhile. Might remember something." He trudged dejectedly across the yard.

Fiona grabbed her arms. "What are we going to do? I just feel sick. Why did we not think about all the steps first? This is a disaster, and what was Murray going to do with the recipe if he found it anyway?"

Bryce put an arm around her shoulder. "Let's take a walk. I think I might have an idea to work out."

Chapter Forty-eight

Tom and Liam, I am so grateful you'd take your day off to come and help." Bryce shook hands with both men.

Tom smiled. "You did sound a little tense and worried. Let me see if I understand the problem. You're ready to run the first batch of the Highland Dew, but there's a problem with Gavin's specifics?"

"That's about it. Gavin doesn't remember the specifics. I haven't told him you were coming yet. I wanted to be sure this might work, and I think Liam is the only one who can answer that."

"Answer what?" Fiona came up from the office. "Hi, Tom. Liam."

Bryce looked around. "Okay. Since Liam is the Master Distiller and has tasted each of the whiskies in the cellar, I thought he might be able to walk Gavin back through the steps and have him describe them verbally. I know his memory isn't great, but physical memory might be better."

Tom nodded. Liam spoke up. "I think it's worth a try. I know for myself that I do a lot of my tasks by rote. If you asked me how I did it, I might not remember."

Fiona looked skeptical. "It makes sense, but I don't know if Dad will feel pressured."

"How about if he just goes with Liam? Slow and easy. No pressure. And anything he can describe will be helpful."

Fiona agreed. "Let me explain it and bring him out. Bryce, why don't you and Tom meet me on the front porch?"

Bryce got Tom a beer and they settled in expectantly.

"This doesn't have to be a problem." Tom took a swallow and leaned back in the wooden rocker. "If we know his barley purveyor, his cooper, and can figure out any malting quirks, we should be able to replicate the product. The water's the same and the storage the same." He smiled at Bryce. "Good call to bring Liam in. There's nobody better to identify subtleties of taste. Believe me. He studied those samples you sent and was really impressed with the nuances."

"That's what I'm hoping. Sure would be nice to have Gavin's notes, though." Bryce sipped her beer into the resulting silence.

⁂

Fiona paced in the kitchen. She didn't want to talk. She wanted her dad to have a moment of clarity and remember how he did his life's work for so many years, or at the very least, where he put his notes.

The hands on the clock didn't move. She wiped every surface for the third time when she heard voices at the back door. "Bryce," she called through the living room.

Her dad walked in, followed by Liam. "I really enjoyed working with you, but I think we're done for today." He laughed. "At least I am. Will you excuse me?"

He shuffled off toward his room, and passed Tom and Bryce in the living room.

"Please sit down," Fiona said. "Can I get you a beer or something else, Liam?"

"I'd really like a beer. Thanks."

The tension was thick, and no one wanted to ask. Finally, Fiona couldn't stand it any longer. "Was he able to remember anything?"

Liam took several swallows of the beer and sighed. "Yeah, he did pretty good. I guess he's been doing the same with the new lads. Explained some of the history that changed. They originally used apple wood to heat the malt. Probably added a nice flavor. And he still can discern the taste he wants."

He took another drink. "Unfortunately, he's pretty vague on some of the details. I think I might be able to reconstruct some information by taking a careful look at the next barrel that comes to us for bottling. Maybe one of the 1998 ones. If I can check the barrel and take apart the layers in the whisky, I might have a better handle on what's missing. No guarantee, though."

Bryce smiled. "That's a really good start. I hoped you could figure some of this out. Man, you're good."

"Will it be enough to make the Highland Dew?" Fiona asked.

"I think we'll just have to try a batch and then make adjustments if necessary. Then try again," Tom said.

Bryce stood as both Tom and Liam did. "We'll keep looking. Thank you both for coming. I'm sure Leo would say the same."

As their car left, Fiona started to cry.

"What's wrong? We got some good information." Bryce came over and sat beside her.

"I don't know. I'm relieved but still scared this

will all blow up."

"I know how you feel, and I'm worried, too. But you know, we might be able to blend the new whisky in three years with some of the older stuff. We'd have to call it something different, but that could work." Bryce stood up and stretched. "If it's okay with you, I think I'll go out to the office and go through some of the old invoices to see who their original purveyors were. Who knows, they might remember somebody who worked here back then who remembers some details."

"That's a good idea. I never would've thought of it." Fiona started making a list on a piece of paper. "Since you'll be around, I'm going to run over to the store and get a few things. Tomorrow is Dad's birthday, so I want to make him something special. Maybe you could bring those files into the kitchen so you could listen for him?"

"Sure, I can do that. You take your time." Bryce kissed her forehead and left for the office.

Fiona finished her list and grabbed her shopping bags and purse. She stopped. "If I don't check that recipe, I'll be kicking myself." She dropped her stuff and snatched her mum's cookbook off the shelf and dropped it on the floor. It bounced and dozens of small and large pieces of paper flew everywhere.

"Dammit to hell! What else can go wrong?" She swiped tears from her eyes and swept all the papers into a pile and slapped them on the table. "This can wait." A quick look at the recipe and she was out the door.

Bryce waved as she sped down the driveway.

Chapter Forty-nine

Bryce spent an hour going through the accounting records. Once she had a few names, she went through the file folder marked "1990s." It was a thick folder. What she wanted was a name or an address for the companies that provided the barrels, barley, or other services.

After an hour, she had found a few leads. She got up to get a drink and noticed the mess of paper at the other end of the table. Fiona must have been in a hurry to leave such a mess.

She dug in the fridge for a beer, and sipped it while she stared at the mess on the table. "Aw, be a sport and clean that up."

First, she separated them in to piles by similarity—age, handwriting, size. Some of the older ones intrigued her. Small delicate handwriting with a fine-pointed fountain pen. Mysterious ingredients with odd measurements. A few must have been in Gaelic. She set three plain envelopes aside.

Bryce just started to look through the cookbook for strays when she heard the car door slam, and Fiona clattered up the steps with some noisy packages.

"Here, let me help." Bryce held the door and took the bag heavy with beer.

"Thanks. That took longer than I planned." She set bags all over the counter and table. "I ran into Bert Coe in the parking lot. He worked for Dad—at least, oh, twenty years ago. I was still in secondary school." She handed Bryce items for the fridge. "Apparently, he moved to Edinburgh eight years ago and apprenticed in one of the large bottling companies. Just retired and moved back."

"How closely did he work with your dad?" Bryce folded up bags and stowed them under the sink.

Fiona smiled. "Exactly what I wondered. I asked him to come by next week to surprise Dad and catch up on old times."

"He might be able to help." Bryce picked up her notes. "I found a couple of names and numbers: one for a fella at the Speyside cooperage and the other at Crisp Maltings. That was listed as barley." She shrugged. "Maybe this guy Bert could shed some light."

"Shed light on what? We got another mystery?" Gavin stood in the doorway with his cane.

"Come, sit. We were doing some detective work to find out about your suppliers hoping that might help." Bryce pulled out his chair.

"What's all this?" He picked up a stack of recipes.

"I dropped Mum's cookbook and Bryce was kind enough to pick up the mess. I wanted to make you something special for your birthday."

Bryce brought a bottle from the living room. "Would anyone care for a dram before dinner? All this talk about making whisky made me thirsty."

They all took a seat and sipped some Highland Dew while Fiona and Bryce took turns telling Gavin what they had found out about suppliers and Bert coming to visit. All the while, Gavin was picking through the scraps of paper and reading the notes. His eyes misted up as he read notes from Mary and from his mother.

"You okay, Dad?"

"There's a lot of our history just in these old notes and recipes, Fi. I'm glad we kept them." He opened one of the envelopes and found a handful of snapshots from Fiona's childhood. He handed them to her. Another envelope held a small amount of cash.

"What do you suppose Mary was saving this for?"

Fiona was explaining the photos to Bryce when her dad slapped the table.

"These are my notes!"

Chapter Fifty

By Monday afternoon, it was all-hands-on-deck. Bryce had set up a schedule and an outline of what they needed in order to start a new batch of Highland Dew. Assembled around the table were Gavin, Brian, Gary, Fiona, and Bert Coe. While Gavin and Bert were trying to put together a list of what they needed, Brian and Gary were reviewing the invoices from Crisp Maltings, and the Speyside cooperage.

Bryce went outside to take a phone call from Liam. "Okay, I have some paper. Go ahead."

"From what I could figure out, they've always used oak Bourbon barrels. The six special-edition barrels were sherry casks. Here's the oddity—in the oldest samples, I can just barely detect apples."

"You know, that was the first thing I noticed when I did the blind test. I really think that was what made it unique." Bryce shook her head and smiled. She had underlined the word "apples." "We have found the source for the barley and the barrels. It looks like sometime in the early nineties they started using the maltings from Crisp. For a while, they did a few small batches here using a combination of coal and apple wood."

"That's interesting. I also think that was detectable in the Distiller's Edition."

"I need to get back. As soon as we can, we're

going to start the first batch. Keep your fingers crossed that we've got all the ingredients we need."

"Let me know."

Bryce reported Liam's comments, and when she mentioned the apple flavor, Gavin smiled and nodded. He began messing with his pipe, which meant a story was coming. Fiona winked at Bryce. Now conditioned, Brian and Gary sat back for the story.

"When all this started back in the early part of the eighteen hundreds, makin' whisky was illegal. Hell, the monks were distilling spirits since the sixteen hundreds. Anyway, your great-great-granddad got caught and fined so many times that he quit. He started making cider from the apples in this valley. Got away with that, so he tried aging it a bit more and made some good hard cider. They had to build a bigger cellar to keep it.

"When things cooled down, your great-great-grandmother helped set up the still and started making whisky. Stored the barrels right behind the cider." He laughed. "Granddad was in the clear. She kept all the records hidden. When their boy married, his wife learned the secrets from Great-grandmother. Eventually, they paid the excise men for a license."

"So that's how the recipe ended up in the cookbook," Fiona said.

"No one would think of lookin' in a woman's cookin' stuff."

Bryce nudged her. "Good thing you tossed it on the floor." Laughter broke out.

"That was an accident!" Fiona argued.

"A heavenly accident, I'd say." Gavin winked at her.

The next few weeks flew by in acute anticipation. There was still work to be done, and Speyburn sped the number of barrels they bottled to the maximum capacity they could muster alongside their own product.

Fiona fought between elation and panic. They had designed and ordered a new sign, and Bryce had just gone down to direct the installation of two large sign posts.

With fall around the corner, Fiona busied herself with young Robbie planting new flowerbeds and adding decorative stone. And since the men had power washed the house, she wanted to get the trim painted. All the while, in the back of her head, she weighed several options that might give her and Bryce a way to live together. It frustrated her to say goodbye every evening and watch Bryce drive the few miles to her cottage. Her fantasy was to add onto the house, or build a separate house for her dad—or for them. As the sales increased, the financials ceased to be a worry.

Bryce came running from the office. "It's time."

"For what?"

"Your Dad's gonna check the second distillation." She stopped and hugged Fiona. "Come on."

"I'm not sure I understand."

"I don't know the particulars, but a sample in the spirit safe is being tested to be sure that the amount of alcohol being produced is between sixty and seventy percent."

Fiona laughed. "Well, that helps."

When they got into the still room, Gavin was standing at the spirit safe with Brian, whispering and fiddling. They were both smiling. Brian stepped back. "It looks like we're on schedule. Time to start filling some casks."

Gavin leaned down to them, grinning. "Too early to tell for sure, but it looks good. I'll stay to switch it, then I think we should celebrate. How about we go somewhere for dinner?"

Fiona and Bryce looked at each other. "Why not?"

"Let's ask Brian and Gary," Bryce said. "I know they have family to get home to, but maybe for a drink."

It was settled, and Bryce offered to make a reservation at the Highlander Inn so they could tell Billy.

Fiona and Bryce walked back to the house. Fiona finally admitted to feeling relaxed. "Do you think we could talk about inviting a few people to celebrate this?"

"You realize it'll be at least three years before we really know how this will taste."

"Yes. But we solved the mystery, and we have whatever information Dad can give us. I think we should thank the people who've helped us."

Bryce smiled. "You're right. We can start making lists. Say, do you think I should contact Helen?"

Fiona shoved her forward. "Arse."

Chapter Fifty-one

The fall weather in the Speyside region turned everything rich and golden. The distillery buildings were restored and painted. Even the house looked warm and welcoming. The flowerbeds were neat, the bushes trimmed, and the porch furniture repaired and stained. Fiona had marked out a special area in the apple orchard for chairs and tables. She hoped to provide tastings and simple snacks.

Meanwhile, Bryce had been busy on the phone with local and American distributors. She wanted to be sure the official rollout of their product would be well received. Tom Hobart assured her he'd have samples ready.

Brian and Gary had been working on a secret project in the warehouse. The whole building was off-limits for weeks.

Gavin checked on the production every day to be sure those barrels were treated like new babies. While still a little unsteady, Gavin MacDougall was once again feeling the pride of his heritage. John MacDougall, and especially his wife Helen, had started small and struggled mightily; in the end their legacy had survived. He was especially proud of Fiona. She had assumed the mantle of responsibility, and had grown into a very efficient manager.

Bryce was up early checking her notes. Tom had promised he'd get the new bottles there by noon.

"Sign. Right." She dialed the local rep. "Hi, this is Bryce Andrews. I'm checking on the sign installation for the MacDougall Distillery? That'll be perfect." She had driven to Elgin to be absolutely sure that the sign looked exactly as she'd ordered.

Next call was the Taste of Speyside in Dufftown. She'd enjoyed eating there and the owner was thrilled to put together some options for lunch. When she hung up, she looked at her watch. Billy had promised to order some Champagne and she needed to check on that, too.

"Hello, may I speak to Billy? This is Bryce Andrews."

"Oh yes, he said if you called to tell you the wine is in the coolers and he'll be there by noon."

"Thanks."

She changed clothes and got ready to drive over to the celebration.

❧ ❧ ❧ ❧

Fiona finished sweeping the porch and smiled at the spot-on appearance of the whole place. When she heard a car, she stuck the broom in the house and went out to greet Bryce. When she rounded the corner, there was a bright red convertible parked and two unfamiliar figures getting out. It only took a moment to recognize Reggie Ballard.

"Hi, Fiona. We just had to come by and congratulate you on your success," she drawled. "Bryce told me that the MacDougall Distillery was back in business." She handed Fiona a bouquet of roses.

"I wasn't expecting—"

"Oh, this was a surprise for me, too. Let me introduce my good friend Matt Takata. He's with Suntory—BIG distributors."

"How do you do." He bowed and shook her hand.

"We're awfully busy today…is there something I can do for you?

"We don't want to keep you, but Matt asked if you might be interested in a proposition?"

Fiona felt completely blindsided. "A what?"

He took a step closer. "I have looked into your business and your remarkable product Highland Dew. I realize you have been working with Global Distillers and Distribution, and I am prepared to double their offer per barrel. Cash."

Fiona staggered backwards and bumped into a porch step, where she promptly sat. "What are you saying?"

Reggie sat beside her and gently explained. "Suntory would like to represent you at twice the rate Global offered."

"But…don't you work for Global?"

Meanwhile a truck and a van pulled in delivering supplies for the party. Brian was directing the table and chair placement while Murray was busy moving chairs.

"Well, yes, but I'm acting as a kind of consultant."

"We certainly don't want to intrude, but once I discovered this treasure I did not want to wait, you understand," Mr. Takata interjected.

Fiona spotted Bryce's car in the distance. "Yes, I do. Why don't you both come inside and I'll find my father. He's the one you need to talk to." She ushered them both into the living room. "I'll be right back."

She hurried out the back door as Bryce drove up and stood staring at the red sports car. "Don't tell me, your dad bought a new car." She started to laugh.

Fiona shushed her and hustled her to the office. "I want you to remain calm and listen. That car belongs to Matt Takata, I think, from Suntory."

"What?"

"Just listen. He was brought here by Reggie. And just offered me twice what GDD is offering."

Bryce's face turned crimson and she began to stammer.

"Stop. I have not said anything, yet. They are in the living room waiting to meet Dad so he can tell them about MacDougall Distilling." She grinned. "I thought they might like to talk to Tom Hobart about their offer when he gets here."

Bryce sat down in the office chair and whistled. "Boy, they might even be happy to talk to Ian. How do we keep them in there?"

"Leave it to me." Fiona smiled and winked.

❧ ❧ ❧ ❧

"Just set the chairs over there around the long table," Fiona said.

She was lucky the town church had some extra tables and chairs. They didn't charge, but Fiona put cash in an envelope as a donation. She waved as the volunteers finished setting them. There were enough seats for twenty people. She had figured fifteen or so, depending on how many Brian invited.

Gary arrived with the plates and utensils.

"Hi. I'm so glad you're here."

He set the box down. "Is there something else I

can do??"

"Let's put those on the table." She took some of the plates and napkins. "Brian is holed up in the warehouse and won't divulge your secret plans."

"I'll go see what he's doing. Brian told me his family would ride over with mine in a little while."

Bryce came out of the office just as a car pulled in, and she waved. "It's the food." She jogged over to help carry trays while Fiona cleared off the food table. Then she introduced her. "Fiona, this is Karen, who was kind enough to drive over. This is Fiona MacDougall, manager of the business."

They took out several trays, all covered with plastic wrap. Everything looked delicious. All different small sandwiches, and other finger foods and pastries.

"These are all okay without refrigeration if it doesn't get too warm. You might want to put towels over to be safe."

"Thank you so much. We'll get those trays back to you." Bryce handed her a check and some cash.

They'd just waved goodbye when a van pulled up, and out jumped Billy. "Champagne delivery, ma'am."

Brian and Gary came up just in time to help with the coolers. "Any beer in there?" Gary asked.

"Matter of fact, there is." Billy clapped him on the back.

Bryce leaned over and whispered, "Are they still in there?"

"Yup, I asked Dad to explain the distillery history to them. Should take a while." She smiled. "Besides, their car is blocked in."

"So, what's the big secret, Brian?" Bryce asked when he passed her.

"Oh, you'll find out in a bit."

In rapid succession, the families arrived, followed by two of the guys from their cleaning crew. Everyone gathered under the trees and introduced themselves.

"Fiona, I'd like you to meet Kurt Morgan and his wife Katie. They are the token American distillers around here."

Fiona grinned. This was exactly what she hoped for. Family. She glanced over her shoulder to the front porch and spotted Gavin puffing on his pipe and gesturing to his bored guests, who looked a little shocked.

"Come over and meet everyone, Dad."

"We will in a bit," Gavin said.

Another van arrived, and Tom Hobart stepped out and waved. Bryce went to meet him. Fiona watched as they stood near the back of the van and whispered. A horn interrupted them and Bryce trotted off down the driveway.

"Hi, I'm Barbara Townsend, Brian's wife. This is our daughter, Tabitha."

"It's so nice to finally meet you. I can't tell you how much we enjoy working with Brian." Fiona shook her hand.

Tom came over. "Hi, Fiona. So nice of you to invite us. Liam will be a little late—I made him work. Oh, there's Gavin. Who is he talking to?"

"A surprise. That's Matt Takata from Suntory, and GDD's own Regina Ballard. We're hoping Ian will be here soon. We thought all of you would enjoy hearing what Matt and Reggie have to say."

Fiona uncovered the trays and encouraged everyone to grab a plate.

Bryce returned, breathless. "Whew. That was the sign installer…"

"I want to go see," Fiona said.

"Hold on. I'd like to wait a little. I was hoping Ian could be here. Let's wait till everyone has gotten something to eat and we'll open the bubbly. Okay?"

"I suppose. I'm just so excited to see it."

"Promise. You won't be disappointed. Where's Tom?"

"Up talking to Dad and our surprise guests." She pointed. "Let's open some of the Champagne."

Billy had joined the men on the porch, so Fiona and Bryce started to open bottles. Another car pulled in and parked closer to the house.

"It's Liam," Bryce said and waved. "Let's hand these out." She took a few glasses to the guests and Fiona started with those at the tables. When everyone was served, Fiona handed one to Bryce. "Here's to us. We actually pulled this off."

Bryce smiled. "Yes." She looked around. "What an adventure this has been."

"I'll say. I hope the ends definitely justified the means." She winked.

They clinked glasses and drank.

A black Range Rover pulled in. With the tinted windows, Fiona couldn't see who it was.

Chapter Fifty-two

"Here, hold this. I'll check. Are you watching the company?" Bryce started for the car as Ian Smith emerged. "Ian, I'm so glad you came."

Fiona joined her. She hadn't met him, but had heard so much about him. He did look like a proper British squire.

"Hello, Bryce. I've brought you a surprise." He pulled open the back door, and Leo Edelman stuck his head out and slowly stood.

"Oh, my God." Bryce stumbled. She walked over and embraced him. "How…when did you…I don't—"

"When Ian called to tell me the good news, I had no choice. This is worth celebrating, so I came as a surprise."

"How in the world…?" She hugged him tightly.

"Are we in time to help celebrate? Oh, this must be Fiona." He took her hand.

Fiona stood with her mouth open. Bryce's boss came all the way from the States for their little celebration. "I'm so glad to meet you. Bryce says such wonderful things about you."

"She's been a very special member of the family." He took Fiona's arm. "Do you think you might find me something to drink?"

"Of course, but we have another surprise." She quickly explained the surprise visit and the offer, and steered them to the porch. From a distance, she could see the color drain from Reggie's face as she whispered to Takata. Bryce was already there with some Champagne.

Leo climbed the steps slowly. "Ms. Ballard, this certainly is a surprise. Here to congratulate Bryce? And Matt, I haven't seen you in years. But I guess a leopard seldom changes his spots. Hoping to cash in?"

"Leo, good to see you looking so well. I heard you had some medical issues."

Leo turned to Tom Hobart and asked, "Do you remember the case law on...what was it, Ace Distribution VS Global in 2001?"

Tom recited the case like an experienced jurist. It was a similar incident where a company tried to poach a client and ended up losing their license and paying an enormous fine.

Leo smiled. "Mr. Takata, I hope my message is clear, because my understanding is that Ms. MacDougall and her father are not interested in your illegal offer." He walked over to Reggie and put an arm on her shoulder. "Reggie, disappointed is not a strong enough word. I will expect your resignation on my desk in the morning." He turned and walked down the steps. "Tom, I think we should have a chat."

❧ ❧ ❧ ❧

Bryce moved cars to let the unwanted guests depart. Reggie tried to talk. "Bryce, this was all a terrible misunderstanding. We've been close for so long, and I know I can explain if..."

"Leave. Now."

Reggie grabbed her arm. "Bryce, please. We've known each other for a long time and you know how much I care about you. Can't you please just listen? For all we've shared, you must know how jealous I get."

Bryce shoved her behind the red convertible and grasped her shoulders. She took a deep breath to keep from screaming or striking Reggie. In a low voice, she growled, "Wasn't it enough that you nearly derailed this whole deal and my relationship with Fiona? But, you had to fuck over the whole company including Leo? With Suntory? What the hell were you thinking?"

"I guess I wasn't thinking clearly," Reggie mewled.

"Get out, and don't ever contact me again."

"Oh, Bryce, you are being so unfair when I all I've ever done is try to help you."

Bryce opened the car door. "You need to get some help, Reggie. You're a sick woman.'

Most of the guests had no idea what transpired, and Billy did a great job keeping plates and glasses full. Few even noticed the red sports car racing down the driveway.

For the next hour, Bryce poured Champagne and introduced Leo to all the players. He was especially delighted to see Billy again. He took some time talking to both Brian and Gary—who looked star-struck that he'd come over to them. Finally, she introduced him to Gavin. The two men connected immediately. Two seasoned whisky veterans.

At one point, Tom tapped his glass. "Could I have your attention? Before I forget, I'd like to introduce the new ad campaign for the Highland Dew." Liam brought over a box, and Tom pulled out a bottle with the new label for McDougall Family's Highland Dew. Everyone oohed and ahhed.

He then pulled out a bottle of the Distiller's Edition 1989. Even Gavin was stunned. It was even more detailed, with gold lettering.

"How did you…?" Gavin asked.

Liam said, "Remember when I asked to test a cask from the older run? Well, since we had it, thought we may as well bottle it. So, we have three hundred bottles for a special advance release." He opened the carton and pulled out four of the Distiller's Edition and five of the 1998 batch.

Even Leo was flabbergasted. "Good work, fellas. I hope one of those is for me." Bryce picked one up and took it to him.

Fiona followed suit and handed one to her father. "This is for you. Your living legacy."

He wiped tears from his eyes with his handkerchief and sniffed. "I thought we were done for. That, all this"—he waved his arm—"was gone. The MacDougall family heritage would end on my watch." He took Fiona's hand. "You believed when I didn't. You resurrected this place." He motioned to Bryce. "Without you, Bryce…your support, your ideas, your many connections to all these people…it wouldn't have happened."

The tears fell freely for him and his extended family. He held up the bottle and everyone else hoisted a glass. "Slainté."

Bryce wiped her face. "There's one thing more. If you'll all follow me down the driveway. Ian, would you take Gavin and Leo in that golf cart?"

When they were all gathered. Bryce took hold of a large drape covering the new sign. "This is the dawn of a new day."

The bright white sign with dark green lettering read: MacDougall Family ~ Distillers of Fine Whisky, Est.1870.

And hanging below on brass chains and smaller

sign which read: Townsend & McClure, Ltd.

Brian and Gary stood slack-jawed then high-fived each other and hugged. "This is awesome," Brian said. "We have a little surprise, too. Since our whisky won't be ready for some time, and it's important to get the Dew up and running, we started a little enterprise in a small section of the cellar. We are aging some cider in small oak barrels and plan to sell it."

A laugh rippled out. Then Gavin said, "Very enterprising and clever. I think you might have a great idea to help the young whisky."

They all applauded and gradually moved back up to the house.

Bryce and Fiona lingered by the sign.

"It's beautiful, Bryce. How did you get it so perfect? I love the green and white. And what a nice thing for Brian and Gary."

"I worked with Tom's designer so the sign and the label would match. He's got a whole ad campaign ready for the whisky."

"But when did you have time to do all this engineering?"

"Actually, I think Ian and Tom were in cahoots. I'm sure Ian dangled the idea in front of Leo, which made it irresistible."

Fiona stopped and looked up at the crowd. "We have quite an extended family, don't we?"

Bryce paused. "And a lot of responsibility."

Fiona took her arm. "I think we'll be okay. We have quite a team behind us. You know, Leo looks nothing like I imagined. Dad really likes him."

"Good thing." Bryce laughed. "He was the man behind this whole strange artisanal whisky thing. Bet he'll want to showcase this for the trade show next year."

"Bryce, will you be able to talk to him while he's here about your future? I'd sure sleep better if I knew."

"Let me see how long he'll be staying. I could drive down to Glasgow to meet with him. Or wherever."

Brian and crew drove down and stopped. "Thanks for everything. This was just mind-boggling. We're so honored to be part of this legacy. We'll see you Monday."

"Thanks for your hard work. See you."

Gary was right behind and waved. "Thanks, you guys."

When Bryce and Fiona reached the porch, they noticed the Champagne had stopped flowing and the whisky bottles were open.

Leo was holding court. Tom, Liam, and Ian were seated at one of the tables. Billy was loading his van. Gavin and Murray were nowhere in sight.

"Let me thank Billy, and I'll be back." Bryce trotted to the van. "You were so great to come out here and bring this great Champagne. Please take the rest back with you."

"Bryce, this was great. I'm so happy for you, and I was thrilled to see Leo again. Pressured him a little to come by the inn."

"You know none of this would ever have happened if you had not blind-tasted the Highland Dew—our Cinderella whisky," Bryce said.

He laughed. "That was only the beginning of your adventure. You made some solid connections and helped several people along the way. You should be proud of what you accomplished."

She waved as he drove away. It was true—so much had happened in the past few months. But the job wasn't quite done. She hoped Leo would see fit to let her stay. Not just for her sake, but for Fiona and her father.

The men were standing and ready to leave.

"Bryce, I'd like to meet with you, Tom, Liam, and Ian next week. Ian can call with specifics. I'm very proud of you and all you've done here for Global, as well as all the other people. The MacDougalls are exactly the people I want to represent. Now you get some rest."

"Yes, sir. Thank you so much for coming all the way over. It means the world to me that you were here to share it."

Leo nodded, and Ian patted her shoulder. "Well done, my dear. I think we'll be talking soon." She watched them as they disappeared in the dusk.

Fiona came over and put an arm around her waist. "What a day."

Bryce draped an arm across her lover's shoulders. "You said it."

"Let's go sit on the porch." Fiona pulled her along.

When they got there, she noticed a glider. "Where did that come from?"

Fiona laughed. "Believe it or not, Murray found it out back and he fixed it, sanded it, and stained it. He brought it over earlier."

Bryce sat. "And we can both sit together."

"Shocking, I know." Fiona sat and put her arm around Bryce.

"Is your dad…?"

"Oh, he's in an excitement coma. I went in to check on him. He's snoring. This day wore him out. But, Bryce, I've never seen my dad so happy." She leaned over and kissed Bryce just below her ear, then her neck.

"Are you sure you want to do that?" Bryce moaned.

"More than anything." She continued down to the shirt collar, which she pulled away.

Bryce closed her eyes and felt her insides melting. Even breathing was difficult.

Fiona unbuttoned the first two buttons and kissed across Bryce's chest.

"I'm having a little trouble not fainting…"

"I'll catch you. Let. Go." She slipped her hand under the shirt. "Bryce, I don't want to lose you. Ever," she whispered.

Bryce could barely make her mouth work. "Why would you…oohhh…lose me."

"What if Leo wants to send you back?" She caressed one breast gently.

The fog began to clear, and Bryce stopped Fiona's hand. "Wait. Did he say something to you?"

"No. It's just that I overheard the guys talking about what an incredible asset you are to the company."

Bryce shook her head clear. "I'm not sure that means anything. I'll know more when I meet with them." She sat up and took Fiona's shoulders. "There are two things that are for certain. I love you more than anyone I've ever known, and I do not ever want to be away from you. And two, I'm proud to work for Leo and I'm grateful for all the opportunities he's given me, but I will quit tomorrow if it means leaving here." She pulled her close and kissed her deeply and passionately.

Fiona opened her eyes and took a breath. "Oh. Okay." And she returned the kiss.

The indoor lights clicked on as the last rays of color faded through the apple orchard boughs from the western sky, and two doves called softly to each other.

MacDougall & Son

DISTILLERS OF FINE WHISKY

1870

HIGHLAND DEW

3621

The History behind Highland Dew

The history of Cardhu—which was written *Cardow* in the beginning—is closely connected to the history of two women: Helen and Elisabeth Cummings. Helen and her husband John Cumming ran a farm at Cardow in the late eighteenth/early nineteenth century. It is known that in 1816 John was convicted for distilling without official license three times. Distilling to small extents was usual for the farmers at that time, and nearly no one cared for licenses. They just couldn't afford it.

At Cardow, it wasn't John but his wife Helen who distilled, and she was known to have an eye on approaching excise officers and warn farmers in the neighborhood by setting up a red flag. Helen didn't just only distill for their own needs; she also sold her whisky from her kitchen's window, it is said.

In 1824, the Cummings could afford to buy a distilling license after the Exise Act of 1823 had reduced duties. They bought new stills, and in the beginning were helped selling and distributing their whisky by their friend George Smith, later the founder of The Glenlivet.

After John died in 1846, his wife Helen and his son Lewis carried on running Cardow Distillery.

The distillery and farm officially were handed down to Lewis, and in the following years he employed a brewer and a malt man. When Lewis passed away in 1872, his wife Elisabeth—supported by her mother-in-law Helen and her two young sons—carried on operating the distillery. Seeing the demands for whisky grow, Elisabeth bought new ground not far away from the previous farm and built a new Cardow distillery using the same water sources. It could produce three times more whisky than the old one.

In the year 1893 Elisabeth made a very important decision: she sold Cardow to John Walker & Sons for 20.500 pounds, and ensured her family to hold shares in Walker's company. She died one year later, and didn't have the chance to see the success of her wise decision: under the shield of the big company, Cardow could stand the hard times caused by the whisky market crash in 1898.

In 1899, the stills of Cardow were doubled and the distillery was connected to the railway by building a new road.

Distillers Company Ltd.—today Diageo—acquired the distillery in 1930. In 1960, a reconstruction and expansion followed the increasing demand for whisky in the post-war era.

In 1965, the word "Cardhu" became a trademark, and the brand was used to sell the whisky as single malt. In 1981 the name of the distillery was also changed from Cardow to Cardhu—a lightly different spelling for the original Gaelic word that means "black rock."

About the Author

Barrett Magill a retired RN, a writer, and Golden Crown Literary Society Award Finalist who published six novels in four years with Bedazzled Ink including: Damaged in Service, Defying Gravity, Dispatched with Cause, Deliver Us From Evil, Balefire, and Flights of Fancy before joining Sapphire Books. Her new YA entitled The Dreamcatcher was released in January 2017. Balefire was re-released in June 2017.

She is a member of the Western Women Writers of New Mexico, the Land of Enchantment Romance Authors, Romance Writers of America, Golden Crown Literary Society, and the Petroglyph Guild.

Barrett enjoys mountain views from two acres of prairie in New Mexico's high desert with her three dogs.

http://www.facebook.com/Barrett-Writes

http://barrett-writes.com/

https://twitter.com/BarrettWrites

http://www.sapphirebooks.com/barrett

http://highlanddew.com

Check out Barrett's other books

The Dreamcatcher - ISBN - 978-1-943353-67-5

High school is rarely easy, especially for a tall, somewhat gangly Native American girl. Add a sprinkle of shyness, a dash of athletic prowess, an above-average IQ, and some bizarre history that places her in the guardianship of her aunt. Then normal high school life is only an illusion.

Kai Tiva faces an uphill struggle until she runs into Riley Beth James, the extroverted class cutie, at the principal's office. Riley shows up for a newspaper interview, while Kai is summoned for punching out a classmate.

Riley is the attractive girl-next-door-type whom everyone likes. Though a fairly good student, an emerging choral star, and wildly popular, she knows she'll never live up to her older sister. She makes up for it with bravery, kindness, and a brash can-do attitude.

Their odd matchup is strengthened by curiosity, compassion, humor, and all the drama of typical teenage life. But their experiences go beyond the normal teen angst; theirs is compounded by a curious attraction to each other, and an emerging, insidious danger related to mysterious death of Kai's father.

Their emerging friendship is tested as they navigate this risky challenge. But the powerful bond forged between them has existed through past lives. The outcome this time will affect the next generation of Kai's people.

Balefire – ISBN – 978-1-943353-91-0

Silke Dyson is a free-spirited artist and teacher struggling with a vision impairment as a result of a physical altercation. Kirin Foster is a pragmatic Type A writer for a travel magazine with great opportunities for travel, and a growing restlessness.

Their lives intersect at thirty-thousand feet during a tropical storm. With plans lost in the ensuing confusion, they form an unlikely friendship. The relationship strengthens in the warm tropical sunshine of the Belizean Cayes.

To their surprise, they discover a real connection with backgrounds in Milwaukee. Back home they continue an easy rapport with common interests and mutual friends.

Sometimes a random spark of kindness or caring can kindle a small flame. With patience and serendipity, a small flame can grow into a balefire—a beacon of hope to guide a pair of lost soul's home.

Other book's by Sapphire Authors

Razor's Edge (American Yakuza) – ISBN – 978-1-943353-81-1

Luce Potter lives by a code of honor. Push her and she shoves back, harder. There's only one problem: Luce has just found out that revenge is a knife that cuts both ways. Now that her lover Brooke has survived the attack on her life, Luce has only one thing on her mind, and his name is Frank. Unfortunately, someone walks into her life that she didn't see coming.
Brooke Erickson has survived an attack so brutal it's left a permanent scar on her soul. All she wants to do now is go home and finish recuperating with her lover, Luce Potter, by her side. An unexpected event puts Brooke at the head of the Yakuza family. Can she command the respect necessary to lead it through the crisis?
Luce and Brooke's worlds are upending. Can each do what's necessary to survive and return to a new normal?

Lavender Dreams - ISBN - 978-1-943353-59-0

When Sarah Chase got on the ferry to Bainbridge Island, she left her lover, her job, and her past behind. She didn't know that in the course of one day she would meet a woman who might be the girl of her dreams, change her career path, create a new family, and find herself in a fairytale mansion with two of the quirkiest little old ladies imaginable.